UNDER A SKELLIG SKY

BREDA JOY

POOLBEG

Published 2022
by Poolbeg Press Ltd
123 Grange Hill, Baldoyle
Dublin 13, Ireland
E-mail: poolbeg@poolbeg.com
www.poolbeg.com

The moral right of the author has been asserted.

A catalogue record for this book is available from the British Library.

ISBN 978-1-78199-705-5

Typeset by Poolbeg Press Ltd

www.poolbeg.com

ABOUT THE AUTHOR

Breda Joy is a native of Killarney, County Kerry. *Under a Skellig Sky* follows her debut novel *Eat the Moon* (2018) into the the Poolbeg Press stable. She is also the author of three books of non-fiction.

A graduate of the M. Phil. in Creative Writing Programme (2010/2011) at Trinity College Dublin, she has had poetry published in literary journals including *The Stony Thursday Book*.

She was a finalist in the 2016 GreenBean Novel Fair at the Irish Writers' Centre, Dublin. She has been shortlisted for the Francis MacManus Short Story Competition (2011); long listed for the *RTÉ Guide* Penguin Ireland Short Story (2012); a winner in the inaugural Trócaire/Poetry Ireland Award (2012), and a winner in the Kerry County Council One Act Play Competition (2005).

A winner in the ESB National Media Awards (1997), she has worked as a regional journalist with *Kerry's Eye* and *The Kerryman/Corkman* newspapers in Killarney and Macroom, as well as with the Leader Group in Melbourne.

ACKNOWLEDGEMENTS

I can't have been much more than four years of age when my mother called me to the breakfast table of an English couple and their little daughter who had brought her own miniature cutlery set on holidays with her. The encounter with these guests in our streetside Bed & Breakfast is my earliest memory of this sector of Ireland's tourism industry.

Over the years, I've stayed in various B&B's and Farm Guesthouses as well as having had short stints working in some as a student. I knew many of the women at the heart of this sector through our family grocery shop also. Eventually, as a journalist, I came to write about their life and times.

I would like to acknowledge their spirit of entrepreneurship, financial independence and genuine care for and interest in their guests as the chief inspiration for this book. They were and are fiercely competitive businesswomen who, at the same time, often created bonds of kindness lasting generations with guests. I felt it was timely to record their contribution through fiction because the emergence of Airbnb and other factors have led to a more impersonal accommodation sector in Ireland.

The theme of loyal and supportive friendships between

women is very much at the heart of this work too. I've been blessed through my life with the best of friends from so many different walks of life and countries. The soundest of women! Thank you, one and all. And let me give a moment of loving remembrance to the ones who have passed.

Thank you to my fine son, Brendan, who gives the deepest meaning to this confounding caper of existence.

I appreciate deeply the feedback given to me by the readers of the near-finished draft of *Under a Skellig Sky*. The encouragement of Liz O'Brien, Marion O'Donnell Cronin and John Magee, Killarney, and Mary O'Connor, Derrynane, gave me great heart.

Thanks also to Mary O'Leary for one or two good yarns that I wove into the narrative. And thank you to Mark and Jean Eldred for their advice on the work of the artist.

My mind can only wonder at how Poolbeg's Paula Campbell manages all the aspects of publication from choosing book covers to liaising with writers and retailers. Thank you, Paula, and everyone else at Poolbeg Press.

The chief 'error detector', Gaye Shortland, is meticulous. Your attention to detail means everything, Gaye.

My agent, Jonathan Williams, must take a bow for introducing me to Poolbeg and setting me on the road to publication. His mantra, 'Onwards and upwards', has been added to my personal store of motivational phrases.

Thank you to all the readers who gave my first novel, *Eat the Moon*, a vote of confidence. I hope my imaginary Skellig cast absorbs you as much.

DEDICATION

In memory of Gisela Willms-Guiton

One wonders in this place, why anyone is left in Dublin, or London, or Paris, where it would be better, one would think, to live in a tent or hut, with this magnificent sea and sky, and to breathe this wonderful air which is like wine in one's teeth.

John Millington Synge, *Travels in Wicklow, West Kerry and Connemara* (1910)

Chapter 1

Mary's eyes sharpened to a seagull gleam when she focussed on the hard cash the husband and wife had handed over at the kitchen door. Vouchers and credit-card payments never delivered the same satisfaction.

"Thank God for loose people," she said, storing away the banknotes under the bright yellow china hen on the worktop.

Carol had stopped midway through stacking the cereal bowls in the dishwasher, glancing over her shoulder. She was going to chide her mother yet again about leaving too much money lying around the house but she was distracted.

"Excuse me? Loose people. Are we talking about loose morals? That pair didn't look much like swingers."

Mary clucked disapprovingly. "Will you go away from me, you *gligín!* I'm talking about tourists in cars rather than buses."

"So you mean 'privates'," Carol said. She considered introducing a frisson of sexual innuendo but thought better of it.

Carol and her mother had just finished serving breakfast to three Corkwomen, all walkers on the Kerry Way, and the intrepid Dutch couple who had turned up without booking.

Mary was warming up to an interlude of Killarney envy. Carol could feel it coming.

"Loose people or privates," said Mary. "Call them what you like but South Kerry would be lost without them. All the rest are shooting round the Ring from Killarney in coaches and landing back there to the hotels like homing pigeons in the late afternoon. You know they say it must have been a Killarney person who invented the Ring of Kerry trip. They start out in Killarney! And where do they end up?"

"Killarney," Carol repeated dutifully. She started on the greasy plates. "Well, God bless the appetites of this set of privates."

Mary chuckled to herself.

Carol raised her eyebrows. "Are you going to share the joke or am I to diagnose early-onset dementia?"

"Oh, I don't want to be going on and on, and I'm the first to admit that Killarney was good to me, but I just thought of Máire, that old friend of mine from the hotel who started her own B&B. She was complaining to me one day that she wasn't busy enough. When I pointed out that she'd just told me she was full, she said, 'But I'm not turning anyone away!'"

Mary was shaking with mirth. Carol had heard the anecdote before – many a time – but she was glad to see her mother in such good humour. It was the weather. She'd have to ring the date on the calendar: March 24, the day the sunlight came back. The colour register, set at monochrome during the eternal rains of spring, was suddenly suffused with light. The terracotta-coloured garden shed was radiant. Light flared off the windows of the parked cars. But she wasn't going to fall for this flashy visitor: this light was a tourist, a day-tripper just giving a quick look round before the curtains of rain were drawn again.

After the snow had melted in that first week of March, it had never stopped raining. The best fields in the lower reaches of the valley were muddied green skirts, weighted at the edges by grey hems of flood water. Waterfalls foamed white through gulleys in the grey cliffs and, when the winds gusted, the spray was blown skywards like smoke billowing from a chimney.

The March monsoon had continued. Confined to such close quarters with her mother, Carol had perfected the art of selective listening. From her usual station at the easel, she zoned in and out at strategic junctures to minimise reprimands about the silences essential for concentration.

Maybe setting up the studio in the old conservatory opening off the kitchen wasn't such a great idea, but the light was ideal and she was on hand whenever she was needed. The magnolia shrub had grown so much in her absence that it shaded off the space from all the harshness of the southern light. It was ideal: perfect clarity and no shadows. Not that there could be any problem with glare on a damp morning when the sky was a grey shield.

The conservatory had been one of her favourite spaces in the house when she was a child. She'd lose herself in a book in there, stretched full-length on the bench along one side, the muffled tap of the magnolia branches on the glass in high winds a comforting noise.

There was nothing comforting this particular morning about the drone of the television as Mary zapped from one channel to another. Carol much preferred it when her mother was surfing the net on her iPad (she'd joined a computer course in Waterville), but that urge was fitful.

Now she was stabbing the remote control with the urgency of a game-show contestant with the right answer.

"Every kind of a channel under the sun and not a decent programme on any blessed one of them."

Carol examined the cluster of primroses taking shape on the canvas. Miniatures were challenging, but she hadn't the energy for landscapes yet. She was working her way through a series on the first flowers of spring: dandelions, lesser celandines, wood anemones, and her favourite, the delicate wild violets. If she could flog a few of the canvases to the craft shops in Portmagee and Cahersiveen, it would save her from eating into her bank account.

She addressed her mother without turning around. "You mean no documentaries on genocide or the Third Reich on daytime telly? Why don't you try *Loose Women* for a bit of light relief?"

"Yes, and listen to some halfwit twittering on about still being a virgin after twenty-three years of marriage. Like that foolah the other morning on one of those mindless programmes." She switched channels. A weather forecaster was standing in front of yet another diagram of Ireland obscured by overfed clouds. "Would you look at this one? She's like a pull-through for a rifle."

Carol turned away from the easel just in time to catch a glimpse of the petite presenter. "She must be on a diet – cabbage soup and power shakes, I'd say."

She immediately regretted shifting her attention to the kitchen. The worktop in her line of vision was littered with cartons of milk and fruit juice, cereal boxes, egg containers filled with broken shells, marmalade and jam pots, as well as breakfast dishes cleared from the table of the Corkonians who had insisted on eating at half seven, half an hour before the regular starting time.

It was a quarter past eleven. Where had the time gone?

4

There seemed to be no end to the work since she had persuaded her mother to put the house up on Airbnb just before Paddy's Day. Bookings had begun to come in immediately.

Mary had been complaining that business was dwindling and there was no one "off the road". Carol suggested that they try Airbnb as an experiment for six months or so.

"Do you mind if I stay around until the end of the summer?" she asked her mother. "I need to lick my wounds. The Airbnb would generate some extra cash for the house. Just treat me as the hired help and pay me whatever percentage you think is fair."

Mary had been deflated when Carol rang to say she was pulling out of Italy. She had hoped that she would settle there. She was glad to have her home, but she worried about her next move.

"Give it a go by all means but extra people will mean extra work," she said. "Do you think there's any hope of you mending things with Matteo and going back?"

Carol shook her head. "I don't think so. But you never know. I just need some time on my own. He *has* been ringing me. Maybe absence will make the heart grow fonder."

Mary's heart went out to her daughter. "Take your time, Carol. We'll play this Airbnb thing by ear. We can always cancel it if you change your mind. Don't be too quick to write Matteo off. Remember what your father used to say – 'There's so much good in the worst of us and so much bad in the best of us that it evens out'."

Carol was moved by her mother's kindness. "I know, Mam. He's not the worst in the world. There's a lot of good in him. That's what makes it hard."

She had originally thought there would be plenty of time for painting once the breakfasts were served. The idea was that she'd fly through cleaning the bedrooms to have the rest of the day free for herself. It wasn't quite working out like that. She'd hardly had time to meet up with Angela. She'd have to ring her and arrange something. And then there was the question of her mother. Had Mary really complained that much before?

Mary sighed. "I wouldn't have opened until Easter only that you got ahead of yourself. There's more work in this job than people think. You're away so long, you've forgotten the half of it."

Carol had forgotten but she wasn't going to admit it. "Well, if you weren't so dead against me looking for a Woofer, we wouldn't have half the work. We could do up the old den in the yard for them. It was fine for us in the summers when we were kids."

Her mother snorted. "Wouldn't I sound nice telling Margot and Timmy that we were getting a Woofer?" Her voice curdled. "It sounds like some kind of dog."

Carol winced at the thought of her domineering cousin Margot. At least they'd been free of her for a few days. And Timmy – it was a pity that his arthritis prevented him from doing much gardening around the place. He was still only sixty-nine. He'd been her mother's right-hand man when her father was busy at work.

"Willing Workers on Organic Farms. How many times must I explain it to you? They work in exchange for their food and accommodation. They're nearly all young students who want to see a bit of the world. I did it myself. The path down to the cove is all grown over. They'd be great for jobs like that."

"And before you knew it, there'd be a cannabis plantation in the middle of the wood," her mother said. "I can imagine the type of organic farming that crowd'd be into alright."

Carol smiled. "Wouldn't it be an ideal cottage industry in keeping with the enterprises tucked away in the forestry by our resident hippies? Anyway, we'll work something out, I'm sure. We can't afford extra help unless things get rightly going." She turned back to the easel.

The crunch of gravel carried faintly through the window.

A fly couldn't pass the window without Mary noticing. "Is that the New Zealander gone past?"

It was. Oliver Wesley, their very first overseas booking on Airbnb. A Kiwi with odd eyes – one green, one blue – and a distant personality. Maybe he was an iceberg that would melt under the heat of the Kerry welcome. He had requested a plain breakfast at a later time than the other guests because he wanted to get in some early morning cycles. No Full Irish, just yogurt, cheeses and bread. Carol agreed readily – one less fry. Tall, spare and athletic, he had iron-grey hair cut close to his head. He had brought a racer that you could lift with your little finger. Setting out on the dark mornings, he was like a satellite on wheels.

His insistence on keeping the bike in the bedroom hadn't gone down too well with Mary. "Where's he going, bringing muck and dirt into the house? That's a beige carpet in that room, I'll remind you."

She had looked at Carol as if she had twenty-two heads when she'd accepted a booking for him, a single, for seven nights on Airbnb.

"You know I have a soft spot for singles, but seven nights?"

"There's hardly going to be a stampede before March is out," Carol had said.

Mary hadn't got over her initial animosity. She sniffed in disapproval now. "I find it more than strange that he can't sit down to breakfast at a normal time with everyone else. It's odd too that he doesn't want us cleaning the bedroom while he's here."

Carol could feel a prickle of irritation. At this rate, she'd have to clean out the den and turn it into a studio for herself. "He's hardly an axe murderer. And it's less work. I'm not going to argue with that. He's living in the heart of London. I suppose he just wants peace and quiet."

Mary frowned. "I don't know. I've a funny feeling about that fella. Remember all those cases of women going missing up around Kildare and Dublin? It usually boils down to some oddball floating around on his own."

"Well, I have to hand it to you – a mother's intuition. He's got that strained look. The bedroom will be littered with body parts when he leaves. Just say a decade of the Rosary that ours won't be in there with them."

Mary shook her head. "Mark my words." She turned off the TV. "He's a strange fish if ever there was one. Burning lights into the small hours – God only knows what the next electricity bill will be."

Carol pointed at the dining-room door and put a finger to her lips. "*Shhh*, for God's sake! I've just heard him come in. Keep it down or we'll end up on TripAdvisor. You're forgetting that he doesn't have the fry. That's a big saving."

She brewed a pot of coffee and took it into the dining room where the visitor was poring over *The Irish Times*.

When she got back into the kitchen, she switched on Radio Kerry and turned the volume up as a noise-shield to blur the effect of the tirade that Mary had resumed.

"That fruit bowl will bankupt us. If you want to make money out of this Airbnb lark for yourself, you'll have to listen to me. Did you see those three horses of Corkwomen this morning? Cleared the full fries and went on to lay into

8

fruit, yogurt and cheese as if they never saw a bite in their lives before. It's a wonder there's anything left for his lordship. To add insult to injury, I saw them making off with the brown scones. No wonder they can spend a week walking the Kerry Way. It's a cheap holiday. Are we a farm guesthouse or the Vincent de Paul? We'll be halfway to the poorhouse ourselves if this continues."

Carol knew that, at heart, her mother would empty every food press in the kitchen to make sure that no one went away from the house hungry. It was just that the walkers had gone overboard. And she knew too that she wanted Carol herself to have a generous share of the profits over the summer. But the last thing Carol wanted was her mother to feel that she was a financial burden.

"Ah, Mam, doesn't everyone rave about your breakfasts? You're hardly going to start cutting back at this hour of your life."

Mary smiled. "I suppose not, girl. It was just that those three madams got on my wick this morning. I never saw anyone to eat that amount. I'm a bit tired too because we were up that bit earlier for them. And we're still behind ourselves. We'd want to clear the last table as soon as he's finished and put the dishwasher on."

"*We? We?* Does that mean you're going for the operation?"

"What operation?"

Carol grinned. "The one to separate your arse from the chair. What else?"

Mary opened her mouth to reply but the sound of a car in the drive drew both their attention. She was stricken. "Surely the next booking isn't landing yet, and not a bed made?"

They both relaxed when they saw the post van pulling up outside the front door. Carol went out to greet the postwoman and lingered on the doorstep to savour the brightness of the prodigal sunshine. She stood there and inhaled the fresh spring air with the pleasure of a woman on temporary release from the fumes of sizzling rashers and an egg-pan crackling like a second Krakatoa. The smell of the kitchen was so dense she could have carved the fries out of it. Three-D printing was only trotting after her.

She sniffed the sleeve of her blue sweatshirt. She was a 'Full Irish' on legs. What of it? The birds were singing louder, the hydrangeas swelling with buds. Bare branches of the beech trees were conductors' batons swaying in the surges of wind. She'd seize the brightness and take a quick walk to blow the cooking fumes out of her lungs. Grabbing a blue fleece from the hall, she set off. Her energy level was so high she wanted to skip. Such a shame that adults gave up skipping. Then she spotted the lone Kiwi – Private Oliver Wesley – moping along the drive. How had he finished his breakfast so quickly?

The last thing she wanted that morning was to be landed with someone to make talk to on her walk. She considered cutting through the wood to avoid him. But, on the other hand, she felt a longing to connect, to have a decent conversation. She recalled an article she had read about a woman who had carried out some incredible ocean crossing on her own. The woman had spoken of her appreciation of looking into the eyes of another human being when she finally reached land.

Then again Private Wesley might be escaping from human eyes (one particular pair of eyes even) – from chatter and the whole shebang, to savour time on his own. There was something in his gait, though, that gave her the sense that the opposite might be true. And if her instincts were wrong, she'd just vamoose.

Her mood lightened when it dawned on her that he'd be ideal material for a positive TripAdvisor review.

She could read it already. '**Carol, artist and daughter of the owner, shared her morning walk on an enchanting coast road as she gathered material for her new collection of paintings. Her local knowledge was invaluable. Glenosheen can't be recommended highly enough.**'

Needs must. He couldn't help it if he was as dull as ditch water. Still, better that than blinding her with bull.

So, what would her opening line be? The weather, of course, the old reliable that kept Irish people connected in an age-old conspiracy against the elements.

Putting on the charm for 'the people' was second nature to her since she was a child. She smiled brightly as she gained on him.

"The rain is due in soon, according to the forecast. I thought I'd get in a quick walk before the clouds open. Do you want to tag along?"

The grateful expression on his face made her feel guilty about her reluctance.

"Are you sure you don't mind?" he said.

"Of course not."

He didn't look totally convinced. "I really don't want to intrude but it does make a big difference when you get to talk to the locals in any country."

They fell into step. Carol was used to driving conversations. She was riffling through her file of topics when Oliver got there before her.

"I think I will take your advice and cycle over to the island later."

Carol had briefed him about Valentia Island the evening before.

11

"I'm looking forward to it," he said. "When you're in a car, you're insulated from everything really."

"Insulation is your only man around here when the mad winds are sweeping in from the Atlantic with gallons of rain. But you're blessed to pluck this fine morning out of the March weather."

Oliver grinned. "I have all the gear. I'm an addict really. If I don't get out, I get withdrawal symptoms."

The old estate wall ran along the left-hand side of the road while a grassy ditch enclosed the farms on the opposite side. Carol loved the old wall. She pointed out some of its idiosyncrasies to Oliver. Flat stones were wedged one on the other. At various points, the stonemasons of old had come across boulders in their path and incorporated them into the wall, stacking flat wedges of stone on top.

She liked to imagine what thoughts had filled the stonemason's mind as he whistled and worked: the girl whose eye he was looking forward to catching at the crossroads dance, the jam jar of coins he was steadily adding to for his passage to America? Or was he a married man torn between pride at his wife's news that there was going to be 'an increase' in the family and the worry of another mouth to feed.

She stopped here and there to take pictures of the wall, her eye taken by the pattern of lichens or tiny plants growing between the cracks.

Oliver threw back his shoulders and inhaled deeply. "The trip over here is worth it for the air alone. That writer had it in one."

"Which writer?" Carol hated non sequiturs. She hoped he didn't share her mother's habit of emerging abruptly from her own thoughts to make references that bore no relation to what had gone before.

"Oh, my apologies. I'm speaking about your great writer, John Millington Synge. Can you believe I planned this trip on the strength of a single sentence from him?"

Nothing would surprise me, having come across every variety of a tourist growing up, Carol felt like telling him. Yes, we have a right one here. Slightly daft in an absent-minded-professor class of a way. He was the sort that a mother might be afraid to release into the world, but who glided on without a bother, mainly because people like herself took them under their wing.

While all that was running through her mind, he explained how he'd bought a copy of Synge's *Travels in Wicklow, West Kerry and Connemara* in a bookshop near Charing Cross. He stood at the side of the road and closed his eyes – in preparation, she guessed, for delivery of the quote.

"'*One wonders in this place,*'" he intoned, "'*why anyone is left in Dublin, or London, or Paris, where it would be better, one would think, to live in a tent or hut, with this magnificent sea and sky, and to breathe this wonderful air which is like wine in one's teeth.*'"

She was gobsmacked. "That's really beautiful. Are you sure it's about Kerry, though? I thought he spent all his time on the Aran Islands?"

Oliver grew animated as he listed names of places that Synge mentioned in the travelogue. "He spent a lot of time up the road from here near Rossbeigh. He devotes a whole page to the Glenbeigh Races. He's quite funny about them. I'll show you the book if you like."

Carol threw her arms in the air. "Oh, I believe you, though thousands wouldn't. It's a fright that a total stranger has to tell you something about your own place."

Oliver grew serious. "I didn't mean to –"

13

Carol punched his arm playfully. "*Arrah*, I'm only slagging you. Don't mind me."

Oliver related a section of the book where Synge described meeting an old man, on the coast road near Glenbeigh, who had talked about the famous Irish warrior Fionn and his men, the Fianna.

"And then he pointed to a neck of sand on the coast and told Synge that that was where Oisín had been drawn away to Tir na Nog – the Land of Youth."

Carol spluttered with laughter. "*Tír na nÓg*."

"Oh, sorry for mispronouncing it."

He was obviously stung. There went the TripAdvisor review gurgling down the drain.

"No, *I'm* sorry – that was rude – but you made it sound like eggnogg."

"It's OK."

Carol stopped dead in the road. "So, you read about Oisín, and that's what attracted you to Glenosheen – the Glen of Oisín."

Oliver nodded. "I mightn't have come here only that your house popped up on Airbnb soon after I'd read the book."

"Well, that's gas – I mean, funny. Because we've only just gone up on Airbnb this month as an experiment. My mother has always registered with Fáilte Ireland but this is a new venture. My venture, really. For as long as I stay around."

"Well, lucky for me that you're trying it out," Oliver said. "I'm going to stop talking now and allow you to enjoy your walk in peace."

"I'm fine out, but you can't really take in your surroundings if we're yapping too much. If you want to ask me anything, don't feel you need to zip your mouth entirely. Anyway, I need to take a few photos to give me ideas for my paintings. When I'm finished the spring flowers, I'm planning a series called 'Meditations in Stone'. But I'm doing more thinking than anything else. Thinking and ducking the easel too often."

She took out her phone and zoomed in for a close-up of a boulder set into the wall. White lichen clouded the spaces between the emerald coating of moss. Her ear caught the music of the invisible stream coursing along the gulley on the other side of the road – one of her favourite sounds. She picked up on the energy of the turn of the season: the sheen on the lemon lesser celadines smiling from the grass verge, pockets of primroses in the ditch, the summoning light, the skittish breeze, the sky ballooning into a blue expanse above her. Even subtracting a few points for the ripe smell of slurry wafting from a nearby field, it was a good time of year to come home. A good time to be alive, even if she still didn't know her arse from her elbow in terms of what she was going to do with her life. *Not* coming to a cinema near you soon: *What Carol Did Next.*

She wandered on taking more photos and became so absorbed that she completely forgot about her walking companion for a few minutes. Then, she glanced over her shoulder. He had fallen behind and was studying a pair of listing wrought-iron gates sunk into the earth at the entrance to a wilderness of shrubbery. A colonnade of beech trees, leading up the centre, edged an open space that was obviously a driveway before briars and saplings had taken over.

She retraced her steps to where Oliver was standing.

"Please tell me I'm seeing things," he said, pointing into the wilderness. "Surely those can't be New Zealand Tree Ferns?"

"Correct," she said. "They're nearly as common as

15

furze in some sheltered pockets around here. Up in Dublin, they'll only grow under glass in the Botanic Gardens. The Gulf Stream creates such a micro-climate down here that they can survive quite happily outside. And you're wondering about the avenue of trees, no doubt. They used to lead to the 'Big House', the mansion that the estate walls were built around to keep out the locals unless of course they were admitted as cheap labour. An English family owned it. The head of the family in the late 1800s was a botanist. He made it his life's work to colonise it with all sorts of exotic trees and shrubs, lots of them from your neck of the woods in the Southern Hemisphere."

The rumble of a tractor sounded behind them. Carol motioned to Oliver to stand well in off the narrow road. The driver waved from his perch on the blue tractor as he passed, drawing a slurry-spreader splattered with mud. A whiff of sulphur blew back to them.

"There's your champagne air now for you. The farmers will tell you it's the smell of progress."

Oliver chuckled and they continued to walk.

"But they left, the family?" he said. "Left a lifetime's achievement behind?"

"Oh." She glanced at him. "They were burned out – like so many other Anglo-Irish families in the 1920s while the War of Independence was raging."

"Oh, yes, of course," he said, a little embarrassed. "I do know about that."

"They went to England and never came back. Rumour had it they fell upon hard times. And now the wilderness is claiming back the semi-tropical garden every year. You should walk up there – have a look – only three walls of the house were left standing and, now, screened by the

16

luxuriant growth, the ruin has taken on the air of Sleeping Beauty's palace."

By this time, they had climbed to the top of a steep hill. There was an open gateway to their left.

A sea wind met them with force as they walked towards a two-storey, stone-fronted house standing on a rise. It was the holiday home of a wealthy American family who had relatives visiting in turn through the summer.

"The Thumans spent the odd Christmas here in the beginning, but the bad weather put them off," Carol said. "We call the father the Chicken Pie Baron. Apparently he's made a fortune from them. Money or no money, it's the same old story with holiday homes. Dark windows at night. One less neighbour to rely on. No children to keep the national schools open."

Carol was forging ahead towards the lawn that a scattering of boulders rose through like the backs of whales when she noticed that Oliver was hanging back again. What was with the man?

"Isn't this private property?"

Carol tutted. "Of course it is. But they leave the gate open to give any would-be burglars the message that there's nothing worth breaking in for. Come on, they won't mind."

"Are you sure?"

"Of course I'm sure. We can wave to them on the security cameras."

Oliver frowned. "I'd prefer –"

She went back, stepped behind him and pretended to push him. "*Arrah*, come on! I'm only letting on about the cameras."

The sloping lawn ended at a ditch topped by two whin bushes, sculpted by the wind to lean landwards. Carol stepped up on a boulder and beckoned to Oliver to follow. She didn't look out to sea. She knew what lay out there. Instead, she waited for Oliver's expression. She wasn't disappointed. His eyes lit up and his jaw slackened. Way out on the horizon, the two Skellig islands reared up out of the waves. The sky above them was leaden – the promised rain was on the way. *Sceilig Mhichíl* and *Sceilig Bheag* – Skellig Michael and Small Skellig. They could have been christened 'cloud-piercers' because of their needle-like peaks.

Grey clouds had unrolled from the horizon. Carol had often seen the view more startling under a blue sky but the islands were always dramatic.

Oliver was silent. She let him be for a few minutes.

"Well?" she said finally.

"Magnificent," he said.

Carol wheeled out the old reliable, not that the term was fair to the description which was the best she had ever come across for the Skelligs. "An English writer described them as two drowned cathedrals rising out of the sea."

"That's perfect," Oliver said in a faraway voice. He turned to her before looking back out to sea. "This reminds me of the first and only time I saw Gibraltar. We were driving for miles and miles down this motorway. Then, suddenly, there it was, looming out of the sea. I know it's not quite the same thing – Gibraltar is a peninsula – but the effect is similar even though these islands are far out to sea."

Carol didn't want to interrupt his rapture but she was growing cold standing in the sea wind. If they didn't get a move on before the mass of cloud swallowed the sun, they'd be perished.

"Believe me, this is absolutely nothing compared to actually visiting Skellig Michael."

"I'm definitely coming back here to take that boat trip," he said.

"Hope you won't have to battle through crowds. *Star Wars – The Force Awakens* – really put Skellig Michael on the map!"

Suddenly, a wayward squall laden with the rotten-egg-aroma of slurry tore towards them from a field near the house. Carol waved her hand in front of her face. "From the sublime to the ridiculous. Come on, we'd better skedaddle before we suffocate. We need to get back before it pours and my mother sends out a search warrant for me. I knew the morning was too good to last. I haven't even started the bedrooms yet. Anyway you'd want to be making tracks for Valentia, even though I think you're nuts to cycle there with the rain on the wing."

As they retraced their steps, Oliver kept his neck craned to take in a view of the Skelligs for as long as possible. The grey bulk of cloud continued to expand across the sky towards the headland, and puffy white clouds scudded across the diminishing blue like sailboats in a headwind. Gulls sky-skated in slanting white clusters, their cries carrying to the headland.

Carol was just turning in the gate for home when she felt Oliver's hand on her shoulder. She jumped. He pointed to the wall beside the gateway: a stark latticework of branches fanned out on the stonework in a formation of shadows. She took out the phone and snapped a picture.

Chapter 2

Margot Bradshaw's black Mercedes pulled in under the beech trees. It was barely a year old. Nothing but the best for our Margot. Carol was consoled by the sight of her mother's 2018 Toyota Yaris holding the side up. She called out a commentary to Mary from the window.

"It's Cousin Margot – Mrs Efficiency herself. She's applying some fresh lipstick – her signature scarlet, no doubt."

Mary was flustered. Her niece unnerved her. "She could be applying Valspar for all I care. Come on, quick, put some order on this place or we'll never hear the end of it."

Carol darted across to the worktop to push three cereal boxes into a press but one of them fell back out again, scattering cornflakes all over the floor. "That's all I need. I must have gone tragically wrong in a former life."

She grabbed a dustpan and began to sweep the cereal into it.

"*Does the clutter not get in on you, Carol?*" she said, mimicking her cousin. "*How do you keep up with the ort with the season beginning?*" (Art was gentrified to *ort* in Margot-speak) She dumped the breakfast debris in presses, the fridge and the bin, and ran a dishcloth along the worktop surfaces. "I swear that woman must have an in-built radar that tells her to turn up when the kitchen is looking like a tip."

20

Mary muttered, "Her radar must be on overdrive at that rate."

Carol tripped over a cat that let off a squeal. "Oh my God, how did she sneak in here again? Ah, Mam, get that *piscín* out the door before Margot lands in. I can't believe she has this effect on us. You'd swear she was the Fáilte Ireland Inspector or something."

"Don't even mention that word *inspector* to me." Mary poured some milk into a bowl and reversed across the kitchen floor. "Here, *puss-puss*! Come on out the door!"

Carol looked out through the conservatory. "Thank heaven for small mercies. She's on the mobile phone." She pulled out a drawer of the dishwasher and fed in some blue willow-pattern breakfast plates.

Mary returned from her cat-disposal mission and cleared her own breakfast bowl and mug from the kitchen table.

Margot had grown up on the posher side of the O'Connell family. Her grandparents had taken up an offer of the Land Commission in 1953 to sell off their small rocky holding wedged between the mountain and ocean and moved to the 'Promised Land' of County Kildare where farms were being carved out of former landlords' estates. They were part of a general wave of migration from the poorer farm holdings of Kerry and Mayo to the lush grazing lands of Kildare and Meath.

Carol's father John used to tell of the lonesomeness in the townland when the others watched Margot's grandparents pack beds, furniture, pots and pans, and all their belongings into the lorries that moved them. They took away eight cows, a horse called Billy, forty sheep and the dog, Shep. All they left was the cat that had gone missing on the day of the move. John said the cat had Christian sense and refused to leave the Kingdom of Kerry.

The sadness at the exodus was mixed with envy because John's uncle and aunt had already travelled to Kildare to check out their new home and returned full of excitement. A fine new house, a cowshed with concrete floors and glass windows were waiting for them on the fifty fertile acres. The contact persisted through the years with the Kerry O'Connells travelling up from the mountains and valleys to visit their cousins.

Margot's father was the first of his generation to go to university. He graduated from University College Dublin as a doctor. Every summer they rented a house in Waterville and, in between golfing, drove out to the valley on visits.

Margot was a model of perfection from the very start, with a glossy black helmet of hair and an endless selection of designer dresses bought on shopping trips to Dublin. In her mid-fifties, she was fifteen years older than Carol. Armed with a law degree, high-achieving Margot had moved to London and worked her way up to partnership status in a small legal firm. She had two grown-up children from her short-lived first marriage to a Mayo solicitor with a high opinion of himself and an excessive interest in a series of fawning secretaries.

On a visit to Glenosheen, Margot, who had since married Richard Bradshaw, an English investment banker with industrial-strength patience, and snapped up an abandoned farmhouse and ten acres in the valley on impulse. She restored the building as a bijou farm guesthouse based on an agri-tourism venture she had visited in Sardinia. When her legal firm was bought out by a rival company, she moved over with a pot of money to lodge at the end of one of the valley rainbows and a boundless zeal to get any relatives she was in contact with to achieve their

full potential. Carol was firmly within her sights on that
score.

The long-suffering Richard commuted to an investment
bank in London via Kerry Airport on the days he wasn't
working from home.

Yes, Cousin Margot was a force of nature, Carol reflected
as she took a bobble from her apron pocket and tied back
her hair. She retrieved her paintbrush and affected an air of
nonchalance at the easel.

Mary turned on Radio Kerry and sank back into her
armchair just as her niece blew through the back porch.

Margot shook the rain from her coat. Her eyes raked
the disorder of the kitchen table in search of a place to set
down the bunch of rhubarb she was carrying.

Carol feigned surprise. "Is it yourself, Margot? Oh, rhubarb!
Great. You know we love it." She took the ruby-coloured stalks
and deposited them on top of a bag of potatoes inside the back
door, sensing Margot watching her as she did so. "Another crop
coaxed from Timmy's green fingers. Aren't you lucky that Mam
loaned him to you? He's a treasure of a man."

Margot looked grim. "Treasure isn't exactly the word
soonest to my lips when we're talking about Timothy Healy."
She was glancing around the kitchen which still looked
untidy despite the hasty offensive on the detritus of the
breakfast. "Really, Carol, doesn't the – "

"No, Margot, the clutter doesn't get me down."

Carol never ceased to marvel at how Margot, a woman
who stood only four foot eleven in her stocking feet, could
be so forceful.

Margot threw her eyes to heaven. "I've told you before.
I've the number of a very good Feng Shui consultant living
in Ballinskelligs. She moved over from Surrey."

Carol laughed. "Herself and half of South Kerry. And I've told you I'll give her a go when you try this excellent hypnotherapist in Tralee to rid yourself of that positively anal obsession with ultra-clear worktops."

Mary stood – she could see a spat shaping up between the two cousins. "Sit down there, Margot, and I'll make you a cup of tea."

"Herbal, please. I'm detoxing. Let me have a look at the packet to see the constituents."

Carol interrupted. "Will you get over yourself, Margot? We're hardly going to poison you."

Margot was hovering beside a kitchen chair. "The last time you offered me camomile, the expiry date was two years and three months old."

Mary sat back down. "I never in my life heard such a brouhaha about a simple cup of tea. Will the pair of ye give over? Aren't you going to sit down, Margot? You're making me nervous."

"I don't mean to offend, but after I got home from here on Tuesday, my good navy suit was positively covered with white hairs." She plucked the cushion from the chair with the tips of her fingernails, dropped it on the next chair and sat on the very edge of her seat.

Mary ignored the disapproval in their visitor's voice. "That must have been Jacinta, sister of Francisco and Lucy, a litter I christened after I'd been watching a documentary on the Children of Fatima."

Carol placed a mug of tea in front of her cousin. Margot was toying with the teaspoon and becoming progressively more ill at ease. Carol observed her looking at Mary with a tightness around her scarlet mouth.

Mary was warming to the topic of the cats. "It's

strange, but I never liked cats to begin with. It's just that I got a name for being kind to animals and, before I knew it, people were landing me with kittens. And I'd prefer to give them a home, rather than see them ending up in a bucket of water. I try to get as many of them as I can neutered but some of the divils are so wild we can't catch them in that special cage. You'd want eyes in the back of your head to keep them out of the house."

Carol realised that, to used a mixed metaphor, her mother was barking up the wrong tree with the cats. Margot was in warpath mode. There were any number of give-away signs – a fixed look in the eye, a stiffness in the posture, fidgeting with her gold chain, all akin to a cat sitting still but twitching its tail in annoyance. Margot was waiting to pounce. Carol asked her if she was alright.

"I'm fine really except that . . ." She hesitated.

Carol attempted a feeble diversion with the weather to stall the inevitable. Whatever was coming was not good. "Will we get any break from the rain at all? The tumble drier is eating electricity." She gabbled on. "That reminds me of the parish priest who was transferred to Allihies down on the Beara. When he was asked what he thought of his new parish, he said, 'Allihies! A great place for drying clothes!'."

"Actually, Mary has already told me that one – several times," Margot replied drily. "But this conversation about cats brings me to the reason for my visit this morning."

Mary had launched into a story about Jacinta's latest litter and either hadn't heard Margot's remark or was wilfully ignoring it. Whatever it was, Carol could see her walking them deeper into trouble. Margot had had it in for the cats for some time.

"You should have seen them – like three balls of snow," Mary said. "Not a sooty smudge on them, even though I'd swear it was that blackguard, Lucifer, was the father."

Margot's tone was clipped. "I heard."

"About Lucifer?" Carol asked.

"Not him. His progeny," Margot snapped.

Carol sensed big trouble on the horizon but Mary trundled on unwittingly out of the trenches and into the death zone.

"The only problem with Jacinta is you couldn't watch her. Soon as the kitchen door was open to the hall, she'd be off up the stairs looking for a soft nest to have the kittens. It's only natural after all."

"Oh yes, a nice soft nest she found," Margot said grimly. "Or so I was told. The birthing process has become, I'm afraid, an official complaint to the Farmhouse Association. It came up at a committee meeting of the Kerry branch last Friday. I was deputised to let you know about it." She paused. "I hate to tell you this, Mary, but we had to hint at the slightest touch of Alzheimer's to copperfasten the defence case presented to head office."

Carol took refuge behind the easel to hide the fact that her shoulders were shaking with laughter.

Mary heard her snort. She rose out of the chair. "I don't know what you find so funny. Is it such a joke to see your mother insulted? I know who's to blame for this. That miserable weed of a Dublin woman. All airs and graces just because the husband was a doctor and they lived in Dalkey. She fancied herself as some class of an archaeologist just because she was taking a night course. I had a pain in my head from listening to her going on about ring forts."

"A consultant, mother."

"A consultant, how could I forget? I whisked the poor mites away as soon as she came pounding at the kitchen door. And we gave them a brand new duvet, changed every single stitch of clothes on the bed. He was very nice about it, but she had an old sour look stuck on her puss."

Margot sprang to her feet, looking over her shoulder at her trousers as she did and frowning. "I really don't want to be upsetting your mother, Carol, but I don't seem to be getting through to either of you. You don't seem to appreciate the gravity of the situation."

Carol stretched her arms out. "Come on, Margot, we're talking about the premature labour of one fecking cat indoors. It's hardly going to upset the cosmic order, is it? *News Flash* – 'Cat Bed Scandal Rocks Kerry Tourism'. If they were Americans, they'd have been delighted and the nativity scene would be a hit on YouTube at this stage."

Margot glared at her. "Certain standards have to be met if we're going to effect optimum positioning of the product in an increasingly competitive market, especially when Killarney is hogging the show. It was never more crucial than it is now with the Wild Atlantic Way branding and the *Star Wars* publicity offering us an advantage."

"What about the USPs you're always ranting and raving about?" Carol said, affecting a posh tone. "Unique Selling Points?"

"Come off it, Carol, you're not proposing some mangy cat as a USP?"

Mary frowned. "What did she say?"

"She said she'd love another cup of tea."

Mary's lips contracted to an anorexic line, but she said nothing.

Margot pointed to the cluttered porch behind her. "I really don't want to interfere but there's a grave problem here. If you're not prepared to up your game to meet the extra visitors from this . . ." she sniffed, "this Airbnb venture, you shouldn't have got involved. Really, Carol, you should think things through. I'm sorry to repeat myself but standards really have to be met."

Mary's restraint couldn't survive another reference to standards. Two red spots were burning on her cheeks. "You lecturing us about standards and you with just two seasons under your belt! God help your guests, banished to their bedrooms with top-of-the-range teamakers and satellite TV. No welcoming cuppa in the sitting room. Some farmhouse!"

Margot took a deep breath. "Our property is located on ten acres of farmland, I'll have you know. If I choose to run my house along tight business lines, I can't be faulted for that. Making a profit is hardly a subversive activity."

Carol flared. "Whatever about subversion, making money seems to be an obsession with you."

Margot's face flushed underneath the perfectly applied foundation. "Don't tell me you're setting yourself up as some Joan of Arc of the B&B sector?" Her voice rose to an operatic pitch. "*Sterile as my house might seem to some, at least my guests aren't plucking cats' hairs from the upholstery or feline placenta from the duvet!*"

Mary's eyes bulged. "You're not in the business a wet week and you have the gall to talk to me like that in my own house? I've worked in hospitality for over fifty years. The third generation of visitors are returning here."

Margot paused and took a deep breath. She was obviously hauling out the best nuggets from her personnel training. Something along the lines of 'How to deal with a flaky employee who loses it'. Her voice was calm when she spoke again. "We must think of the good of the entire Farmhouse Association. If one unit is under-performing, we will all suffer in the long run."

Carol had had enough of the lecture. "Save it for the book *'How Endlessly Motivated Margot Can Turn Disorganised You into a Clone of Herself'*. Just drop it now, or I'll be tempted to deliver a few home truths."

"Home truths? Home truths?" Margot did a dramatic twirl in the middle of the floor. "That's rich coming from someone presiding over this – this disaster area. The tsunami left more order after it."

She took another deep breath, a technique from her corporate mindfulness sessions, and began again, wearily this time.

"I've put my reputation on the line by persuading the Farmhouse head office to overlook this – this isolated incident with the cat. But I can't stand idly by and let this continue. Can you assure me something is going to be done about these cat incursions?"

Carol surrendered to despair. No one dictated to her mother, especially in relation to 'God's creatures'. She turned Radio Kerry up another notch as she saw her mother's eyes darken and bore into Margot.

"Can you assure me that you'll take your interfering nose out of my business in double-quick time?" said Mary. "You're as good as accusing me of operating a cat hotel."

Margot grabbed her coat and headed to the back door, speaking over her shoulder. "As you wish, Mary. I'm leaving but I may just have to take my concerns to a higher authority. This could well call for a Fáilte Ireland inspection."

The door slammed.

Mary walked over to the radio and turned it down. Carol dashed across and turned it up again, stabbing her finger furiously towards the dining-room door. "The Kiwi's having a late breakfast – again. I forgot all about him."

"She'll never draw an inspector down on us," Mary said without conviction.

Carol felt a weariness settle on her. "We're going to have to make the peace with the divine Ms Margot. And, whatever about a bleddy inspector, if the wrong person takes umbrage about the cats or anything else on TripAdvisor, we're scuppered."

Chapter 3

Carol O'Connell was the first to admit that her life was a series of half-baked decisions. She changed direction every five or six years, shooting off her chosen course as abruptly as a tourist who sights a signpost looming up at the edge of the Ring of Kerry road and lunges left or right without warning (like rental cars rolled off assembly lines minus the regulatory indicators as it seemed to Kerry people doomed to drive behind them every summer).

She got an impulse to rearrange the essential furniture of her life in the same way that others might revamp their homes. Out with the old, in with the new.

Getting a new suite of furniture, replacing curtains with blinds, shedding a pine kitchen for a minimalist look might be the height of adventure for some, but Carol was operating at a totally different level: relationships were jettisoned, jobs thrown up and an airline ticket bought for a new country with incredible ease.

As a teenager, a nomadic existence had been the last thing on her mind. Her first option had been to stay in the valley to work on their small holding and help out with the farm guesthouse. Anything to be near Jimmy. But her parents insisted that she broaden her horizons. In her mother's book, that signified putting as wide a distance between Jimmy O'Sullivan and herself as was educationally and geographically possible.

Carol became a rebel with a cause. If they didn't want her at home, then she'd show them. She enrolled in the Crawford College of Art in Cork City, worked on a bread stall in the English Market and in a night club to make extra money.

On her first visit home, she wore a bicycle lock and chain around her neck, accessories for a denim jacket, mini-skirt and Doc Marten boots.

Her mother arched an eyebrow when she met her at the doorway of Killarney Railway Station, but held her silence until they were in the car.

"Did you mislay your bike?" she enquired casually. "Or is it just an identity crisis?"

Carol was prepared. "It's a statement."

Mary tutted. "You look as if you're dressing yourself from the storeroom of a bicycle repair shop. I'm glad we're arriving home under the cover of darkness."

Carol levered her Doc Martens onto the dashboard and muttered, "Passive aggressive as usual."

"Lucky for you, madam, that my anger is more passive than active."

There was no telling what look Carol would have embraced when she arrived home at weekends. She veered from Anna Karenina to rock chick to *Vogue* model.

At the house her father paused his reading just long enough to look out over the top of the *Irish Independent* and take in the latest transformation.

Carol kissed him on the top of his head on her way to the fridge.

"Is my chauffeur ready for the trip over the hill?" she said with a smile.

Her father pretended it was a chore. "Of course he is, given the grand fare he's expecting."

The banter was always the same. They'd catch up on the week while he drove her down to Portmagee to meet Jimmy. Mary didn't approve of her rushing straight out the door after she arrived home but, for the most part, she'd given up nagging.

"There's no talking to her," she said to John when he came back. "That fella has her head rightly turned."

"Hold your peace, Mary. These things run their course. The more you try to pull her away from him, the more she'll run to him. And, you know, he's not the worst in the world."

John's main worry was that Carol had invested her entire heart in the relationship. She had rushed headlong into it. She wanted Jimmy for keeps. He knew that the young lad was mad about her too, but not to the same degree. And, as a man, he recognised that Jimmy had a wandering eye. The Sullivans were known for it. Carol had tears in her eyes on a couple of nights when Jimmy dropped her home. She confided to her father that they had argued over girls he had been chatting to. John had advised her not to be too jealous but knew it was useless.

On those Friday nights, Carol couldn't wait to step through the door of the Fisherman's Bar when she would search out the light in Jimmy's eyes as they met hers.

The summers were wild. The sound of the exhaust pipe in Jimmy's red Ford Escort van was loud enough to wake the dead. If they weren't heading off to car rallies in Cork or Killarney, there were music festivals in Kenmare, Clare or Galway. They'd pitch her small tent in some field a farmer had converted into a camping site, stumble back in the small hours and wind themselves around each other in two sleeping bags zipped together while the rain beat down on the canvas. Often, they didn't even bother with

the tent and slept in the back of the van which smelt of
fish and damp overalls.

Muddy festival fields, the tang of vinegar and the smell
of cooking oil from chip vans, the hum of generators, the
beat of a bass guitar echoing in the cavern of her head,
Jimmy's kisses tasting of Guinness and joints, splitting
headaches in the morning.

And heading home to face a different variety of music.
Jimmy's father ranting and raving about being left to run
the boat on his own on the busiest weekend of the year –
it was always the busiest weekend of the year on the pier
– and back in her own house where her mother was like a
worn record. "No thought for the work you left me with
but you'll have your hand out quick enough when you're
heading back to college."

Two peas in a pod, that was Jimmy and herself from the
summer they did the Leaving Cert right through her three
years in Cork. Looking back as an older, wiser self, she
could see how they were sealed in their own cocoon,
oblivious of their families. Everyone else was superfluous.
They had 'the dream'. From this distance, she wondered if
they had truly shared the dream or was it her vision alone of
Jimmy in the boats, of herself teaching art in Cahersiveen,
Killorglin or Kenmare, anywhere within driving distance of
the valley.

Back then, her boundaries were defined by the Skellig
horizon and the spine of the MacGillycuddy Reeks. That
was her world, sufficient in itself. She couldn't wait for
Friday evenings to head back down to South Kerry,
leaving behind Cork City of the church spires and stacks
of houses climbing the sides of its terraced slopes.

Two peas in a pod until the evening she searched out

his face and his eyes held guilt rather than welcome. Just a single look and she knew he was gone from her.

She couldn't eat, couldn't sleep. Her stomach burned so badly she felt as if it was coated with a paste of cayenne pepper. She faded away until her clothes hung loosely around her scarecrow frame and black shadows ringed her dead eyes. The valley grew small, the neighbours watchful. Her parents' concern was suffocating. Maybe her mother had been right all along: there was a bigger world out there.

Carol's brother, George, was older than her by eighteen months. Michelle was a good six years younger than her. The age gap between Michelle and herself meant that they had never been overly close. Carol's relationship with George came somewhat easier, framed in sarcasm and slagging of their different lifestyles. With Michelle, it was different. Carol always found that she was treading water with her younger sister, flailing for some common ground between personalities that were polar opposites. There was the left-over unease too from teenage years in which Carol felt she came off second-best in her mother's eyes. With maturity came the understanding that Mary had possibly converted her pent-up grief at losing her third-born infant son, David, into love of the new baby girl, Michelle, whose arrival had surprised them all.

In the beginning when friends and relatives still expected Carol to make something of herself as George and Michelle had done, they would quiz Mary as to her progress. A friend told Mary about a son who was taking the 'scenic route' to his eventual career choice. The term was a godsend and Mary trotted it out whenever she was questioned about Carol.

The friends smiled indulgently when Mary said she was 'young, cracked and airy'.

"*Arrah*, she'll grow out of it," they'd cluck. "At least she's not on the drugs . . ."

Even that observation tailed off in a question, or so it sounded to Mary.

Eventually, the questions were superseded by compassionate looks on the rare occasion when Carol's name came up. On the other hand, there was no shortage of chat about George and Michelle and their achievements.

In the early years, Mary had encouraged Carol's wanderlust in the hopes that it would help her heal from the break-up. That was when she thought it was a phase, a prelude to weighing anchor and knuckling down to an occupation some way resembling a career. She had revelled in the despatches from Earl's Court, Nice, Chamonix, Moritz, Queenstown, Fairbanks, Greenwich Village. She was living vicariously, drinking in the experiences she'd never even have dreamt of.

Working in a high-class London hotel to see how things were done over there had been Mary's one ambition, but then she had married John, crossed the Laune Bridge on the way back from her working life in Killarney and settled into Glenosheen just a valley away from the farm she'd grown up on.

Even if Carol was a rolling stone, Mary had the consolation that she was able to feel at home wherever she found herself. She could create a home out of nothing, fashion a living space that even the most nervous and edgy of individuals could relax into like a shell. Her eye for colour was key. She was her mother's daughter in this respect at least.

John and herself had cringed when they delivered Carol to her first flat in Cork City, a drab basement on Wellington Road with a window looking out on a grubby footpath. When they called again, she had transformed it into a Mediterranean haven with a can of blue paint, lemon throws and a potted plant. She dashed off bright, bold canvases to match her surroundings.

Thrift shops were an Aladdin's Cave for Carol. When the time came to move again, everything went back into the shop after friends got first choice of the leavings. Any excess went ahead by post, and she was ready to leave with her ancient rucksack. She worked in burger joints, language schools, fish factories, and in the seafront restaurants, bars and shops of harbour towns. Every chance she got, she painted and sold her work in markets. She would have loved to paint full-time but she'd never have made enough money to survive.

When winter came, she headed for the mountains and the snow. For her twenty-fifth birthday, Mary and John paid a small fortune for her to take a course in an exclusive culinary school in Knightsbridge. The investment paid off dividends. She found work catering in alpine holiday homes owned by investment bankers and opulent enough to have doubled as sets for James Bond films. She gave art classes to groups of ex-pats and taught English to locals.

And when she tired of that, she tended the 'nearly dead and the newly-weds' on the cruise ships circuit for a couple of seasons.

Mary blamed herself in a way for the gypsy lifestyle of her youngest daughter. If she had given her time to work things out for herself, instead of insisting she had to go to college immediately, maybe things wouldn't have ended the way they did with Jimmy and she wouldn't have run scared from the heartbreak. She had only wanted the best for her.

"You'll have to go to college like George," Mary had told her. "By all means go and see some of the world when you've a qualification behind you. When your father brought me back here from Killarney, I vowed that my own children would have more opportunities. None of you would bury themselves down here. Education is the key to every door, especially for a woman. As beautiful as this place is, it's the graveyard of ambition. Once you put down roots on the southern side of the MacGillycuddy Reeks, you close off so many options for yourself. Look at it this way – you can do the degree in art, add a fourth year to get the H.Dip and a teaching job near home. Four years might seem like a long time to you now but college years will fly. And you'll be home for the holidays."

Carol was far too smitten by Jimmy O'Sullivan for Mary's liking. Love? A seventeen-year-old knew as much about love as a pig knew about a white shirt. Mary's secret hope was that the relationship would fizzle out once Carol put some distance between herself and home. What did they say? *Be careful what you wish for.*

In time, young Jimmy went on to marry a Dutch psychotherapist-turned-weaver whom he'd met on the boat one summer. They were rearing six wired-to-the-moon blond children, all home-educated and breastfed until the age of three, of course, and conversant with the basic yoga poses by the age of eight. Mary had done everything in her power to discourage Carol from pinning her future on Jimmy but, given the assorted specimens she'd brought home to Glenosheen in the years that followed, she allowed herself the occasional twinge of doubt. But all anxieties and other uncomfortable stirrings were subdued by a post-dinner gin and tonic. A double measure, of course.

The last in the line of men borne home to the valley by Carol had been Matteo, a secondary school teacher from Ornavasso, a nondescript valley town north of Milan and close to the Swiss border. Mary had to admit that Matteo was by far the best of the specimens. He had a permanent, pensionable job which was more than could be said for the shower of hippies who had preceded him. Still, there was something about him that Mary couldn't quite put her finger on. She wondered why he hadn't married. The words uttered by Timmy, workman-cum-sage, when Carol had brought home a divorcee from New Hampshire, came back to haunt her: "All these lads have some story following them."

Carol had been down on her luck and her money when she met Matteo in London. He was over on a stag weekend with his friends. She was working as a chambermaid in a small hotel in one of those 'upstairs downstairs' side streets off Earls Court Road and renting a room long-term in a hostel. She had forgotten to replace the toilet roll in a bathroom. When she knocked at the door, Matteo opened it and locked his amused brown eyes on hers.

"What do they say?" he began as he looked down at the double roll. "You must be afraid of Greeks who come with gifts."

Carol laughed. "You nearly have it. *Beware of Greeks bearing gifts*. The trouble is I'm Irish and I don't think the Greeks had toilet paper on the gift list."

His face lit up. "Irish? I wanted my friends to go to Dublin. I want to go to Ireland for ever."

39

"Dublin isn't Ireland. When you come over, you have to go south. South to the mountains, the lakes and the sea."

He leaned against the doorjamb as if he was prepared to stand there all evening. "I come from the lakes and the mountains. We have all. But I will travel south if you take me."

What an Italian Romeo, she thought. Yet she sensed a genuineness behind the flirting. He invited her to *The Phantom of the Opera* that evening.

For Carol, aged thirty-five by then, love began over that toilet roll in Earls Court. She upped sticks and moved to Ornavasso, set on the floor of a valley where marble had been mined for the *duomo* down in Milan.

Matteo was steady, appreciative, kind and, well, not the sort of man you'd kick out of bed for eating crisps. He lacked the spontaneity of the harum-scarum partners of the past but she had grown tired of the insecurity. Or so she felt then.

Matteo's lifestyle was quieter than she had been used to. He wasn't keen on parties or having friends around to the house. That wasn't an issue until she began to make friends in the valley. And then there were the lapses into morose silences (artistic temperament) and his budgeting (he cut the toothpaste tube in half to extract every last bit of it). But whenever she took to making lists of positives and negatives, the positives won out.

As well as teaching woodwork in a local school, Matteo made fine art furniture in his spare time. She loved the smell of wood shavings and furniture oils in his workshop. His creativity and passion for the beautiful pieces he produced was a side of him that attracted her hugely. In turn, he encouraged her painting.

"You are so good," he said. "It is a tragedy you cannot paint all the time."

One evening she came home from work in Milan to discover an object draped in a white sheet in the middle of the living-room floor. Matteo was standing in front of it, beaming from ear to ear.

"Oh my God, Matt, it's beautiful!" she screamed, when he pulled the sheet aside to reveal an easel made from polished walnut. He had worked on it during free classes in school to surprise her. She threw her arms around his neck and kissed him.

Matteo's family, the Ceruttis, conformed to every stereotype of a big, welcoming, raucous Italian clan. They enveloped her, and she relished their warmth.

She found work teaching in an English language school in Milan, and ran art classes for adults in Ornavasso every winter. The valley was so much bigger than Glenosheen but she felt instantly at home. Lake Maggiore and other beautiful but commerical tourist resorts were within striking distance.

The biggest problem was the language. Matteo had reasonably good English but most of his family and his friends spoke only Italian. She worked hard at becoming fluent, but the fact that she wasn't a native speaker often left her feeling like an outsider.

Ornavasso was a 'plain Jane' kind of town. It fitted like a comfortable pair of slippers. She called it the Cahersiveen of northern Italy.

A mountain away lay its fairytale neighbour. Orta, a mediaeval town set on a lake, reminded Carol of *Romeo and Juliet* the first time that Matteo taken her there on a cold and bright March morning. They wandered the narrow streets on the lakeside. Cavernous shops with entrances as narrow as the width of a door lined the main strip that tourists followed. One shop sold nothing but dried mushrooms, the smell of them so woody it was almost solid in the air. Ancient flights of steps enclosed by towering garden walls climbed to a quiet road overlooking the monastery set in the middle of the lake.

"This is my soul town," she said on that first visit.

Carol drove to Orta every week, sometimes with Matteo and at other times with the women friends she had made in the valley. Even when the hordes of tourists arrived in the summer she found solitude on the high road.

"You think you own the place," Matteo joked.

"Or maybe Orta's taken ownership of me," she replied.

He stopped on the road, took her face between his mittened hands and kissed her cold cheeks. "You two ladies have the same beautiful spirit."

It was a blue-skied day with a lively wind hurrying in off the lake. They climbed the steps to the high road to look out on the island monastery and the snow-capped mountains stretching away to the horizon. Secretly, she hoped that Matteo would propose to her there one day but not just yet. She wasn't to know that she would be confronted with a very different decision in her Italian heaven.

It was strange that it was here of all places four years later one January afternoon that she had the sensation of being mugged, so strong and immediate was the pang of longing for home that hit her. The intensity of the feeling was ridiculous given that she'd been back in Kerry the previous November, but her legs grew weak and she sank onto a low stone wall, ignoring a concerned look from an elderly couple approaching her. She wanted to be with her own people, the people who spoke her language, to walk the mountain road and look out on the Skelligs. She wanted to squelch her bare feet into the springy bog and watch water, dark as treacle, cover their whiteness.

Was she losing her senses? Once she had got the taste of far horizons, she always said Glenosheen would hem her in. Even after a week's visit she was itching to be off again. Hadn't she headed for the airport without a moment's thought in November?

January never sat easy with Carol at the best of times. She didn't hold with the truck of resolutions because she knew she wouldn't keep them. And that made her think of her lack of discipline. She questioned what she had achieved to date. Self-doubt set in.

January would inevitably roller-coaster towards her fortieth birthday in December. It was a milestone that concentrated her mind. If she was going to be anywhere when she was forty, it couldn't be home. And she couldn't be alone. Matteo and herself had hit another patch of turbulence but things would settle. She was probably overthinking, overreacting to the new negatives appearing on the list. No man was perfect. Not even Matteo who was so proud to relate that his name meant 'gift from God' in Hebrew.

It was the quietest time of the year in the language school. Maybe she would follow through on this aching for home and burn it out. Just for a couple of weeks. Enough time to gain perspective on the life she had with 'God's gift' in Ornavasso. Enough to satisfy the curiosity sharpened by rumours reaching her from home that Jimmy O'Sullivan and his psychotherapist weren't the happiest of campers this weather despite their Swiss Family Robinson set-up.

Chapter 4

The throb of a motorbike engine carried through the open kitchen window. Carol and her friend Angela smiled at each other knowingly.

Angela tapped her watch. "Half three on the button. You could set your watch by him. Did you ever see a man like him to keep to a routine?"

Carol nodded. It was on the tip of her tongue to remark that Timmy's times of arrival coincided with mealtimes. Even though he had moved into a sheltered housing scheme in Cahersiveen twelve years previously, he never left a day pass without calling to Glenosheen. He had a nose for the *tae* brewing. He could arrive in the kitchen mid-morning or mid-afternoon, or for any of the three main meals. He never affected the forced politeness of country people who felt duty-bound to say they had just got up from the table at home, even though their stomachs might be hitting their backbones. Timmy's initial acceptance of a 'cup out of the hand' always evolved into the chair being pulled out to rest the legs and a full-blown conversation.

"What do you think of the motor bike?" Angela asked.

Carol got up to take an extra mug from the press and flicked on the kettle switch. "I was codding him that I'd nearly like it for myself."

The two friends stood at the kitchen window, watching Timmy park.

"Timothy Healy," Carol said, her eyes filled with affection. "Did you ever come across a man that everything has worked out so well for?"

"*Shhh* – don't let him hear us talking about him," Angela said softly. "Everything? Well, not exactly everything, but with the houseen from Social Services and then the pension a few years ago, he doesn't know himself. And not forgetting the famous bike. That Barbara Winters was a living saint the way she looked after him. Pity she had to move back."

After Timmy qualified for the pension, he limited his work to light gardening jobs because arthritis was taking its toll. One of the gardens belonged to an American couple, Robert and Barbara Winters, who had retired to Ballinskelligs. When Robert died, Barbara sold up and went back to Long Island. Sorting through their belongings before the move, she made Timmy a present of a blue-and-white Passport Honda. A little of the foam was showing through the saddle but, apart from that, it was perfect. Barbara told him it had been manufactured in Japan in 1980. They had shipped it over from America in the container of belongings they brought to Kerry with them.

"Robert would have dearly loved for you to have it," she said. "He couldn't believe you were still riding a pushbike at your age and with your arthritis."

Timmy had to go through the ritual of refusing to take it at first, though he was petrified that she would take him at his word. "Ah, missus, that's far too good to be giving away. You'd get a good price for it in one of those magazines people sell things on. *Fair Deal* or *Done Deal* or one of those things."

But Barbara was well-used to Kerry customs by then and knew how to assess polite refusals. "No, Timmy, my mind is made up. This Honda has your name written all over it."

The offers and the refusals shuttled over and back three or four times until Timmy felt that he wasn't too eager in accepting. "Well, if you're really sure about it, I won't say no." He took a step forward and shook her hand firmly. "I won't forget you for this, missus. Or himself neither, God rest him. I'm sure he has a bed in heaven."

Barbara told Angela later that she had to turn away abruptly so that he wouldn't see the tears welling up in her eyes. When Angela praised her kindess, she shrugged off the compliment.

"Robert always looked out for Timmy after we had learned of his life story," she said. "I was only carrying out his wishes."

Timmy made his entrance with his motorbike helmet under his arm. It was like one of his limbs. The kitchen chair screeched on the tiles as he pulled it out from the table.

"Damp old day, ladies, but it'll be blowing past us on up to the Reeks in no time. I passed the missus on the road. I suppose she's off into Cahersiveen for the shopping?"

"At least that's where she said she's gone, but God knows where she'll end up," Carol said. "After the business yesterday morning, she could roll up to the United Nations to hire in a peacekeeping delegation."

She noted that Timmy didn't make any enquiries as to 'the business'.

"Any news around the place?" he asked. He was making a dog's dinner out of being casual.

Angela added some more boiling water to the kettle

and poured him a mug. "If *you* don't have the news, nobody has it. Any word from the palace east the road? Word has it you did a turn in her ladyship's garden yesterday."

Timmy sat up straighter in his chair and helped himself to two fig rolls from the open packet. "Oh my Lord, there is something up alright now that you mention it. She nearly took the pillar off the garden gate when her car screeched into the yard. She was farting fire. Says I to her, 'Aisy, woman dear, don't go giving yourself a heart attack. What's ating you?' Says she to me, 'I'm at the end of my tether with the pair below'." He nodded ominously towards Carol. "The highest thought in her mind is to draw the tourist bosses in Dublin down on ye. That was the story by her yesterday anyway."

Carol slammed down her mug. "So she gave you an earful, did she, knowing full well that you'd come running with the story? I know her game."

Timmy nearly choked on the last crumbs of his biscuit. "'Pon my soul, you know I won't breathe a word of anything to another living soul."

"Not until you run into the next living soul around the next bend," Carol said, boring her eyes into his.

Angela made an attempt to soothe him. "It's alright, Timmy boy, we know you're caught between the two camps. But your heart is in the right place."

Carol couldn't help herself. "It's just that your mouth is all over the shop."

Angela glared at her and she softened.

"Yes," she went on, "the great Margot did arrive yesterday morning bearing gifts of early rhubarb planted by your very own hands. Maybe she thought Mam would bake a tart and we'd sit down to dine as she pegged pearls of wisdom at us."

"In all fairness, she –" Timmy began, but Carol put up her hand with more authority than a guard directing traffic at an intersection for the Killarney Races. He judged that another biscuit was the wisest course.

"Will you let the poor man have his spake?" Angela implored.

Timmy glanced at Carol. She said nothing. He ventured out on the brittle silence. "It's like this. I think her gander was up to start with because she knew ye had two visitor cars that morning and she had only the wan belonging to a perished-looking pair from Holland or Germany or somewhere ordering fecking stuff with no meat for breakfast, and the sausages and rashers she bought were going to waste. 'And the cost of everything,' sez she to me. On top of that, the auld High Five was playing up."

Angela and Carol had given up correcting Timmy's 'gander' and 'High Five'. He thought gander made a lot more sense than dander and he refused point-blank to memorise Wi-Fi. 'Ye know what I'm on about,' he'd say.

He diverted the conversation to a Cork couple who'd bought a bungalow at the far end of the valley. The husband was the son of a local man who had left the locality as a teenager. Angela knew the topic was a distraction but she played along.

Although Timmy wasn't born in the valley, he had inherited the mania of certain country people for tracing the connections of anyone who crossed their path.

"That crowd are like a brace of briars," he said as he presented the research he had painstakingly eked out, tracing marriage connections stretching back generations. There was nothing that frustrated him more than a family of blow-ins without even a strand of a web to start him off. Still, he'd blunder on valiantly with a list of questions in the hope that he'd find some link, however tenuous.

"But, tell me, who was she herself before she married in there?" he'd say. "I heard tell that her people were originally from Glanmore, but one of them came by a farm of an uncle and aunt who had no family of their own."

He was sore disappointed on the rare occasion that his enquiries led him down a cul de sac.

"But that's the way i'tis anyways," he'd finish glumly. This was the signature phrase to round off any of his conversations, a lilt of the voice to draw a happy conclusion, a drop of a few octaves to signal an unsatisfactory outcome.

For acquaintances like Robert and Barbara, unadulterated blow-ins with no connections this side of the Atlantic, Timmy compensated by taking an intense interest in their children and relatives. The unconscious irony was that he hadn't an inkling who his own relatives were.

Angela, a townie and a blow-in to the valley, wasn't remotely interested in Timmy's genealogical research into the new owners of the bungalow. She sighed. "I'm afraid it's a bit more than the car count that's bothering Margot. She's obsessed with her great scheme for 'labelling the product and repositioning us on the global market' no less. Something tells me, Carol, that the only label yer cats will make is the one on the Old Time Irish marmalade jar. Since she came back from London, she's always been frustrated about our lack of drive in the Farmhouse Association."

Encouraged that the heat had well and truly switched from him, Timmy chipped in with another observation. "Hasn't she the ears burned off every other TD and councillor looking for something to be done about the High Five?"

"Well, we'd all benefit from stronger broadband," Angela said. "I have to hand that to her."

Timmy relaxed. "I suppose you can take the woman from the city but you can't take the city from the woman."

"That's it in a nutshell, Timmy, old stock," Carol said. "You should get into marketing yourself. Tell me, how do you find the long-suffering Richard? Or should I say 'Mr Margot'. She must have him hen-pecked."

"*Arrah*, grand out. It's all water off the duck's back to that man. He's a gentleman. Himself and myself do have great chats down the garden when he's home for weekends. Margot calls it his therapy."

Angela was gathering up the mugs and taking them to the sink, despite Carol's protests that she would wash them. "We'll all be needing therapy before this is over."

Timmy gave a laugh. "That Richard has a sense of humour. 'Timothy,' he says to me. You know the quare way those English have of talking. 'Timothy, in the unlikely event that she is ever to find me with another woman, I shall go straight to the crematorium, and not wait for her to kill me.'" He continued to laugh at the story that the two women had heard over fifty times.

"Sure you're like a mouse, yourself, in front of her," Carol said. "'Yes, Margot, no, Margot. Wasn't it the best thing that ever happened to the place to have you come away from that auld London?'"

"Sure, you can't blame a man for wanting to keep on the right side of her."

Carol went over and squeezed his shoulders. "You know right well I'm only blackguarding you. There's enough upset around the place today."

"D'auld bread and breakfast is tough going right

enough. I don't know how ye hold at it morning, noon and night."

"Willya stop your *plámásing* – always telling us what we want to hear," Carol said.

Timmy winked. "What other way would you have me? Any morning a tourist asks me what class of a day we're going to have, I tell them it has all the signs of being grand – even if it will be out in the day. That sends them off happy. And, if they drive far enough out of the shadow of these godforsaken mountains, they're sure to catch some bit of sun. Am I right?"

Carol and Timmy both laughed but Angela didn't join in. She was looking into space, a lost expression in her eyes.

Timmy was grave. "I said, 'Am I right, Angela, girl?'"

Startled, she pinned a smile on her face. "Of course, you are. You're always right, Timmy. Down the right side of you, anyway."

Carol noticed the dark circles under her friend's eyes. "You're gone very quiet on us. Penny for your thoughts."

Angela's laugh was forced. "Hold on to your money, girl. I'm run ragged. I can't even remember what my last thought was. I was probably trying to remember how many rashers were left in the fridge."

Carol sniffed out a cover-up. "Don't tell me you're on 'Alcowatch' again, watching for the signs of a break-out."

Angela held up her two hands and crossed her fingers. "We did have a bit of an upset but it's calm seas, thanks be to God. He's busy with the early lambs. And he's back at the meetings."

Carol had an uneasy feeling as she caught the practised lightness in her friend's voice and the hope in her eyes. But she didn't want to chase Angela away with a heavy line of interrogation. She opted to set her at ease. "I was going to ask after the boys but I lost my train of thought. How're they doing?"

Angela beamed. "Fantastic, thanks be to God. Gearóid is coming up to six months in that bar in Atlantic City. A record for him. I'm on WhatsApp to him a couple of times a week, and on Skype every Sunday. And Seán . . . ." She looked at her watch. "Oh my God, is that the time? I'll have to collect him soon. He doesn't know himself since he got that job bag-packing in the supermarket in Cahersiveen. He's saving for a new Kerry jersey. I'd be lost only for Kerry Parents and Friends."

Carol had to grudgingly admit that Brian had one saving grace. That was his devotion to Seán. There wasn't a football game from the smallest club match to the All-Ireland in Croke Park that the father and son weren't seen at.

It hadn't been like that from the start. In the first few months after his son was born, Brian couldn't accept the diagnosis of Down Syndrome. He had turned to the drink – yet again.

Angela credited his change of heart to the legendary Kerry footballer Mick O'Connell, who lived on Valentia Island with his wife, Rosaleen. The couple's son was also born with Down Syndrome. The loving bond between father and son, who were both great Kerry supporters, had given hope to many a disheartened parent. Brian saw them together at a match when he was still struggling to come to terms with Seán being Down Syndrome. If Micko could handle it, then so could he.

The only pity was that Brian had such a volatile relationship with his firstborn. Gearóid did all the right things but it was never enough for his father. The irony of it was that when Gearóid turned eighteen and went on weekend drinking sprees, there was hell to pay. The final straw was over the milking. Gearóid volunteered to cover the milking five mornings a week when he wasn't at college in Tralee, but he wanted Saturday and Sunday off, especially during the football season.

Brian wouldn't hear of it. It was all or nothing.

So, in his second year of business studies, Gearóid took a J1 Visa for the States and didn't come back. It was breaking Angela's heart that he was illegal and couldn't come and go as he pleased. She was nervous about how he would fare in Trump's America. She had nightmares of him being picked up and handcuffed. But, like everything, she made the best of it.

When Gearóid went away, Angela embarked on learning how to use every App available to contact him. One of her teenage nieces gave her a crash course on the mobile phone and iPad. Snapchat, Viber, WhatsApp all became second nature to her. She'd never have bothered with Facebook only that she discovered how easy it was to message rather than making a phone call. And when Gearóid finally caved in and accepted her friend request, she could follow his life through the photos.

She'd taken to jotting down pieces of news in a notebook to prepare for their phone conversations. She resisted the impulse to report on who had died. He'd accused her of sounding like the Radio Kerry death notices after she'd began a few calls with news of deaths in the parish, mostly older people he hardly knew. It was hard maintaining a relationship with a child an ocean away but, she consoled herself, that was the story of every second family in South Kerry. England, Australia, the States and Canada had taken the best of them.

Carol hugged Angela as she left. "Thanks for giving your time to the manic depressive. I'll pull myself out of this. Margot's attack might be the wake-up call I needed."

"Steady, Carol, that might be going a bit too far. Just get cracking with the tidying. And keep those fecking cats outside."

Timmy had located a whiskey bottle in the corner of the worktops and was examining it. She knew he was figuring that levels had dropped since he had last shared a hot whiskey with 'the missus' (he had never called Mary by her first name even though there wasn't much more than twelve years between them).

"It's what you call damage limitation, Timmy. If I can't sleep, I get up in the middle of the night and make myself a hot one. Only for that bottle and Angela, they'd be arriving in white coats to cart me off to some clinic. Dublin, of course, to keep the shame from the door."

Timmy spoke so softly and quickly she had to strain to catch his words. "It's not for me to be saying but you might have some company up there in d'auld clinic wan day."

"What do you mean?"

"Don't tell me you didn't hear about your neighbour?"

"Not Brian again?"

"Who else?"

Carol's stomach went into freefall. Brian was on and off the drink as often as the weather changed. Even when he was off it, he was no great shakes. He was always a 'Flash Harry' – the biggest tractor, the swankiest car. He'd nearly milk the cows in a suit if he thought he wouldn't get spattered. Some farmer he was, cruising around in a BMW and doused in aftershave with the capacity to stun at fifty yards.

"The poor thing, landed back in the same crap again thanks to the useless git of a husband, What chance had Angela to confide anything when there was so much blabbing about Margot and the stupid argument? She had to listen to me raving, and all that poison swirling around in her own head."

"That's the cratureen out the door. Taking care of everyone and herself missing out. The drink is a curse. Brian has her heart broken with it."

Carol was trying to remember when she'd last seen Brian. He'd seemed fine in himself then. A bit edgy, maybe, but he was always like that when he was on the dry. Angela, of course, was really happy in herself. He was after promising her the sun, moon and stars.

Carol had desperately tried to believe it, for Angela's sake. There was no point in warning her not to get her hopes up. But she bought into it too because Angela was well due a lucky break after all she put up with from her husband.

She asked Timmy how long he thought it had been going on.

He shrugged. "The divil had been at it a *fwile*, but he's after straightening himself again. She had me around the farm last week ferreting out bottles from ditches and all over the place. I found them them in cattle troughs, shtuck in between the hay bales." He half-laughed. "He was like a hen laying out. God help us, it isn't right to make a joke out of it. If the man would stick to pints itself. But, no, goddammit, it has to be that cursed wodka."

Carol was pacing. "I can't believe I was so stupid not to recognise the signs in Angela. Then, again, she's hardly been over here in the last fortnight. That was sign enough."

"Sure she was putting the good face out like the

55

cracked jug on the dresser," Timmy said. "She was sore disappointed he was gone back on the hard tack and didn't want to be bothering anyone with her troubles. On it, off it. It's hard to keep up with him but he's on the dry now and he's going around like a cat. I'm getting the evil eye for clearing out his store."

Carol vented her bitterness. "I suppose Angela was killed from trying to hold the place together as usual. Nothing like the Real Ireland that you'll never find in a tourism ad."

Catching some of Carol's fire, Timmy had a go at Brian's family. "Clane useless his crowd are to her any time he breaks out. She's left with all the work. Just because Angela was a townie, and not from a good enough side of town for them. Do you remember the way the poor girleen thought a poor heifer was sick when Brian told her she was 'thrown up' at the mart and had to be brought home? There was no call for the way he laughed at her."

A spray of spit flew from his mouth as he warmed to the subject, and Carol couldn't insult him by wiping her cheek.

"Damn glad of her they should be, the way she kept the place from going under the time he went buckhouse and sunk a fortune into all that farm machinery. Bank money – there's no trust in it. The bank was quick to lash it out and quicker again to look for it back."

Carol glanced around the kitchen. It was all very well Angela saying she'd help her get the place in order, but now that Carol know the pressure she was under, she couldn't have her around the place like a skivvy.

Timmy went into mind-reader mode. "Don't worry, girl, Brian is throwing a dacent shape at keeping on the strait and narrow for now. And this place will sort itself out. Faith then, I know it will. Though, God knows, it will take a small miracle with the cut of the kitchen. But that's the way i'tis anyway."

Carol did a double-take. She had switched off from listening to the reassuring banter until the 'small miracle' kicked in. "Get out, you scut. You're beginning to sound like you-know-who."

When Timmy was gone, she gave a lingering look at the easel before reaching under the sink for a basket of cleaning materials and rags.

Chapter 5

The trouble with living in the virtual world of serial killers, in Angela's experience, was that you found yourself casting a jaundiced eye on random strangers. For instance, just that morning, she'd been queuing behind a greasy-haired man in a Euro shop in Killorglin. He was in his mid-thirties or so, wore a black hoodie, grey runners and a preoccupied look. There were two bottles of bleach in his basket. Immediately, she imagined a crime scene.

"Next, please," the cashier called, startling Angela from her daydream.

The supposed serial killer broke into a broad smile as he walked away from the cashier towards a woman with a baby in a buggy. He didn't look so forbidding when the serious expression had evaporated.

Angela was reading a copy of Patricia Cornwell's *Red Mist* that she'd picked up in a charity shop. Now that the tourist season was kicking into life, she'd have time to read only at night. It was a good job that she went to bed earlier than Brian. He couldn't stick a light on in the bedroom. Even her discreet reading lamp was too much for him.

She paid the girl and slipped the three Toblerones into her bag with a guilty feeling. She'd eat one that night as she lost herself in the crime world. She'd have been rushing around enough during the day to burn the equivalent number of calories. The chocolate would have to be polished off before Brian saw it. Her twin addictions of chocolate and thrillers were his pet hates.

They had been in the sitting room on a Sunday afternoon only a fortnight earlier when he'd summoned her out of an American women's prison with a caustic statement that was supposed to pass for humour. "The Killer Queen. I suppose you'll clock me with a blunt-force instrument and cut my body into tiny pieces. And while my mortal remains are floating down the Inny to the sea, you'll be perched on the riverbank gnawing away at a Toblerone like an otter."

Angela peered at him over her copy of *Red Mist*. A red mist of her own was hovering. "I'd never be as obvious as that, Brian." She detected the barest flicker of uncertainty in his eyes as if he suspected she might just harbour such murderous thoughts.

But he responded just as quickly. "Why couldn't you read Maeve Binchy or honest-to-God romances like any normal woman? Whenever I call into the bar and it's quiet, Sheila Enright has some romance on the go on the counter."

Angela's stomach lurched. Brian was never done going on about the barmaid when he was drinking. She couldn't tell whether he was referring to a visit to the bar from ages ago or recently. If she questioned him, he'd accuse her of thinking that he was after breaking out.

The sickening way he spouted on about that wan was enough to capsize the mind of any woman. The drink really brought out a spiteful side in him. And much of the nasty remarks had to do with unfavourable comparisons with Ms Perfect Enright.

How she always wore sexy tops – practically pouring

herself over the counter with the pints. 'You're always stuck in the same old duds.' Wonderful Sheila was always back from some concert or holiday. 'There's great go about her.' The figure on her even though she had to be well into her forties and had four children at home. 'It would make all the difference if you lost a few pounds.' The sense of humour she had. '*Arrah*, you'd never get the joke.' He even had the cheek to come home during a bender with a flier for *Slimming World* that the divine Sheila had given him.

Angela read another paragraph of *Red Mist* to distract herself from the annoyance he caused her by elevating his barmaid's reading tastes beyond her own. She visualised him incarcerated in a small cell in the Georgia women's prison in the company of a butch serial killer.

He was disappointed with the lack of reponse to his jibe. "What are you smiling at?"

She looked at him wide-eyed. "I've just come to a scene in the morgue. They're always my favourite."

He shook his head. "I've always said that sanity tests should be compulsory for all women before marriage."

Angela's smile didn't falter. "I'm with you on that one." She licked her index finger and turned another page.

He flicked from channel to channel with the remote. "Nothing but rubbish. It's enough to drive a man to drink. I'm going out for a walk."

Angela should have felt relieved when he left the room. Seán was out visiting cousins in Waterville for the evening. The house was quiet, the fire warm. She tried to deny the tell-tale signs. He wasn't after breaking out. He was just in a mood. She was overthinking again. But she had a right to be annoyed. She couldn't be pussyfooting around him just because he was on the dry. *If* he was still on the dry.

Why couldn't she be like any normal woman? The cheek of him. Why couldn't he be like any normal man? She must have done something woeful in a former life to deserve this sentence of living with such a contrary man.

It was always a relief when he gave up the drink and she was spared the tormentation of his falling in the door, spouting every kind of rubbish. There was the honeymoon period when he busied himself with work and fitness. He was delighted with himself. Even if he acted as if he was expecting some kind of prize for sobriety, she tolerated it as the price that had to to paid for his good humour and peace in the house.

But the relief eventually gave way to tension when he began to crave the drink again. He'd fight with his toenails, she maintained. All he'd do was sit in at night and watch television. If she suggested going to Tralee or Killarney for a concert or a film, he'd say the drive was too much. She'd become watchful for the signs of an impending break-out. And that's what she was doing now. It was the old warfare in her mind and she hated herself for it.

In the early days, he'd say that he was off the drink so long that he was no longer dependent on it. He could handle it now. A couple of glasses would do him. No need need for binges. He was in control. She bought into that delusion once or twice. But Brian never bothered with a cover story at this stage. He simply hit the bottle again without explanation or justification.

What kept her with him? She often asked herself that question. A woman on a TV talk show once said that it was the central heating that kept her in the marriage. Some people said half a loaf was better than no bread. Emotionally, she was surviving on a few crusts when Brian

61

was drinking. She couldn't live with him, she couldn't live without him. Where would she go? What would she do? She left school too young. She had never qualified at anything. This was home for the boys and herself. It was her duty to hold it together. She had invested too much in the boys, the farm and in her marriage to let it go.

It wasn't all hard going. When Brian was off the drink and back to his real self, he was full of fun and affection. When he put his arms around her and ran his fingers through her hair, she was eighteen all over again.

No couple could be happy all the time. To look at Facebook, couples were living the dream but that was a front. Only the other day, she'd seen a post by a woman she knew claiming that she was 'feeling blessed' with her 'hubby'. She knew for a fact that 'wifey' had to be dug out of 'hubby' on a night out in Killarney when he ignored her in the bar for twenty minutes while he chatted to an ex who was down from Dublin for the weekend.

At least the Bed and Breakfast was keeping him sober for now, she tried to convince herself. Once the people were in the house, she could count on him to turn on the charm. Yes, his two 'charm taps' would be gushing full on. There would be less arguments.

She had to give him credit in one department at least. He never held a grudge. Once they had both said their piece, the issue was forgotten and they moved on. He brought that from his late father.

That was easy enough for him, really, because she was never one to bark at him. She left so much go for the sake of a quiet life. It wasn't worth the hassle. Carol lectured her on her passivity, told her she was suppressing her anger and building up a bank of guilt, but it was in one ear and out the other.

Angela was so glad that Carol was back home. There wasn't a day that she didn't feel the better for meeting her. She had a knack of making you feel good about yourself. But Carol had little or no tolerance for Brian or, as she so delicately referred to him, 'that excuse of a husband of yours'.

Angela was loath to sell out on Brian's good points. "Sure the drink is an illness. He's the best person in the world when he's off it. He can't help it. Isn't it running right down through the generations? He couldn't escape it."

There was always something to blame for the latest break-out on the drink – a cow dying, an argument with one of the boys, a pain in his big toe. With Gearóid away the problem was that the milking and the farm work fell back on her when Brian was on the beer. It wasn't fair. Yet, strangely for a townie, she loved the farm life. She was always hoping that Brian's next stretch off the gargle would be the one that would last.

In the meantime, the farmhouse business gave her a new lease of life when the summer season rolled in. It put a distance between herself and her problems. She had less time to dwell on her own woes when she was concentrating on the guests and making their stay enjoyable. It was good for Seán too. He helped her out with the breakfasts. He loved getting tips from the guests, who adored his open personality.

She missed Gearóid so much, though.

The longing to see him was even sharper when the first anniversary of his leaving home had come round in January. This would be his second summer in America. Illegal. And all for nothing. If only his father wasn't so stubborn. If only he recognised what a good son he had.

Chapter 6

The winter that Carol turned twelve, work began on the extension that had been a dream of her mother's ever since she had worked in the Great Southern Hotel in Killarney and longed to start a business of her own.

Mary loved her children but she also loved her work and her independence. The early years back home in the valley had been very difficult. She hankered after the bustle and purpose of her hotel days in Killarney, the banter between the staff, the pleasure of compliments from satisfied guests, many of whom returned year after year.

As head housekeeper, she had been in charge of a fleet of girls who kept the bedrooms shipshape. There was nothing she couldn't deal with. Whenever there was a problem, she was the go-to woman. Every so often she had to calm a hysterical girl when a befuddled bat had fluttered through the window from the Virginia creeper on the exterior wall.

Winter was the season that Mary came into her own. She superintended a revamping of the rooms, choosing new wallpapers, singling out carpets in need of replacement, donating bed linen and towels with slight imperfections to Saint Vincent de Paul. Her eagle eye swept over the front lobby with the blazing fire that greeted guests inside the revolving front door. She took in the reception desk and the bar to make sure that everything was shipshape and welcoming when the guests arrived. First impressions were everything.

Flower arrangements were her speciality. She alternated between dried flowers in winter and, from May onwards, rhodendrons, roses and a host of other colourful blooms from the hotel garden. She adored Christmastime when great swathes of decorations garlanded the foyer and bar. Pride of place went to a towering fir tree decorated all in white.

Mary had initially tested the water for a B&B business of her own with two bedrooms in the house. She firmly believed that all women should pursue education and work as long as possible. When her children were young, the task of raising them distracted her but she was never fully satisfied. Then, her friend Máire started a Bed and Breakfast in two rooms in the family home in Killarney in summertime. The friend's children were evicted to a small caravan in the back garden to facilitate the enterprise.

John was sceptical when she first proposed the idea. "If you think I'm going to put up with strangers traipsing around the house and asking me questions, you have another think coming."

Mary produced a sheet of writing paper from her apron pocket and handed it to him. He read the figures, the estimated profits from renting the children's two bedrooms for the summer with the cost of food subtracted. The rudimentary spread sheet was her trump card. John had been worrying about the cost of college almost since the day she told him she was pregnant with George. She knew that a black-and-white column of figures would sway him more than any discussion. He was sold on the idea with one small reservation.

"No child of mine is going into a caravan. We'd be the talk of the place."

Instead, he drylined the storage shed across the yard, insulated it and put new lino on the floor. He broke a door through into an existing outside toilet that was a relic from the old days. This was spruced up with new tiles and a new sink and toilet bowl.

George, Carol and Michelle were delighted with the prospect of having their own den that smelled of fresh paint and looked so spacious and hollow without a stick of furniture in it.

Mary came up with the idea of getting two new sets of bunk beds. They were delivered one day while the trio were at school. When she brought them across the yard to see the 'surprise', they immediately began to argue about who would get the top bunks.

She registered with Bord Fáilte, the precursor to Fáilte Ireland, and joined the Irish Farmhouse Association. And so the family was inducted into the world of Bed and Breakfast or, as Timmy joked, "Bread and Breakfast". Purists would argue that the farmhouses were very different from the B&Bs because they included the farm experience, but Mary never had any truck with the terminology. She was a businesswoman out to provide the best possible experience for her guests.

For Carol, the seasonal routine of packing all their clothes and belongings into cardboard boxes to migrate across the yard became second nature. Once they had moved, Mary transformed the two rooms with crisp sheets, vases and heirloom furniture pieces in strategic positions. Every second season, the walls were freshly wallpapered. It was almost like reclaiming her old life in the hotel. It bothered Mary that she couldn't offer en-suite bathrooms, but the fact that it was a farmhouse holiday covered that. To compensate, she fitted shell-shaped wash basins in each bedroom. She promised herself that when her dream extension came to pass, she'd have beautiful en suites in avocado green, Robin-egg blue and plain white.

As word of mouth sent more and more visitors to the door, she talked about the possibility of an extension, but John said she was overreaching herself. "We're grand out as we are. What do you want going killing yourself with extra rooms only to make yourself a bank manager's slave?" But the dream had taken hold and his words fell on deaf ears.

While the original two bedrooms met Mary's exacting standards, they paled into insignificance when her design sense was let loose on the extension which represented a blank cheque for her creativity.

Mary had a bank account of her own from her Killarney days. She added steadily to her nest egg every summer. For years she had been stockpiling light fittings, lamps, sheets, rugs, furniture, pictures and ornaments to embellish the extension. A lot of her acquisitions went up into the attic. She stored more under the bed, in the wardrobe and in big boxes stacked against the bedroom wall until John complained that they wouldn't fit in there themselves.

Hard as he tried to hide it, he too was bitten by the bug and added to the store of objects from time to time. The yellow hen was one of the first things he bought her. He had forgotten her birthday – yet again – and she was in a sulk. He landed back from Cahersiveen the following evening with a brown paper parcel wrapped up in string.

"Lovely, just what I needed," she said sarcastically when the china hen was revealed in all its glory.

He stood there beaming as if he'd presented her with the crown jewels. "It suits you down to the ground.

You're always saying, 'I'll do it myself, said the Little Red Hen'."

Mary hissed, "*It's yellow!*"

"What's wrong with that?"

"Nothing, nothing."

With that, he stepped forward and whipped off the cover with a flourish to reveal a tiny burgundy-coloured leather box in the bowl underneath. "Crack open that egg now!"

She opened the box to discover a pair of gold earrings inset with pearls. She kept a straight face. "She's a good laying hen, alright. I might hold on to her."

Her sister, Agnes, brought the best of sheets and bedspreads from New Jersey whenever she visited. A keen bargain hunter, Mary waited for the sales. At home, she'd unpack purchases like a set of matching wall lamps or an ornate mirror and show off the 'before' and 'after' prices to John.

"How do people pay the full price? They must have more money than sense."

John would look at her with a deadpan expression. "At the rate your treasures are growing and by the time you have call to use them – if that day ever dawns – the National Museum itself won't have space to hold them."

Every night in bed she decorated the rooms in her mind. Her favourite flowers – fuchsia, honeysuckle, montbretia and lily – inspired her colour schemes. Four big pictures she had bought in Mackey Shea's in Killarney were chosen to complement the colours. There was a seascape, a forest, a girl in a tangerine dress sitting under a lilac tree, and a garden scene dominated by a purple tree that, years later, an Australian visitor told her was a Jacaranda.

Wallpaper was pretty and it disguised a host of faults, but newly plastered walls would be ideal for painting. The extension had remained a dream of Mary's until a modest legacy from an elderly aunt in Greystones and a dig-out from a sympathetic Killarney bank manager, who knew her business acumen from her stint in the town, had turned it into a reality.

When the work finally started, Mary thought that the stones would never stop coming up out of the patch of backyard where a cluster of outhouses, including a piggery and calf byre, had been demolished. Time had already done half the job on the sheds which John had earlier replaced with a modern concrete structure set a field away from the house. The ground underneath them was a bed of stones of various sizes.

The *rat-tat-tat* of the digger bucket flinting off rock echoed around the valley and inside the chambers of her head until she heard the staccato beat, even when the machine driver took a break from this rooting and tearing. Finally, a patch of level brown earth was ready for the foundations to be dug.

Every day, Mary watched the extension rise block upon block, windows first appearing as empty squares, blond timbers meeting each other under the rap of hammers, individual slates slotting together to become a roof that, along with window frames and glass, closed off the box that became two ground-floor bedrooms and then two upstairs bedrooms overlooking the sea two sloping fields away.

Next came the smells of wet plaster, varnish, paint and, finally new carpet, as the hollow space filled and softened. Tiles and bathroom fittings were delivered in big boxes. The notion of four en-suite bathrooms was the talk of the valley. A procession of locals arrived to see the work concluding on what Timmy had taken to calling 'The Southern', the hotel that Mary had cut her business teeth in.

When Timmy first arrived in Glenosheen, he swallowed down food with so much urgency you could be forgiven for thinking he was afraid that it would be his last meal. He even took to squirrelling away cuts of bread and cold potatoes in his bedroom. John had always kindly maintained that Timmy's obsession had everything to do with the meagre portions in the orphanage in Tralee.

Mary had to take him aside and explain things delicately to him. "Keeping food in the bedroom will only attract a horde of mice, Timmy. You'll always have enough to eat with us."

As gently as she spoke, he fidgeted with his fingers, one hand grabbing the other. He glued his eyes to an invisible spot on the ground between them.

"Now, don't think I'm cross about this," she said. "I'm not."

Mary knew there were no words to convince Timmy that he had washed up in the valley of plenty. Only time and kindness would win him over.

He had arrived that first day as a helper on a delivery truck from a big hardware shop delivering beds. He'd found work in the shop after he left the orphanage. Mary brought the driver and himself into the kitchen for something to eat. Timmy tore into the cold bacon and tomatoes as if he'd never seen a bite in his life before. He practically drowned the meat with HP brown sauce from a bottle.

Mary and the driver exchanged glances over his head. She poured Timmy another cup of tea, cut him two more slices of brown soda bread and a big skelp of bacon before calling the driver outside the door on a pretext of checking the invoice. When she returned, she asked Timmy if he'd like to stay on and work for them. This was typical of Mary. She operated on instinct – with a little research thrown in – and the driver had confirmed that Timmy was a sound young man in his mid-30s, who was struggling to make ends meet ever since he'd left the orphanage. After paying for digs in a pokey room in the home of a cantankerous woman, he had very little to survive on.

John was out every day on his farm advisory work, and the garden and fields were getting a bit too much for him, even though he'd be last to admit it. Her own hands were full with the guesthouse and the three children, who were like the steps of the stairs.

"You'll be free to work on other farms in the valley as well if you want," she explained. "If you get sick of us here, you'll have no problem striking off wherever your fancy takes you. But you'll be guaranteed a wage and your bed and your keep at Glenosheen for as long as you want to stay with us."

It nearly broke her heart to see the way hope and doubt flickered alternately in his eyes when she made him the offer.

"What will they say in the shop in Tralee?" he said. "Maybe they'll complain me to the orphanage. They were very good to give me the job when the Brothers asked them."

Mary reassured him that everything would be fine. "My husband, John, will sort all that out. We're good customers. I'm sure they'll be glad to hear you're getting a start in the country and a berth with a family who'll look after you."

Inwardly she smiled at the thought of John's reaction to the new addition to the household when he'd get home.

He gave her free rein in the house. There was that trust between them. In turn, she welcomed whatever creatures or visitors he landed home with. Whenever she wanted to run with the extension or to get stuck into some activity in the parish, he'd advise caution before eventually giving her her head. The most she'd hear from him was, "Are you sure now you're not biting off more than you can chew, girl, with the children and everything to look after?"

John and herself were a good team. Many's the person who took the road to Glenosheen to ask their advice either singly or as a couple. There were some who went out the valley road with more in their pocket than they had come in with and others who left with a lighter heart and clearer mind.

Mary knew that her impulsive decision to offer Timmy a home was her biggest solo run. But taking in people who had fallen on hard times was part and parcel of growing up in South Kerry when John and herself were children. Elderly bachelors or single women in dread of being sent to the 'County Home' because they had no children to care for them often finished out their days with neighbours. They contributed to the household with their pension books. Beggarmen or 'knights of the road' stopped off for a night's shelter, sleeping in the hayshed or on fireside chairs. In the old days an armful of straw or hay would have been spread on the kitchen flags for them.

Mary remembered waking up one morning and coming down to the kitchen to find an elderly man in a black overcoat asleep in a chair with his stockinged feet inside in the range oven. It was part of the family lore that he had made his way back to Cork City and slept under a bus for heat in the station. Some poor driver didn't realise he was there the next morning, rolled over him and killed him. Mary never forgot the misfortunate man with his feet in the oven.

The afternoon Timmy accepted her offer to come and live with them, he said he'd need to go back first and get his clothes. Again, the driver shot her a look and said he'd collect them from Timmy's digs and give them to the next bus he heard going the road to Cahersiveen. Mary patted the shoulder of the gangly young man with the tight black curls. "In the meantime, we'll get you anything you need in town. I can put the price of it against your first week's wages. We'll put a camp bed in the attic for you until John gets a mobile home from the Council for you. You'll be a great help to me around the place because I can barely stir with the three *gearcachs* hanging off me. We'll fatten you up soon enough." The last promise never came to pass. Timmy never rested long enough to put on as much as a pound. But the thing was that, although he lived in wellingtons from the day the first pair were bought for him, he grew to take on a distinguished look, the aspect of a gentleman who would have appeared perfectly at home in a drawing room with a snifter of brandy in one hand and a cigar in the other. The older he grew, the more the sense of consequence emerged, but he was oblivious of it.

As Carol entered her teens and became a voracious reader, she began to imagine Timmy speaking as a character out of an English period drama. But his actual speaking voice was totally at odds with his physical bearing. To her, he could have been 'Sir Timothy' kitted out in a smoking jacket discussing the state of his shares in Bougainville copper or cricket results from the home counties.

Carol, named for her December birthday, and Michelle

73

and George, named for their parents' love of the Beatles, were constantly at loggerheads as children but, from the first day Timmy crossed their threshold, they had adored him. Their father, when he got over the surprise of finding an extra face at the table on returning home that evening, set out to teach Timmy everything he knew about gardening and farming. Timmy was an eager disciple in every way. Before long, he was picking up the expressions and the accent of the natives.

"There's no fear of any weeds being found on Timmy's grave when he shuffles off," one of the elderly neighbours was to remark as his appetite for work was noted.

George was unexcited about the bedrooms in the extension but Carol and Michelle begged to be allowed sleep in the upstairs bedrooms until 'the people' began to arrive for the tourist season. Tourists were always called 'the people' in the house, a throw-back to the lingo Mary had assumed without question until Agnes, home on a visit from the States, had challenged her, "What are you calling them 'people' for? Aren't we all people?"

When Mary had first started taking in paying guests in the two existing bedrooms, the term slipped into the language of the household.

"We have to keep the extension rooms good for the people," she told the girls. "I want to have them perfect for the summer. I can't have you putting marks on the walls or messing the place up. Look at the cut of your side of yeer bedroom, Carol."

George weighed in on the side of the girls. "Oh Mam, go aisy on them. You're always going on about the people. It's always 'Stay quiet and don't wake the people' and 'Tidy up everything before the people land in on us.' All the good stuff is kept for them."

Michelle was his rear gunner. "He's right, Mammy. Once the summer comes, it's always 'the people, the people, the people'. I'd say you wouldn't even talk to us only that you want to us to do the jobs for the people."

Mary laughed. "What a pair of Orphan Annies I have in Carol and yourself. My extension is hardly off the ground and ye want to be installed in it."

Carol went over to the window that was open to allow the paint to dry. She looked out towards the garden and the sea view opening up beyond it. "I'd love to to wake up in this room. Just give us a few nights in here when the beds come. I promise to be tidy."

Mary put her hands on her hips and began to protest but Michelle cut in on her. "It'd be like being on holidays ourselves. We could be your first tourists in the new rooms. And then we'll be two Cinderellas sent out to the den for the summer."

There were four good-sized bedrooms in the house and one small attic room. Carol, Michelle and George were evacuated to the den across the yard in the summer. The three of them resented being shunted out there but there were compensations. They could have their friends around – the bunk beds were a great attraction when first delivered.

Mary eventually relented in the face of Carol and Michelle's pleas. She promised them a couple of nights in her 'Southern' or 'Buckingham Palace', titles that were circulating in the valley. She was so happy to see it taking shape because she had suffered doubts more than once that it would ever see the light of day.

In spite of her projections of the income it would generate, John still worried about the costings.

"The money will come," she told him. "Everyone needs a dream, and this is mine."

As the final touches were being made, she forbade John and the children from entering the four rooms. She picked wild rhododendron, furze and lilac from the garden. The flowers were arranged in antique china jugs – one with a kingfisher perched on a branch and the other, a Royal Doulton with a geometric green-and-blue pattern. Two Belleek china vases in pale yellow and cream were also called into service.

The windows were paintings in themselves because the views from each was taken up by trees and the sea.

Mary's favourite room was christened 'Chestnut'. In May it framed a section of the old chestnut tree heavy with candle blossom. A stack of soft yellow and green towels placed on a marble-topped washstand in a corner reflected the soothing colour scheme of the room.

Beside this room on the first floor was 'Beech' because it overlooked a magnificent copper beech and, across the green expanse of fields, the sea. One of the nuggets of information that John like to share with the guests was that the beech tree was also known as the 'widow-maker' because it had an aptitude for falling suddenly on any poor individual innocently walking by. Mary used to warn him against telling the story. "For God's sake, they're on their holidays. Don't be depressing them."

For 'Beech', she had chosen a Wedgwood blue with hints of ivory and subtle touches of pink in the cushions, curtains and bedspreads.

Downstairs on the ground floor, 'Camellia' was painted in a cream that was offset by bold scarlets and blues she had chosen after she had seen a feature on the artist Paul Gaugin in a Sunday newspaper. Beside it, 'Honeysuckle' was a more dreamy merger of gilt, yellow and gold.

The en-suite bathrooms, tiled from ceiling to floor and complete with deep baths, were her pride and joy. The original bathroom got a facelift too with black-and-white chequered lino, pine wainscotting and gleaming white paint. A shower was installed at the head of the bath. Agnes sent her a matching shower curtain with black-and-white designs. A long rectangular mirror with a white frame created the illusion of more space.

When the extension was finally complete, it gave Mary the deepest pleasure to survey all her work. The starched net curtains billowed in the evening breeze. Each object and colour were in perfect harmony. Her back ached but the twinge stole nothing from the pleasure of knowing she had created something so welcoming and pleasing to the eye.

Who were the guests that would rest their heads on those soft pillows and what would their own stories be, Mary wondered. Her own crew were finishing their tea downstairs in the kitchen. The children's chatter and John's deeper tones rose faintly to her at intervals. The bedrooms had been her own private preserve for days. As well as working on them for a couple of hours daily, she had walked into them at odd times of the night to steal glimpses of the work that was fast approaching the finishing line. Now it was time for the unveiling.

She crossed from the new hallway to the creaking landing and called down the stairs. "*I'm ready! Come up!*"

They all trooped behind her into 'Chestnut' to begin with. It was a help that the evening sunlight filtered through the candle blossom at that minute. She pulled back the curtain to reveal the green-and-cream picture filling the entire frame. Their eyes said it all. Even George was impressed.

John clapped her on the back. "Well, wasn't that the best day's work I ever did to bring you back down from Killarney? This room is done up so well, I feel like moving in here myself." He stepped forward and sat on the edge of the bed, pretending to test the mattress.

"Get off my good bed before you wrinkle it," Mary said.

The final act of the ceremony was to put up the swinging sign on the pole that had been sunk into the ground beside the entrance gate. A Dutch artist living outside Cahersiveen had painted the sign: '*Glenosheen Farmhouse Accommodation.*' The words were set against a background of the sea. The same man had painted small name-plates on wood for the bedroom doors. The motif of the leaves and flowers matching the names of the rooms were repeated on large wooden lozenges that served as key-rings.

Once the season, one week ran into the next. Mary had the satisfaction of seeing her income triple with the extension. She stored the takings in a blue metal cashbox that she kept under their bed. John teased her at night when he saw her counting the notes and rearranging them. "Is there a thousand extra in there since the last time you counted? I should be looking for my own cut for supplying your people with so many tips about the local attractions."

Mary smiled. "You're only jealous."

As the children grew older, they took turns cleaning the bedrooms. They were delighted with their modest wages. Maybe 'the people' weren't so bad after all.

Chapter 7

"Did you have many last night?" Mary enquired, turning off the TV to give Angela her full attention.

Angela said she had two couples. Carol asked her to stall her report until she plugged out the iron and put away the ironing board.

"This place is worse than a Magdalen Laundry," she said, nodding at the neat stack of sheets and pillowslips in a basket on the floor. She pulled out a chair and sat down. "Fire away now."

Angela opened by giving the low-down on a Galway couple who, at a guess, were in their forties and who acted as if they had both discovered love second time round. "It was all 'love' and 'pet'. They were so luvvy-duvvy they nearly fell into each other's eyes over the fry. He even put the milk into her cup for her before she poured the tea."

"I kinda like that," Carol said dreamily.

Angela was looking at the biscuits. She knew she shouldn't have a second one but her sweet tooth won out. "Well, come to think of it, so do I. My fella wouldn't think of doing that in a month of Sundays. He wouldn't even notice me at the table not to mind putting milk in my cup."

Carol debated whether or not she should venture a leading question to prompt Angela to open up about Brian's latest drinking binge, but her friend didn't appear worried – on the surface anyway. Maybe Timmy had been exagerrating. Or maybe Brian had steadied himself and given it up again. And then again Angela might be delivering an award-winning performance at covering up, an act Carol herself could carry off with aplomb when required.

To listen to Angela's good-humoured take on the guests, you'd imagine she hadn't a care in the world. The other pair, she related, were two young Italian honeymooners. So impossibly young-looking that they'd pass for teenagers, especially the thin slip of a girl with black hair cascading down her back.

They reminded Angela of Brian and herself at that age. Their togetherness, their simple delight in each other touched off a secret spring inside her and released a pang of regret. She had said a little prayer that her little Romeo and Juliet would fare better than she had. All this she kept to herself, telling her audience, "That young pair never stopped taking pictures of the sheep and ate only gingerbread and marmalade for breakfast."

"If they were all like that, we'd save a fortune," Mary said, topping up Angela's mug and nodding at the biscuits. "Have another. By the way, Angela girl, any developments on the western front?"

Angela sighed and took a biscuit. She told Mary that she had rung Margot after the breakfasts were over and found out that she had three cars the night before. Enough to improve the humour. Timmy had already been on the phone to deliver a car count not alone for Margot's house but every B&B on the main road between Cahersiveen and Glenosheen.

"I think the thaw might be setting in," Angela said.

Mary rubbed her hands. "I knew it was all hot air by

her. Weren't her mother and myself always as thick as thieves?"

"I thought you couldn't stand the sight of her," Carol said. "Go on, Angela."

Angela looked at the two of them in turn. "I persuaded her to come back over and make the peace. It wasn't easy, mind you, but she did admit that she could have been a bit over the top."

Mary's face brightened. "Well, that was big of her. You have to give her her due for that. I'm warning you, Carol, don't let your mouth run away with you when she lands. I don't want you making a song and a dance about it."

Right on cue, the crunch of gravel heralded the entrance of another car through the gates. The three of them looked at each other. Could it ever be? Carol's stomach fluttered as Margot's chariot emerged between the two banks of hydrangea. The sensation took her surprise. She hadn't realised that the altercation was taking that much of a toll. Three deep breaths, and thoughts of loving kindness.

She looked out the window. "Would you believe it? She's got Wing Commander Timothy in the passenger seat."

Angela whispered to her. "For my sake, give it your best shot, Carol. I can't keep on going indefinitely like a ping-pong ball between her ladyship and the pair of ye."

Margot advanced across the gravel as briskly as her black stilettos would allow her to and made her entrance. Carol had to admire her guts in making the first move with the olive branch. She wanted to demonstrate that she appreciated the gesture.

"Thanks for coming back over," she said. "We'll go into the dining room. I think we could both do without the audience."

Mary half-rose in her chair to follow them but Carol signalled to her furiously behind Margot's back to stay where she was. Mary waited just long enough for the door to close. Then she blistered across the kitchen floor with Timmy on her heels. She mimed a command to bring a chair over to the door, and stationed herself there with Timmy beside her like a sentry.

Neither of them noticed Angela's face darkening as if a mask had slipped. Her shoulders slumped and her face clouded. There was a faraway look in her eyes.

Margot and Carol positioned each other on either side of the breakfast table nearest the window. This wasn't the most opportune choice from Mary's point of view because it was the farthest table from the door.

Margot's face was deadly serious. "I hope we can deal with this problem in an adult way – minus the schoolyard hysterics of the day before yesterday."

There was something about the domineering tone that eroded some of the cloud of universal oneness that Carol was endeavouring to wrap around herself. Before she could take even a single breath, the words were out. "If you hadn't come across so high and mighty, you wouldn't have got my back up and I wouldn't have been so sharp with you."

"I won't even go there." Margot had a habit of punctuating every few sentences with a sniff. "I take your point about my manner but you can't deny that things aren't exactly shipshape around here."

Carol felt a gloom descending on her. "Don't rub it in. I admit I left things slide. And you can imagine the battle with my mother wanting to do things one way and me arguing for another. She can be so stubborn."

82

At the other side of the door, Mary flared and began to get to her feet. "I'll give her stubborn!"

Timmy motioned for her to sit down again. "Wan of ye, two of ye. The apple didn't fall far from the tree."

Carol knew she'd have to swallow her pride for peace sake. If the disagreement continued to simmer, her concentration on her painting would suffer. She had rehearsed the grand gesture, allowing herself one note of defiance for pride's sake. "This isn't easy for me. Personally, I think you're sticking your nose in where it doesn't belong but because of 'Catgate' and the complaint, I know things are going to have to improve around here. You have my word. Satisfied?"

All she had stopped short of was going down on her knees in front of the white goddess of the Farmhouse Accommodation sector.

For that reason, she couldn't believe her ears when, instead of acknowledging her great sacrifice, Margot stated, "There are just a few teensie weensie points to run over with you."

On the other side of the door, Mary was fit to be tied. "The strap! I'll give her teensie weensie if I get at her."

Timmy put his fingers to his lips and hissed, '*Shhh!*'

Angela had dropped her head into her arms on the table.

Carol gritted her teeth. She suspected she was venturing into a territory far beyond the ken of deep breaths.

"I must admit I was excessive when I said I'd get on to Fáilte Ireland," Margot said. "Can we agree that I'll give the place a quick once-over, and there will be no need for outside agencies?"

"Isn't that good of you?" Carol said quietly.

Margot, caught up in her own mission, missed the

sarcasm masked in her cousin's level voice. "Only when you're ready, of course."

Mary was bristling. "Let me at her, the condescending madam!"

Timmy knew he could only hold her back for so long. "*Resht will you, resht!* Give her enough rope to hang herself."

"She has enough rope to hang all the cows in Kerry at this stage," Mary snorted.

"I didn't want to mention this the other day because I felt I'd so much to say as it was." Margot was sliding farther and farther out on thin ice, oblivious of the danger. She interpreted Carol's mildness as an acceptance of the obvious sense of the advice she was bestowing on her. "But I think you should know that three American women turned up at my door a couple of weeks ago, having been turned away by your mother. They were most upset."

Carol winced. She had a feeling she knew what was coming. The three women had been so fussy about the beds that they'd lain out full length on them. One of them had bounced around so much that Mary had declared to Carol in a loud voice that maybe it was a trampoline she wanted.

Margot more or less related the same details. "They were shocked by your mother's treatment of them. She's alleged to have told them, 'Look, Goldilocks, ye'd be better moving on and testing the beds in some other house if my mattresses don't meet yeer standards. The Hotel Europe in Killarney might be more in yeer line.' Is that true, Carol?"

Carol had adored the Goldilocks line. She had been relieved that her mother had dispatched the three fusspots. Not that she could confess this. It took her all her efforts to maintain a poker face. She nodded solemnly.

Outside the door, Timmy winked at Mary gleefully. "Good on ya, missus!"

Mary made a wholly unsuccessful attempt not to look pleased.

Margot motored on to the next item on the agenda. "Obviously, there's one matter that we're particularly worried about."

Carol felt that she had passed into an out-of-body experience. Her voice sounded curiously detached. "And what might that be, Margot?"

Margot stretched out her crimson nails and inspected them. She was still looking at them when she spoke. "The cats. I know it's a tricky one since Mary is so attached to them, but there is an amount of them. I noticed a few mangy specimens as I came in. Inbreeding, I suspect. One unfortunate creature appears to have no tail. At the risk of sounding callous, I have to suggest a cull of some sort might be in order. Or else ship them over to Klaws, that animal charity in Kenmare."

Mary was dumbfounded. "Are my ears deceiving me?"

Timmy knew that there would be no holding her back now. "She wants a hit list drawn up for those innocent craturs, and pour auld Lucifer is at the head of it on account of him having no tail. Didn't I always tell you he belonged in the *ezoo*?"

Carol's internal mercury zoomed towards her head. "Let's be quite clear about this for fear there is any misunderstanding down the line. You want to become the self-appointed inspector of our house. Furthermore, you are calling for a pogrom of the cats."

Margot groaned. "There you go again making a melodrama out of it. I know for a fact that Klaws will rehome the cats for a reasonable donation. And they don't all have to go. Anyway, it's not healthy for Mary to be so obsessed with cats and watching TV. Have you ever thought of enrolling her in the active retirement association? It would do her the world of good."

Timmy didn't even attempt to restrain Mary as she rose out of the chair and burst into the dining room.

She charged towards Margot. "Active retirement, the cheek of you! I haven't given half my life showing hospitality to people from the four corners to be dictated to by the likes of you, family or no family!"

Margot leapt up and took a step backwards.

Mary advanced, stabbing her finger centimetres from her face.

"I'm only trying to be helpful," Margot protested.

"Helpful, you killer of cats!" Mary said. "Helpful, you jumped-up madam! You landed back here from London with more airs and graces than the Queen. Well, you can take your airs and graces and shove them where the sun don't shine!"

Margot shot an appealing look at Carol. "Talk sense to your mother, for God's sake."

"Frankly, Margot, I think it might be better if you left now," Carol said.

Margot stood up to leave. "You are going to give serious consideration to what I said?"

"I'm only the paid help," Carol said. She nodded towards Mary. "This is the woman of the house."

Margot took a few steps towards the kitchen door, then paused. "I'm appealing to you, Mary, be reasonable. Times have changed and you have to change with them. There are hygiene considerations."

Mary flared at the mention of hygiene. "You won't come in here playing the dictator like your mother before you. Flouncing around the place with that 'I am the doctor's wife' stamped all over her smug face."

"Mam, there's no call for that," Carol said.

At the sound of the raised voices, Angela lifted her head out of the cradle of her arms and drifted into the dining room. She looked as if she had woken from sleep.

Mary had the bit between her teeth and there was no holding her back. "Call my house dirty, would you? You have a short memory. Do you not remember the summers down here, and the way you were dragged up? That mother of yours gadding around with big notions. Running up bills in Tralee and Killarney for her finery, flaunting herself to every Tom, Dick and Harry in the golf club, driving your poor decent father demented."

Margot's face was pale. Carol was so shocked at her mother's outburst that she was lost for words.

Angela's voice filled the silence. "Stop it, Mary, stop it right now."

"I didn't come here for this," Margot said, her voice trailing away with the stranglehold of tears. "You've left me no option but to bring in Fáilte Ireland." She put her fist to her mouth and fled through the kitchen.

Mary was defiant. "What are ye all staring at?" But her voice lost its certainty under the scrutiny of three accusing pairs of eyes. "Someone had to stand up to her."

Carol shook her head. "We know that but, God, why did you have drag up all that old stuff about her mother and father?"

"It's the truth, isn't it?" Mary said with even less conviction.

"Ah Mam, the whole parish knew it was true back

then but that doesn't give you the right to go throwing it in her face."

Timmy found his voice, and added to the general gloom. "They'll be the dear words for you yet, let me tell you, missus." His words met with a deafening silence. When no one else spoke, he launched forward again in an awkward bid to round things off. "But that's the way i'tis anyway."

Mary finally caved in under the weight of the wave of disapproval bearing down on her. "She roz the temper in me. I'm sorry now but what's the good in that? I just wanted to knock the high and mighty look off her face."

"You certainly succeeded in that," Angela said glumly. "I never thought I'd see the day when I pitied Margot but when I saw the look on her face as she flew past me . . ."

No one had the heart to say anything else.

A mobile phone rang.

Angela reached into her pocket and answered it. Her face grew serious, and she walked out into the kitchen. Carol followed her.

"Yes, I'm listening. Go on." She paused. When she spoke again, her voice was frantic. "*Look, if you have something to say, just come out with it. For the love of God, you're frightening me. Just tell me.*"

She paused again.

Carol and Mary looked at each other. Timmy wrung his tweed cap in his hands.

"You're what? I don't believe you."

She dropped the phone on the floor, slumped to her knees and rocked over and back with her arms clutched tightly around herself.

Carol ran to her. "Angie, Angie, what is it? What's wrong?"

Angela looked up. "It's Brian. He says he's leaving me. That we're finished."

Carol reached down, grabbed her two hands and lifted her up. She guided her to a kitchen chair.

"Come on, tell me what's going on with him," she said.

But Angela wouldn't meet her eyes.

"Not now," she said. "Not now."

Chapter 8

Hindsight is a mighty faculty. Looking back on it, Carol knew she should never have gone to the funeral, especially with all the tension generated by the falling-out with Margot setting her on edge. She could count on one hand the number of times she had met Vincie since they were at secondary school together. If she was honest with herself, she was probably hoping that she'd get a glimpse of Jimmy. A glimpse would have been a fine thing. Instead, she had walked smack into him on the street after she had parked the car.

The day was wet and breezy. Who would have believed that she had flown home to snow almost a month earlier? Still, it had been a beautiful homecoming. The Reeks were great mounds of vanilla ice cream. Even on the coast, snow had rested at the sea's edge at Derrynane.

She bowed her head against the rain as she walked towards the church. In her hurry, she barely noticed the figure leaning into a doorway to light a cigarette.

He straightened up as she passed. "Carol, is that you?"

She turned in surprise. It took her an instant to recognise him. "Jimmy?"

He had put on weight. It changed his face. Only for the voice and the blue eyes, she wouldn't have recognised him. The most disconcerting thing was his teeth – gleaming white, as if he'd stepped off the set of *Baywatch* instead of the pier at Portmagee. He must have gone for implants in Budapest or somewhere. She knew it was all the rage during the boom. She made a mental note not to expose her own aged incisors.

"I heard you were back. You haven't changed a bit," he said.

She couldn't return the false compliment. Neither could she lie. "God, Jimmy, whatever about those teeth, your eyesight must be failing. Anyway, good to see you. How're you keeping?"

"*Arrah*, I'm on the ball. I'm out and about. That's the main thing, isn't it? And yourself?"

"Tearing the devil by the tail. Getting used to being home again. I can hardly believe how fast the weeks are flying. March is nearly out the door." She waved her hand in the direction of the church. "I suppose we're on the same mission."

He nodded. They walked on side by side. The rap of a cleaver on the meat block carried from the butcher's. A café door opened and released warm air and the aroma of coffee. The breeze caught a blue plastic bag and sent it waltzing down the street.

"What's the real story about Vincie?" she asked. "I'm hearing every class of a version."

Jimmy shrugged. "Hard to say. The spring was always a hard time for him. He'd either take to the bed or the bottle. He went on a bender the week of the snow and kept going until last weekend. Herself was talking about shipping out and taking the kids with her. He was found in the sea the other evening."

Carol shivered, whether from the dampness of the rain settling on her thin jacket or the thought of Vincie she

91

wasn't sure. "I heard too many stories like that from home when I was away. I don't know what's gone wrong with this country."

Jimmy took a drag of his cigarette. The smoke blew in her face. "It got mortal bad during the recession. People were under fierce pressure. That was another thing about Vincie. The banks were on his case about the mortgage. Like a lot of people, Vincie lost the run of himself and built a mansion of a house. But we're not going to solve it this morning, girl. It's enough that we're above the ground ourselves. How're things out in Glenosheen? Your mother must be a good age now."

They made small talk. She steered the conversation towards him by enquiring about business on the boats, about his children. When she asked about his wife, he threw his eyes to heaven. The expression pleased her more than it should have.

He looked at his watch. "Come on, we've time for wan before the Mass."

She hesitated. Tongues would wag if she was seen going into a bar with him. "We'll be the talk of the town."

He laughed. The deep, musical laugh she remembered so well. A current burbling over river gravel. "And what of it? No harm to give them something to talk about."

The previous night pushed its way past them into the fresh day with a breath of stale beer when he opened the bar door. He took a last drag of the cigarette and threw it on the kerb. Carol glanced up and down the street as she followed him in. None of the people heading towards the church seemed to take any notice of them. But, as a seasoned corner-of-the-eye observer herself, she couldn't be sure.

She took a seat on her favourite bench inside the

window while Jimmy went to the counter. A neat pyramid of turf sods smouldered coldly in the fireplace. Every stray gust down the chimney blew out the peaty smoke that was so much part of home for her.

Jimmy returned with two steaming hot whiskeys. "Look on it as medicinal. We could do with a bit of heat to warm the bones."

She resisted the impulse to point out that the rain had softened the air.

He knocked a bar mat from the table. When he went to pick it up, she noticed a bald patch on his head. At least he hadn't opted for a hair transplant – yet. Suddenly, she felt a pang of sadness for their young selves and all the years that had separated them.

The bar was empty and silent except for the television taking the attention of the barmaid at the end of the counter.

"I can't believe he's lying in that box up there," Carol said, staring into the bottom of the glass as if in search of an answer. "'He was such a live wire in school."

When she looked up, Jimmy was staring at her intently. "Makes you wonder what it's all for. Makes you think you should go for what you really want in life instead of getting stuck in a rut."

Carol sensed the barmaid's gaze turning. The sound of the church bells signalled the start of Mass. She dispatched the last swallow of the tepid whiskey and rose to put on her jacket.

"What's your hurry?" Jimmy said. "That Mass will be going on half the morning. The new curate believes in slowing it down to make it meaningful. The problem is that he gets so carried away with the meaning at times that he forgets whether 'tis a man or a woman he has in the coffin."

Taking the empty glasses, he headed to the counter again.

The barmaid was on full alert, eyes taking in Carol from head to toe. If she did, Carol sucked the whiskey from the piece of lemon in her mouth, bit the heat from the cloves and stared her out of it.

"I thought Glenosheen would have been a slow death if I didn't get out, but now I wonder what I gained by running away," she told Jimmy when he returned with two steaming glasses. "Maybe I should have stood my ground but we'll never know the answer to that one, will we, Jimmy? You seemed to have got the better part of the bargain."

He shrugged. "I've a grand bunch of kids, I'll grant you that. And the boats are booming. The lift started with the Wild Atlantic Way. I used to go to a few of those auld tourism shows to promote the place. They had no more interest in Portmagee than the cat until the Wild Atlantic Way came along. Then, *Star Wars* really drove the thing on. Traffic jams in Portmagee, bate that. We're flying really and my kids are great but sometimes I wonder what if yourself and – "

Carol waved her hand. "Stop it, I don't want to hear any of that *raiméis* out of you." The truth was that she was flattered that he wondered the same as she did, that he was prone to the same 'what if's' after all these years. The volume of her voice was higher than she intended. The antennae were twitching behind the counter.

The mournful sods of turf had finally come to life and the flames performed a blue dance in the hearth. Suddenly, the glasses were empty again. Carol headed to the counter this time. Her only regret was that she had rushed out the door at home without her breakfast. The hit from the whiskey was stronger than it should have been.

The warm glow inside melted her reservations about the barmaid. They chatted to each other while the kettle boiled. "*Arrah*, I don't know how long I'll stick around. It could be six months. It could be forever." Now, spread that one good and thick around the town, Carol thought.

As she walked back with the two glasses, she caught sight of the clock on the wall. If they hurried, they could slip in at the back of the church and who was to know but that they'd been there all the time.

Jimmy wouldn't hear of it. "The graveyard will do us fine. We'll be grand. Vincie won't take a blind bit of notice. Sure, he hasn't been inside the door of a church in years."

The next thing Carol knew he was whispering confidentially how 'herself and himself' weren't sleeping together any more. Very hard altogether it was on a man to have to do without the physical side of things. He attempted to smile at Carol but it turned into a leer. She read the naked lust in his eyes as he reached across the table and took her hand.

She drew back abruptly. "Angela told me that you were seeing that dolled-up wan from Kenmare back then before we broke up, but I wouldn't believe her." Her feelings were as jagged as if they had only parted the day before.

"Ah Carol, pet, that was only a fling. If you'd held your cool, I'd have been back to you like a shot. Angela would have been better off minding her own bleddy business. Her own marriage isn't anything to write home about." He leaned across again and stroked her face. "Don't be like that."

Carol swung her head violently to the side. "You have no idea what you put me through. And leave Angela out of this. She was only out for my good which was more than I can say about you."

Jimmy was rapidly morphing into a cornered rat. "Lave it, will you, lave it! What's done is done. I have enough to be listening to at home without you starting on me."

Carol suddenly felt weary. Here she was sitting in front of a discontented, balding, middle-aged man, not even a pale ghost of the carefree, curly-headed teenager who still went whistling through her dreams. "OK, OK. We'll let sleeping dogs lie. For old times' sake."

When he arrived down with two more whiskeys, she proposed a toast. "To our departed selves. To the Jimmy and Carol that were. May they rest in peace!"

Jimmy clinked his glass with hers. "Amen, sister." At least he'd maintained his sense of humour.

"That's more like it. That's my old Jimmy. Keep it that way like a good man and we'll be sucking diesel."

The church bells tolled again. Carol stood up and rapidly sank back down again. Second attempt. She put great concentration into walking steadily towards the front door. She waved gaily to the barmaid. The grand exit. Let the last hour be our finest. Or our worst. Or however it went. She couldn't remember the expression clearly.

Jimmy followed her. Her head was a great distance away from her feet. The warmth of the bar fell away from them in the open air. She shivered as they stood looking down the street. The honeyed brown coffin with its gold handles was gliding over the heads of the crowds in the churchyard.

They walked to the edge of the crowd and pressed in between the warmth of the bodies. There were sidelong glances but Carol ignored them. She held her breath to contain the whiskey fumes. None of the funeral parlour chatter here, only the sound of the bell pealing, and the shuffle of feet across the concrete yard towards the gate.

When the crowd melted away on to the street, Carol found herself standing in the churchyard beside Jimmy. His arm snaked around her waist. To add insult to injury, she was hiccoughing. She tried to disengage from him but the arm was a clamp and her mind was set to slow motion.

Slow motion was not the term she would have used to describe the locomotion of the tall red-haired woman in an Aztec jumper and pink harem trousers who was advancing on them. The warrior queen, with coordination presumably honed by years of yoga, hit Carol a stinging slap across the face.

"Another one of them that has no interest in a man unless he has a wedding ring on him, I imagine," she snapped, before swinging round to a dismayed-looking Jimmy. "There's more women hanging out of you than ornaments off a Christmas tree."

Carol's cheek was burning but she felt strangely detached. She was analysing the mix of Dutch and Kerry pronunciation in the woman's words and marvelling at her use of idiom.

By the time the hand went on to connect with Jimmy, it had become a clenched fist. Something told Carol that this was a set routine. Nausea was setting in. She gripped the car keys in her pocket. She needed to get home. And fast.

Chapter 9

The fourth day of the row with Margot was never-ending. The atmosphere was dragging Carol down. She packed her mother off to the hairdresser's in Cahersiveen for the afternoon to take Mary's mind off things.

"I know it's not your day but ring up and I'm sure Eileen will fit you in," she said.

Mary went to the mirror. Her hair was perfect. "I could get another couple of days out of it but it will do me good to see the outside world. It's not just her ladyship. All this rain is depressing me. Check the fridge there to see if we have enough milk. I know we're out of mushrooms and tomatoes."

Mary had been going to the same hairdresser for years. Eileen O'Donoghue may as well as have been running a counselling service. She was one of the wisest women Carol knew, as confidential as the confessional. No stories travelled. If anyone could shift the dark mood that had settled over Mary since the morning, it would be Eileen. The only pity was that Carol didn't have the time to go herself. Margot had refused to be pacified when she followed her out to the car. Carol wondered if she had been too hasty taking flight from Italy and her problems with Matteo.

If it wasn't bad enough that the two German women had taken up two rooms, one of them had managed to sleep in the single *and* the double, credit that. Carol flew through the bedrooms and filled the washing machine. They'd used a rake of towels. At least she didn't have to deal with the problem of hen parties and fake tan that Killarney B&Bs and hotels were rife with. She felt tired. Thankfully, there were no new bookings for that night.

She put the kitchen in order and scrubbed the floor. Jacinta and two of her friends, fur ruffled by the breeze, were eyeing her hungrily from the kitchen window. You could feed those cats the day long and they'd still be putting on the starved act. She placed a carton of cat nuts in the shelter of the turf shed. Margot did have a point. The cats were a problem. Still, the farm menagerie was much reduced from previous years.

All through her childhood and her teens, her father brought home 'lame ducks' that farmers couldn't be dealing with: sickly calves, orphaned lambs, ancient collies. Their small farm came to be known as an unofficial animal sanctuary. Some animals were delivered to the door, others were dumped. And still more turned up of their own accord as if guided by an invisible radar of welcome and care. Carol missed the menagerie. Maybe the universe would deliver!

Carol had a theory that whenever life dished up troubles, the universe compensated by sending good things her way. It was delusionary, she knew, but wasn't it as well to be deluded positively rather than negatively? The strange thing was that it regularly worked. Given the way things were panning out, she hoped that a wave of goodness was building up out there somewhere and heading in her direction.

In the meantime, there was always the comfort of a soya latte and gingernut biscuits. She reached under the table to the cardboard box of back issues of *Kerry's Eye* that she had been threatening to dump for weeks.

"But I haven't gone through them all yet," Mary had protested when Carol had seized the box earlier. "The older the paper, the more interesting it is. Did you ever notice that?"

Perversely, that seemed to be true. Despite herself, Carol picked up one of the papers and began to leaf through it. Three or four pages in, she came across a picture of a group of Skellig boatmen accompanying an article calling for the season for landings on the island to be increased a few weeks on either side of the May to September limits. There was Jimmy in a yellow waterproof jacket standing to the left of the group. She turned the page in double-quick time.

Three deep breaths. She had been dipping in and out of Buddhism for years – mindfulness in its purest form, in contrast to the corporate commodity being served up to stressed-out executive types for ridiculous sums. Leaving things go was an acquired skill. Even Timmy had his own version: 'Lave it off.'

She closed her eyes, focused on the peace within and closed the newspaper. She opened her eyes again and dunked another biscuit in the coffee. She was still gazing into space when her reverie was interrupted by a soft cough behind her. She jumped and wheeled around.

Oliver, alias the Kiwi, was crossing the floor with a bunch of flowers and a bottle of wine. "Apologies, I didn't mean to startle you."

Carol exhaled loudly. "God, you put the heart crossways in me."

He took a step towards the kitchen table as if to deposit his offerings there. But then he thought better of it and took a step towards her.

"You've been so kind and helpful to me since I arrived."

He handed her the bouquet and the bottle. "And it's just that I couldn't help overhearing the *um* . . . the frank exchange of views in the dining room a few days back. I had forgotten my bicycle lock and came back for it. You and your mother seemed so upset that I wanted to make some gesture, but I waited until now."

He was blushing like a teenager. Carol didn't fully know what to make of him. She had dismissed him as cold and standoffish initially but, after half a week observing him, she deduced it was a natural shyness that took time to wear off. The best thing about him was that he drank in every morsel of information she gave him about the area and followed her suggestions. Down through the years she'd learned that you could exhaust yourself delivering insider tips over breakfast only to discover in the evening that the guests had gone in a totally opposite direction.

There was an intelligence in Oliver's eyes too. When he had first arrived, she had him down as a man in his sixties. A grieving widower maybe. A college professor going through an existential crisis. An IT consultant trading the cyber world for nature. The mind boggled. When she dropped fresh towels into his room one morning, she saw his passport lying on the bedside locker. A quick peek revealed that he was fifty-two since the end of January.

Wine and flowers. The chrysanthemums were woeful – the best the local supermarket could muster. She'd have been just as pleased if he'd carried half the ditch in. Not that March had much to offer yet except for the lingering daffodils. The eagerness in his face was touching. She couldn't remember the last time anyone had given her flowers. Well, without being choreographed.

She put the offerings on the worktop and opened a press to get a vase. "Ah, Oliver, there was no need to go doing that at all. But I'm glad you did. You're too kind. I'm embarrassed now. Guests are on holiday to escape from the real world, not to be landed with a king-sized dollop of conflict like the one you were served up in the kitchen that morning. It looks like we're going to have to review the sound barrier."

Oliver looked at her nonplussed. His odd eyes, green and blue, reminded her of the shades of Ballinskelligs Bay on a cobalt-skied day. He looked away quickly. She must have been holding his gaze an instant too long.

Get a grip, Carol girl.

"Sound barrier?" he asked.

The eyes incident had distracted her. She had lost the train of the conversation. What the hell was he on about? She racked her brain in panic. She was having one of her mother's senior moments.

The corners of his mouth curled in a smile. A gorgeous smile.

He knew she was struggling. *Feck*. Then it came to her. "Oh, the sound barrier! That's Radio Kerry in the mornings. A twiddle of the volume button and the news, deaths and weather will muffle any coughs, arguments or kitchen crises. Or so we thought."

Oliver reassured her. "Oh but it does, for the most part. I am totally conversant with the death rate in Kerry at this stage."

Carol laughed. "That's insider knowledge. Have you acquired a grasp of local geography yet? At times, the radio makes it sound as if more people die in North Kerry than South Kerry."

He paused, as if deciding whether or not to divulge secret information. "Actually, reading atlases and maps is a hobby of mine. I have a big interest in place-names. You certainly have some strange ones in Kerry. I haven't the foggiest idea how to pronounce Gnee-ve-guilla. The pronunciation seems to bear no relation to the spelling."

Carol laughed and told him how. "At least that's our version. You'll hear another one on RTÉ. But coming back to our own radio sound barrier, I wonder what went wrong with our system."

Oliver hesitated before picking his words carefully. "Well, that lady . . . Margaret, is it?"

"Margot."

"Margot was operating at rather a high pitch. She sounded frightfully passionate. Do you think she really will lodge an official complaint?"

Carol was taken aback. She hadn't realised he had heard so much. She'd have to make light of it, although the thought of extra hassle made her weary. Out with the good old B&B face. No point in providing fodder for TripAdvisor. Her smile was as bright as it was false. "Storm in a teacup. I'm sure it will blow over before you can say 'The Force Awakens'."

Yep, she'd definitely elbow Daisy Ridley out of the way at the next Oscars.

Oliver had been distracted from the kitchen fracas. "So you're a Trekkie fan. I must confess I don't know the first thing about it."

"Neither do I really, but I felt I had to educate myself when I came home and saw how Star Wars fever had gripped the place. You can't go into the post office in Portmagee without tripping over stuff about the film. I

103

couldn't be serving up breakfast and going '*duh*' at the mention of Yoda or Darth Vader. Sure they're like family to me now."

Carol reminded herself of a wild bird feigning a broken wing and setting off in the opposite direction from the nest to distract the attention of a predator. But Oliver wasn't so easily distracted after all.

"Maybe you could still talk this Margot out of lodging an official complaint."

Carol threw back her head. "I'm not quite ready to grovel just yet. Anyway, if she goes ahead with it, my mother can take the blame for driving her over the edge."

"Do I detect a note of obstinacy?"

"An entire symphony. I wouldn't *plámás* her if my life depended on it." She added quickly. "*Plámás* means sweet talk or flattery."

"If you don't mind me saying so, your livelihood might depend on some sweet talking."

"You're a well of consolation." She gave him an appraising look. "Can I have your word that none of this is going to end up on TripAdvisor?"

Oliver put up his hands. "Of course you can. I'm sorry if I sound as if I'm meddling. There I go putting my foot in it again."

Carol laughed. "Apology must be your middle name, Oliver."

He looked down at his feet. He was blushing again. Carol never meant to be as sharp as she sounded. She regretted making him feel uncomfortable.

"The first Health and Safety rule of this house is to take nothing we say to heart or you'll end up with a nervous breakdown. And that, my dear tourist, would be way up the line from a few kittens in a bed in the Fáilte Ireland list of offences."

Oliver visibly relaxed. "I do tend to take things too seriously . . . oops, just caught myself. I think I felt an apology coming on again."

Carol took a corkscrew from the drawer and handed it to him. "Here, you do the honours. I'll probably break the cork or something." She took two glasses from a press and put them on the kitchen table. "We'll have a wine and art interlude to lighten up."

Oliver opened the bottle. "Shall I pour?"

"Pour away. Are you interested in art?"

He nodded. "That's one of the advantages of living in London. You can nip in and out of the Tate or the National Gallery quite easily."

"That would be a dream existence for me." She took a sip of the wine and looked at the label approvingly. "*Mmm*, good bouquet. Wonder if your taste in art matches it. Come over here and have a look. Don't be afraid to be honest."

Oliver looked at the watercolour of the delicate fern-like plant growing from the crevice of a stone wall. "Ivy Leaved Toadflax," he murmured, taking another sip of wine.

He put Carol to shame. She had spent all that time getting the detail of the plant correct and she hadn't given a thought to its name. She wasn't going to parade her ignorance, though. He was taking his time in coming up with a response. She began to feel unaccountably nervous. Oliver bent in close to the miniature. After what seemed like an age, he spoke in a considered tone. "It's an exceptionally good likeness. It reminds me of Dürer's painting, *The Great Piece of Turf*. I really like your style apart from one aspect. I'm not so sure about the grey you've chosen for the stone. There's a blue hue to it that doesn't seem quite right."

Carol clinked her glass with his. "I *am* impressed. That's what I felt myself but I wanted to hear it from someone else. It's too late now to sort that grey out but I'll bear it in mind for my primroses."

"That's the challenge of art, isn't it? Finding the courage to go back to something again and again."

Everything he was saying was reassuring Carol more and more that she was on the right track with her work. "And another challenge is to know when to leave well enough alone. In life as well as in art." She smiled up at him. "You can't believe how good it is to be able to have a conversation like this with someone."

Oliver's eyes brightened with pleasure. "I was afraid I was getting too profound and boring you."

Carol gave one of those shrieks that always made her wince when she heard herself. "*Au contraire*. It's such a novelty to have a break from B&B-speak."

She pulled a tea towel from the back of a chair, tied it around her head like a scarf and launched into a soliloquy.

"*It's so hard to get a dacent rasher – they're all water when they hit the pan. The eggs are the same. Free range, moryah! Do you know that orange juice is one of the worst stains to get out of the carpet? What are they putting into it? It's a way quieter than last year. There's no-one off the road. Only for the bookings we'd be empty. That Airbnb is putting us out of business. Every second one is at it now. Thank God for the bit of sunshine or they'd never leave Killarney. The drier is going night and day when we get the rain. Sneem and Waterville are choked with buses. Will we ever see the day when a bus will stop in Cahersiveen again? They'd want to be sorting out that greenway. It could be the makings of us.*"

She whipped off the tea towel and took a mock bow.

"*Bravo, bravo!*" Oliver said, applauding her. "I had no idea we guests caused so much trouble."

Carol was breathless from her monologue. "There I go again, shooting my mouth off. Please tell me you're not a spy in the pay of Fáilte Ireland."

Oliver's expression was deadpan. "For a bright woman, you took a long time to rumble me."

For an instant, Carol believed him. But then he began to laugh and his face was transformed. He looked so attractive when he wasn't being awkward and self-conscious.

"You should laugh more often," she said. "It suits you."

She crossed her fingers behind her back. Please God you haven't gone too far, Carol girl. His eyes crinkled. And he didn't even blush. A silence held between them, a comfortable silence that Carol wasn't even tempted to rush in and puncture with a funny remark.

Oliver was the first to break the spell. He drank the last of his wine and rinsed the glass at the sink. "I'm keeping you from your work. I presume you have to put a programme in place to prepare for this inspector – if he or she does materialise. If I can help in any way . . . I'd be happy to. This place is really special and I'd hate to see it sold short."

Carol topped up her own glass. "I badly need to cultivate a sense of urgency in myself. You're very kind to offer but I can't imagine what you could do unless, of course, you want to undertake the kidnapping of my mother's entire feline family?"

Just then, the back door opened and Mary walked in,

her eyes a lighthouse beam flashing from the wine bottle to the pair of topers and back again.

Oliver's sense of ease disappeared instantly.

"Oliver here has just volunteered for active service in our fight to hold on to our cherished Fáilte Ireland shamrock," Carol said. "I've recruited him to relocate the entire cat population with the help of Klaws over in Kenmare. That was after I plied him with wine and got him to confess that he's an SAS officer working out a defection plan."

Mary delivered one of her speciality cobra looks. "What kind of an impression are you giving our guests?"

"Guest, mother, singular. Chill. We're in the kitchen. No need to put on the act. Sit down and have a glass."

Oliver pulled out a chair for Mary. He offered her a glass of wine but she shook her head, glaring all the while at Carol. He looked from one to the other as if trying to work out the most effective peace-making strategy.

"I travel extensively, Mrs O'Connell, and, trust me, your house is truly splendid. A marble fireplace in the dining room, breakfast on fine bone china, fresh flowers everywhere, and oh those gardens. As for your cats – they are such characters."

Mary's face softened with every line of praise for the house. At the mention of the cats, she beamed. "If only you were around to trot that out for the inspector – if Margot carries out her threat to draw one down on us."

Carol moved to press home the advantage. "Your hair is gorgeous, Mam. They must have a really good conditioner."

Mary touched her hair lightly. "Eileen's marvellous. She knows my hair like the back of her hand." But then her gaze shifted to the bottle of wine and her eyes hardened again. Before she could open her mouth, Carol was off again.

"Oliver, would it surprise you to learn that my mother hasn't washed her hair in – how many years is it again, Mam? But don't be alarmed. There is an explanation."

Mary scowled. "Carol, I'm warning you. How much of that wine have you drunk? In the middle of the afternoon, I ask you!"

"Ah, Mother, you won't be shipping me out to Talbot Grove for treatment any day soon. What harm is a glass or two? The bottle's a present from Oliver – a consolation prize for our state of warfare." She turned to Oliver. "Since my mother qualified for the pension, she treats herself to a wash and set every week. Her pension treat."

Oliver's expression grew sombre. "You know my own mother used to do exactly the same thing. The only problem was that she insisted on going out to the salon one winter Saturday. We think that's how she caught the pneumonia that took her from us. Do be careful, Mrs O'Connell."

Mary clucked sympathetically. Oliver was evidently storming down the inside of the course with the wind of a concerned son at his back. "Don't mind your Mrs O'Connell. Call me Mary."

Oliver had relaxed again. "Why, thank you, Mary. And I am serious about my offer to try and help you deal with this inspector crisis. If it does arise."

Carol was relieved to have her mother back on side. She felt re-energised and ready to tackle the house. She pressed the cork back into the wine bottle and put it into the press. "The worst of it is not knowing the day or the hour. It's like waiting for Godot. Come to think of it, did he ever come, Godot?"

"I don't believe he did, actually," Oliver replied.

Mary's beatific interlude suddenly evaporated. "Give over your old rubbish talk, Carol." She waved her hand around the kitchen. "At least you got something done when I went to town. You need to get the skids under you to have the place in order for that South African couple due in this evening. You know we're practically the only farmhouse open this early. Most people are waiting for Easter to put up the sign."

Oliver began to reverse towards the door leading into the hallway. "I really should be off now."

"Don't mind us," Carol said. She turned to her mother. "What South Africans?"

Mary looked stricken.

Carol was in shock. "I thought that was tomorrow. Look, don't worry, we're fine. The room is ready. I can nip to the shop if they have any food fads."

"Will you listen to her?" Mary said, turning to Oliver. "Where was she got? Little do any of the guests in the dining room know what I'm putting up with. Had you an idea?"

Oliver was itching to escape. "Well, *um* . . . " he stuttered.

Carol stood up and pulled a basket of cleaning materials from under the sink. "I can never decide what's the strongest aroma wafting through the house any morning – the smell of grilled rashers or burning martyr. I have got through the bedrooms – only have to do the shower rooms."

Oliver offered to help her, but Mary cut in immediately. "Don't be cracked. We can't have the guests turning into the hired help."

"Off you go on that bike of yours," Carol said.

When he left the room, Mary just sat there staring into space. Carol felt a twinge of guilt. Maybe she had overdone the wine.

"Are you not turning on the telly, Mam?" she asked.

Mary just sat there.

"Are you alright?"

More silence.

"Look, I'm sorry for larking around. You know me, I don't mean anything by it."

When Mary eventually spoke, her voice was weary. "Carol, girl, you know I don't take a blind bit of notice of you. It's just that I can't abide being on bad terms with anyone. I went too far with Margot. I'm mad at myself for upsetting her. And I'm not the best in the world at mending fences."

The words struck a deep chord with Carol. She hated conflict herself and could never rest easy until she had made her peace with the person she had fallen out with.

"Sure none of us are angels, Mam. Don't go beating yourself up about it. We'll sort things out." She took the remote control and flicked through the channels. "Distract yourself there with some programme. I'll fly through the shower rooms and, when I come down, I'll throw a nice herb omlette together for us."

Climbing the stairs felt like an effort. Normally, she bounded up without even noticing the steps. When she'd left Italy to come home, she never bargained on the domestic landmines she was tripping on. Every problem has a solution, she told herself. She repeated the phrase over and over in her mind. She'd throw off the anxiety in two shakes of a lamb's tail. Well, maybe a half-a-dozen lambs.

111

Chapter 10

"How in the name and honour of God, Timmy, do you think I could go away and leave the house empty while Carol is off gallivanting in another corner of –" Mary's voice jumped a few octaves higher – "*the Wild Atlantic Way!* And I'm left here on sentry duty in case the blasted inspector drops out of the heavens?"

She thumped the table. The two mugs rose up like chorus members in *Riverdance*, the teaspoons rattling inside them.

Timmy was cursing himself for drawing down Johnny McCarthy's funeral. He knew Carol had spent an entire day working in the house after her outing to Bolus. He wasn't to know that she had taken off again to Valentia Island that morning after the bedrooms were done. Herself and the New Zealander on bikes – he was leaving the next morning.

"You'd think Carol would stay around the place a bit more," he ventured, "especially since she was the wan that wanted that Airbnb set up."

The sympathy had the desired effect. Timmy was familiar with Mary's outbursts. They were rare and short-lived.

She pointed to the enamel breadbin. "Take out some porter cake there, and I'll wet the tae. *Arrah*, I can't blame Carol. She did have the bedrooms done before she took off. And there's no bookings for this evening. It's enough to have one of us cracking up. I'm fit to jump out of my skin any time the front doorbell rings."

She pushed a mug of tea towards Timmy.

"Tell me what happened to Johnny, anyway? I heard he was in the hospital for tests, then I heard nothing a'tall."

Timmy savoured a bite of the cake. It was moist and spicy. He'd watched Mary tip an entire bottle of Guinness into the mixture. "He went very quick for a finish-up. D'auld heart carried him. Of course there was a wakeness in that family. I thought one of ye might have showed a face, missus. Ye'll be missed."

Going to funerals was like a hobby for Timmy. He rarely missed one. There was one day when he had mixed up times. When he walked up to the mourners, he realised that he didn't know a single one of them because they had only moved into the area a few months earlier. But there was nothing for it only to continue around the mourners shaking hands and expressing sympathy.

"I'll just have to send a Mass card," Mary said as she walked over to the mirror hanging on the wall inside the back door. She examined her reflection. "I'd swear all this caper is after putting years on me." Her voice was exasperated.

"Aren't you the picture of health and elegance?" Timmy said, throwing an admiring glance at her powder-blue cashmere twin set set off by a string of pearls. "You're the dead spit of the Queen Mother."

Mary frowned. "Given the fact that the same woman is dead at the moment, that's hardly a compliment."

Timmy back-pedalled. "The Queen. Sure that's who I meant. Queen Elizabeth herself."

"Lizzie has a few years on me yet." Mary sank into a

chair and rested her chin on her two hands with a mournful look. "What's it all for?"

Timmy knew exactly what she meant. At some point every summer, she posed the same question. And he could nearly predict his answer word for word. "I often wonder what you're doing drawing all this work down on yourself every summer, missus." He had used the identical prompt last summer, and the summer before that.

It was time to take a different tack. "Weren't Carol and yourself doing fine out until this inspector malarkey blew up in your faces?" He waved towards the bare worktops, the gleaming floor tiles, the vase of Oliver's flowers on the windowsill and three cats forlornly staring in at them. "But you're on top of it all now. The place is like a palace. You could ate your dinner off the floor."

Mary took the brush and swept around the range. "I could never understand the sense of people saying that. What business would anyone having ating off the floor?"

Timmy took inspiration for his finale from the banished cats. "And the cats haven't put as much as a whisker inside the place in days."

Mary's eyes had been brightening but, at the mention of the cats, they darkened. She went to the back porch and filled a dish with cat nuts. The cats were parading up and down the windowsill, tails erect as pokers, when they saw her approaching with the food.

"Oh my poor *piscíns*," she said, opening the window and putting the dish outside. "If they as much as darken the doorstep, Carol is after them like a lunatic."

"The craturs," Timmy agreed. "They mustn't know what hit them."

She took a blue-and-white J cloth from the side of the

sink and began to wipe down the surfaces. "That's enough of my *ollagóning*. I can't be burning the ears off you with my sad story."

She threw back her shoulders and swept the mugs off the table. Timmy hadn't finished his tea but he let it go.

"You know as well as I do, Timmy, that it's the B&B that keeps me alive. I love to see the people coming. The most of them are fine dacent people, though we do get the few *glugars* from time to time." Her eyes took fire. "Do you know that Carol caught some *dullamoo* drying clothes with the hair drier in the bedroom last week? I ask you. They were after washing them in the hand basin with the shampoo, I imagine. But where was I?" Her face softened. "Oh yes, the nice people. A lot of them come to me with their stories. I could write a book with what people have told me. I know we're going all the time in the summer but the winter is long and dreary enough. If I ever gave up, I'm afraid that would be the end of me. I know the place had got quieter but I was managing fine with the few that were coming. I'm half-sorry now for letting Carol sign us up to the Airbnb. I'm a Bord Fáilte woman and a Farmhouse woman all my life."

Mary had a heart of gold. Timmy couldn't bear to see her troubled. Her mood was shifting like the light coming through the conservatory. The sky was a mass of grey cloud, but every now and then the sun came and went in bursts so abrupt that you'd think the Man Above was controlling it with a switch.

"Sure you're only trying to help her out for a while," he said. "When she gets back on her feet, she'll be out the gap again before you know it. For as long as I know Carol, she's like a bird flitting from one branch to the next. And aren't you still a Bord Fáilte woman? You have a foot in two camps, if you ask me."

Mary looked thoughtful. "As long as I'm not run into the ground by the time she's ready to spread her wings again. She's all mad plans about bringing some animals around the farm again. What am I going to do with her menagerie if she takes flight? She was talking about getting bees the other day. Bees, I ask you! I'd look nice left with a hive of bees."

Timmy was facing a serious challenge in putting a gloss on Carol's hairbrained schemes. "You have a point, missus, you definitely have a point there. But sure 'twill all work out in the end." He wheeled out the old reliable which, like a cup of tea, covered all eventualities. "And any day we're above ground is a good day." Then, out of the blue he asked, "Do you think there's something stirring?"

Mary regarded him carefully. His remark caught her left-side. Eventually it dawned on her. "What interest could she have in that long streak of misery? He can hardly string two sentences together for himself." Even as she spoke, she doubted her words. For all his blather, Timmy was one of the shrewdest judges of character she had come across.

"I don't know too much about that," he said. "He seems to be coming out of his shell."

Was that a hint of smugness she detected in his response? She didn't want to let him know that he had stolen the march on her with his observation. Some distraction might do the girl no harm. She'd been up and down in herself since she came home. She didn't want to let on she'd missed the Italian but the break-up had knocked the stuffing out of her. How must she feel facing forty in December without a secure job and a home of her own, especially when the other two were so settled?

"I can't imagine her taking that fella seriously," she said. "And, anyway, I don't believe she's completely done with that Italian."

"*Arrah*, you're right, missus. Maybe it's only part of d'auld bread and breakfast making people feel at home. She's gone mad for cycling with him all the same." Suddenly, he was all attention like a gun dog cocking his ears. "Did you hear that?"

Before Mary could answer, he shot out the back door. She looked through the window and saw him re-appearing on the far side of the lawn where there was a view across to the mountain road and the blue lights of an ambulance. Timmy must have heard the siren. The same fella could hear the grass growing.

At the same time, Oliver and Carol emerged from the driveway on their bikes at speed. Mary was surprised to see them back. She laughed to herself. Maybe Carol's nose had been itching when they discussed Oliver and herself. But her amusement died away as she saw the pair of them approach Timmy and begin a serious confab. Carol's hands were flying. Not a good sign.

"Come in, damn ye, come in," Mary muttered. She could see Oliver dropping his bike on the lawn beside Carol's. Things had to be deadly serious.

Timmy shot ahead of them and burst in the back door. "Good God, missus, it's desperate to the world altogether!"

"What's the matter?" Mary said sharply.

He waved towards Carol, who had just walked in. Her face was grim.

"We were cycling past the turn-off for Angela's place," she said, "when the next thing we saw was an ambulance coming screeching down the boreen with the blue light flashing." She paused to take a gulp of breath. "It had hardly passed us when Dr Hennessy drove down after it. The same surly boyo would have driven past me only I stood out from the verge with the bike in front of me. All I could get out of him was that Angela was after taking a turn and they were rushing her to Tralee."

Mary pulled out a chair and sat down. "I hope some of her family will be in Tralee to meet it. I wonder is she gone to the Bons or the General."

Carol pulled out a drawer and scrabbled inside. "I'll go myself, straight away. Where *are* the car keys? Since we tidied this place I can't find a blessed thing." Her voice was agitated. "I knew something was wrong. I had this feeling. Why didn't I just sit down with her and make her talk about it. Of course there was no time. Nothing but rush, rush. Story of my life."

"What do you think happened?" Oliver said.

Carol snapped. "I don't know what to think. Will somebody find those keys for me?"

"I'll drive you," Oliver said. "You're too upset to sit behind the wheel as it is."

Mary addressed her softly. "Simmer down, girl. You'll get to Tralee in plenty time. We have no idea how long it will take to get her a bed. Hasn't she a younger sister married in Tralee? Annette. Someone is bound to ring her." She turned to the three of them. "Does anyone know if she was on her own?"

Timmy half-closed his eyes in concentration. "I know there was a blue car with a French registration there last

118

night, but I suppose they took off in the morning. Come to think of it, I did see the red Micra of that sister-in-law, Theresa, flying up the road when I was coming over here. You know, that poker-faced teacher wan married to the bank fellow from Wexford that has a path worn up and down to the betting office?"

Oliver's eyes widened at the flow of speech from Timmy. In spite of the seriousness of the situation, he had to bite his lip to stop himself from smiling.

Carol caught his eye and winked. "You're a mine of information, Timmy. Theresa – Mrs Soroptimist herself."

Mary frowned. "We have no Soroptimists down here."

"Well, if we had, she'd be in the thick of them," Carol said. "The same woman could run the country for you, given half a chance. What was she doing up there? She wouldn't even give Angela the time of day when I knew her."

The three of them trained their eyes on Timmy, the oracle.

He began hesitantly. "I couldn't be rightly sure. Herself and the other sister that's retired from the County Council – you know the wan that'd put you in mind of a plainclothes nun – have been around the place a lot since himself took off with that melt of a . . ." he paused and reconsidered, "that new girlfriend wan he met when he was drying out."

Carol gasped. "The what?"

Timmy was taken aback. "I only heard the other day, but I thought she'd have told you, Carol, ye being so close and all that."

Carol was dumbstruck and, going by her mother's face, so was she. She couldn't believe that Angela hadn't confided in her.

Mary was fuming. "The cheek of him. Poor Angela will need all the help she can get to cope with this." She snorted. "She's blessed with the pair of sisters. It's a pity they didn't make some attempt at straightening their brother out before this." She followed their gaze towards the window. "Who's landing now?"

Carol looked out. "Stone the crows, I thought she'd never darken the door again."

Margot took two steps into the kitchen and stood there stiffly. Her hair was askew and there was a ladder in her tights, Carol noted. Things were serious.

"I came to let you know but, obviously, you've heard. Poor, poor Angela. Theresa rang to tell me." She began to gabble with nerves. "I met Theresa through a night course in Waterville – 'Finding Peace in a Frantic World', ironically enough." She puled herself together. "The guards rang Theresa after a French tourist found Angela collapsed in a bedroom and contacted the emergency services." Her voice wavered but she inhaled deeply and continued in an acid tone. "Brian's mobile was powered off."

Mary's voice was low. "There's more to this, isn't there?"

Margot twisted her hands nervously. "I don't know if I should say."

Carol could hardly tell her she was among friends. "She didn't. She couldn't have . . ."

Margot nodded. "There was an empty pillbox on the bed beside her. I blame myself. If I hadn't been caught up in this marketing drive and this nonsensical argument with you. If I hadn't been so – "

Mary raised her hand and stopped her. "We're all guilty of our own blindness, all at fault for spinning around in our

120

own little worlds, barely noticing the troubled look in the eyes of those around us."

It fell to Oliver to pose the question that was on all their lips. "I know it's hardly my place to enquire, but how is Angela? Did the doctor say anything?"

Margot swallowed hard. "He couldn't be sure but he felt the amount of pills on their own weren't enough to . . . you know. But it was too serious to take any chances. He wants her to be pumped out. What an awful fool I've been. If everyone wasn't in such a spin about this inspector, Angela mightn't have ended up in this mess."

Mary waved her to the table. "Will you come over here and sit down, for God's sake. I told you not to go drawing the whole thing down on your shoulders. I shouldn't have said those things about your family. It was unforgiveable. I should have taken back my words before this but, for what it's worth, I'm very sorry."

Margot leaned over Mary and hugged her. Mary looked decidedly uncomfortable. She didn't do physical displays of affection.

Carol caught her eye as she endured the clasp. She couldn't resist the opening for a joke. After all, it was black humour that had sustained the Connells through all their troubles. "This gets more like 'Little House on the Prairie' a la South Kerry any minute. Steady on there, Nellie, or you'll smother Grandma."

Timmy glared at Carol. "I don't know what the smart comments are about. It's not one bit funny. That poor girleen gone off in the back of an ambulance. If I thought 'twould come to that, I'd have said something myself about those wans."

Three pairs of eyes swivelled towards him in unison.

Carol's voice was urgent. "What do you mean? What wans?"

Timmy sounded surprised, impatient even. "Didn't I tell ye already? D'auld sisters. Didn't I say they were haunting the place this past week? As if she wasn't demented enough without them."

Margot was recovered enough to remark primly, "I know Theresa. She's quite nice really."

Timmy snorted. "Nice, is it? All they're worried about is keeping the land in the family. Once they heard he wanted to sell out and take his half, they were in behind Angela like rear gunners to try and get him to stall the digger. I'd like her job. According to Brian, farming is a dying business, what with Brexit an' all. He said now was the time to get out."

Margot persisted. "Maybe they were only trying to help her. Who are we to say?"

Timmy got up from the chair and drew himself up to his full height. Carol had never seen him look so serious.

"She was in no fit state for having the wind put up her about solicitors and court cases and how the boys could lose out if the farm went under the hammer. I came to the back door one evening and they were drilling her like sergeant majors. Then, yesterday evening, she was there in the kitchen all alone, her head buried in her arms and she sobbing her poor heart out." His voice quavered. "I'll curse myself to the end of my days that I walked away, but I thought she wouldn't want me to see her in that state." Tears started to course down his face. He rubbed the sleeve of his jacket furiously across his eyes.

Carol nudged Oliver in his direction. Oliver put his hand on the older man's elbow as tentatively as if it were red-hot metal.

Just then, someone knocked at the door leading out to the hallway. The door was slightly ajar and a man's face materialised in the opening. The thin face gave the appearance of being disembodied as the man peered around the door. He had a wispy beard that reminded Mary of a goat.

"Hello. Can I help you?" she said, opening the door wide and revealing a second man and two women in the hallway behind them. She was in no mood for dealing with people.

"I'm Dave," he said. The accent was American. "This is my wife, Martha. " He pointed to a couple on the doorstop. "That's Beth and Joe. The guesthouse we stayed in outside Killarney rang ahead for us."

Her heart sank. "But I have nothing in the book until tomorrow night. For Saturday, that is. I'm sure of that. I see that you're down for dinner. We normally don't do dinner. That's why I remember." She shot a look across the room at Carol. "Check the book there, Carol. We have no booking written in for today."

The bould Dave was adamant. "No, I'm sure it's today. Friday. Don't you remember Mrs O'Leary called ahead to make the booking? She recommended you so highly that we changed our itinerary to spend one night on the Ring of Kerry, instead of rushing on to the Dingle Peninsula."

Carol got a flutter of anxiety. Surely she had written down the booking correctly? She remembered the phone call as clear as day. She crossed the room to the book and flicked through the pages rapidly. She had made a wrong entry for the day. Where was her head?

It was time to resurrect her meagre experience of amateur dramatics garnered from lead roles in a few school plays. Roles that George had declared 'perfect for the drama queen' at the time.

"Here it is," she said brightly, stabbing her finger on a blank line and snapping the book shut in double-quick time. "It's just that we've had some bad news that distracted us from your arrival, but you needn't concern yourself about that. Follow me and I'll show you to your bedrooms. Then, when you bring in your bags, you can sit into the dining room just off the hall here and I'll get you some tea and coffee."

She left the kitchen and pulled the door firmly shut behind her.

Mary turned to the others. "She'd lose her head only it's tied on to her. How did she put it down wrong? I must have been at the hairdresser's when she took the call. I wouldn't have made that mistake. That's the end of the hospital for her. Margot, can you make sure, please, that Angela's sister has been contacted and will be in there? That crowd are down for dinner too and we've no shopping done."

Oliver opened his mouth but Margot beat him to it. She sniffed a crisis with all the heady excitement of a beagle at a drag hunt.

"Oliver, you're on your holidays," she said. "You've had your quota of domestic drama for the day. Leave this to me now."

He nodded. "If you're sure I can't be of assistance, I'll leave you to it. I really don't want to intrude." He felt as if he was withdrawing from a military command as he left the kitchen through the back door to retrieve his bike from the lawn.

Timmy caught up with him on the driveway and gave him a conspiratorial wink. "That's the wisest course. Lave them at it." He threw a leg over the Honda and tightened the helmet strap around his neck. He glanced at Oliver, his face suddenly grim. "I hope that poor girleen will be alright."

Oliver paused with one hand on Carol's bike and another on his own. "From what Margot says, she should be alright. But she's going to need a hell of a lot of support when she comes home."

"She won't be lacking in help. For the life of me, I don't know how she's going to cope with the antics of yer man this time out, though. But that's the way i'tis anyway. Mind yourself, now."

In the kitchen, Mary was dictating a list to Margot, while Carol, settling a paper doilie on the tea tray, reminded them that one of the four was a vegetarian.

"That's all we need," Mary sighed.

Margot was undetered. "A vegetarian. That's nothing. Try cooking for a vegan. I have an arsenal of lentils and beans at home. I'll bring them all over when I come back from town for the shopping. Are you sure you have everything down?"

Mary nodded. "You're really getting us out of a hoult. I won't forget you for it. Wait there a minute until I get my purse."

Margot waved her hand as she headed for the door. "Don't worry about it. You can fix up with me later. I'm delighted to be able to do something for you. Poor Angela's mishap puts everything into perspective. We'll all muck in together." Suddenly, she looked down and saw the ladder in her tights. She might as well have been told there was a death in the family. "I'm flying home first to change these."

The effort of putting on the B&B face for the people had temporarily distracted Carol, but the full force of worry and guilt sucked her back down with the treachery of a boghole. "Oh Mam, I feel awful that I'm not going to Tralee to be with her."

Mary was firm. "Feeling awful or worrying isn't going to improve Angela's situation one iota. She's in the right hands now. Your time will come when she's discharged. We'll all have to be one hundred per cent there for her then." She lowered her voice and pointed to the dining-room door. "Now, pull yourself together and go in there and put talk on that crowd. That's what you're good at. Give them plenty of porter cake. We're going to have to butter them up after the quare reception they met with."

Carol switched on the radio. "Better get the sound barrier in place. God only knows what the next act will be in this soap opera. *Fair City*, eat your heart out." She paused. "Where did Oliver go? It's his last night. What a note he's going out on!"

Mary studied her expression as she spoke. There it was – a softening around the eyes as she said his name and the faintest hint of regret in her voice when she mentioned the last night. Timmy, the old fox, was right. Carol was going to miss the awkward New Zealander who had turned out to have a kind heart, odd and secretive though he was.

"Put his name in the pot. We'll make sure his last supper is one that he will remember too."

When Carol turned to take the tray into the dining room, she could feel her mother's gaze lingering on her knowingly. "What's up with you, Mam?"

"I wonder if it will really be his last supper."

A surge of gratitude carried Carol into the dining room where four faces turned to her expectantly. "Where did you say you're all from?" she said, setting down the tray.

"Philadelphia."

126

"Philadelphia? Lovely altogether. And what do know about the Ring to start with before I share my own list of favourite places set back from the autobahn. Sorry, I mean the main route."

Chapter 11

Mary scrolled down the tablet screen. "How about this one? Jamie Oliver's Vegetarian Shepherd's Pie. Sounds very filling. It's got lots of lentils in it. Margot brought over a rake of them in every colour going. There's only one problem – the amount of natural gas they'll generate will raise the roof."

"That goes with the vegetarian territory," Carol said, thumbing through a battered copy of a Crank's vegetarian cookery book she had bought in London when she had been trying to impress a boyfriend who was partial to rainbow-coloured jumpers, dreadlocks and veggie food. "Chernobyl, here we come."

She was still finding it hard to get used to Mary's prowess with the internet. Every time she heard the tablet mentioned, for a split second she imagined her mother reaching for a box of pills. Then, it would come to her that she was dealing with her mother, the born-again new technology wizard. That was the advantage of having such good night classes in rural areas. If she was still around in the winter, she'd have to look up a few. The winter. Best not to think about it.

Carol was a confirmed Luddite. She worked her way around the internet on a need-to-know basis: email, word processing and Facebook were her limits. Anything outside that sphere didn't interest her. She knew she should invest in an iPad and a Kindle but she doubted if she would have the motivation to learn how to use them. Besides, any additional expenses were strictly ruled out until the Airbnb revenue began to flow. This didn't stop Mary delivering regular mini-lectures encouraging her to brush up her IT skills. She had just finished one on Ada Lovelace, 'mother of the computer as we know it'.

"She was a mighty woman when you think of what she was into back in the 1800s," Mary said. "She was a brilliant mathematician. You should Google her name and read up on her."

Carol snapped the cookery book shut with an exaggerated sigh and dropped her chin on her hands. "Well, Professor Ada, high priestess of Google, can I rely on you and the mercurial Jamie Oliver to get me out of this fix?"

Mary adjusted her glasses on her nose and peered out over them. "If you hadn't mixed up the booking and we had plenty of notice, I'd have sent you into the veggie section of one of the supermarkets. Anyway, American food is processed to within an inch of its life. They won't know the difference."

"You don't know the health freaks, Mother. Everything has to be so 'free from' that I don't know how the producers end up with anything to put in the package. And don't mention the milk. The time I found a café tucked away between the bookshelves in a Chicago Barnes & Noble, the woman behind the counter listed so many different types of milk to go with my coffee: skim, low fat, full fat to name but a few of them. I can't remember the half of them. I was floored. Daddy had some craic about that when I told him. We only had good old-fashioned milk back then."

Mary smiled but Carol detected a shading of sadness in her face. "I suppose he'd have thought that anything to sell a few extra gallons of milk for the poor farmers couldn't be a bad thing. Anyway, we shouldn't be drawing down the trouble of a dinner for four on ourselves. I gave up that lark years ago."

She had learned from the Americans that a daughter of one of her old Killarney friends had rung up from her farm guesthouse with the booking. She explained that they would only come if there was dinner available. They wanted to minimise their driving on the Kerry roads.

"Simple mathematics," Carol said. "Multiply twenty-five euro by four and you get a hundred. Simple, that is, until you find that two of them don't eat onions, and one is a vegetarian. That's not counting the one who's in mortal dread of anything processed. She's the most straightforward one, as it turns out, because, when you think about it, we don't eat anything processed apart from those packets of cooked ham."

Mary was more than apprehensive about the dinner. Carol had great ideas but she was often slow on delivering them. She knew that money was an issue, but she was hesistant about mentioning it because Carol was so independent. She decided to bite the bullet.

"You know that I have no trouble giving you a loan until you start making some money. I'd prefer to see you getting ahead with your painting rather than slaving in the kitchen."

Carol blew her a kiss. "I'd hug you only I know you'd cringe. You know I didn't come home to be living off you. Besides, the pair would be haring off to get a solicitor if they heard I was dipping into their inheritance. Hand Jamie over here and I'll see what I make of him."

The kitchen was cosy with the heat from the range. Rivulets of rain ran down the window and the conservatory glass. It all felt suffocating to Carol. She wished she was over in Tralee beside Angela's bed.

Mary handed her the iPad and started folding the red serviettes that would complement the red carnations she had pilfered from Oliver's bouquet: carnations mixed with last year's rose hips and a few miniature daffodils foraged in the garden. She had taken out a pair of crystal candleholders and red tapered candles. The dining-room table looked fit for a photo shoot in *Good Housekeeping* with the fire blazing in the antique black marble fireplace behind it.

"That should knock the socks off them," Mary said, nodding at the tableau visible through the open door. Carol didn't reply. Mary knew she was lost in her own world. She spoke more loudly this time. "Now you can see the sense it made not to go to the hospital, I suppose?"

Carol shrugged. "We could hardly have ordered in take-aways from Cahersiveen for them. That's the worst about this business. You're tied to it."

Mary bit her tongue. You should have thought of that before you launched your Airbnb project, she thought. "The main thing is that Angela is OK. And you have to admit that preparing the dinner and dealing with the visitors is keeping your mind off things. When your father died, work was my salvation."

Mary's voice was so firm that Carol looked up from the tablet screen that she was only barely focusing on anyway.

"I could never understand how you could turn around and deal with a houseful of people after the funeral. I thought it was so cruel when you were still in shock. I had so much pity for you. You should have had time to grieve on your own."

Mary set the ornately shaped serviettes to one side and took two wooden butter paddles to make butter balls, adding to the aesthetics of the dinner table. "It might have appeared cruel to someone looking in from the outside, but it was the work that kept me from going under. I went through the motions every day, clung to the routine like a lifebuoy. When I closed the bedroom door at night, it was a different story altogether. I fell to pieces." She paused to sink a knife through the pound of soft butter. "I was able to absorb the fact that your father was gone only by degrees. I used to compare myself to a frozen river with what was left of the water flowing deep below the icy surface. If the entire reality of it had crashed over me, I would have been washed away. Bit by bit, the thaw set in and I allowed myself to suffer his absence. That's when I learned the awfulness of that word 'gone'."

Carol shivered. "I'm so thankful that Angela isn't *gone*." She wore a slight frown as she gave her attention to the recipe on the screen.

Watching her, Mary was enveloped by the tenderness and the protectiveness she had experienced as a young mother. She wished that Carol would settle like her other two children. She wasn't sure if she would ever be fully content in South Kerry when most of her age group were gone and those still there were caught up in rearing their children and, more often than not, in commuting to work elsewhere in Kerry. Oliver had sparked some light in her but, pairing her off with a good man, be it him or some other one, wouldn't be the solution either. Carol's paintings would have to take off if she was to be truly content. She would have to start a novena to Saint Anthony. He hadn't left her down yet.

The onion-free Guinness Beef Stew was simmering in the green Le Creuset pot on the range and the rich fragrance filled the kitchen.

"A stew without onions, I never heard the bate of it," Timmy said when Carol gave him a sample bowl.

The vegetarian shepherd's pie was browning nicely in the oven, as was a rhubarb meringue and sponge dessert that Mary had whipped up.

Carol was proud of her own innovation with the topping for the shepherd's pie. She had mashed sweet potato in with the regular potatoes and added cream plus a shake of nutmeg. Tea lights glowed in small crystal holders set between the red candles.

All the effort was rewarded by the exclamations of the two couples, Dave and Martha, and Joe and Beth. Joe insisted on Carol and Mary joining them in the dining room for the meal. Carol didn't mind because she enjoyed giving advice on the best things to see not only around the Ring but also in Ireland generally. Mary grudgingly agreed to sit in. She wasn't in the mood for 'making talk'.

Timmy refused to join the party but bolted back a hearty plate of the stew before heading for the hills.

There was an empty setting at the table. Carol had tried to persuade Oliver to join them but he made the excuse that he wouldn't feel at ease with the Americans.

"I'm putting out a setting for you in case you change your mind," she said. "Please don't abandon me to my usual fate of being the 'talking machine'."

133

"I have a few odds and ends to organise for the morning. It's an early start to get to Kerry Airport."

"A few tits and bits, I suppose," Carol said, deadpan.

"I beg your pardon?"

Carol grinned. "That's Timmy's version of titbits."

Oliver smiled back. "You're a gas woman."

Carol replayed the conversation to herself at the dinner table when she took a break from being the hostess with the mostest chat. She must have been smiling faintly to herself because Mary kicked her lightly on the ankle to bring her back from orbit. She reluctantly gave her attention to the people again. They weren't bad sorts, really, but she kept imagining how different the evening would have been if Oliver had got over himself and joined them. She still held out a little hope that he might appear. Meanwhile, she glanced around the table and put on a bright smile. "Has everyone got enough of everything? There's plenty more soup in the kitchen if you want any, but you'll need to leave space for the main course."

They all made appreciative sounds and complimented her highly on the basil and tomato soup. All except Dave, who was the silent type. He reminded Carol of the grim faces carved into Mount Rushmore. Martha compensated for him with a stream of talk. The intelligence forwarded from the guesthouse in Killarney was that Martha was his third wife, a fact that didn't appear to bother her in the least. Carol was intrigued as to how a man with such a stony demeanour could be motoring along in a third marriage.

About an hour before dinner Martha had used the phone in the kitchen to brief the next guesthouse on their dietary requirements. She explained that Dave found the mobiles too expensive for landline calls, and she offered to pay for the call. Asked for her surname, she had replied 'Wilson', faltered, and then scotched the first name and replaced it with 'Wright'.

Mary and Timmy were observing her indiscreetly from the table.

"Mr Finally Wright," Mary whispered.

Timmy spluttered over his stew.

When the visitor replaced the receiver, Mary moved in for the kill. "I love your jeans. Gloria Vanderbilt, I'd say." A compliment designed to set the victim at ease.

Martha ran a manicured hand glistening with rings down her thigh. "Yes, they're a wonderful fit. Do you have that brand in Ireland?"

"Of course we do. I have an eye for quality." The scene was set for a probing question. "Is it fair to ask you if Dave and yourself are on your honeymoon?"

It was like taking candy from a baby. Martha related how Dave's first wife had died young. When he remarried, Ethel and himself had moved into Martha's neighbourhood. Martha and her first husband, Harold, had been a foursome. Ethel passed away, followed by Harold.

Timmy was hanging on every word with the same concentration he'd afford an intricate commentary on a football game.

"George ended up spending more time with me," Martha said, her face lighting up. "One thing led to another, and we got married at the Cliffs of Moher in the pouring rain last week. And now we're on our Irish honeymoon wearing these matching rings we bought in Galway." She held up her hand to show off a shining Claddagh ring.

Mary was genuinely touched by the childlike pleasure in the American woman's face. "I'm half-jealous of you. I

135

can never get over Americans. Ye'll have a cut at anything no matter what stage of life ye're at. Half the Irish are afraid to get married a'tall. Take Timmy here for instance."

Timmy was taken aback at the reference to himself and looked embarrassed.

Mary was sorry for putting the spotlight on him. She diverted it back to herself. "As for the rest of us who lose our partners, we're very slow to get going again."

Timmy gave a broad smile. Martha looked at him quizzically but Mary was off again.

"You're a great bit of stuff," she said. "I hope you'll be very happy. You deserve it for venturing out again."

Martha was puzzled. "A great bit of stuff? What do you mean?"

"It means that you're a powerful person, full of get up and go," Mary said. "You fit the bill exactly. A lot more women would never have stirred outside the door again."

As Martha left the kitchen, she was positively glowing from the praise. She stored up a 'great bit of stuff' for future use.

Mary turned to Timmy when a safe interval had elapsed after Martha had left the kitchen. "Well, that beats Banagher. That man hasn't a stray word to throw to a dog, not to mind a cat, and he's on his third marriage to a grand woman. What do they see in him?"

Timmy grinned. "He must have some little gimmick. It's powerful altogether when you think about it. The only place that fellow will see seventy again will be on a door."

Carol walked in on the tail-end of the conversation. They brought her up to speed. "I think it's great. I haven't made it out the gap even once. I might ask them to give a mini-seminar under the title 'Hot Tips from the Multi-married for the Altar-shy'."

Mary was applying her lipstick. "Should Timmy and myself sit in on the talk? You're altar-shy yourself, Timmy."

Timmy threw his eyes to heaven. "I had a few skirmishes along the way but I always escaped. Thank God I got off lightly."

Shortly after the visitors had arrived around noon, Mary had come across Dave snooping around the dining room. He had picked up a silver ladle from the sideboard display and was studying the stamp by the light of the window when she had walked in. He started when she spoke.

"Yes, it's the genuine article. My husband loved collecting antiques. He bought the set from an antique dealer in Cahersiveen." She laughed. "And left me with the job of polishing it."

As Dave handed her the ladle, she noticed the Claddagh ring with the gleam of newness on it. She asked him if he knew the verse that went with the ring. When he shook his head, she asked him to hold out his hand. She held it in her left hand while she pointed out the symbols of the heart, hands and crown while she recited. "*I hold your heart between my hands and crown it with my love.*"

Given the alarmed look in the American's eyes as he pulled his hand away abruptly, Mary was afraid for a second that he thought she had been flirting with him. Then, she heard a soft cough behind her. She turned in time to register a displeased expression flitting across Martha's face before she converted it into a false smile displaying an array of expensive dental work.

"I was just giving your husband a blast of the verse that goes with the Claddagh," Mary said brightly.

"Oh," Martha said in a relieved tone.

Jealous of me, Mary thought to herself as she retreated to the kitchen, God help her head.

Beth and Joe were Martha's sister and brother-in-law she learned. Joe had got his very first passport to travel to Ireland with them. He was none too impressed with the weather. Beth and Martha had travelled together before. Beth wasn't altogether pleased to be hitched to a discontented husband on this trip.

When Carol served up the main course, her guests were so genuinely appreciative that she opened a bottle of Pinot Grigio. She caught Mary's there-go-your-profits look when she arrived in with the bottle but, what the hell, they seemed like genuine people and she could do with a glass herself after the flurry in the kitchen.

As it turned out, Joe and Beth were over-enthusiastic about the wine. Carol began to regret her decision when she noticed Joe appropriating the bottle for himself. But Mary had registered his attachment to the bottle too. Her hand shot out like a greyhound from a trap and topped up all the glasses, favouring Carol, who had to take a deep breath to maintain a serious face.

On top of being a guzzler, Joe was given to whining. "Your roads are so narrow. We lost a wing mirror in Connemara. And the rain – good lord, it never stops."

Carol took a slug of wine and threw out a few conversational decoys, steering clear of the old reliable Trump for fear she couldn't contain herself if any of the Americans were fans.

Beth was wired, constantly contradicting Joe and Dave, and circling on the perimeters of the conversation, waiting for an opening to lob in totally unrelated anecdotes.

Dave loosened out after the wine. Carol made sure to top up his glass. Soon Martha and himself were a vaudeville act, teasing each other with good humour. Even though the two-hander came across as rehearsed – jokes that might even have been tossed out in their previous marriages – there was obvious affection between the pair.

Old Dave might just be a dark horse, Carol thought, but Martha was fortunate to leave the dining room in one piece.

When Carol had initially served up the steaming plates of Guinness casserole, Beth had sniffed the air like a tracker hound. "Oh my God, that smells divine. What is it?"

Carol gave a quick run-down on the recipe: "Guinness, wholegrain Lakeshore Mustard, carrots and mushrooms braised with the Kerry beef."

"Looks wonderful."

As Carol returned to the kitchen, she called over her shoulder to Martha, "Your vegetarian shepherd's pie is coming up next."

Martha was already scooping a spoonful of gravy complete with a succulent mushroom from her husband's plate. "That tastes awesome. Do you have a portion for me?"

Carol wheeled around in the kitchen door as she tried to process Martha's conversion to the casserole. "But it's beef. You said you're a vegetarian. Do you mean you only want the gravy and the veg?"

She had barely finished the sentence when Martha speared a cube of beef with her fork while Dave feigned shock and pulled the plate towards himself.

"Oh, someone told me you get better food in Ireland if you say you're a vegetarian," she said, chewing the beef with relish. "I hope you don't mind but I'll have what

139

Dave's having." She was quite unconcerned about her confession.

Carol deliberately didn't look at her mother. She pulled her lips back from her teeth like a sheepdog snarling. "Of course you can have some. There's loads in the pot."

She closed the kitchen door securely behind her and shot directly across the floor and out through the back porch. She threw her head back and uttered words of Anglo-Saxon origin to the night sky, then added, "Vegetarian, my arse!"

By the time the table was cleared and the dishwasher stacked, Mary and Carol were both yawning.

Carol was taken aback at how exhausted her mother looked. "You go away up to bed. I'll reset the table for the breakfast."

Mary didn't protest. "It's nice to be nice but you'd swear they hadn't a bed to go to. And what did you think of our alleged vegetarian?"

Carol laughed. "All that trouble picking out a recipe for her! She thought she'd get better food! What will they come out with next? I thought it was fantastic that they were on their third marriage, though, fair play to them. There's hope for us all yet. Even you, Mam."

Mary turned away sharply. "I can't keep my eyes open. See you in the morning."

Carol put the abrupt retreat to the stairs down to tiredness. Not for the first time, she wondered if she'd done the right thing starting the Airbnb. She pulled out a tray to gather the last of the glasses from the dining-room table. There was a soft knock at the door to the hall. Her heart sank. Surely none of the four were back. She had given them her all.

The door opened gently and Oliver walked in.

"Here," he said, taking the tray, "give me that. I'll help you finish up and we'll have a cuppa."

Carol's tiredness vanished.

Chapter 12

Carol had rehearsed the comedy routine about their alleged vegetarian, honing the lines calculated to best get a laugh out of Angela, but as she glanced across from the driver's seat all she caught was a smile as watery as the sun trying to break through the grey sky overhead. Angela was so pale and washed-out looking. Her eyes were the worst: they were dead in her head.

They had parked in the car park at Ballinskelligs, sheltered from the sea by the sand dunes. Delinquent bursts of rain blew in through the opening to the beach, pelted against the windscreen and shook the car slightly.

Angela had come home from the hospital that morning. When Carol had rung the house, Theresa answered the phone. To give the sister-in-law her due, she had sounded concerned and genuinely caring. There was enough concern for Carol to cut her some slack on the flash of overbearing attitude. And, Theresa got brownie points too for agreeing immediately that a walk on the beach at Ballinskelligs would do Angela some good after being cooped up in the hospital.

The abject failure of 'Carol the Comedian' prompted a change of tack. She decided to put her money on the tried and trusted shoot-from-the-hip approach.

"Are you sure you should have come out so soon? You're as white as a sheet."

Angela didn't reply. The windscreen was fogging up. She leaned forward and cleared an oval look-out with her fist.

Carol turned the car key and let her window down a fraction, admitting spits of rain that were cool on her cheek. A seagull wheeled in over the car park. "I'm not going to force the talk out of you if you prefer to be quiet. You know me. I can talk enough for both of us." She cursed herself silently as soon as the words were out. That's great, Carol, more jollity, she thought. Can you never shut up?

Angela had caught a tendril of hair that had come loose from her ponytail and was twisting it around her index finger. Her voice was hoarse when she began to speak. She coughed and began again. "And I can scarcely talk at all. The hospital? Two nights in there was more than enough. Anyway, I didn't want to become one of those bed-blockers with all the poor people waiting hours in Casualty to get in. Casualty was like a war zone with so many people on trolleys. It took some effort to convince the doctor that it was safe to release me into the care of my two . . ." her voice hardened, "my three guardian angels. I had Annette vouching for me as well." She reached up and turned the rear-view mirror towards her. She touched her face with the tips of her fingers. "The cut of me. Those black circles. I've turned into a right old hag." She pushed the mirror away from her in disgust. "Do you think this was the way he was seeing me all along?"

Carol was consumed by sympathy for her friend and rage at the toerag who had knocked all the life and self-belief out of her. "Stop torturing yourself," she said gently. "You've just endured over two days in our so-

143

called healthcare system – not a luxury spa. That's enough to make even a Rose of Tralee look like an understudy for the Hag of Beara."

She could tell that Angela wasn't even listening to her. Her eyes were remote. The sound of a stomach rumbling broke the silence.

"Was that you or me?" Carol asked.

Angela sighed. "Probably me. I haven't touched more than a couple of natural yogurts since . . ."

Carol knelt up on the driver's seat and reached into her wickerwork basket in the back of the car. She pulled out a flask. "Take that, please, madame." She twisted around again and placed two pottery mugs on the dash.

"These are my favourites," Angela said, examining the pattern of blackberries, bees and brambles on the mugs. "A man from near Waterville used to make them."

"I know," Carol said, twisting back into her seat. "I was sore disappointed when I heard he had passed away." She unwrapped a tinfoil package of bread. "I prepared a VIP picnic for you. I was hoping we might get a break in the rain but we'll have to make do with this mobile sauna."

"Just like our trips to the beach as kids," Angela said, pouring the coffee slowly and releasing its aroma into the clammy vacuum.

Carol offered her a slice of the fruit bread from the tin foil. "Mam's experimenting again. This time it's white soda bread with cranberries and apricots mixed through. A fistful of macadamia nuts too. A gourmet version of the old-fashioned currany cake."

She watched Angela hesitate before selecting a slice and biting into it. Her heart rose as she saw her smile with pleasure and eat some more.

"*Mmm*," Angela said. "What's the jam? It's gorgeous."

Carol spoke through a mouthful of the cake. "It's quince jelly. A batch from last summer. Mam rooted way into the back of the press to find a jar for you. She was afraid it was all gone. Some people prefer it with cheese but I eat it with anything."

Angela's eyes welled up and when she swallowed there was a lump in her throat. "Ye're so good. I'm such a stupid, stupid eejit."

Carol faked a bossy tone. "Shut up and eat your cake, woman. There I was thinking I was doing so well with my gourmet picnic and you go off blubbering on me." She pulled a tissue from a box in the dash, and handed it to her. "Big blow now for Mammy."

Angela smiled in spite of herself. She took another piece of cake from the package. "You know the funny thing about me was that no matter how deep the crisis was, I never lost my appetite. Well, until now . . . I remember pouring my heart out to you after one of Brian's episodes and, in the middle of it, wondering if you were ever going to open the packet of Chocolate Kimberleys."

"That's why they call it comfort eating, I suppose," Carol said.

Angela threw her eyes to heaven. "And I suppose that's why I'm the size I am."

"Will you go way outa that! I would die for your curves. I'm a total stick insect no matter what I eat."

The outside world had disappeared behind a veil of condensation. Carol was getting groggy. She opened both windows another fraction. The rain blowing in from both sides was cold. She felt more alert.

Angela shivered. Her face clouded. "I wonder what she

looks like. You know who I mean. I've never seen her. No kids by her. Well, up to now . . . She probably looks like some class of a model."

Carol had got one or two reports of Brian waltzing around the streets in Killarney with your wan, arms wrapped around each other like teenagers. One friend had rounded an aisle in the big Tesco on Park Road and walked straight into them holding hands. The bleddy fool. The older the goat, the giddier.

The best description relayed down the Ring of Kerry road was that she was like some sort of a Sindy doll: masses of dyed, wavy blonde hair (wait till she had the hand out for the price of the highlights), liberal use of black eyeliner, and long, skinny legs. She had feet as big as seine boats and teeth that wouldn't look out of place in a horse, the friend had loyally reported.

Carol was keeping all her information in reserve for use at a more judicious time. "She's not worth wasting your thoughts on. It's him the fault lies in, not you. Don't you forget that. Anyway, what a great prize she has in him."

The pep talk was wasted. Angela had a faraway look in her eyes. "Imagine him meeting her at one of those AA meetings. Would you credit it? I was plain diverted when he was going to them so diligently. I let myself trust him again. It wouldn't have hit me so badly only that I was after relaxing back into trusting him. There must be one like me born every day. You can understand how it could happen. All that common experience. All that talk about their problems. No wonder he fell for her."

Carol could hold her tongue no longer. "Fell *on* her more like the story. For God's sake, stop being so fecken understanding! I'm sorry about the language – I know –

but sometimes I despair of you. Show some temper. He's a Grade A boll– " She caught the warning look in Angela's eye and cut her colourful title short. "It's absolutely desperate what he's gone and done. After all those years you stood by him and kept his head above water."

"Don't you think I know all that, but what can I do? I have to try and keep my own head above water now." Angela opened the car door and spilled the remains of the mug of coffee out onto the ground. She hurled a half-eaten slice of cake away from her. A seagull swooped and picked it up.

"I wonder how his digestive system will cope with the cranberries and the apricots," Carol said drily.

Angela pulled the door shut and slumped back in the seat. "I wish to God I could get angry but all I feel is this bleakness, this awful loss of energy. When he phoned me the other day, my heart plunged like an elevator crashing from the top floor right down to the bottom. Even to put one foot in front of the other is an effort. Only for Seán I'd throw in the towel. I have to keep going for him. And I didn't mean to – you know – I'd never have left him alone. I just wanted all the mad thoughts swirling around my head and the awful upset in my stomach to go away."

It was taking Carol all her strength to hold back the tears. "I wish you had told me how bad you were feeling. I had no idea it would take you to the brink. This is not you, Angela girl."

Angela blew her nose. She rubbed her temples. "My head is killing me. This crying isn't helping. It'll have to stop. Look, I didn't know how bad I was either. I'd get cruel waves of desperation but then I'd pull myself together. I had to. I never intended to . . . It's just I went into that room to make the beds. It was a French mother and daughter. The daughter was suffering from depression, it turned out. I was wrecked tired. I only had a couple of hours' sleep the night before. I woke at four o'clock, and the thought of them was like a big stone in the pit of my stomach. When I went into the bedroom, I just wanted to sleep and sleep. The tablets were on the locker. The funny thing was I don't think I'd have taken them only the bottle of mineral water was right beside them." She paused, and added bitterly, "Evian. So healthy. I thought of Alice in Wonderland tumbling down that hole. But someone must have been looking out for me that day." Her voice trembled. "Maybe my poor mother up there." She took a deep breath and continued. "Whoever it was, the two French guests had forgotten their camera. It was the luck of God that they came back for it and found me slumped on the bed."

Carol's tone was breezy. "That was a lovely holiday story for the visitors to take home and all – how they came back to their cheery Irish farmhouse to find the woman of the house comastose in their bed. And who's been eating my anti-depressants?"

Angela punched her in the arm. "You're desperate, Carol O'Connell."

"But there's a bit of spirit coming out in you, Angela, girl. We want more of that and less of the other. Anyway, how're the two saintly sisters-in-law treating you?"

"I thought they'd be mortified at what I'd gone and done. Disgraced the family and the parish and all the rest of it. But they've hidden it well if they are. I'd have been stuck in the hospital till the weekend only that they came full square behind Annette when she vouched for me.

They're beginning to suffocate me, though. When one goes away, the other turns up. It's like 'Watch One Hour with Jesus'. They're at me to go for counselling, but I don't know. I've taken the sign down until Monday. Thank God there were no bookings for these few days."

Carol opened the car window and put her arm out to test the weather. The rain had stopped. The sun was an intense silver disc burning through the solid wall of grey cloud. She turned to Angela as she opened the car door. "Come on before we suffocate in here." She jerked her head towards the wind-blown car park. "This is as good as it's going to get." She pulled a small rucksack from the back seat and put it on.

Ballinskelligs was Carol's personal sanctuary whenever she was troubled. The waves tumbling towards the shore had a gentleness and a music that she knew nowhere else. If Angela was going to find a balm for her bruised spirit, it would be there in the shelter of the bay where the Skellig monks were said to have settled when they abandoned Skellig Michael.

They walked into the wind, warming up as they increased their pace.

McCarthy's Castle, set on a rocky outcrop at the beach edge, was cut off by the tide. Angela told her about a project a local artist had carried out on the castle.

"She got everybody to gather up hundreds of empty glass jars for her and she made candles in them. The candles were lined along all the castle's windowsills and wall tops and lit at twilight." The bare memory of the floating island of twinkling flames brought the light back into Angela's eyes.

They chatted about their teenage days haunting the

beach to catch glimpses of the Dublin and Cork boys who returned every summer to holiday homes and caravans.

"Do you remember those blond twins from Cork City?" Carol said. "I was stone mad for the wild one. 'Twould take me of course. And the pity of it was it was the quiet fella who had the crush on me. I could never get it right."

Angela looked out to sea and across to the Beara Peninsula, a misty grey outline on the horizon. "Do you remember the solicitor's son from Dublin? Such a fine thing. I couldn't believe it when he asked me out. We had a lovely summer. We wrote to each other for months, but the following summer he never showed up. He had an uncle and cousins in New York and they shipped him over to them."

Carol laughed. "Maybe they thought he'd go native if he spent too much time down here. I was watching a documentary about the artist Paul Gauguin lately and the life he had in French Polynesia. I know we're not an island down here but we are a sort of a paradise for all those families who keep coming back here."

Angela gave an absent-minded response and went a few steps ahead. Carol knew she was slipping away again onto the fast-track of her thoughts. And that's the way it would be, coming and going. Carol knew the state well. She'd lived through it herself. You'd sit in front of someone, listening to what they're were saying and managing at the same time to replay conversations in your head or invent conversations you wanted to have to explain your viewpoint to someone who wouldn't understand it in a month of Sundays.

She quickened her pace and fell into step with Angela. "What did the Cork mother shout when her son got into difficulty swimming in Ballinskelligs?"

Angela shrugged.

Carol felt rage boiling inside her at thought of the hurt Brian was responsible for. It hardly seemed worth delivering the punchline of the old joke but she pressed on. "*Help, help, my son the consultant engineer is drowning!*"

Angela's attempt at a smile was dismal. "Maybe we should turn back. I don't like the look of the sky."

Carol burst ahead with exaggerated strides. "Come on, we'll at least make it as far as our secret garden."

Angela frowned. "If there's anyone in the house, we'll be cleared off. The last thing I need now is aggro."

Carol gave her a playful push on the back. "Who's going to be there at this time of the year? Trust me."

A few hundred yards up the beach they reached a shallow stream flowing rippling over dark sand. They turned and followed it through a break in the sand dunes. They climbed a bank onto a lawn, on the far side of which the stream curved away towards a two-storey house. Upstream, a small weir broke the flow into tumbling whiteness.

Carol caught Angela glancing nervously towards the house. "Don't worry. That's how the rich are different. You can own a paradise like this and scarcely visit it."

She led the way to a boulder with a piece of bleached driftwood shaped like a gigantic boomerang leaning against it. The breeze had dried the big rock. They leaned against it and looked out towards the sea. Great beams of sunshine were descending from the pewter sky like stage lights. A flock of dark birds came darting over the water. Carol loved the way they wheeled and turned as one. She wished she could find the same synchronicity. It might make life easier. But, then again, she was never meant to fit in neatly with a flock. She'd probably take a wrong turn and ruin the harmony. Better off on her own. Better off to concentrate on those silver rays. What contrast for a picture!

"Look at the way that light is coming through on this dull afternoon," she said. "Who would have thought? I'd have come home for one of these skies alone. Let me try and catch it."

She took some pictures with her phone. Then she pulled out a sketch pad and some charcoal from the small backpack and began to fill a page with bold, black strokes. While she sketched, a vast window opened in the centre of the cloud mass and a waterfall of light streamed down the sky.

She handed Angela the sketch pad briefly while she took another photo. Then, she resumed her drawing.

"The thing about this coastal light is that it can disappear in minutes. You have to work fast."

Angela watched the play of quicksilver on the water. "What a privilege it is to be miserable in one of the most beautiful places in the world."

Carol made no reply. She was lost in the drawing. Finally she added a few more lines and held the pad out at arm's length to study the result. She was satisfied. Turning to Angela, she held out the pad. "There, a present for you. Those heavens are breaking through especially for you. It's your personal light show."

Angela protested. "You need the sketch to paint from. I couldn't take it from you."

"Honest, I don't need it. I have the photos. I'll mind it for you till we get to the car. And when I finish the painting, that's going to be for you too."

"No, I can't –"

"Repeat after me. 'Yes, yes. *Thank you, thank you.*' Come on, no more of this auld 'I'm not worthy' nonsense."

Angela took the pad. "Yes, thank you, but how can you make any money if you give so much away?"

Carol stood up and stretched. "You get back what you give away. That's the law of the universe. This is your first walk towards wellness. This light is shining for you."

The beams were still flowing into the waters of the bay.

Angela stared at them. "I'd like to think it is. I think I'm feeling a small bit better." She indicated the width of a few centimetres between her finger and her thumb. "Maybe about this much, but it's something nevertheless."

They picked their way down the grassy bank and retraced their tracks across the beach. When they looked up again, the beams had gone and the sky was darkening.

Carol linked her arm with Angela's. "Let's start a rumour. They'll say we've turned."

Angela laughed bitterly. "It's a wonder I haven't turned with all I've been through."

Carol warmed to the topic. "It's not too late yet, you know. Find a lesbian lover. Better again find a vegan, sock-knitting German lover in a hemp jumper and move her in. That'd shake them up good and well, wouldn't it? The family farm with a pair of gay lovers in occupation."

Angela bent in two with the laughter. "Do you know what? I nearly would to see the look on his face!"

Carol jumped up and punched the air. "*Whee*, you're laughing! I don't believe it. You may as well have told me my lotto numbers have come up. I knew the Ballinskelligs magic would work. Don't say a word. I don't want it spoiled." She grabbed Angela by the hand and started running. "Come on. We'll race the rain to the car."

Chapter 13

Eoin McCarthy was the obvious choice when the summons arrived. It was years since she'd been in his office, but little had changed, apart from a bronze patch of damp extending across the only clear stretch of aged wallpaper inside the door. The rest of the wall space was covered with shelves sagging under the weight of yellowing bales of paper sheets with curling corners. How and why he still kept all the files was a mystery. The airless room smelled of damp. The sash window rattled when a cattle lorry trundled past on the street.

"Couldn't we say that I wasn't long home from Italy and that I was having a hard time adjusting?" Carol suggested. Before he had time to reply, her mind lit up with a better idea. "Say I wasn't myself – that I was recovering from a broken relationship."

"And go making cannon fodder of yourself for the *Kerry's Eye* and the rest of the papers, Carol girl," he snorted. "Not at all. Least said, soonest mended. Lave it to me, and I'll manufacture the extenuating circumstances."

"But I was thinking –" she began.

"You're up to your oxters in hot water, so don't you be thinking about anything. I'm in the business of damage limitation. Are you heeding me? There's a visiting judge next month. Wisha, you'd never know our luck. We won't

154

bother with adjournments. Best to get it over and done with."

She had managed to keep her looming criminal status – innocent until proven guilty and all that – concealed from her mother, but for how long she didn't know. It had never occurred to her that she could end up as a news item in the local papers until Eoin had clued her in. Country life – was there much bothering them?

Angela was hardly a fount of consolation. She related how an acquaintance had left a mountain of parking fines stack up after she had been told that the governor of Limerick Prison would turn her away because they were short of space and had bigger fish to fry than non-payment of trifling fines.

"Oh, but wasn't she welcomed in and locked up for the night in a cell with a *mane* class of a woman," Angela related.

Just what Carol wanted to hear.

When she left the office, she tried to put the case out of her mind but the worry of it was always there. She never imagined the hearing would come round so quickly, but four weeks sped by and there she was, a defendant at the April sitting of Cahersiveen District Court.

"All rise now, the court is sitting," announced a tall man wearing a tweed jacket and hugging a sheaf of folders to his chest as he emerged and took his seat at a table in front of the judge's desk.

The judge followed him, and sat on a chair with a high back.

This rising and sitting was a bit of a contradiction in terms, Carol mused as she got to her feet with the rest of the gathering in the tiered seating of the public area. But she was in no position to play the court jester, especially since Judge Andrew McNamara was only sitting in for the day as a substitute for the regular judge and was an unknown quantity. He adjusted the black gown on his narrow shoulders and scrutinised a pile of documents through a pair of filigree spectacles perched at the end of his nose. He looked up briefly to scan the full house gathered for the eleven o'clock call-over of the cases.

Grey hair, ashen skin, thin mouth. She wouldn't be surprised if the piercing eyes under the bushy brows were grey too. A study in monochrome – so apt for a man dealing in the black-and-white facts of the law. Not that his legal brain would be taxed by her case.

She had arrived twenty minutes early in the hopes of avoiding detection by small-town eyes gawking at the misfortunates heading through the courtroom door. She could imagine the running commentary if she was spotted.

'Surely that's not Mary O'Connell's daughter landing in. No, not the youngest one – she's a national teacher up in Dublin. Mary was like a paycock when she got the call to training and headed off to that college for primary school teachers. Married well so she did. Some high-ranking guard. Yes, you're right, the eldesht lad is an accountant up in Galway. Word is he owns half of Salthill. This is the middle wan. That's right, how well you have her. Touch of the hippy about the same lassie. She landed back from Italy or Spain or one of those other foreign places over that direction at the start of March and brought the shnow with her. Looking as if she hadn't pulled a comb through that tangle of black curls for the pasht six months, so she was. Where was she got? When Mary sails into town, you'd swear she was dreshed for a wedding. I wonder what's bringing the daughter in here today?'

Daylight from three dusty windows set high on one wall was nullified by fluorescent bulbs on the ceiling. The murmur of conversation and the smell of fresh coffee carried from the front door where a cluster of defendants were postponing their fate. '*Just Do It*' read the slogan on a tee-shirt worn by a thin young man sitting in front of Carol. Bet he was sorry he did.

Apart from the bench of four suited solicitors and seven or eight guards sitting in a row on the opposite side of the room, there was only a handful of people in the courtroom when Carol arrived at quarter past ten. She selected a position in a middle row and made herself as inconspicuous as possible. She glanced over at the guards. She couldn't distinguish her captor from the others. A few right-looking farmers' sons but one or two handsome cuts of fellas that could have made poster boys for a Templemore recruitment ad.

Their faces were so young. How the hell had she reached the stage of life where she fitted the cliché of guards appearing boyish? It wasn't reassuring to realise that it had crept up on her.

When she first came in, Eoin McCarthy was engrossed in conversation with an elderly man, a farmer at a guess, but at the sound of her footsteps he looked up. 'You'll be grand,' he mouthed, giving her the thumbs-up.

Though her father had been ten years older than Eoin, they had been the best of pals. They golfed together in Waterville, Dooks or wherever the fancy led or misled them, took in race meetings in Killarney and Listowel, sank a quiet few pints together in Mike Murt's on Friday nights. Eoin, a portly man with a florid complexion, had the look of Churchill about him. Her father had been as thin as a whip. 'Laurel and Hardy,' was their nickname in the local.

Eighteen years since her father passed away. He'd be eighty-four if he was still alive. An aneurism. She'd never forget getting the phone call in London. She still got wistful when she saw an older man whom, she imagined, looked as her father might have looked at that age. Friends told her that she'd never marry because no man she ever met could live up to him. Personally, she thought it was because no man could put up with her contrariness. Plus she'd found neither a man who didn't bore her after six months or, likewise, no place interesting enough to put down roots for life. That was until Matteo came along and introduced her to Ornavasso and Piedmont. Yes, that gave her the notion she might just be capable of settling down in one place with a man without the fear of never-ending boredom setting in. She sighed. That notion had got the high road and here she was, the returned émigré, waiting her turn in the local courtroom.

The scribes had their biros at the ready to record the cases. They were perched just to the left of the tweeded court clerk who was leafing through the records of the damned. Carol imagined her own entry on the charge sheet – Carol O'Connell, Glenosheen, Skelligmore, County Kerry. Her adventure with the law would be transferred into the notebooks of the two reporters. One was a redhead who looked so serious that you'd think she was going to be hauled before the judge any second herself. At a guess, she was in her late twenties. Stop frowning, Lois Lane, or you'll have wrinkles before your time. Clark Kent was a different proposition. Handsome in an unshaven and swarthy way, he exuded arrogance. Carol sighed. How well she knew the ambitious type. He'd be editor while the little carrot-top was still doing the rounds of the courts in a rust bucket that began to disintegrate as soon as she paid off the final loan instalment.

As the court clerk called out names, people stood up in the courtroom and made their way down to the front. Solicitors bobbed up to plead their cases. Carol was surprised at the liberal sprinkling of eastern European names mixed through the local ones. There had always been a quota of German, English and Dutch blow-ins but these defendants were working people, going by the fines for motoring offences and drunk and disorderly charges. The melting pot that was South Kerry had obviously taken on some extra blends during the boom that had crashlanded in 2008. And they had made it through to the recovery that had given Carol the encouragement to come home in 2018.

Her stomach rumbled. Did it sound so loud to everyone? The hunger pangs and the nerves were working together to sharpen the anxiety she felt as she anticipated her own name being called out.

Suddenly, someone farted and a smell of sulphur thickened between the benches. The *'Just Do It'* guy, sandwiched between two friends, began to shake with silent laughter. One of the friends snorted. The judge shot a burning look that must have singed the ears of the court clerk as it passed.

"*Silence in court!*" the clerk called.

Eoin had drilled Carol on what to do when she was called forward, how to look suitably contrite and full of regret. There had been no need to take acting classes for that. Boy, but she was full of regret now. Regret at going to the funeral, at accepting Jimmy's invitation to go for a drink, at having that extra one, two, three.

159

"*Arrah*, just come for the wan. For auld times' sake." That's how it began.

How stupid she had been to forget the inevitable Kerry follow-on. "Sure what's your hurry? A bird never flew on wan wing. Wan more won't kill ya. Sure when will we meet up again?"

Well, she had been the bird that attempted flight on one drunken wing. Well, more accurately, attempted to drive on two drunken wings. How could she have been so thick?

The court clerk put one page aside and cast his eye on the next listing.

"*Carol O'Connell!*" he called.

A flush rose up Carol's neck with the heat of a flame and burned through her cheeks. What a voice. There was an actor lost in him. His real calling was on a West End stage. Her name echoed around the courtroom, out the front door, up along the street and out the road. In a few seconds, people forty miles up the Ring of Kerry road in Killarney would be cocking their heads as they heard her name boom through the streets. Her legs felt like rubber as she squeezed her way past two men and a woman and out onto the steps.

Please God, don't let me fall, she thought.

All she needed was just one person to recognise her and carry the story. Someone would relate it to Timmy Healy alias *News of the World*, and he'd be on hotfoot to her mother with the report. She'd have to postpone the inevitable and get there first.

She held her hands behind her back, grabbing the left wrist with her right. Her fingers were sweating too much to interlace them. She squeezed her wrist tightly. The guard was reading from a little black notebook with flip-over pages. Not the type of black notebook she had hoped to end up in. He was so grave, she could imagine him emerging onto the birthing bench in a miniature uniform. He had observed her driving erratically on a bend on the Waterville road. What if he had a Freudian slip and said *erotically*, she thought madly. Driving erotically. She could feel the ends of her mouth begin to curl into a nervous smile. For feck's sake, Carol, look tragic, it shouldn't be hard. She dug her fingernails into her palm.

The evidence continued. When he had opened the car door, she had fallen out towards him. Her eyes opened in alarm. Mother of God, this was news to her. There was a ripple of faint laughter in the body of the court.

"*Silence in court!*" the judge barked.

From the corner of her eye, she detected a burst of enthusiasm that set the reporters' pens zipping across their notebooks to fuel a headline fest. Mr Letter-of-the-Law Garda, he without sin, resumed his montone delivery.

A breath test proved positive. Hell it did, he was probably under the influence himself from passively inhaling her vapours. She was conveyed to the Garda Station where a further test was carried out. The concentration in her breath had sealed it. No need for blood or urine samples.

Carol visualised herself floating under the ceiling of the courtroom in an out-of-body experience. It was the ideal location to make out which men were developing bald spots and which root treatments were overdue. But the two sticky wet patches of perspiration under her arms brought her back to earth.

Eoin was addressing the judge. Phrases bobbed past her like flotsam in a current. "Guilty, my lord. Totally out of character. Comes up from a respectable family. Fully accepts the gravity of the offence. She was deeply affected by the tragic death of an old schoolfriend whose funeral she had attended that morning. A language teacher by profession. Disqualification will be a severe handicap. Applying for a postponement."

Then it was the judge's turn. Was that a fleeting expression of compassion in those grey eyes? Please God, no. Flint she could handle but not sympathy. Sympathy would reduce her to tears. She met his gaze with as neutral an expression as she could muster. Come on, throw the book at me. I deserve it. Just get it over, so that I can get out of the stocks.

"What is your attitude to drinking and driving?" he asked.

This was it, her big moment. She'd speak from the heart. To hell with the reporters. Here she comes, ladies and gentlemen of the press, the remarkable Carol O'Connell, human cannonball.

"I'm only thankful that I didn't injure anyone or worse. I've been haunted by the thought that I could have killed someone. I never thought I'd ever drive in such a state, and I'll make it my business to never *ever* let it happen again."

Her sentence was meted out. A two-hundred-and-fifty-euro fine and a three-year disqualification from driving. The disqualification was postponed until October on Eoin's request. He had already informed her that it was likely to be reduced to two years when they re-applied to the court in two years' time. Two years – God only knows where she'd be then.

Before she knew it, she was back in the bench, so mentally exhausted that she decided to sit out the rest of the hearing in order to meet Eoin and find out how she could pay the fine and get the whole sordid episode over and done with.

There was one case left. It was the farmer she had seen Eoin speak with before the judge came in. He was seventy if he was a day. He could have been any of the sheep farmers her father had dealt with in the valleys around South Kerry in his work as an agricultural adviser. Carol had often travelled around with him in the old Ford Cortina at weekends or on her school holidays. By the time she was twelve, she could have practically written a dissertation on sheep scab and EU subsidies. She loved the tea in the farm kitchens, the big black-and-white collies bounding down the laneways to meet them, the walks on high fields and the exuberance of the wind blowing in off the Atlantic.

She could have met this man a hundred times – cheeks ruddy from the elements, body spare and muscular from climbing mountain slopes after sheep, words rationed out as if they were a dwindling stock. His weathered hands contrasted with the snow-white shirt cuffs. When he was in the witness box, his birdlike wife grasped the handles of her old-fashioned black handbag so tightly that her knuckles were waxen.

This simple country man, it was alleged, had punched a neighbour in a dispute over a gorse fire that had spread into his land and threatened a hayshed. The prosecuting solicitor, not long clear of college from the look of him, kept up a barrage of questions like a terrier. The cross-examination was all a variation on the central question, "Did you assault my client?"

Hard as the solicitor tried, he couldn't get the country man to give any response other than, "He burned my land".

Carol was so full of admiration for his refusal to budge an inch that the tension ebbed from her body and a faint tongue of spirit flickered through her exhaustion. She felt relieved when the judge dismissed the charges against him. At least the day had gone well for someone.

"All rise now, the court is over," the court clerk declared. The judge disappeared through a door and into his chamber.

Carol made her way down to Eoin. She had a bundle of notes ready in her bag to hand over to the clerk. An unwelcome dent in her savings.

"There's no two ways about it, Carol girleen, but you could have killed someone driving in that state. Thank the Man Above that you had no accident. There was no one hurt. That's the main thing."

Carol hung her head. She couldn't argue with that. She had a lot to be thankful for. But the court was only chicken feed compared to the cross-examination that faced her before Judge Mary O'Connell. With a heavy heart, she faced the coastal road home, wishing the journey would go on and on.

She spent half an hour fidgeting around the kitchen but still she couldn't pluck up the courage to break the news to her mother.

"You're like a hen with an egg," Mary said. "What ails you?"

Carol took a deep breath and regarded her shoes as she spoke. "I was in court this morning. I was disqualified for three years for drunken driving."

Her mother's face was impassive. "I figured you'd get as much, given the state of you that day."

"What? How did you know about that?"

"How did I know about that? *Me?* Sure you had barely stepped out of the car when the entire parish had it. I was one of the first to know." She tapped the side of her nose. "Central Intelligence."

Carol sighed. "The network. I should have known. Why didn't you say anything to me?"

Mary shrugged. "I knew it was going to come out at some stage. I was waiting for you to tell me." Her eyes grew cold. "The thought of the damage you could have done is the frightening thing. If you ever again get behind the wheel of a car with drink on you, don't you dare darken my door."

Carol felt as if she was four years old. "It won't happen again, I can assure you," she mumbled.

"I can't wait for the papers to come out next week," Mary said drily. "We'll have great reading. You'll be the talk of the parish." She caught sight of her daughter's downcast face and relented. "*Arrah*, you'll only be a two-day wonder before they turn their attention to someone else. We've faced worse."

She was grateful to her mother for being so magnanimous but she couldn't shrug off the thought of the carnage she might have caused. She turned to the best therapy she knew.

Chapter 14

Carol stood back from the easel, her fingers interlaced around a mug of honey and lemon to absorb its warmth. She dipped her head to itch her cheek off the shoulder of her fleece and stamped her feet. The thermals under her jeans were a godsend. She set the mug down between the tubes of paint while she pulled a square of paper from a kitchen roll and blew her nose. All she needed now was the head cold to travel to her chest.

For a change, she had experimented with *Skellig by Night*, a gleaming moon silvering the ocean in front of the islands. Margot's words came back to her. 'Dash them off.' Given the modest price she was asking to get herself established, that was exactly what she should be doing, but she ended up putting as much effort into every painting as she would for a royal commission.

"For the last time, I'm telling you to come in to the warmth of the kitchen!" Mary called. "You'll catch your death out there."

"I think I already have. But if I come in, the heat will send me into a coma and I'll get nothing done. Another half an hour and I should have finished this one."

Spurts of water plunged down onto the windowsill outside, an unwelcome reminder that the cleaning of the shoots was overdue. The windows were beaded with raindrops. At least the rain saved her one job – cleaning the glass. Drops on the upper panes, streaking down fastest, reminded Carol of amoeba under a microscope.

All the shrubs in her view were shaking like mad things in the south-westerly wind. The scarlet rhododendron was a freestyle dancer given over to the beat of wind music that only it could hear. The shrub paused between gusts, only to throw itself over and back when the wind picked up again. The poor blossoms would be in fritters before the day was out. Already, some of them had fled across the gravel.

It was the third consecutive day of constant rain. Puddles on the driveway dimpled in the downpour.

She could hear Timmy chatting to her mother in the kitchen.

He came out with another beauty. "'Tis endless, like. Endless. Rain, rain, rain. 'Tis enough to make you want to emigrate. But that's the way i'tis anyhow."

Emigrate. That was rich. She was the returned-to-the-rain emigrant. Not that Ornavasso would ever pass for the Costa del Sol. She took another square of paper from the kitchen roll on the windowsill and blew hard on her tap of a nose. Then she picked up the mug and knocked back the remainder of the lemony drink.

She could feel an enormous sneeze coming on. Serving breakfast hadn't helped. She'd lit the dining-room fire for ambience sake, but gusts of wind had reversed the smoke back down the chimney and made it billow around the room.

Mary insisted on not cleaning the chimney until the jackdaws had had a chance to rear their brood. They had been nesting in the chimney for generations. Love of nature was all very well but lighting the fire on a windy

167

day, as Carol had discovered, was tantamount to a health-and-safety issue. Another gem for TripAdvisor. '**It was a wonderful stay until we were removed by ambulance, suffering from smoke inhalation.**'

Carol's mind drifted back to a day when her father had assembled all the rods for the chimney-cleaning ritual. The first rod up the chimney was attached to the flat brush that sent a shower of soot falling into the grate. As a child, Carol knew all about the jackdaws' love of shiny things. She waited for a diamond ring or a sparkling brooch to descend with the pile of twigs. She was rewarded once with a gleam of gold – a lipstick compact.

She reached for another square of kitchen roll. Between daydreams and nose-blowing, the day would be gone on her.

A few strokes of the brush and she was restored to her world again, a hand in a glove, a pea in a pod. She felt so at home with the work. Why did she always find it so hard to go back to the easel after she had broken the continuity? Immersed once again in the pleasure of painting, she reprimanded herself for having postponed the inevitable.

Another squall hammered a handful of rain against the window. If the rain didn't let up, no visitors would make it through the veils of mist to the front door. A stubborn hope followed fast on the heels of her doubts. This was going to work. A small but steady trickle of business was coming through. Yes, there were too many of the blasted one-nighters, but that's what you had to do to gain a footing on Airbnb. Washing bed linen and cleaning showers after people who stayed just one night was too much work. As soon as she was established, she'd change the setting to a minimum stay of two nights. The weather wasn't encouraging people to stay longer either. Trouble was they'd been four months waiting for skies to clear – a bit of a stretch even by Kerry standards. Maybe the 'Wet Atlantic Way' was a more accurate branding for the coastal route.

Carol forgot the cold as she concentrated on finishing the moonlit Skellig which would bring her total of island scenes to four. If she kept the pace up, she'd have enough paintings to supply shops in Portmagee and Cahershiveen. And Oliver was encouraging her to set up a website and go for the online market.

Twenty past four. Suddenly, she felt the cold and the hunger. She had eaten nothing since noon when she'd wolfed down a bowl of home-made chicken soup which was her mother's medicine.

When she got back to the kitchen, the pair at the table stared at her as if she had two heads.

"Look at the cherry-red nose on you," Mary said.

"You'd swear she was knocking back the brandy," Timmy guffawed.

Carol swept low in a mock bow. "Thank ye kindly. That does wonders for my ego."

"I'm sick of telling you to go to the doctor and get an antibiotic," Mary said. "You're doctoring yourself for the past couple of days and it's worse you're getting. The smell of garlic off you would knock a horse. I hope you don't have it it in your socks again. Lacing the soup with it is bad enough."

Carol took a tub of moisturiser from the shelf beside the mirror and applied it gingerly to her red nose. "Give me a couple more days. If I'm not better by Monday, I'll go, I promise."

Even though there was the prospect of more money coming in from the paintings, the thought of shelling out fifty euro to the doctor made her nervous. The last time she'd checked her bank account, she couldn't get over how the balance had dropped by a couple of hundred euro. Her financial affairs would make a church mouse look like a Russian oligarch.

At first, she thought she'd been the victim of cyber crime but when she went through the statement it all depressingly added up. Petrol was the worst offender. The sooner she was off the road, the better. Maybe the disqualification was a blessing in disguise. The few trips she had made to Killarney to maintain her link with the outside world weren't cheap.

Opening the fridge door, she peered in to select the makings of a sandwich.

Just then, Margot breezed in the back door. "Hello, all. Any news?"

"No," Mary said, "we were hoping you might have some."

Carol set out a wooden board with olives, avocado, Macroom mozzarella and Mary's crusty brown soda bread fresh from the oven that morning.

"Dig in, everyone," she said.

"All in good time," Margot replied, heading for the conservatory. "I want to see how your latest offering is coming on."

Carol grabbed a slice of bread and followed on her heels.

Margot gasped. "That's fantastic. I want it for myself."

Carol was torn. "I owe you big time, but the shop is waiting for it. I can't disappoint her. I must keep to my commitment. The business will be great for my cash flow."

"Don't mind me. You can do me one like it later on. Don't worry about the money either. I told you to cut back more on your spending and concentrate on getting the Skellig scenes finished. After the May Bank Holiday Weekend there will be lots more people coming to stay."

Carol mentioned that Oliver was talking about coming back in May for a weekend, but she'd prefer to get a couple of nights in London in June instead. She ignored the knowing look that Margot shot her.

"I'm looking forward to some decent conversation," Carol said and, noting her cousin's arched eyebrow, added quickly, "Present company excepted."

"He was the dream guest," Margot said. "He took no notice of the rain. I could do with a few of those."

"He was easy around the house too – no big demands," Carol said. "He was such a good listener that I had to remember to ration my own words. Some hope of that." She pictured Oliver sitting across from her at the kitchen table. She almost forgot she was talking to Margot. "There was some indefinable quality about him."

Suddenly, she noticed that she'd been speared by Margot's gimlet eye and her focus sharpened. Too late. She had given too much away.

"He's an old soul, someone who's been around before," Margot said levelly. "I've only come across one other man with the same quality."

Carol was intrigued. "Who?"

"Your dad."

Before she could process her astonishment at Margot's profundity, her attention was taken by the apparition of a man strolling into the kitchen outside the line of vision of anyone but her. Clad all in brown tweed and sporting a mustard cravat, he looked like a stray from the Wexford Opera Festival. Passing the mirror, he paused to straighten the raven-black toupée set at a rakish angle on his head.

It was all unfolding before her eyes like a slow-motion car crash. Her mother and Timmy were nattering at the table. Margot, having shared her epiphany, had reverted to type and was telling her to see to the leaking gutters.

The man coughed loudly. Mary wheeled around towards him, her face the picture of dismay. She hadn't even the composure to configure her 'Fáilte Ireland' mask.

Not another man on his own, Carol thought. She'll be driven cuckoo by them.

Mary recovered enough to address the surprise visitor. "Where did you spring from?"

The stranger looked alternately from the floor to a far corner of the ceiling as he spoke. He said the back door was open and he had let himself in. "The front doorbell doesn't appear to be working. I hope I haven't arrived at a bad time."

Mary, making a snap judgement on his appearance, decided it was certainly a bad time. "Actually, we're in the middle of a family crisis so we won't be taking any further guests tonight, but I can recommend another farmhouse if you like."

The man's eyes switched from the window back to the ceiling again which made it easier to observe him. Carol noted that the top of his shirt was open, offsetting the impact of the cravat. The shirt had to be a size too small for him. He showed no signs of answering her mother. She checked for a hearing aid. Negative.

She was just about to repeat her mother's communication at a higher pitch when he spoke.

"Actually, I won't be requiring a room here. The name's

Arthur McKeown. I am on contract to Fáilte Ireland to carry out inspections. But if this isn't a convenient time, I'll call back."

The kitchen took on the appearance of a tableau at Madame Tussaud's until Margot sprang forward, grabbed the visitor by the elbow and steered him into the dining room. Timmy bolted for the back door.

Carol's mission was to calm Mary, who was in a state of high agitation.

"Come on, Mam," she said. "Sit down and rehearse the apple-cheeked granny knitting at the hearth for him when he comes out. Relax."

Mary sat down, her mouth twisted in a mutinous pout. Instead of knitting, she stabbed the needles into the big ball of wool. "Relax. Easy for you to say. Relax and she inside poisoning his mind with God only knows what."

Carol opened her eyes wide. "I thought she was your new best friend."

"*Get over there and see whose best friend she is!*" Mary hissed.

Carol performed an exaggerated mime of tiptoeing across the floor to the door. She whispered over her shoulder as she went. "Maybe she's trading sexual favours to save us. I'd better not tumble in the door on top of them." She knelt down and put her eye to the keyhole.

Margot was glaring at the inspector. "I've spent five minutes explaining to you that you're looking at the original complainant in person. Can you not accept that there's been a radical change in circumstances and I'm withdrawing the complaint? In other words, you're here on a fool's errand."

Hands clasped behind his back, the said Arthur was

studying an antique clock on the mantelpiece. "*Hmm,*" he said.

Margot stamped her foot on the wooden floor. "I don't believe you've listened to a single word I've said!"

Carol winced at the anticipated pockmark on the wood.

The inspector kept on facing the fireplace as he spoke. "I get the distinct impression that you're a very knowledgeable woman. You might tell me one thing."

The implied compliment took some of the heat out of Margot. "And what might that be?" Her tone was suspicious.

The inspector strolled across to the window and pressed his nose to the glass. "Where can I catch a game of bingo around here? And do you have an idea what the jackpot is?"

Margot's jaw dropped. "You've got to be joking."

The inspector's breath was clouding the window. He stepped back and traced a game of noughts and crosses on the glass. "Not in the least, I assure you. I contracted the obsession on one of my early inspections – an antidote to the tedium of Irish provincial life and an alternative to sitting in drab hotel bars watching the locals turn more oafish with every pint swilled."

Carol drew back from the keyhole and put her fist in her mouth. Her shoulders were shaking with mirth. Mary was going to get out of the chair but she waved her back and resumed her sentry duty at the keyhole.

Margot was flummoxed. "There's bingo in Killarney in two nights' time."

"And after that?"

"After that? How long do you intend staying?" The volcano was rumbling.

Carol was grateful to see Arthur – surely they were

going to get to know him on a first-name basis – emerging smack-bang into her line of vision.

He walked towards Margot, stopped a few paces short and addressed the ornate lampshade above them. "That's rather a strange reaction coming from the person who summoned me here. You hardly think I could justify the trip on the strength of inspecting just one premises. I'm here for an extensive tour of duty." He paused, double-clicked his heels and looked straight over Margot's head. "And I'm staying at your house as a guest of the Farmhouse Association."

Carol fell back on her heels and laughed silently.

Mary hissed at her, asking what was so funny.

"Give me a minute," she mouthed back.

Margot's complexion was the ruddy terracotta of a Portmagee lobster. "At Primrose Lodge? That sounds most unorthodox. I've had no contact from the office.'

"Mrs Bradshaw, I will have you know that I am an independent contractor engaged by Fáilte Ireland for my expertise. How am I expected to carry out a proper inspection without an element of surprise?"

"Exactly what inspection are we talking about?"

Arthur plumped into one of the fireside chairs and assumed a languid posture with a hand supporting his chin. "I'm carrying out a root-and-branch inspection of the entire area. I thought I'd made that clear to you. Primrose Lodge is on the list too, naturally."

"Mr McKeown, I am not in the habit of repeating myself but this is all very unorthodox." Margot was enunciating every syllable with the concentration of a student at an elocution grading.

"Don't worry, Mrs Bradshaw, I'm sure you will come through with flying colours."

Margot glared at him.

Carol darted back across the kitchen. She rubbed her knees while she delivered a summary of the exchange to her mother.

Mary couldn't disguise her glee. She clapped her hands. "Oh my God, she's after drawing an inspection down on the whole parish. The rest of the Farmhouse members will have her guts for garters. I can hear them cackling already. One ringing the next in panic. Like hens flying from the fox in the henhouse – feathers flying."

But suddenly the two of them grew sober, each knowing what was on the mind of the other.

"How do you think we'll get on ourselves?" Mary asked.

Carol paused. She knew how much the Fáilte Ireland approval and the official shamrock emblem meant to her mother. "Look, we can only do our best."

Mary looked stricken. "Surely he won't start with us. I'm nowhere near ready."

"Over my dead body. If he throws any shape, I'll concoct some story."

Carol pulled out a chair and sat beside her mother, staring at the dining-room door. The ticking of the clock had never sounded so loud.

Chapter 15

Mary often had occasion to ask herself if she was running a farm guesthouse or a centre for asylum seekers. She pictured the house beaming out radar signals specifically coded for people who needed to escape from the world. Mixed in among them was a generous quota of her oddities or, as John had preferred to call them, her strays. Not that he wasn't averse to landing home with strays of both the four-legged and two-legged variety.

A lot of women in the farm guesthouse sector would prefer to see a pair of serial killers, even a family of serial killers, arriving on the front doorstep rather than a dreaded single taking up an entire bedroom, especially at the height of the season when there was a killing to be made.

Mary was different. She always had a soft spot for the pariahs of the bed and breakfast sector – lone tourists, especially women travelling on their own. But everything in small doses. Lately, they seemed to be attracted to Glenosheen in droves.

Singles didn't hold a monopoly on 'quareness' by a long shot but Mary swore she'd want to be in the full of her health for those that came with every figary about dietary requirements and bedroom comforts. The full of your health and possessed of a poker face with custom-fitted pulleys to keep the corners of your mouth yanked well-down when they started in on stories that defied every form of reason and logic. Yet, the very ones that spouted *ráiméis* could deliver their own brand of wisdom. Life had taught Mary never to sell anyone short. Tourists brought more to the door than cash.

The afternoon that she opened the front door to Suzanne Villeneuve, she immediately gathered that this was no ordinary woman. The large black-faced toy sheep the woman was cradling in her arms was a not-so-subtle pointer to her individuality. Individuality was Mary's code for eccentrics (Carol drew more on imagery such as 'box of frogs' or 'space cadet').

"*Je suis Quebecoise*," the individual said, practically leaping across the threshold.

"No need to translate," Mary said immediately. "I've got schoolbook French."

"And I have impeccable English," the woman said. "A legacy from my London cousins. The French was a momentary lapse." She held out her hand. "Suzanne Villeneuve."

"Mary O'Connell at your service."

She noted that the visitor's hand was surprisingly petite for such a large woman. Suzanne had no distinguishable shape because her body was lost in the folds of an ankle-length midnight blue-and-mauve velvet dress. She had grey-blonde hair scraped into a bun. Her hazel eyes beamed from an unlined face, and were framed by long coal-black lashes. When she registered her visitor's unblinking, wide-awake look, Mary instantly thought of a doll Agnes had sent Michelle from America one Christmas in the annual gift hamper of toys.

Apart from the cuddly sheep which signalled a woman

178

marching to the sound of her own stylised drum, there were no major alarm bells ringing for Mary yet.

Mary fetched tea and soon they were ensconced in the sitting room off the front hall, a small fire burning in the hearth to take the chill out of the bracing spring afternoon.

From the instant Suzanne had crossed the threshold, she had given Mary no cause to open her mouth. She spoke as if she was rehearsing for a one-woman show, which in fact she turned out to be, giving a blow-by-blow account of her seven-day journey from Dublin across to Galway and down the west coast.

"I've booked nothing in advance," she said. "I like to be free to go where the spirit takes me. I was actually heading for Kenmare today when I noticed the light hitting your beautiful sign and picking out the colours. The valley was calling to me. I knew instantly I was meant to be here." Striking her chest in a general approximation of where her heart was submerged, she said, "I felt it here."

She had a brace of anecdotes about so many B&Bs and farmhouses that Mary's heart sank. Not another one-nighter. Her mind began to drift away until Suzanne began to tell her about her stay with a Clare farmer, who apologised for the lack of a breakfast.

"He explained that his wife was gone to a place called Knock on a pilgrimage," she said gaily. "*Knock*. I thought the name was a joke at first. You know, of the 'knock, knock' variety." She leaned forward and took another sip of tea from the china cup she had raved about when Mary brought in the tray. "He had simply no idea where anything was in the kitchen. I asked him if I could grab some cereal and make a coffee. He gave me carte blanche. The situation didn't bother him in the least."

Suzanne laughed so heartily at her own story that her shoulders shook.

"He was a lucky man that you took it so well," Mary said. "How did he expect to get away with that? They mustn't have heard of the dreaded TripAdvisor in the west. You know, I have a daughter here who's waging guerilla warfare on it. She lets them away with nothing."

Suzanne wiped her eyes with the back of her hand. "Oh, she's so right. I never believed 'the customer is always right'. A false dogma in my book. But I don't think TripAdvisor would have worried this man. What was causing him great concern, though, were your alcohol driving-limits and the way in which your police are implementing them so strictly." She began to parrot a soft Clare accent that left Mary awestruck. "'*There's a big quietening down in the country pubs. Everything is tied up altogether. It's an expensive racket now if people have to pay for a taxi to get home. Shure you're knackered again in the morning with those fellas out with the breathalyser. The country pubs are finished altogether. It's going to have an awful effect down the road.*'"

She stood up when she finished and took a bow.

"How did I do?"

Privately, Mary was staggered that her guest had stayed silent long enough for the Clareman to utter so much. "How did you remember everything he said?"

"Oh, I've always had tremendous recall. It's my gift."

Mary made a mental note to limit her own utterances and to warn Carol to do likewise.

"By the way, I'm happy to pay the full single supplement," Suzanne said. "I get the impression that singles aren't always welcome. In fact, I've noted a dramatic dimming of the light of welcome whenever I'm rumbled as a solo traveller."

Mary could well imagine the looks. But, before she knew it, she was remembering all the places Carol had travelled on her own.

"You'll do no such a thing," she said. "Just pay me exactly half what the room would cost two people. It'll come back to me some other way."

Suzanne jumped to her feet again with an agility that belied her weight, dropping her sheep to the hearth rug in the process, and enveloped Mary in a bear hug that constituted the greatest challenge to her osteoperosis in some time.

Mary had been dozing by the fire when the doorbell rang. She had withdrawn to the peace and quiet of the room to read *The Irish Times*. Now she eyed the paper surreptitiously. It was the Saturday edition. A guest had left it behind. There were some really interesting articles in the features section, and she wanted to get back to it.

Suzanne was rambling on again, absentmindedly stroking the sheep's fleece. "Of course, my mother told me I spoke my own language even before I learned to speak in English or French. She spent quite some time trying to narrow down what language group it belonged to. The nearest she could come to was Basque." She seemed utterly unaware of how bizarre a capability she was confessing to.

Mary took a sip of tea from her cup and replaced it on the saucer. She always kept to the custom of welcoming her guests with china, unless of course they came with kamikaze children. Then, they got mugs. Today, she had chosen the white Arklow set edged with gold.

Emboldened by Suzanne's apparent lack of awareness, Mary got her to elaborate. "At what age were you speaking this different language and when did you stop?"

Suzanne warmed to the topic. "My mother said she couldn't exactly put a time on it because she had left some months go by, thinking it was simply gibberish. I was almost a year old when she finally realised I was speaking a language of my own and she began to take notes – phonetically of course. The pity is I don't have the notebooks because my father said he wasn't going to indulge '*l'enfant*' in any foolishness and threw them into the fire. But he didn't get seriously worried until I had passed the usual time for learning to speak normally. I was almost three years of age and I hadn't articulated a word of French."

Mary put another two sods of turf on the fire. The room had heated up in no time. She returned to her chair. The sunlight was hitting the back of her head and she was beginning to drowse. If Suzanne kept talking at this rate, she'd nod off. To keep herself alert, she asked another question. "If you continued speaking it until you were three, surely you remember a few words?"

Suzanne shook her head and her eyes grew serious. "It's one of the greatest losses of my life that I don't remember any. Every now and again I will get the sensation of a word or a phrase hovering somewhere just on the edge of my consciousness but, hard as I concentrate, I can't seem to grasp it." She brightened again and hugged the sheep to her. "But you'll never guess what was the most amazing thing about my language?" Her eyes were wide as saucers.

Yes, I've done it again, Mary thought. Is there a force field around me attracting the craturs who aren't really for this world? She composed her face. "I haven't a clue to God what it was, Madame Villeneuve." She had a feeling that she was going to be enlightened in double-quick time.

"Suzanne, please, plain Suzanne." She leaned forward in her armchair and squashed the sheep beneath her ample bosom. She dropped her voice. "I could speak to animals and they understood me. Mind you, we lived in an apartment in the centre of *la ville du Quebec* and I didn't have access to many animals apart from cats and dogs. But our dog, Misty, carried out every single command I gave her. You know, I miss that most of all. Think of the fun I could have had with that in Ireland."

Indeed, Mary thought to herself. The wonder of it all, she marvelled, was that Suzanne, if she could be believed, had operated effectively as an estate agent right up to her retirement the previous year.

Switching tracks after the language interlude, Suzanne grilled Mary with the diligence of a professional about property values in Kerry, the impact of tourism on prices, and the interest shown in Killarney and Kenmare as retirement havens.

She nodded intently as Mary related how so many seaview properties had been bought up for a song during the hungry fifties and sixties when the children of small farmers headed for Britain and America, and the lights went out one by one in the abandoned stone houses.

"So many of them were reinvented as holidays homes and even year-round homes for foreigners mad enough to take on the Irish winter," Mary said. "More had the roof slates ripped off by storm winds. Doors sagged on hinges, sheep wandered in and out, fuchsia took root in earthen floors and saplings grew from chimney stacks and wall tops." She waved her hand. "You can see it every couple of miles around here. There is one big advantage to rural depopulation, though," she added, realising from Suzanne's glazed eyes that she was succumbing to the heat of the fire.

The prompt worked. The visitor regained her focus, and refocused on Mary, who counted it as a coup that she'd caught her attention.

"The absence of artifical light has won us entry into the gold tier of the Dark Sky Reserves of the World. We've had film crews coming from Japan and every whole place to point their cameras up at the carpet of stars that's supposed to be every bit as dazzling here as in places like the Grand Canyon and the North Pole."

"That's really something," Suzanne responded, but her voice was vague. She looked over her shoulder towards the window. "What a collection of cats you have."

Mary followed her gaze and scowled. The sunlight was showing up the smudges and paw-marks on the window panes. No matter how many times she cleaned them – correction, how many times Carol now cleaned them – the cats rubbed up against them.

"Ah, I have a fondess for cats. I'm known for it, with the result that anyone looking for a home for a litter of kittens or a stray cat ends up travelling from miles around to drop them at our gate. I've a small fortune left with the vet for neutering but I can't seem to curb the population."

Suzanne, the calculating real estate agent, seemed to have slipped away, replaced by a softer woman. "You have a good heart, Mary. I could sense it as soon as I saw you. Never regret your kindness to animal or human. It all comes back to you."

Mary sighed. "I hope you're right. I'm in hot water over those cats more times than I care to think."

Suzanne stretched out luxuriously. Mary noted that her ankles, like her wrists, were remarkably slender for such a large woman. A silver bracelet adorned her left ankle above which a tattoo of a yellow rose was just visible, its tendrils twining down towards her heel.

Suzanne yawned, revealing a set of perfect white teeth. "I feel so much at home here. Would you be able to keep me for three nights? I eat like a bird, just yogurt and fruit for breakfast, none of your artery-clogging fries."

Mary thought of the saving on food and the break from laundry and cleaning. "Not a problem. You'll be meeting my daughter Carol later. She's giving me a hand this summer."

"If she's anything like her mother, she must have a heart of gold," Suzanne said, reaching for the newspaper.

She turned the pages, reading out headlines here and there until she came to a news report on homelessness.

"I was really shocked by the numbers of people on your streets in Dublin," she said. "What's worse, I discovered that the children skipping along the corridor in my hotel were homeless too. We've got the problem in Canada too, but I was surprised to learn it was so extreme here."

Mary nodded. "Carol can't get over it either, especially the families. There was nothing like that before she went away."

Suzanne frowned. "The problems of the homeless makes me wonder about my business. I am happy to be out of it now. Property prices put homes out of the reach of ordinary people."

"If only there was some way of reversing the population

gap between cities and valleys like ourselves. We're dying for the want of people. Houses are lying idle, schools are struggling to stay open while up in the cities young families are stuck in hotel rooms with hardly room to swing a cat. It's reckless altogether. But what can we do?"

A silence fell between the two of them. Mary expected Suzanne to rush in and fill it. Instead, she sat up rigidly, closed her eyes and breathed in deeply.

Mary was nonplussed. She coughed gently.

Suzanne waved a hand in admonition. "*Shhh*, I'm channelling. I see a woman and a child on a narrow road." She hummed under her breath. The humming changed to singing. Then, her eyes shot open like a doll rising out of a box. She fixed Mary with a stare and shouted '*Bon courage!*'.

Mary put her hand to her chest. "*Jesus, Mary and Joseph, you frightened the life out of me!*"

"That's my gift to you," Suzanne said quietly. "*Bon courage.*"

Mary didn't know whether to laugh or cry. The sad look in the visitor's eyes made her uneasy.

"Yes, be of good courage," Suzanne said. "I see trying times ahead for you but, remember: *bon courage*. Repeat it to yourself. Be of good courage and you'll come through. I know you will."

Mary tried to be casual. "*Bon courage*. Another aspiration for me to join with the old ones. I suppose it can't do any harm."

Suzanne rubbed her eyes and yawned. "This channelling is taking more and more out of me every time."

Mary glanced over at her guest, whose eyelids were drooping. Very soon they closed and her jaw, that overworked jaw, sagged a little.

Mary padded towards the door, a gentle snoring reaching her ears as she turned the old porcelain knob as quietly as she could.

She gave one final look back at the reposing figure. Yes, she certainly did attract them.

Chapter 16

The fella said he'd organise a lift to Killarney for Sharon, but she told him she'd take her own car. He looked at her quare like. None of the other collectors had cars. They had nowhere near the money to buy cars. Signs on, they were doing street collections for charity.

The fella said his name was Charlie but she had her doubts about that.

"Well, an excuse for a car like," she told him. "An old lady I did a bit a cleanin' for had it in her garage for years. She had to give up drivin' cos the sight was gone bad on her and she nearly done herself in the last time she druv it. She told me to take it away if I could get it goin'."

An excuse for a car was right. She just about made it through the first NCT, an' she doubted very much if she'd get through the next one. Whenever she got stuck in traffic for a long while, the thermostat shot up. She had half-a-dozen plastic bottles of water lined up on the back seat for the journey to Killarney. Just in case.

Killarney. The word was fairly zinging around her head. It was a ticket to Disney or a fun fair. A foster family she had lived with had taken a holiday cottage there for a week wan time. They were the best family of the lot. Crackin' good until the auld fella got a new job in Galway, an' it didn't really suit them to bring her with them. Could have bin an excuse too.

Maybe they were after getting tired of her. Hard as she tried to be good an' friendly with the daughter who was a year older than her, she never felt as if she rightly fitted in. Same old, same old. The best times were when the auld fella was working away somewhere.

But she couldn't really blame any of them. Didn't they bring her to Killarney? 'Twas like bein' in a big picture book with de mountains and lakes. There was a carnival right in the middle of the town, burstin' with lights and loud music and excitement. The smell of popcorn and the rubber of the bumpers, candyfloss sticky on her fingers, the hiss and the jangle of the rides. Birds' Bazaar, they called it.

It was Carnival Week when they were there. There were competitions every night. You got free tickets whether or not you won anything. Mad it was – in a good way. She won a big set of paints in the Wild Flower Competition. Gave it to the daughter to soften her because they had a fight that night and she had a big puss on her. And the ma was delighted with her for doin' that.

De fella on the bumpers kept givin' her special looks that week. She was twelve but big for her age, never had a boyfriend. Was too scared of dem. Every evenin' she looked forward to his smile. But the daughter noticed. She got jealous and started pussin' and told the mother. Sharon got a big talkin' to. All for nottin'.

How long ago dat was. Twelve goin' on thirteen years. Sharon felt sad. She'd been happy dat summer. Happy as you could be when your ma was drinkin' herself stupid half the time, when you da was all loved up with some jade and didn't want to know ya, and you were watchin' yourself all de time for fear you'd feck up with de foster family an' piss dem off, nice an' all as dey were.

If she had one of dem crystal balls back then and looked ahead, she'd have saved herself a loada hassle. If only she hadda listened to de foster mother, she'd know that smiley boys could be trouble. Well, the wrong wans anyhows.

The wrong wan. Darren had started out good. He didn't mean to be a wrong wan. And no matter how quare he went with de drugs and all the rest, he gave her Lisa. He didn't plan to, no more than she planned to have a baby at seventeen. But he done a good thing despite himself.

Lisa was the best thing dat ever happened to her. She was seven now. The best thing in the world. The pain of her ma goin' away to London left a big hole inside her but Lisa filled it right up to the top. The old haunty, sad feelin' still came knockin' at Christmas and birthdays but it never lasted for long. Lisa was a cure for any bad mood. And now she was bringin' Lisa to Killarney. They'd find a farm or somethin' around the place to see lambs. But she couldn't tell the collection fella that Lisa was comin' too. He mightn't give her the job if he knew. A girl in the hotel had told her about him. She said he was a bit of a langer but not to take any crap from him. Just put a hard face on ya, she said, and let him know ya wanted the right money at the end of the day. It was a good charity – suicide prevention. People gave loadsa money for it. And the collectors got a good cut.

Sharon felt good about collectin' for dat. It might have been her ma's story when she died in London. She thought her ma only got stuck in the drugs when she went over there but she didn't know for sure. But she met some nice people in an Irish centre and they helped her to get clear of dem. Her ma was makin' a big effort then. She even writ two letters to Sharon sayin' she would come over an' see her. But then there was some kinda strike at the rehab centre an' she had to leave for a few days. She was found dead after an overdose. The word came through social workers. The wan in London said Sharon's ma didn't do it on purpose. Her system was so clean after bein' off de drugs that the dose was too much for her. Sharon wanted to believe de story with all her heart but sometimes . . . Whatever the real story was, she was still glad to be able to collect for suicide.

She had a mobile number to ring da fella when she got to Killarney on the Friday morning. He'd give her a collection bucket, stickers and a bib when she met him. If he paid her enough, they'd drive around the Ring of Kerry. She was sorry she'd made that promise to Lisa. She kept singin' '*We're going to see the King of Kerry*'. Lisa was so excited that Sharon made up her mind to travel down on Thursday an' book into the cheapest hostel they could find.

She was sick and tired of the hotel they were stayin' in. She had a small bit of the children's allowance saved in the Credit Union and she'd dip into that. She loaded their good stuff into the boot because you'd never know who'd come snoopin' around in the hotel.

And so they were on the road with April showers comin' and goin' as they left the city behind and headed out into the open country beyond Ballincollig. The John Spillane song, 'Johnny Don't Go to Ballincollig' came into her head. Her ma used to sing that wan. It used to drive her spare.

The big sky over the green fields was switchin' from blue to grey every couple of miles.

"*Rain, rain go away, come back another day!*" Lisa sang as the wipers whooshed over and back.

"Didn't I promise you a big surprise for Easter?" Sharon said to her.

"Yeah, Mammy, you're the best. We'll keep drivin' and drivin' right through the golden gates of the King of Kerry's palace."

Lisa was wearing a purple fleece, blue jeans and her favourite sparkly blue shoes with lights in the heels. A woman in the Vincent de Paul shop had a granddaughter the same age as Lisa and kept all her cast-offs for her when she got to know them. Lisa was small for her age and the granddaughter was the opposite, so it worked out well. Still, Sharon would have liked to buy brand-new clothes for Lisa more often than she did. It pained her to see how her little second-hand princess had learned not to ask for new things, though the longing showed in her face when they passed shop windows. For that reason, she kept away from shops as much as possible.

"Will we see horsies in Killarney? And baa lambs too?"

"We'll see the horses but I'm not too sure about the lambs. They're out the country a bit. I have to watch the petrol."

Lisa's face dropped. She had a dog-eared book about farm animals. The lambs were her favourites. Of course, Sharon had fed her with stories about going to the country to see them when she was small herself.

"We'll do our best to find the lambs," she said. "They can't be too far from the town. Tisn't Africa we're goin' to."

They were driving past the wide river outside Macroom. A bridge sat on the water surface – the only sign of the the village and the farms that had disappeared underwater when the valley was flooded to build a dam.

Just then, the song 'I Can See Clearly Now' came on the radio. Sharon turned the volume up to the last.

Lisa covered her ears with her hands. "*Mammy!*"

Sharon caught the feeling of the tune. The rain was gone. She could see clearly now. They were on the open road to Killarney. The stuffy hotel was behind them. She shouted out the song, beating time on the steering wheel with her left hand.

The walls and gateway of Macroom Castle came into view as they crawled through the town square in a line of traffic. Sharon silently cursed the thermostat that was creeping higher and higher in the clock on the dash.

Lisa bounced up and down. She pointed to the castle walls. "*There, look! That's where he lives! The King of Kerry!*"

Sharon shook her head. "No, that's where the King of Macroom used to live."

Lisa wrinkled her nose. "That's a funny name but they're lucky to have their very own castle."

Sharon had been in Macroom a couple of times. She knew the castle had long since disappeared and that only the entrance gate and outer wall remained. She didn't tell Lisa. They'd lost too many dreams already.

After the road climbed up out of Ballyvourney, the sky was in a grumpy mood over Kerry. The sour look of it made her think twice about their adventure. Going away somewhere special was always nice but it made coming back to the real world twice as hard. She had a terrible habit of crossing bridges even before a sound of water was to be heard.

When they reached the top of the County Bounds, the sky had cheered up. A rainbow arched right across the valley below them. The Kerry mountains reared up like waves ahead of them. Lisa was snoozing in the warmth of the car.

"Wake up, dozy Cronin, and see what the King of Kerry has organised to welcome the Cork princess."

Lisa's sleepy eyes came into focus. They lit up when she saw the rainbow. "Oh, that's beautiful!"

Sharon checked the mirror and pulled in on the hard shoulder. "Come on, we'll have to get a selfie with that."

Outside the car, the giddy wind pulled at them. Sharon was sorry she hadn't put on their jackets. It was perishing. She knew the phone camera was useless but the rainbow was so beautiful, she had to try it. She took a selfie with as much as possible of the rainbow behind them. She took several more of the rainbow itself. Lisa snuggled into her mother as another gust rose and pulled at them.

Sharon took a bottle from the back seat and opened the bonnet. The radiator glugged it down. Lisa was watching her fill it. When they turned around, the rainbow had disappeared.

Lisa frowned. "Aw, it's gone away so fast."

Sharon put her arm around her. "That's the thing about rainbows, pet. Ya never know where they will turn up or disappear. That's what making chasin' rainbows so much crack. This one was our lucky charm."

Lisa face brightened. "Wouldn't it be great if we found the pot of gold in Kerry?"

She made Sharon feel hopeful again. "You'd never know what we might find in Kerry. Off we go again."

Sharon could remember hardly anything about Killarney. All she could recognise for sure was the church with the stone steps climbing up to it like stairs. It was straight across the street from where the carnival used to be. It was a let-down to see the dull car park without all the rides and the lights. She reminded herself that she had been there in the summertime.

After she parked the car in a quiet side street and taken a chance on not putting up a parking ticket, she stopped a red-haired woman walking an enormous golden and white dog and asked directions for the place where the horses and carriages parked up.

"You mean the jarvey stand," the woman said, pointing all the way down the street. "Keep going straight down there and you'll find them all around the bend from the Town Hall."

Sharon admired the dog, and asked if it was alright for Lisa to pat him.

"Of course you can," the woman said. "He's as gentle as a lamb. He's a cross between a husky and a boxer."

"What's his name?" Lisa asked, wrapping her arms around the neck of the dog which had obligingly sat down on the footpath.

"He's Milo," the woman said. "He's like a rock star here. Everyone loves him."

Sharon had to practically drag the little girl away from the dog. She knew that Lisa would be mad about the horses. They walked along the footpath looking at the line of them. One of the jarveys was eating his sandwiches up high on the front seat of his carriage. He was sharing pieces of the bread with three crows perched on an iron bar at the front of the carriage.

Quick as a shot, Lisa asked if she could feed the birds too. She had absolutely no shyness. She was ready to rush right into the next adventure. Sharon was glad she was so different from herself, but sometimes she worried where it would lead her.

"We don't want to be botherin' the man," Sharon said.

"It's no bother at all, as long as these boyos don't take fright and fly away," the jarvey said.

The crows did flutter into the air as Lisa shimmied up the carriage wheel but they landed again when she sat on the long cushion.

"What's your horse's name?"

"That's Dolly. She's having a bite to ate too."

The horse had her head buried deep in a canvas bag of oats which was tied around her neck. She was munching hard. Pigeons and crows hovered nearby. They were waiting to peck any stray grains of oats that escaped from the bag.

The man replaced the lid on his lunch box. He had one piece of crust left.

"Watch this," he said, throwing the bread away from the carriage and high in the air. One of crows swooped and caught the bread. It flew away with the other two crows in pursuit.

"There goes Jacko," he said. "He's called after Jack O'Shea, one of the best Kerry footballers ever. Jacko could pluck any high ball out of the air."

The man was so kind that Sharon dreaded refusing if he asked them if they wanted to go for a drive. When he didn't ask them, she wondered if he guessed they hadn't much money. It was as if they were marked out. Maybe it was their clothes. She didn't know for sure. All she hoped was that their fortune would have changed before Lisa became aware of it. As it was, she wouldn't allow herself think that her little girl noticed already.

The driver packed away his lunch box and flask. "Now that you know Dolly and Jacko, you might as well know my own name. I'm Joe. And who have I here?"

Sharon introduced them both. Joe said they might as well meet Dolly properly when she took her head out of the feed bag. He untied the blue twine securing the bag around the horse's neck. Dolly lifted her head clear, stray grains falling from her big lips as she continued to chomp.

"*Yuck*," Lisa said. "Her teeth are so big and yellow."

"That's because we can't find a toothbrush big enough for her," Joe said. "Anyway, she doesn't need one because she doesn't eat sugar."

"Can I rub her, please?" Sharon asked.

Dolly was completely black apart for a white star in the centre of her forehead. Sharon lifted Lisa up level with her head. Joe asked Sharon for her phone and he took a picture of the two of them. He told them if they were still around at half five, he'd bring them for a drive as far as McDonald's, but they'd have to walk back into town because he would be heading home.

That evening all Lisa could talk about was Dolly. How she'd held the reins to drive her out the road, how the bells had jingled on her harness and how the star on her forehead had shone so brightly.

They walked the town that evening, the streets busy with Irish families on a break. Music spilled out the doors of every second bar. Down on the main street, crowds circled two buskers.

"Can we stay here for ever?" Lisa asked.

"I wish we could, pet. I wish we could."

"But wishes can come true, Mammy, if you wish hard enough. Do you know what?"

"What now, chatterbox?"

"I'm going to wish on Dolly's star."

Sharon was stunned. "Well, that's the best idea I've heard in ages. I want to wish on Dolly's star too."

They spent the night in a hostel. Because it was a bit

early for tourists, the owner gave them a room of their own. Sharon felt her stomach clench as she paid over the money. When she checked her purse, she thought she should have more than that left. The few things they had bought all added up. She dreaded the thought of having to put more petrol in the car.

The avenue where they'd parked ran between two terraces of old stone-fronted houses. She'd left the car outside the one house that had window boxes. The boxes were black with two bright red hearts apiece carved into them. Geraniums and small blue flowers that Sharon didn't know the names of were crammed into them.

"Wouldn't it be lovely to have a house like this?" Lisa said.

"Yeah, pet, it's like a place the fairies would be livin' in."

The next morning she had to meet the Charlie fellow in the big car park. She left Lisa in the lobby of the hostel. She told her she wouldn't be long and warned her not to budge. They'd already brought their stuff back up to the car.

It was no problem finding Charlie in the car park. Three other fellows and two girls were clustered around the boot of a car. Only he was 'Seánie' now. She said nothing. He was handing out plastic collection tubs and orange bibs with the name of the charity printed on them. He allocated all the shops they were to collect outside. Sharon got Penneys.

One of the girls asked about collection permits. He took a drag of a fag and glared at her. "Don't be worrying your head about effin' permits. That's all squared with the boys in blue."

Sharon went back to the hostel and collected Lisa. "You know I have the power to turn into an invisible woman," she told her daughter.

The girl was skipping along beside her mother. "You're only pretendin'."

"Naw, I am not pretendin', Lisa Cronin. Just you wait. When I get to Penney's door and hold this collection box in front of me, it's goin' to be like a magic cloak coming down on me. No one will see me."

"Ah, Mam, tell the truth. You're only teasin' me."

"Ya might as well be invisible when you stand stock still as a collector. Either they don't see ya or they don't want to see ya. Just watch and see for yourself."

Sharon told her that she could go around some of the shops while she was collecting but not to go any further than Quills at the end of the street. She wasn't to stand beside her because people might think it was odd.

It was a day of April showers. Cars crawled up High Street with wipers whishing. When it rained, Sharon stood in the shelter of Penneys' doorway, the warm air and smell of new clothes wafting around her. But the doorway was bad for business. She was more invisible there than she was out on the footpath. She killed the time looking at the people and listening to them. She couldn't get over all the Cork accents she was hearing.

A rich-looking wan crossed the streets towards her. She was dragging out of a fag. Sharon turned her face away from the acrid smell of the smoke in the fresh air. She didn't know which was worse: fag smoke or the fumes from the vapes. To think that she'd been a smoker herself until she got pregnant with Lisa!

The rich-looking one had a big thick head of highlighted blonde hair falling below her shoulders. Sharon imagined the cost of getting that done – a bleddy fortune. She wore a grey wool coat, black trousers and high black shoes with sparkles on the toes. A girl, who looked about ten, was at her side. Another dark-haired woman, who looked no way as rich, was already standing at the shop door with a teenage boy.

The blonde woman greeted the dark one. "What're you doin' in Killarney, girl?"

"Same as yerselves. Down for a break." She smiled at the young girl. "Look at her. She's the head off the dad – the head off him, I tell ya."

Sharon stood there like a statue while the conversation played out in front of her. If business didn't pick up, she'd be getting a poor return for her day. Then, a young fellow hardly her own age came along. He was a bit sallow and she couldn't make out whether he was Irish or a foreigner because he smiled but didn't speak. He reached into a pocket of his blue rainjacket and took out a ten-euro note and put it in her bucket. She tried to thank him for being so generous but he had disappeared through Penneys' door. Once the shower passed, she switched back to the footpath in the hope of catching some of the passersby.

Everyone walking in and out of the shop carried paper shopping bags. What was it like to have enough money to buy whatever you wanted? Maybe they had credit cards to put it on the never-never. She hated the worry of owing money again. She'd taken a loan from a moneylender to pay for the tax and insurance for the car. Never again! The interest kept going up and up. It took the help of the Vincent de Paul and the Money Advice and Budgeting Service to get his claws off of her.

The rain returned but Sharon stayed out on the path to try and get a few extra people. The door was a dead loss. Her runners got wet and it soaked into her socks. Her feet grew cold. She could make do with any sort of clothes but she hated cheap shoes. They always left the water in. There was nothing worse than cold wet feet. She stamped up and down.

Where was Lisa? She was never out of sight for more than five minutes. She tried not to get anxious. She felt bad asking her to walk around the shops to kill the time, but what else could she do? Looking in the wide door, the racks of spring fashion taunted her. What was it like for a little girl? Lots of the people passing in and out were obviously families from Cork and other parts of the country on their Easter holidays. She wondered if they were as happy and as together as they looked.

"I'm waiting for my women." The voice startled her because she'd been the invisible woman for so long. A youngish man standing beside Penneys' door was speaking to her. He tipped some coins into her bucket. "I'd better go in and find them in case they have the shop bought up."

As she walked back to her spot at the edge of the path, she was nearly knocked over by a girl in full flight. Their eyes met and they recognised each other. It was one of the other collectors from the car park.

She shouted at Sharon over her shoulder as she passed. *"Get goin'! The guards are on to him!"*

Sharon didn't want to believe what she was hearing. *"What?"*

"No permits! Guards! Get outa here!" She legged it up the street.

Sharon had no choice but to head back down the street to look for Lisa. She had a hunch. On their way up to Penneys, they'd passed a hippie-looking fellow in a top hat setting up a puppet show. He had a black-and-white collie with him.

When Sharon reached the open space beside the Laurels Bar, the family of puppets was dancing to the music. Up at the very front, Lisa was crouched beside the collie, stroking his head.

Sharon swooped down and caught her hand. "Come on!"

When they pushed their way out through the circle of people, they walked smack into a garda running towards High Street. Sharon began to apologise but the garda shouted to his counterpart across the street. *"They're all after running out of New Street, but I think there's one left outside of Penneys!"*

Lisa looked up into her mother's face. Their eyes locked. Sharon yanked her in the opposite direction to the two uniformed figures.

Chapter 17

Arthur slapped a black briefcase down on the kitchen table. Thoughts of Trump and the nuclear button surfaced in Carol's mind. She elbowed her mother. Neither smiled. They watched him snap the case open and reach inside to take out an old-fashioned dictaphone and a pair of binoculars.

Carol arched an eyebrow. "Tools of the trade?"

Arthur tapped the dictaphone. "This, yes." He picked up the binoculars. "Birdwatching is my passion. You know, I can identify the likely nesting place of a sedge warbler from a couple of hundred yards."

"Isn't that wonderful!" Mary assessed him with all the ease of a bomb-disposal expert approaching a suspicious parcel.

Arthur appeared oblivious to the two women. "This must be a paradise for bird lovers." He stalked across the kitchen to the window and trained the binoculars on the driveway. "Good lord, what large cats. They're positive beasts."

Mary gave a wry smile and murmured, "That's from all the little birdies they've been feasting on."

Carol tried to convert a snort of laughter into a cough and ended up sounding as if she was choking. She filled a glass with water and gulped it back.

Arthur swirled around. "Are you sure you're alright?"

he said, addressing the dining-room door.

"It's just nerves really," she said. "My mother and myself are well aware we're in the dock, so to speak. I suppose you'll want to get down to business."

"Well, you know what they say – innocent until proven guilty." He guffawed loudly enough to be heard at the Carhan Bridge.

Mary bristled. "I'll have you know I've no intention of submitting myself to the mercies of any kangaroo court."

"*Shhh*," Carol pleaded, but Arthur was marching into the conservatory.

"As I thought, a much better view from here. I just cannot get over these cats. Incredible. How many are there? There must be at least a dozen."

Carol's heart was sinking. Surely there weren't that many of them? They must have recruited their pals from the neighborhood to protest at their eviction. She looked at her mother, twisted her finger to her temple and addressed the Grand Inquisitor's back. "This entire business has been quite a strain on us. My mother, you must realise, doesn't enjoy the best of health. The anxiety has affected her blood pressure. You'd do us a great favour by putting us out of our misery as quickly as possible. And you might take on board the fact that we think Margot's complaint was vexatious to a large degree. Not that that matters now that she has withdrawn it."

Arthur seemed reluctant to tear himself away from his safari outpost. "For heaven's sake, you make me sound like the state executioner!" he called into the kitchen.

"I've come across some gazebos in my day but this one takes the biscuit," Mary hissed. "Do you notice he hasn't looked us in the eye once?"

Suddenly he materialised beside them with the binoculars swinging from a strap around his neck. He plucked up the dictaphone from the table. "Let's get down to it. I'll start with the dining room."

Mary and Carol watched him from the doorway. He zipped around the room, recording as he went "Dining Room – three tables, mahogany sideboard, silverware display, fresh floral arrangement."

"What's this in aid of?" Mary said.

Carol whispered. "Search me. Some kind of inventory. I wonder if he knows himself, the same fellow."

"Yes, an inventory," he said, cruising across the room.

Carol flushed. There was nothing wrong with his hearing, whatever social deficiencies he might be manifesting. Their only option was to brazen it out.

She pointed towards the stairs. "The bedrooms next, I presume. Just head on up and I'll be with you in a jiffy."

Jiffy. Where the hell did she pull that word out of? She'd be talking like him before he left. She was a pure parrot when it came to picking up accents and speech mannerisms.

She'd done her best with the bedrooms, but she knew the bathrooms were dated. There was no disguising tiles that were well past their sell-by date. Angela had drafted in Magda, the Polish woman from Portmagee, to help them. Carol couldn't get over the girl's mix of the Kerry and Polish accents. Everything was 'like' and 'you know, like' and 'I was telling my husband, like'.

She had called Carol and Angela 'love' so often that it began to grate on Carol's nerves. No man had ever lavished so many endearments on her. She had to admit, though, that Magda was a powerful worker. She barely stopped for a cup of tea.

The house was spick and span from top to bottom after the efforts of the three of them, but it was showing its age in so many ways: rattling windows, patches of damp, groaning floorboards. The whole place was in sore need of a cash injection. There was no disguising that, no matter how much polishing they did.

The cats were still a worry. Banished to the garden, they were balls of resentment on the prowl for a breach in the defences. They were making fewer attempts at incursions through the back door but they could be holding out for a more strategic assault. She had sent Arthur ahead to the bedrooms because she wanted to run out front and scatter them before he viewed them from an even better vantage-point upstairs.

Thud. Angela and Mary started as the noise reached them from the ceiling. They stared upwards, waiting for another sound but there was only silence.

"Mother of Divine God, what's he at?" Mary said, her face the picture of alarm. "Go up quick for fear he's after falling and cracking his neck. Compensation could be setting in."

Carol twisted her hands nervously. "I don't know, Mam – will I be safe up there on my own with him?"

Mary was taken aback. "What do you mean?"

Carol frowned. "Maybe all the caper by him is only a show. He might be as cute as a fox behind it all. Or . . ." She paused for dramatic effect.

"Or what?" Mary said impatiently. "Is there something none of ye are telling me?"

Carol took a step towards her mother, widening her eyes. "Maybe he's a smouldering sex beast." She hitched up her skirt to her knee. "Should I throw him on one of the beds

206

and ravage him in the interests of a good report?"

Mary flared. "You *gligín!* Give over your cod-acting, and get up the stairs and see what he's at."

Carol headed out of the kitchen, pouting and hips swaying. "If you see the toupée flying past the window, count my mission as a success."

Mary shook her head. "This is no laughing matter."

Carol was never more conscious of every creaking step on the stairs. The sun was shining through the stained-glass panel of the high window and onto the landing carpet. Normally, she admired the play of colour on the fabric. Today was different. Had the carpet always looked that faded?

There was an ominous silence. The door to 'Chestnut' was slightly ajar. She pushed it open and, as she entered, she saw the dusky pink armchair overturned in the middle of the floor. She skirted around it.

She sniffed the unmistakable odour of socks. She followed her nose to the source to the bed end: two socks, one red, one blue, and two substantial big toes poking through. Her eyes travelled to the headboard. Arthur was reclining against the bank of pillows and cushions with his hands folded behind his head. His eyes were closed and his breathing was so even she wondered if he had fallen asleep. There was something childlike and vulnerable about him. Maybe that's why a surprising feeling of compassion for the man in all his eccentricity overtook her. Aren't you the quare hawk that's blown in on top of us with your birds and your bingo and your big toes poking out of your socks, she thought.

Suddenly, he sat bolt upright and said: "Full marks for mattress quality."

She couldn't tell if he was speaking to her or to himself. She moved to right the armchair. Before she could drag it back to its position beside the black marble fireplace, he bounded from the bed and took it from her, apologising to the fireplace as he went. "Sorry about that. I was just checking that everything was thoroughly vacuumed. Not a speck of dust under the chair or the bed for that matter. The acid test."

Carol said a silent prayer for Magda, patron saint of forensic dusting. "I'm delighted to hear you saying that."

He went to the window and stood there looking into the distance. Carol tiptoed to the door of the en suite and glanced inside. She winced. She was seeing the tiles with Arthur's eyes. They had cleared the black lines from the grouting with toothbrushes and bleach, but all the tiles were really fit for was the hammer. A feeling of pity for the old house came over her. Chaotic charm could only carry it so far.

"Penny for your thoughts?"

She jumped. Arthur was at her shoulder. He obviously had no *meas* on her thoughts. If she was waiting for him to hand over pennies or currency of any denomination for her thought processes, she'd need a good book to while away the time.

"Ah, the en suite," he said tragically. He spoke as if he was looking at some elderly relative, once a raving beauty, staring vacantly from a nursing-home armchair.

Bring on the acting skills, Carol girl. She summoned up a bright voice from somewhere down in the region of her shoes. "Yes, I see where you are coming from. It's got that jaded look. But the cash flow is starting already with the . . ." She just stopped herself in time. She had nearly gone and blurted out the name of the dreaded Airbnb to a

208

Fáilte Ireland inspector. "Yes, the cash flow is starting already with the new season and the bit of tweaking I've done to the website."

As she trailed him through the rest of the bedrooms, she felt as though she was on some kind of anthropological field trip observing the behaviour of a rainforest tribesman performing strange rituals.

He traced his finger along the tops of picture frames, burrowed under beds, peered into toilet bowls, pulled back bed linen to inspect mattresses, and recited lists of the bedroom contents into his dictaphone. In the bathrooms, he got down on his knees and shone a torch up under the toilet bowl rims. Francis Brennan, eat your heart out!

The only mercy was that her mother had chosen to stay downstairs. He wouldn't even have made it as far as the second bedroom if Mary had seen him subjecting her life's work to such scrutiny.

The only slight candle of hope still burning as she followed him downstairs – the steps creaking even louder under his bulk – was the enthusiasm he had shown for the views from every window and for the light that cascaded into the rooms.

"Well?" Mary's face was tense as she greeted Carol's return to the kitchen. If it wasn't for her mother, she would have told Arthur to take a hike. They could manage fine without the accreditation. With a good website and Airbnb and the repeat business built up over the years, they'd be fine. But try telling that to Mary. The shamrock and the association membership meant everything to her. Losing the accreditation would be in the same league as excommunication from the Catholic Church.

"Have you time for a cup of tea?" she asked him in the hallway. "A cup out of the hand, even?"

"Thank you very much but I think I'll try to fit in a spot of birdwatching over in Ballinskelligs before I make my next call," he said. "You'll be hearing from me in a couple of days."

Carol tried to put the best complexion she could on the situation, but she couldn't shield her mother from the reality of the risk they faced. "He was really impressed with how well-kept the place is and with the absence of dust. Such a great achievement in an old house, he said. He loved the views. And, oh yes, all that money you paid out on good mattresses at that sale in Killorglin yielded dividends. We gave it our very best shot but . . ." her voice trailed away . . . "but I don't know."

Mary was brittle. "What do you mean you don't know?"

Carol's shoulders drooped. "Sure anything could happen with that fella. I don't know if he's playing with the full deck at all."

There was a sudden glint in Mary's eyes. "Maybe that could be our saving grace. He might be better to us than some cauld, official class of a civil servant lad just out to tick the boxes."

Carol could see that her mother was talking herself up into hoping. She allowed herself to be carried along.

"Maybe you have a point there. Although there is something about him that's not right and I can't put my finger on it."

Mary was in recovery mode. "I know what's wrong with him, and his likes. They're all watching too much of that *At Your Service* and the antics of the Brennan brothers."

Carol laughed. "You mean he's a Francis Brennan wannabee."

"Exactly," Mary said grimly. "And we're the sacrifcial

210

lambs. I'll be relying on the fact that this fella is a bit of a loose cannon to carry us through."

There was a rap at the back door. Carol froze. For an instant, she was gripped with the fear that the 'loose cannon' had doubled back and heard them talking about him. Oh, the relief of it when Margot launched herself into the kitchen wearing a navy and cream ensemble, looking for all the world like the winner of Ladies' Day at Killarney Races.

"I met his lordship against me down the road," she said. "How did you fare?"

"Don't even go there," Carol said. "It's so hard to make him out. That's the worst of it. You can't really be sure what you're dealing with."

Margot was the picture of tormentation. "I know, I know. Nobody knows what it's like putting up with him in the house." She looked embarrassed. "Not that I don't deserve it since I'm the one that drew him down on us all."

"You can sing it, sister," Carol said drily.

"Carol!" Mary said. "Don't be so smart. We're all in it together now. Nothing like an outside enemy to unite the forces." She slapped Margot on the back. "All for one and one for all. We never died a winter yet."

Chapter 18

Mary was suspicious from the word go, but she couldn't bring herself to turn the pair away from the front door at that late hour. Where was a mother going driving that lonesome road in the dark of night, dragging the poor child with her? The mother was little more than a slip of a girl herself. Twenty-three, it turned out. And the child was seven. Or, as she pronounced herself, seven and a half.

"That young wan was out early," Timmy observed when he saw the pair of them the following morning.

Mary recognised the local parlance for a girl that got pregnant at a very young age. She shot him a look. "Don't be so pass-remarkable. She's somebody's daughter." Although Carol criticised her mother for setting her mind to 'suspicious' when strangers turned up out of the blue in the valley, she herself had big doubts about the mother and daughter when she joined Mary at the door.

The mother, who gave her name as Sharon Cronin, was clutching two black refuse bags. She was wearing a shiny peach-coloured tracksuit, and shivered in the cutting April wind on the doorstep. As she haggled for a cheaper room rate, Carol caught a Cork accent. And it wasn't the Rochestown Road.

"Even a small room with one bed will do us. Lisa can bunk in with me no problem."

Mary's heart melted. She told her that she wouldn't charge for the child.

The little girl had blond curls and toffee-brown eyes. She was wearing denim jeans, red ankle-length boots and a baby-pink anorak. When she heard that they were staying, she bobbed up and down. "Can we see the lambs please, Mammy? Please, please, please!"

The mother had dark circles under her eyes. Her brown hair was lank and greasy. She looked strained. "Not now, pet, it's too late. The lambs and the mammy sheep are gone to bed. We'll see them first thing in the morning."

The child scowled. "Sheep don't have beds."

The mother was at the end of her tether and in need of rescue.

Carol crouched down in front of the little girl who huddled closer to her mother's legs. "What's your name again?"

"Lisa," the child mumbled.

"Well, Lisa, your mammy was being a small bit silly when she said the sheep were gone to bed. But she's kind of right too. They're gone to bed on a lovely soft bed of grass in the fields. You can get to see them as soon as it's bright."

As the pair headed into the hall ahead of them, Carol looked at Mary and shook her head. She led them up the stairs to the little attic room that they held back for emergencies when someone was really stuck. It was too small to rent as a bedroom proper. Carol had slept there for a couple of years when Michelle and herself were fighting like cats and dogs. The *Alice in Wonderland* wallpaper was still to the good. Lisa clapped her hands when she saw the skylight over the double bed. "We'll be able to watch the stars when the light is off."

Sharon smiled. "Better than the telly and much, much

213

better than that screen your nose is always stuck in."

After Sharon knelt down to open her daughter's laces and pull off the boots, Lisa jumped up on the bed and wrapped her arms around her neck. "You're the best mammy ever! This is a brilliant holiday. And it's lovely not to have to go to school this week."

Carol watched the mother stiffen at the mention of school. She could tell she was close to tears. "You settle yourselves in and come downstairs for some tea and sandwiches when you're ready."

Before she made the tea, Carol nipped out to where the red Nissan Micra was parked. There was a big dent in the middle of the boot. The old reverse-into-a-pole syndrome. She knew it well. The car had clearly seen better days since it had rolled off the assembly line in 1999.

She turned on her phone torch and checked out the inside. In the well of the front passenger seat, she saw the remains of two McDonald's Happy Meal boxes. But it was the collection bucket for a suicide-prevention charity on the back seat that stopped her in her tracks. She checked the discs on the windscreen. Inspector Carol O'Connell reporting for duty, sir. Insurance, tax and NCT certs all out of date, as she had felt they would be.

Back in the kitchen, she reported her findings to Mary who was making a round of ham sandwiches. She had cut one of the sandwiches into fingers for the little girl and set it on a plastic Winnie the Pooh plate.

Carol took a sandwich and bit into it. The loaf bread was so crusty. "Which of us is going to do the night watch?"

Mary took her time replying. She placed a white paper doily on a china plate rimmed with a sky blue. Whether it was a workman at the kitchen table or a guest in the dining room, she brought an art to every act of hospitality. She arranged the triangular sandwiches neatly on the plate and she checked the place settings as she spoke.

"I suppose you make out half the house will be spirited away over the County Bounds before we're out of our beds."

Carol had left the kitchen door slightly ajar to keep an eye on the stairs. "No, I feel bad about wronging the mother totally, but I wouldn't be leaving any loose cash lying around at the same time. Make sure your hen isn't hatching on any money before we hit the hay. I've written down the registration number of the car. A call to the barracks mightn't go astray. What do you think?"

Before Mary could answer, the little girl's sing-song voice carried from the stairs. Carol felt bad about her suspicions. Maybe there was a logical explanation. She opened the door wide and beckoned them in. She pointed to her mother.

"This is Mary. She's my mammy. I'm Carol. They called me that because I was born at Christmastime."

The little girl smiled. "My birthday's on the first of November. That's very near Christmas, you know."

"I said I'd bring her on a trip to see some lambs," Sharon said. "I knew we wouldn't get much more out of the car. I think it's done for. We were lucky to get as far as your house."

Carol showed them where the dining room was for their breakfast and told them the kitchen was cosier at nighttime.

The sandwiches disappeared in double-quick time. Mary served up two hot wedges of apple tart with the cream melting on top. They met the same fate.

Sharon told them she had always wanted to go to the country in the springtime to see the lambs. Her class had been taken to a sheep farm on a class outing in national school and she had never forgotten it.

On cue, Lisa chanted, '*Mary had a little lamb!*' In her excitement, some of the apple tart went down the wrong way. She coughed and spluttered, sending crumbs flying across the table. She put her hand over her mouth in dismay.

Sharon frowned. "Where are your manners, Lisa? What will these people think?"

Mary tossed the little girl's hair. "Don't worry, *a stór*." She pointed at Carol. "You should have seen what this wan got up to when she was a little girl."

The kind words had no effect on Sharon. She looked troubled. "It's been a long day and she's had too much excitement."

"Yes, it was very exciting when the guards –' Lisa began.

"I said you're watching too many silly games on your tablet!" Sharon jumped out of her chair and caught Lisa's hand. "Come on, time for bed!"

"But . . ." Lisa protested as they headed for the door.

"What did I tell you?" Carol whispered to Mary who had begun to clear the table. Mary put down the plates and crossed the floor to her china hen.

A pet day. Carol hadn't heard the term in years, but she knew exactly what it meant – a fine day snatched out of a run of bad weather, a day when the land exhaled the first mild breath of spring. And it was a perfect description of the balmy day she had woken to.

In at the back of the valley where the Murphys' two-storey house was a full stop on the line of the mountain road, the boulder-strewn slopes rose sharply on either side and amplified the bleating of the ewes and their lambs.

Cliff faces loomed grey above the slopes. An earlier dusting of snow had melted from the peaks but there was no guarantee it wouldn't return. Snow could fall in the upper reaches of the valley as late as May.

Now, it was the end of April and everything was beginning. The fresh green leaves hung limply on the trees sheltering the Murphy home. The bright orange of the rusted corrugated roof of an outhouse was a vibrant contrast set against the new growth. Carol reminded herself to take a picture with her phone when they reached the house. The juxtaposition of the rust and the green would be easy to capture and would work perfectly in a painting.

Lisa was transported by the sight of so many lambs and ewes on the road and in the surrounding fields. She gambolled after lambs that looked as if they were wearing masks. She stopped and gestured towards a pair of lambs.

"What's his name? What's her name?"

Carol was taken aback for a second by the questions. But it dawned on her quickly that the only animals known to a city child were pets like dogs and cats that all had names. "They don't have any names. We just call them the lambs."

Lisa was puzzled. "But everything has a name. They're all different. You can't just call them all 'lamb'."

Carol was at a loss to explain. "There's just too many of them. Even if we tried to give them all names, we wouldn't be able to remember which was which."

Lisa was crestfallen but she still wasn't buying into the adult logic. "They're so pretty. They need names. I can't keep saying, '*Here, lamb! Here, lamb!*'. It doesn't sound right."

Carol decided it was time to pass the ball to Sharon. Surely mothers dealt with that sort of intellectual challenge all the time. "What do you think, Mammy?"

Sharon thought for a moment. Then, her face lit up. "I'll tell you what, Lisa, why don't you make up your own names for them. When you run short, Carol and myself will think of a few more."

Lisa brightened. She scampered ahead, scattering names like confetti. She began with the seven dwarfs and graduated to a host of Disney movie characters.

Carol felt a pang of longing as she watched her. She turned to Sharon. "You're very lucky to have her. She's a real live wire, and she's so happy. You're doing a really good job with her."

Sharon flushed. Her eyes lit up with pleasure and gratitude. "Thanks very much, girl, but I'm only doing what any mother – "

Carold wouldn't allow her finish. "Ah, but nothing. Listen to me. You are doing a great job. We Irish are hopeless at accepting a compliment. You may as well be handing us a ticking parcel that we want to get shut of straight away. Tell a woman that her dress is beautiful and she'll say, '*Arrah*, that old thing. I got it in the sale in Dunnes'. Someone taught me a long time ago that you should answer every compliment with 'Thank you'. Are you ready? Take Two. You're doing a wonderful job of rearing that Bo Peep of yours."

Sharon delivered the broadest smile that had crossed her face since she'd landed at the front door the previous night. "Thank you."

"That's a whole lot better. We'd better catch up with Bo Peep before she herds the entire flock out into the next valley."

There were lambs and ewes with black faces – others had white heads with splodges of black around the eyes and nose.

"These hardy natives are called the Black-Faced Kerry Mountain Sheep," Carol said. "When European Union sheep subsidies were at their highest back in the eighties, my father used to joke that the Texan oil barons were playing second fiddle to the Kerry sheep farmers."

"I can't imagine sheep being worth so much money," Sharon said.

"It's a different story now but, back then, the farmers even had their own annual dance – the Kerry Black-Faced Sheep Breeders' Ball. I heard that some of those farmers had helicopters, but I don't know whether that was true."

They were both keeping an eye on Lisa, who was a few hundred yards ahead of them. A wide carpet of grass, cropped tight by the sheep, unrolled down the road centre. Clumps of rushes sprang from the grass at intervals. Nature had a stubborn inclination to reassert itself despite the best efforts of humans. Carol had once found a sneaker embedded in moss in a wood. The moss had begun to cover the alien plastic of the shoe.

She pointed to the ribbon of grass in the road centre. "See that, Sharon. Forty or fifty years ago when ponies and carts were travelling this road, you wouldn't see a blade of grass here. The metal shoes kept it clear. Am I boring the city slicker?"

"Not a'tall, girl. I loves all this stuff. Sure me nan came from a farm outside Mallow. She was always spinnin' yarns about the old days in the country."

Carol had parked most of her doubts about Sharon in the few hours they had spent together that morning. The young woman's frankness won her over. That and the fierce love and protectiveness she demonstrated for her daughter. The collection box and the refuse bags still

219

niggled, but she had opted for the 'innocent till proven guilty' approach. There was more to the young mother than met the eye.

Sharon was wearing a bright red fleece that Carol had loaned her. Her cheeks were rosy from the fresh air and the walk. "Me nan was mad for Alice Taylor's books. Her nose'd be stuck in dem morning, noon and night. Did ya ever read any of dem?"

"I might have read the one about walking to school through the fields. I don't know for sure. My mother probably has it around the house somewhere if you want to borrow it."

Sharon looked away. "I love the stories but I'm awful slow at the readin'. And the spellin'. I was fierce thick at school."

Carol wanted to reassure her but she was lost for words.

Sharon shielded the sun from her eyes with her hand as she tracked Lisa's progress up the road. "I'm tellin' ya, you should read them all, Carol girl. Dere's nottin' like dem. Except *Heidi*, maybe. When me mam was good, she'd read me stories. I was mad for dem. But I was too slow when I tried to read dem meself. I get ashamed now when Lisa asks me to read a story. The only good thing is she's after passing me out."

Again, Carol felt guilty – she had sold Sharon short by judging her on the tracksuit and accent. She'd never expected her to have such a passion for books.

Lisa ran back to them in raptures. A little way up the road, two black-faced ewes, still heavy with their winter coats, were flanked by a set of twins each. One of the lambs dropped to its front knees to suckle, butting the udder with its speckled head as it fed.

"*Twins, twins!*" Lisa chanted. She paused in concentration.

220

"Jack and Jill." She frowned as she thought again. "Hansel and Gretel."

Below the road, a sturdy lamb stood stock-still on a slab of limestone. A sculpture set on a plinth, Carol thought. He was pure white apart from a mottled black face. He had the look of a lowland Suffolk – much posher than his mountain companions. She took a photo.

Lisa was on the move again. "*More twins!*" Her shriek bounced off the cliffs on the far side of the valley.

Sharon and Carol tracked her gaze in the field high above the road where two more lambs, marked with splodges of blue paint on their necks, were solemn sentries. Around them rectangular emeralds of reclaimed fields stretched away towards the end of the valley floor where amber and brown scrubland took over.

The mountain pass separating Glenosheen from the next valley reminded Carol of a miniature Stonehenge. It had been too long since she'd been up there among the boulders left behind from the Ice Age. But that would be an outing for another day.

The sound of a man calling reached them from the slope on the opposite side of the valley. Carol scanned the mountain to catch sight of him. First, she saw a line of sheep filing horizontally across the mountain face. Then, a black-and-white collie on their heels. It took a while to see his master a couple of hundred feet below on a green patch of grass bordered by a stone wall.

She pointed out the sheep farmer, his dog and the moving white beads to Sharon and Lisa. She got them to listen to the farmer calling out commands to the dog.

He alternated between short phrases and sharp whistles. "*Lass, Lass! Go way out below them!*"

It was Patie Murphy. He had to be six or seven hundred feet above them. The valley floor and the winding river lay between them. He might as well have been only two or three fields away, so clear was his voice.

A drizzle fine as shaken caster sugar descended. Carol was just about to tell her two Corkonians that they'd better turn back when she heard a car approaching behind them. Patie's wife, Sheila, was in the driver's seat and her father-in-law, Dermie, was beside her with a half-grown collie perched on his knee.

Dermie rolled down the window and Sheila called across. "Come back for the tea, will ye?"

Carol said she needed to get home to catch up with work.

"Go away ou'r that, sure there'll be gallons of work and money after us," Sheila said.

Carol laughed. "Haven't you enough to be doing yourself besides entertaining the likes of us?"

Sheila pretended to take offence. "You're not out foreign now with big demands on your time. Give over the politeness. You're promising to call over to us since you landed home and divil a trace we've seen of you."

Carol introduced Sharon and Lisa and said they were down from Cork on a short break to go lamb-watching.

Dermie was nonplussed. "Lamb-washing?"

Sheila snorted. "Ah for God's sake, Dermie, she said lamb-watching.'

Dermie winked at Lisa. "If that's the case, there's a pair of pet lambs shouting for their bottles beyond in the garden. I could do with an extra pair of hands. And what's more, we'll give you a taxi home to save you time."

Back in the farmhouse kitchen, Sheila filled two glass

bottles with milk and topped them up with hot water from the kettle. She strained to pull the two black teats over the bottle tops. Lisa was taking it all in.

Sheila smiled at her. "We can't have the two blackguards pulling them off."

She handed Lisa one of the bottles and gestured towards Dermie, who took the second one. "The Lord and Master will lead the way."

Sheila set the table with a big plate of scones, home-made blackcurrant jam and a dish of butter. She poured steaming hot tea from a blue-and-white teapot with a bamboo handle. A gift from her globetrotting son who'd bought it in Vietnam, she explained.

"Ate up, girl," she said to Sharon.

Sheila was one of the most *grámhar* women Carol knew. Many's the time that she had sat in that kitchen and poured her heart out to the older woman. She had the gift of asking just the right question and in such a kind way that you confided in her.

Carol witnessed her work the same magic with Sharon, setting her at ease with small chat about Cork City and the weather until the young mother visibly relaxed and, by degrees, left her guard down.

"You're making a good hand of rearing that little one, but the worry of everything is written in your face," Sheila said. "Are you trying to carry it all on your own?"

Sharon melted in the face of the kindness. She tried to answer but tears slid down her face and her shoulders heaved with sobs.

"Let it all out, girleen," Sheila said, her voice as soothing as calamine lotion on sunburnt skin. "I know you have to keep the face up for the small wan but she won't want to come back in from those lambs for ages."

Sharon made another attempt to speak but her voice broke. Sheila went over to the worktop and brought back a box of man-size tissues. Sharon took one and dabbed her eyes.

"I thought she'd forgotten all about him but I heard her talkin' to one of her friends from school a few weeks ago. 'Where's yer daddy?' sez the other wan. Lisa said nottin' but the friend was like a dog with a bone. 'Don't ya have a daddy?' she sez again. You shoulda seen the way Lisa threw her little shoulders back. I was so prouda her. 'Don't be silly. Everybody has a daddy, only our daddy didn't marry us'."

Carol had a lump in her throat. Sheila reached towards Sharon and patted her on the back. "She has spirit in her. That's all down to you."

She got up and brought the kettle to the table to fill the teapot again. She poured some fresh tea into Sharon's mug. "Drink up that hot sup there. Nothing like the *tae* and the chat to make us pull ourselves together."

Sharon wrapped her hands around the mug and, sipping from it, told them her story.

"In the beginning when Darren was good and tryin' really hard, I useda imagine the three of us bein' always together, our own little family like. I even dreamed of the 'four of us' with Lisa growing taller and a little sister or brother in the buggy. It was Darren what told me to pretend I was on my own when I went to the Council about a flat, to put on the tears and say that Lisa's dad had done a runner and left me holdin' the baby. When I sez to him, 'I don't like telling lies, Darren', he only sez to me, 'Ah, will ya wise up. Aren't they all doin' it?'"

It had been lovely for a while in the flat, just the three of them, she continued. Darren was so good with Lisa when she was a baby. He swore he'd never go back on the hard tack again. He'd stick with the weed. But then the parties started with friends congregating in the tiny sitting room at night. She'd stay in the bedroom with the pillow over her ears to block out the noise. In the mornings, she'd step over empty cans and overflowing ash- trays, sleeping bodies on the sofa, the floor everywhere. One guy even pissed on her beautiful blue sofa in his sleep. And the bathroom . . .

"That's when the rows started," she said. "He'd clear the fellas for a few weeks, and everything would be fine between us. All of a sudden he'd go quare and he'd have them all back again." Her voice faltered, but she took another gulp of tea and steadied herself. "The neighbours shut their faces on us like you'd slam a door. Even the wans that had been really nice to Lisa an' me. They wouldn't let the kids play with Lisa. That was the worst. The Council sent letters about anti-social behaviour. Some man from the Council came out to talk to me. When he landed a second time, I pretended not to be in."

Lisa was about six when it all came to a head, she said. Sharon found her playing with a small plastic bag of pills in the sitting room. Darren's eyes were bloodshot when she rounded on him about it.

"*Lave it, will ya, lave it!*" he shouted. "*She didn't swalla nottin', did she?*"

"But she cudda have, ya thick fecker," she told him. "I can't do this anymore."

Carol could picture the scene as Sharon related the story.

"He begged an' he begged," she said. "Any time I felt

like givin' in, I kept thinkin' of Lisa holdin' de bag of tablets. He kept promisin' that he'd be gone in a few days."

Carol's mind raced ahead. She could imagine how the story was going to end. She flashed a look at Sheila.

"Then one night I was stayin' with a friend to get a break from all the fightin'," Sharon said. "He brought a big gang of fellas back and they wrecked the place. He didn't come back after that."

She blocked his number on her mobile. The Council man was nice but he told her she'd have to go into a hotel or a B&B while the flat was being done up. And he couldn't promise she'd get the same flat back because of the shenanigans.

They put her up in a hotel. Only for Lisa, she'd have given up on everything, she was so down in herself.

It was a year and a half since she'd seen him. He'd come to see her for a while after they'd moved into the hotel, and the worst of the arguing was behind them. That trailed away when he found a new girlfriend with two little boys in tow.

"You'd think Lisa would forget him," she said. "She stopped askin' for him but, out of the blue, she starts yappin' about things they used to do together."

Carol decided to take the bull by the horns and asked her about the collection box and the car insurance. Sharon looked frightened.

"It's alright, Sharon," Carol said. "If you're in some trouble, we'll try to help you."

Sharon told them about doing the collection in the hopes of making some money, about the guards coming after all the collectors because there was no permit.

"I really didn't know, honest," she said, her eyes appealing

226

to Sheila and Carol in turn. "I wouldnta done it if I knew. I'm in a heap of trouble. I'm afraid to face the Cork road again because they'll be lookin' for me."

Carol groaned inwardly. She had reckoned on the trouble with the car but, despite her instincts, she'd hoped against hope that the collection bucket had been kosher. Now it would be harder to bring Mary on board to help the mother and daughter out, but she couldn't leave them back on the road in that kind of trouble.

Sheila looked at her knowingly. "I think I can guess what you're thinking."

Carol looked at her. "Am I mad?"

Sheila laughed. "Three sheets in the winds, girl. But I wouldn't have you any other way. If you're plotting anything, I'll get on to the brother in Cork."

Carol's heart lightened. 'The brother' was an inspector with the Guards. That would be a start anyway.

Sheila turned to Sharon. "Don't mind us. And don't be worrying yourself too much. You're in a heap of trouble, but you've wandered into a good house. They won't see you wrong."

Just then, Lisa burst in the door with a lamb in her arms and a smile reaching from ear to ear.

Chapter 19

" *R* ome. *Rome*. Are we talking *Roma* even? When were you going to tell me about this little excursion?" Carol's voice rose and and fell with all the pitch and intensity of an opera singer.

"We're only in the second week of May," Mary said in a soothing tone cultivated from years of dealing with recalcitrant children and finicky visitors. "I'm not going until after the June Bank Holiday Weekend." God grant me patience, she thought, where was she got?

Carol knew she was overreacting, but she was annoyed at her mother for not letting her know about her plans. "What will I do if this inspector turns up while you're away?"

Mary waved her hand dismissively. "Forget about him. Nobody's heard sight or sound of him since he took off last week. He's hardly going to show up again. It's obvious that no one took Margot's spouting seriously."

Carol pouted. "I wouldn't be too sure about that. We can't let up for a second."

They were sitting in Mary's gleaming scarlet Renault Clio in the car park in the Fair Green in Cahersiveen. Mary changed her car every two years, a continuation of the custom that John had put in place for her while he was alive. Whenever it was due for a trade-in, she was always inundated with requests from acquaintances and even phone calls from strangers eager to snap up a bargain. "You won't forget me now, willya?"

When Carol resumed whining about her mother's holiday, Mary sat calmly in the driver's seat and inspected her aubergine-coloured nails, freshly painted that morning to co-ordinate with the lightweight mac she had chosen for the outing to town.

She knew her beloved daughter, who was wearing (*shudder*) baggy cotton trousers emblazoned with blue elephants, would have to pause for an intake of breath at some stage – it was a biological imperative – and she'd haul out the concerned phrases and understanding expressions. Unless, of course, she was provoked. She looked up from her nails, eager for a pause. Provocation was to be avoided at all costs.

Suddenly, Carol sneezed. This was Mary's chance. *Ooops*, the 'God bless' represented a lost opportunity. She who hesitates is condemned to another earful. Carol had the bit between her teeth again.

While the turbo stream of words continued, Mary reflected on the nature of conversation. Yes, you were supposed to be a good listener. You were criticised if your head was full of what you were going to say when you got a chance to cut in. As far as she could make out, good conversation in Ireland thrived on interruptions. It was a miracle if a sentence got finished. Anyway, if you were so busy concentrating on what the other person had to say, how could you come up with anything interesting yourself to toss into the conversation? Conscientious listeners gave bores free rein.

She glanced at her watch as casually as was possible. They had started the weekly shopping at noon. The plan was to have lunch at the Point as a treat. It was just gone quarter past one. They were still in plenty of time. Carol had been ranting for ages. She'd soon run out of steam.

Carol was in full throttle again, brandishing the folder of the flight itinerary and the hotel with the verve of an orchestra conductor. "If I hadn't gone rooting for the car manual to find the lever to open the bonnet, I'd never have come across this." She sighed. When she resumed, her voice was a few decibels lower. "I really don't mind you going – in fact I'm glad that you are getting out after all those years tied to the house. What I can't understand is all the secrecy. It seems that our little George didn't lick it off the stones."

It was a three-night break, hardly a month on the Orient Express, Mary reflected. To hell with it. She held up her watch and tapped the face with her index finger and tutted, distracting Carol for an instant.

Mary shot through the gap. "Glad I'm going, are we? You have a nice way of showing it. I wouldn't like to be listening to you if you were unhappy about it." Her voice softened. "I didn't tell you because you'd only be fretting about the breakfasts. I had taken no bookings for those few days. I had it planned since last November – way before you'd decided to come home. I hadn't counted on you starting the Airbnb. How many have you coming?"

Carol pressed the button to open the passenger window. Pressed it fairly savagely, Mary noted.

"I don't know how many are coming in that weekend," Carol muttered. "I'll have to check."

Mary made a grand gesture in the interests of conciliation. "Let Margot know you need Sharon that weekend. I'll cover the cost of her wages out of my pension."

Carol felt a pang of guilt. She had sworn she wouldn't turn to her mother for back-up, but reliance had crept up on her. "Ah, Mam, you make me feel like a monster. I wouldn't touch a cent of your pension. I'll manage the work, and I can pay Sharon myself. I'm sorry for the rant. The bleddy tiredness is worse than I thought. I was awake with the birds again. And they seem to be on night duty this weather."

Mary turned the ignition key and switched on the wipers. "There's nothing worse than insomnia. If you get a good night's sleep tonight, you'll be telling me to go away and enjoy myself tomorrow. You'll be telling me to take a week, maybe. A fortnight, even."

Carol smiled. "Of course I want you to enjoy yourself. It's just that I'd hate to face an inspection on my own. On top of that, I haven't much confidence in myself for the breakfasts."

And I haven't either, Mary reflected, but better keep that to myself. "For God's sake it's the best part of a month away. We'll figure something out. We'll drive on now to get the bit of lunch. I'm so hungry I could eat the hind leg of the Lamb of God."

Mary drove down Main Street. Carol gazed out on craft shops, colourful bistros and galleries that made half of the street stretching westwards from the church into a bohemian quarter. Main Street, the farther up you go the *maner* it gets, the smart-arsed father of one of her friends had quipped. Farther away from the town centre and heading west, the shop fronts and windows grew shabby and neglected. Paint was peeling and abandoned window displays were yellowed by the sun. The ambience was of a street set in aspic. It was as if the hands of the clock had stopped in the nineteen-forties on that western front.

Oh, the town, it climbs the mountain and looks upon the sea. Carol heard again the words of Sigerson Clifford's song, 'Barr na Sráide', in her imagination. The town's anthem and her father's party piece. She grew wistful.

Cahersiveen had so much going for it with the Marina, its old-world character and the mountain and sea surrounding it, yet it never got its act together. So many people asked why it seemed to be the only town on the Ring of Kerry that time forgot. Her father's explanation was that the business people of the town couldn't pull together. Carol wondered what change, if any, there had been in attitudes in the town and around the peninsula in the years she'd been away.

Even the Greenway planned to run along the abandonded railway track between Glenbeigh and Cahersiveen had stalled. One of the first things she had noticed on her drive home from the airport in early March were the home-made signs stuck in ditches on the roadside. '**Cycle Way Yes, CPOs No**.' She knew that CPOs or Compulsory Purchase Orders were hugely resented by farmers.

Her mother switched on the indicator for the turn-off to Renard where the ferry left for Knightstown on Valentia Island.

"Is there any progress on that cycleway?" Carol asked idly. "You know, the Green Way. That would really buck up the town if it got going. I read that the one up in Westport is flying."

Mary was glad the conversation had drifted into neutral territory. "Not as far as I know. There's deadlock between some of the farmers and Kerry County Council. It's a crying shame. They should never have stopped the train back in the sixties but they were starved times. It ended up being an export line for people instead of cattle and fish. The views from that track! Michael Palin would have made a television programme on it by now if it had held going." She gave a little laugh.

"What's funny?" Carol said, nonplussed.

"If I had a euro for every time I had to explain 'Compulsory Purchase Order' to the people, I could fund the whole thing myself," Mary said. "Eminent Domain is what they call it in the States. Remember that. You'll need it."

The island ferry was pulling in to the pier as they parked near the restaurant. A scattering of seagulls wheeled above it like crumpled A4 sheets of white paper. The metal drawbridge connected with the pier with a clang, and the cars drove up the slipway. Five in all, and just three waiting to go on. That was May for you. The season was only limbering up.

They were lucky enough to get a table with a view out of the harbour. Once they ordered, Mary disappeared into the Ladies', to touch up her make-up, no doubt. Carol glanced down at her elephants. She'd picked up the trousers in a charity shop in Kensington High Street more years ago than she cared to remember. Mary had given her the once-over when she came downstairs wearing it that morning, but said nothing. Her restraint was a blessing. Carol had suffered enough comments in the past. "Flower power? That ship sailed in the sixties." That was preferable to "Are you thinking of joining the circus?"

Carol's taste might veer too much towards flamboyance but at least she knew her fabrics. She recognised quality before she tested cloth between her fingers. It sometimes crossed her mind that it was because she could never come close to the elegance of her mother

233

that she had veered in the opposite sartorial direction. Not like Michelle, the model of poise and taste.

Mary crossed the room, pausing here and there at tables to chat, nodding at others. Was there no one she didn't know? The few people Carol could recognise still were the parents of friends and the scattering of school friends whom, she imagined, had stayed behind to marry well, disastrously or just plain boringly. Most of her friends had been siphoned off by hospitals, schools and civil service in the cities.

She wondered what the mothers-who-lunched thought of her now. They probably counted themselves lucky that they hadn't raised a hippy. Poor Mary. Then again, it could be worse. At least she hadn't landed back with some quare hawk in tow.

When Carol was a gawky teenager, who paid more heed to opinions of people than she did now, she had overheard a conversation between two mothers during the break at a school concert. They weren't aware that she was in a toilet cubicle as they chatted at the mirror. "You'd never think they were mother and daughter, would you? It must be hard on Mary all the same. At least, she has that dotey Michelle to make up for her." Carol's cheeks had burned. She stayed in the cubicle until she heard them leave.

As Mary approached the table, she noticed a grim look on Carol's face. "Don't worry, it might never happen."

"What if it already has?"

Just then, the waiter arrived with their plates, saving Carol the need to answer any more questions. She had chosen John Dory and her mother was having black sole. "*Mmm*, this smells good. There's nothing like the fish here. I really missed it."

234

The rain had passed. Waves were glinting in the cold afternoon sunshine. The pier was picture perfect with stacks of lobster pots and seagulls swaggering around them. Between the wine, the good food and the scene outside the window, Carol felt at ease.

"Mam, I'm sorry for being so shrill earlier on. I don't know what came over me. It's after burning out now. Do you know something? I think I've made the right decision in coming back. For now, that is. Let's have a toast to the good life in God's own country in South Kerry."

They clinked glasses.

"I'm genuinely glad you're happy to be back," Mary said, "but I hope you don't feel you have to stay around on my account."

Carol met her mother's steady gaze. The flecks of gold were still there among the sea-green of her eyes. Her father used to joke that the gold was the only dowry she had brought with her, adding that it was treasure enough for him. "Aren't you pleased to have someone around the place to take up the slack?"

"Of course I'm delighted to have you here, Carol girl, but the last thing I want is for you to go burying yourself down here on account of me. I've got used to being on my own and I'm set in my ways. I learned to enjoy my own company a long time ago, and besides . . .' She broke off and took another forkful of fish. "The black sole is just divine . . ."

Carol registered the sentence trailing away. No number of years away blunted her radar for sensing when her mother was hiding something. It was one of a number of evasions she had noticed since she had come home. Mary had brushed her off a few times when she asked whom she had been meeting in Killorglin.

Pinning her eyes on a seagull hovering in the air over the pier, Carol asked casually, "So who are you heading to Rome with? I thought it might be one of your computer group."

A look of discomfort flashed across Mary's face.

Carol let the pause settle. "I hope I'm not blundering in on a big secret."

Mary looked out the window. "Actually, it's a friend from Germany."

Carol knew she was concealing something. "Which one of your friends? Do I know her?"

"Well, it's no one you know, really. It's a newish friend. New to you anyway."

Carol was irritated. "Ah come out with it, Mam. Who is she?"

A blush was smouldering under her mother's carefully applied Elizabeth Arden foundation.

Mary took a sip from her glass of water and replaced it slowly on the table. "Actually it's a he."

Carol felt a ridiculous stab of hurt. She thought of her father. What was worse, she knew it showed on her face.

Mary glanced around the restaurant. No one appeared to be listening but you could never tell when some busybody had an ear cocked. She lowered her voice. "Don't look at me like that, Carol."

"Like what?" Carol didn't want to admit she was reacting like a spoiled child.

"Like your father isn't twenty years gone. Like I'm too ancient for male company."

Carol reached across the table to touch her mother's cashmere sleeve. "Ah Mam, you just took me by surprise. That's all." She struggled to sound light-hearted, casual.

236

This was a conversation to be having with your friends, not your mother. "Do George and Michelle know?"

Mary shot her a look. "Of course they don't. *You* wouldn't even know if you weren't home. Not that there's much to tell anyway."

Carol wanted to know everything but she curbed her impulse to shoot questions across the table. Her mother would clam up if she launched into an interview. She had to be content with the crumbs of information scattered through the time it took them to finish their main courses.

Mary was speaking now at a volume more fit for a secret agent imparting state secrets. Carol didn't want to interrupt the flow of conversation by asking her to speak up. Instead, she leaned her head into the table to catch the details of her mother's German 'friend'.

Klaus, Mary began, had a holiday home in Glencar for years. Since he'd retired three years previously as the financial controller of a small publishing company that produced trade magazines, he had more time to spend in Kerry. He lived for the river. He spent hours salmon fishing on the banks of the tumbling Caragh.

They had met one day when his car broke down on the Ballaghbeama Pass. Actually, he had driven straight into a pothole full of water and it had wrecked his wheel. Mary stopped to help. She drove him into a garage in Cahersiveen with the spare wheel which was flat.

Klaus invited her to lunch in the Bianconi as a thank-you. They'd been meeting off and on ever since whenever he was around.

"How long is it since you first met him?" Carol ventured to ask.

Mary didn't seem to have kept a close track on time.

The car had broken down in February. She remembered that because it was a week after Michelle's birthday. No, not the February just gone.

Thank God for that, Carol thought – at least it's not a whirlwind romance. February of the previous year. She did the maths quickly in her head. "That's a long time to keep a secret, Mam."

Mary arched an eyebrow. "Klaus isn't a big secret. It just didn't seem worth mentioning. Anyway, it's not as if he's been here continuously all that time. His wife would hardly stand for that."

Carol had just taken taken her final mouthful of wine. It went with her breath. She coughed violently. Heads turned all over the room.

Mary filled a glass of water for her. "Drink that," she hissed. "We'll be the talk of the place. What's the matter with you?"

The spasm continued. Carol gulped back the water. Her eyes were streaming. She had to blow her nose. Mary was already halfway across the floor to settle the bill. Carol had intended to pay. It was her treat. Feck. *Hippy Daughter Home Living off Pensioner Mother*. They'd be fattening on it.

Back in the car, Carol waited until her mother was on a straight stretch of the main road before resurrecting the topic. She didn't want to excite her and cause a collision.

"Wife," she said. The word hung in the air between them.

"Wife what?" Mary said tersely.

"Wife as in 'you know right well what'. Wife as in married man. Does Mrs Klaus know about you?"

Mary sniffed. Not a good sign. "She won't fly. They

238

used to come over by ferry when the kids were young. She has no interest in the house now. The damp weather here plays havoc with her arthritis."

"I didn't ask you for a medical report. You're ducking the question. And slow down. There's no need to be speeding, even if you are annoyed."

Mary bit out each word. "I am not annoyed."

The silence lingered. She slowed down.

"Maybe I am annoyed. Would you blame me? What's there to know anyway? When he's here, we meet, we go out. I'm hardly the scarlet woman."

Carol was at a loss what to think. "This is so not you. I hope this German isn't leading you up the garden path."

Two men were cycling two abreast ahead of them, chatting to each other. There was a bend a few hundred yards ahead. Mary slowed to a crawl behind them. There was a tense silence again.

Mary scowled. "You'd think they own the road. Of course, the idea of cycling single file would never occur to them."

Carol thought of Oliver. He was always so careful not to hold up cars. She ventured another remark. "Mam, I'm only concerned about you. I don't want to launch the Grand Inquisition. I just want to know that he's a nice person."

Mary drummed her right hand on the steering wheel. "I'm not sixteen. I'm perfectly capable of looking after myself. Klaus is a good man. Now can we just drop the subject, please?"

Carol looked out the window. "If you want. I just got a bit of a shock. There's no need to be so defensive. It's your own business, I suppose."

Mary moved out slightly to overtake the cyclists, but a

car came tearing around the bend. She pulled in sharply. There was an L on the windscreen of the oncoming car. "Bleddy learner drivers. They should all have speed limiters."

Carol's heart was thumping. Her mother had been too close to the bend to overtake. "Alright, alright, I'm dropping the subject to make sure we get home in one piece."

Mary's knuckles were white from gripping the steering wheel. "Thank heavens for small mercies."

Chapter 20

When Carol and Margot reached the front door of the gallery at the edge of Portmagee, it was closed. A handwritten note cellotaped to the door read '*Back in 15 minutes*'. It had been Margot's idea to introduce Carol to the Dubliner who had opened a pop-up gallery in an old cottage for the summer.

"Typical," Margot tutted. "How people expect to do business is beyond me." She waved towards a middle-aged couple, swathed in matching emerald green tee-shirts and peering in a window. "See what I mean. They could be back in their car and gone before he re-opens."

"Chill, will you?" Carol said. "'Tisn't as if you own the place though I wouldn't put it past you. I hope this guy is as approachable as you say he is."

She was relieved, even though she knew she was postponing the inevitable. There was nothing she hated more than walking into a shop or a gallery to make a sales pitch for her work. She had never given it a second thought when she was young, hungry and overseas. These days, she squirmed at the thought of her paintings being appraised by buyers she knew nothing about. She dreaded the anxiety of waiting for the reaction, the crushed feeling if they rejected the piece, the haggling if a buyer was tight-fisted and didn't want to pay the asking price. Worse again if they hadn't a clue about art. Some of them might as well have been selling cream doughnuts. It was so demeaning to have to justify your work.

All this was running through her mind when Margot barked, "For God's sake, Carol, snap out of it, will you? You'd swear I was dragging you to some kind of a slave market!"

"It may as well be. I told you already how I hate approaching gallery owners but, at least when I was abroad, nobody knew me and I could brazen it out. It's going to be way harder here."

Margot was afraid that she'd bolt. "Think of the money," she said in a gentle tone that was so un-Margot.

"Here I go, the merry prostitute flogging my artistic soul," Carol said drily.

Seagulls screamed under the glaring blue sky at the head of the pier. A young couple with a toddler in a buggy threw bread into the water. With the fierce reputation that seagulls were getting in Ireland, Caroline wouldn't have been surprised if a daring gull snatched the child.

Smells of fish and seaweed carried on the warm breeze. Carol inhaled deeply. It was incredible how the heat wave had erased the gloom of the rain. Forgetting hardship must be part of the Irish psyche, she thought. All would be well, all would be well. And if it wasn't, it would pass. Everything passed.

A man in shorts and a tee-shirt had set up a tripod in front of a line of trawlers bobbing gently at the water's edge. She could see the potential for the photo. And, if he turned around, the colourful shop and bar fronts would be equally appealing though his real opportunity would have been in the early morning light when the colours were so much deeper.

She scanned the horizon. If they didn't get the skids under them at the gallery, the Skellig boats would be on their way back in and she ran the risk of bumping into Jimmy. She cringed at the thought of the knowing looks of the other boatmen. It had been quite a feat avoiding him since the churchyard debacle. Him and his avenging angel.

"Do you know him?" Margot demanded.

Carol brought her exasperated cousin into focus rapidly. "Know who?"

"Mark Hamill. Who do you think? The owner of the gallery. Who else?"

"Of course I don't know him. Isn't that the whole point of you frog-marching me down here to introduce me?"

"That's my point. You don't know him. We'll just go in there. He'll either like your painting or he won't. If he's not prepared to meet your price, we'll go elsewhere. But I can't see a problem. He's a nice person and a good businessman. You only have to look at the gallery to see that. Besides, I've spent a small fortune in there since he opened."

Carol was thirsty. She suggested they call into the post-office-cum-shop down the street. It always had happy memories for her. On Sunday drives they'd stop off there for sweets or, if it was summertime, big creamy 99 cones with chocolate flakes speared through them. If she wasn't lugging the painting all covered in bubble wrap, she'd have bought one.

On their way back down the village, they had to step off the footpath twice because of the tide of people coming towards them. At least it was easy to cross the street to the post office because the traffic was crawling.

"Traffic in downtown Portmagee on a Saturday in May, who would have thought it?" Carol said, shaking her head. "Good old *Star Wars*."

Margot was triumphant. "That's what I keep telling all of you. The ship's coming in for this area. Only to take advantage of it. For the life of me, I couldn't understand why it took so long to persuade you to dash off a few paintings of the Skelligs."

Carol bored her eyes into Margot's receding back as she disappeared into the post office. She quickened her pace, and caught up with her examining a display area full of Stormtroopers, Darth Vader, Luke Skywalker, Princess Leia, Chewbacca and other toys alongside school lunch boxes, water bottles and notebooks with the *Star Wars* logo.

An overweight man squeezing past them in a yellow singlet bumped into the edge of Carol's painting and nearly knocked it out of her grip. On out the door he went without a word. Better and better it was getting.

Margot noted her flushed face. "What's wrong?"

"Can you get me a still water, please? I'll wait for you outside. You can't draw a leg inside here with the crowd."

Margot opened a bottle of water when she came out and handed it to Carol. "You look as if you need this. I hope you're not annoyed with me for one reason or another. I'm only trying to open up an opportunity for your *ort*. You can see the footfall here in the village for yourself."

Carol slugged back the water. "I know you mean the best for me and my *ort*, Margot. I just wish you weren't such a . . ."

"Such a what?"

"Well, such a control freak." She waited for the reaction.

Margot threw her head back and laughed with such force that two panier-laden cyclists nearly crashed into each other when their heads swivelled in her direction. "Control freak. Of course I am. And I make no apology

doubt if he was even going to the meetings over the last few months. It was probably a cover-up for meeting her. That fella couldn't lie straight in bed."

Angela sighed. "He might have been going to a few of them. If he was itself, he wasn't long taking off to Croatia with her to work out their future." Her lip quivered. "And to wreck mine. Oh, and another choice bit. The latest break-out was caused by the worry of how he was going to come clean with me."

Carol leaned back on her chair and placed her two hands flat on the table and exhaled loudly. "*He* was worried. When I think of that arch boll –" She registered the flash of Angela's eyes. "That creature merrily fu –" She paused again. "Merrily having carnal knowledge of that bimbo without a thought of the pain he was causing you." Her words were drops of acid.

Angela put her hands up to her ears. She looked around her with scared eyes before whispering, "There's nothing but mad jealous thoughts doing so many circuits of my brain that I feel I've been possessed by a different person."

"*Screw him!*" Carol spat out the words.

Angela leaned across the table. "Don't you think he's doing enough in that department as it is?"

Carol gave a mock round of applause. "That's the spirit. But I mean financially. Hit him where it hurts."

"I know what you mean. I suppose I have no other option." Her voice was deflated. She sounded more hopeful when she began again. "Margot says that having a baby is the equivalent of throwing a hand grenade into a relationship – especially at his age. Maybe it's all infatuation and he'll come to his senses."

"Mother of God, Angie, you're not thinking of taking him back, are you?"

"We've weathered so much together. There were times when he hurt me so badly I thought I could never love him again. But the old feelings came back with time. You know he hates the destructive side of him as much as I do."

Carol made a play of tearing her hair out. "The greatest pity in all this is that they closed down Saint Finan's in Killarney while I was away. Only for that I'd have delivered you directly to the door and tied the straitjacket myself. I can't believe what I'm hearing. I've seen you shattered into so many jagged, sorrowing pieces, and I've always stood by you when you wanted to give him another chance. But this time, don't even dream of it. *Do you hear me?*"

Angela's shoulders slumped and she sank low in the chair. She looked fit to be stretchered out. "Maybe you have a point about St Finan's. Don't you think I'm sick and tired of being so nice all the time? I'm weary to my very bones of doing the right thing by people. This time, I thought he was finally doing the right thing by me. Instead, look what he served up."

A couple whom she knew to see from the Dromid direction passed by and nodded at them. She kicked Carol under the table, an assault that succeeded in getting her to keep her powder dry long enough for them to, hopefully, disappear out of earshot.

Carol, in fairness, heeded the sign language to drop her voice when she reignited. "It's the unfairness of it all that makes my blood boil. You don't deserve this. You of all people. You're so good to us all."

Angela turned the firepower back on her rear-gunner. "Maybe you should think twice about settling back here. I wouldn't like to see you wasting your life like me, propping up a system that will come tumbling down around your ears eventually."

The change in tack took Carol by surprise. Angela was voicing her own doubts. "I know what you're saying. I'm only flying by the seat of my pants with this Airbnb and I don't know how long I'll last. But something is after bringing me home. A bit like those salmon returning from the Atlantic and heading up the Fertha, the Carhan and the Inny to the pools they started out in. I'm going to let the hare sit until I see if this instinct to return is real or whether it will burn out. Besides, what else could I do now that I've made the commitment to Mam?"

Angela's eyes glinted. "Run away with Mr Darcy."

"Are you sure they didn't medicate you in Tralee? Mr Who?"

"You know right well who I mean. You should have seen the way he looked at you the week he was around. Are you in contact as much as ever with him?"

Carol flushed with pleasure. "He messages me first thing in the morning and last thing at night."

Angela lit up. "That's great, Carol. You must be over the moon. Maybe he'll come back." She brightened further. "Or you could go over for a weekend. London, imagine it. I'd love to see it coming to something."

Carol snorted. "I'm in enough trouble as it is without being down for seducing one of the guests. That'd be a good one for an inspector's file if the self-same Arthur turns up again."

"As Timmy might say, you're two consulting adults. Why don't you go for it? *Carpe diem.* Seize the day, seize the man. Sound guys like him don't walk in the front door every other day."

Carol shook her head. "Friendship is enough for me.

You should know me by now. 'Nice' doesn't cut it for me. There's a flashing light on my forehead saying, 'Come to me, Mr Trouble'. If I walked into a room packed thick as a shoal of mackerel with good guys, it's the shark that'd swim straight for me. Timmy summed it up nicely for my mother."

"I didn't think Timmy was a relationship counsellor. What did he have to say for himself?"

Carol was finishing the last morsel of cake. "Mam must have been talking about some of the misfits I landed home with. According to her, Timmy said, 'Between you and me, missus, that girl'd draw rats'."

Angela's hand shot to her mouth to stop a spoonful of cake flying out on a burst of laughter. "I love it. There's a pair of us in it. Maybe it's time to stop repeating the lunacy."

"That sounds familiar. Come again."

"Margot keeps trying to drill the definition of madness into me – repeating the same behaviour and expecting a different outcome."

Carol tapped her head. "Yeah, I remember, I have that stored away up here in some corner." She pointed to her heart. "The problem is that there is a disconnection with this element down here."

Angela sat bolt upright. "You're right. I'm going to have connect up my own head and heart." She crossed her index fingers as if warding off a vampire. "I'll keep Brian at bay – in the unlikely event that he comes crawling back – if you promise to keep an open mind on Mr Darcy."

Carol felt cornered. "I don't think the chemistry is there. He's great company and all that, but I can't ever see myself jumping on his bones. Anyway, he's a tourist, isn't he, one of the people? Wouldn't that be a great recommendation for the house? I may as well organise *Fifty Shades of Grey* theme weekends. That's presuming we ever see him again."

Angela began to laugh but she stopped and her face grew serious. "Chemistry." There was a shaft of derision in her voice. "The trouble with chemistry experiments is that they can blow up in your face."

Carol was strangely unsettled by her friend's insistence. It was putting her on the defensive and she wasn't used to that. "I like a man with . . . " She searched for an image. "I like a man with pulse, a man with a dash of madness. I think our Mr Darcy suffers from an absence of pulse."

Angela flashed a look of rare steel. "Ah yes, pulse – you know where that always lands you."

Carol looked across the room. "Time for coffee, I'd say."

Chapter 21

It was the second week of May. Pink and white blossom coated the apple trees in the kitchen garden. Popcorn trees, Lisa christened them. A clump of bluebells was an azure island standing out in the middle of all the fresh green growth.

She jumped up from the vegetable bed and squealed. "Look at him, Mammy. He's scary."

An enormous bumble bee was droning through the bells of the borage plant beside her. Sharon ruffled her hair when she ran to her side. "Don't take a blind bit of notice of that fella, and he'll do the same with you. Sure he's only doin' his work."

Timmy trundled a wheelbarrow of compost across the patch of lawn sprinkled white with daisies and yellow with buttercups that looked as if they had been glazed with butter. "Are ye going on strike on me or what?"

"Not on your Nelly," Sharon said. "There's too much job satisfaction for us to go downin' our tools."

She was serious. She had spent the best part of two hours clearing weeds from the long rectangular bed with a hoe. Lisa was helping her with a little spade.

The dandelions were the worst with their thick, stubborn roots stretching into the earth like skinny carrots. Lisa had great fun blowing away the feathery heads of the dandelion clocks. "*One-a-clock. Two-a-clock* . . ." she chanted on and on.

Timmy had planted a small plot of potato drills on Mary's instructions in March. The vigorous stalks were well above the ground. The other five beds were overtaken by weeds. Timmy's arthritis was playing up, and Carol didn't want to put extra work on him. She would have loved to take on the garden where she had spent so many happy days working beside her father. She knew she wouldn't have time for all the work it called for. Even growing one or two of the beds for salads and peas and beans, as her mother had suggested, was out of the question.

When Sharon offered to try her hand at growing vegetables and flowers as another contribution towards her keep, they were all sceptical. Yet no one wanted to come right out and ask where was a city girl going with a vegetable garden. It was Timmy who eventually convinced Carol and Mary to give the mother and daughter a trial on just three beds for starters.

One of Sharon's first requests was for all the eggshells to be set aside in the kitchen. A roasting pan full of them was baked in the oven until the shells were brittle. Lisa was recruited to pound them into tiny shards with a rolling pin.

Sharon regarded the finished product with satisfaction. "There now, that's our anti-slug device. I saw it on the telly. We don't want to be poisoning the poor birds with pellets. If the birds eat the poisoned slugs, they'll die."

Timmy wasn't very enthusiastic about the idea but he agreed to give it a try. "If them lads get their snouts on any juicy green shoots, you can kiss your vegetables goodbye."

Sharon drank in the homespun knowledge that Timmy

shared on that first morning in the garden and in the following sessions with him.

He issued his pair of students with a hoe, trowels, little spades, gardening gloves and a black plastic bucket to collect the weeds in and carry them to the compost heap. He got a kick out of being a supervisor-cum-instructor. They learned how to yank tufts of grass and weeds from the edge of the bed as they weeded to create defined borders enhancing the overall neatness of the vegetable beds.

He took a break from his own labours, his face grimacing at the pain in his back as he straightened up and leaned his two hands on his spade. "Start with the weeding. Always start with the job you like least. Do that every day. If ye don't keep up with the weeding every single day, you can kiss your garden goodbye. Three beds will be plenty for ye for starters. We'll see how we'll go after that."

He was more than impressed with the way Sharon applied herself to the work. No weed escaped her. And, best of all, she had great interest in what she was doing. Whenever he told her something, he could tell she was storing it up. His only doubt was the blasted eggshells.

"Those slugs are the cute boyos," he said. "But we'll give it a try." He admired the earth's black and crumbly texture. It was good rich soil. He reached down and caught up a fist of it to show to the mother and daughter. "This is great earth. Earth brings you two thirds of the way there. It was poor enough to begin with. Himself spent years drawing every class of manure to it. Farmers he knew dropped off bags and trailers of horse manure and chicken manure they had no call to use themselves. Sure they were only delighted to have somewhere to offload it. He brought a show of seaweed up from the beach himself too. It all rotted into the earth to make it rich."

Lisa's nose wrinkled in disgust at his description of the process. Sharon took off her green gloves and began to work the soil over with her bare hands.

"Oh Mammy, you'll get all dirty."

"That's clean dirt, pet. I love the feel of it. It reminds me of the brown flour my nan used to mix in a big bowl to make bread."

Lisa was not convinced. She was fascinated, though, by the glistening brown worms that appeared from under the weeds and between the grass roots. Fascinated and appalled in equal measure. Timmy explained that they were still skinny after the long winter but that they'd be fattening up by degrees. He said they were very good for the earth because they tunnelled through it and brought in the air.

A robin alighted on the rim of the black bucket a few feet away from them. "See that lad. He's just waiting to grab a nice juicy worm to feed the missus and the family. He'll be on our tails all day."

Lisa was horrified. "The poor things." After that, she carefully covered up any worm that was unearthed.

Sharon and herself continued steadily at their task while Timmy went back to the house to have a chat with Mary. Every time the black bucket filled to the brim, Sharon carried it to the corner of the garden where Timmy had brought the old compost heaps back into service. The one on the right was filled with dark, old compost that was ready to use. The one beside it was the beginnings of a new batch and would take a year to mature.

"See all those weeds," Sharon said, tipping the bucket into the space. "They're going to melt together and they'll be dug into the earth again next year to make everything grow. It's called the Circle of Life."

"Just like the *Lion King*?"

"Exactly. You're a smart girl. You must be taking after your mother."

A chunky tree stump rose out of the lawn not far from the compost heaps. Sharon walked over to sit on it and beckoned to Lisa to join her. To their left, a line of newly leafed beech trees were swaying lazily in the lightest of breezes. The bass notes of a pigeon sounded off and on in between snatches of birdsong coming from every direction in the garden. A family of crows was in the throes of a noisy domestic dispute that threatened to drown out everything else.

Apart from the encircling stone wall and the black earthen vegetable beds and the flowers splashing lemon, white and blue, everything was green. Green extending from the glossy vines of ivy climbing the trees to the unmown borders of wild grasses, all alive and swaying.

Sharon hadn't felt so happy in ages. She showed Lisa how to take breaths so deep that her tummy rose with each intake. They watched a robin land on the bed they had been weeding and digging. He fluttered away again and perched between the blossoms of an old apple tree that leaned horizontal to the ground.

"Oops, there they go again!" Lisa said as the crows resumed their argument. Their harsh calls splintered the peace of the paradise.

Sharon shaded her eyes against the sun to make out the two big nests of twigs that were just about visible through the delicate green leafy fingers of the ash tree. "I still don't know if the mother crow is warning other crows away

258

from the nest or having a fight with the daddy crow about something."

The words were hardly out of her mouth when she realised it was a stupid thing to say.

"Just like you and Daddy used to be like when you were fighting," Lisa said.

Sharon put her arm around her child's slender little shoulders and pulled her close. "I thought you'd forgotten all that rubbish. That's why I took you away from those bad times. And now we're having good times again."

Lisa took an age to reply. Meanwhile, the crows had reduced their screeching to a few gossipy caws. "All the times weren't bad. I still miss Daddy sometimes. I wish he'd come here and we'd have a nice house like all the other boys and girls in the class have. And a dog. And a proper car."

Sharon's heart lurched into shadow. She thought she'd explained everything properly, that Lisa understood that her father was 'sick' from the drugs and, unless he got better, they had to stay on their own. She stroked Lisa's sun-warmed hair. "I miss the good times with Daddy too, Leese, but I couldn't have you living like those screechy crows. It would be no good for any of the three of us."

"But how do we know he isn't after getting better? Maybe he threw away those old drugs so that he can live with us again. With no fighting."

The light in the child's eyes and the sound of hope in her voice nearly stopped Sharon's heart. "It's very hard to get better, love, when you're as sick as Daddy. It takes a very long time. We'll just have to wait and see. If there's any good news, I know we'll find out. While we're waiting, we just have to be happy with what we've got every day. Can you promise me to try your hardest to do that?"

The crows began their racket again. Lisa put her hands over her ears in mock alarm. "You're right, Mammy. Anything is better than listenin' to fightin'."

They got back to weeding the long bed. When they reached the very end, they stood back, hands on hips, regarding the dark, weed-free earth. Sharon sent Lisa over to the house to call Timmy to come and see their work. His praise was genuine. Sharon could tell that from his face. He called them over to the glasshouse and instructed them to carry clusters of bamboos out to the plot. He leaned five of the poles against five, and lashed them with cord to an extra pole running along the top. He told Sharon to place two more bamboos at either end.

"It's a wigwam," Lisa said.

Timmy went back to the glasshouse to get a black plastic seedling tray of plants with broad green leaves. "These are runner beans. If ye were starting yeer gardening career earlier, I'd have ye growing them from seed. This short-cut is the next best thing. Now, keep a close eye on me."

The first plant came away easily from the well-watered seedling tray. A tiny plug of soil with a web of white roots trailing with it. Timmy had already scattered a few spades of compost under the bamboos. He made a hole about three inches away from the base of a bamboo and dropped the seed plug in.

"Just lean it the smallest bit towards the pole and cover it up. Simple as that."

The novice gardeners took turns setting the runner beans at either side of the bamboo tepee. When they'd finished, Timmy handed Sharon the watering can to sprinkle the plants. "Are ye forgetting anything?"

They looked at him blankly.

"Do ye want half the slugs and snails of the parish telling their pals about the fine dinner that's to be had in Glenosheen tonight?"

Lisa took off for the kitchen with wings under her feet. She came back with a red plastic bucket filled to the brim with eggshell fragments. They scattered fistfuls of them around the bean plants.

Timmy pushed back his cap and scratched his head. "Let's hope they'll do the trick and we won't have to get the heavy artillery out."

Lisa rubbed her knees. Sharon only realised then how much she was aching from all the kneeling.

Timmy clapped Sharon on the back. "I have to hand it to ye. Ye're two nate little workers. The garden is on the way."

Sharon felt good. If only the crows would shut their gobs.

It's a small world unless you have to paint it. Sharon first heard the saying from a man in front of her in a queue in Dunnes. She never forgot it. It was an even smaller world when you were on Snapchat. Once Cork was behind her, she never bothered with any of the online stuff. She wanted to step off her old world. Glenosheen was the magic door she had stepped through.

Her mobile was basic. She only needed it for calls. The internet was often patchy in the house. That suited her down to the ground. She couldn't be wasting money on credit. Lisa had even given up pestering her to play games on it. As much as she was tempted to check up on what

261

her friends were doing, she resisted. The old world spelled danger. Especially Darren. He was on a mad merry-go-round. Wild horses wouldn't drag her back on to that scary thing.

Glenosheen was a safe distance away from Cork, from leaking shoes, the dread of the next day, from trying to hold on to enough money for food, the boredom of tomorrow, from crawling back under the duvet when Lisa was at school, the fear of meeting Darren around the next corner, from fish-eyed women in the Social making you feel it was your fault you couldn't get a job with hours that fitted around school times.

But it's a small world that the Worldwide Web won't poke its bony fingers into.

A guard came to give a talk on drugs when she was in secondary school. He told them there wasn't a corner of Ireland that you wouldn't find drugs, that you'd be surprised what you'd find in the smallest of villages, down out-of-the-way boreens. They all have their contacts, he said. At the head of the chain was the supplier in Limerick or Cork with links stretching all over.

"And these buckos have their own intelligence network," the guard said. "They'll have contacts everywhere. Small little bods who might owe them a favour in the future, if they didn't owe them money or a turn already. Inside knowledge is only a phone call away. If the insider is slow to part with information, they only have to lean on them or, worse, on their families. From my years of experience, this leaning is an ugly business: petrol through letter boxes, burned-out cars, phone calls in the night. If you ever get mixed up with drugs, boys and girls, this is the crowd you'll be drawing on you."

In sleepless nights when Sharon lay in the old bunk bed in Glenosheen and listened to Lisa's even breathing above her, his words returned to her. But she shrugged them off. That was Cork. This was Kerry. There were no drugs in Glenosheen. They were a long, long way from any trouble. She'd earned this peace. It was owed to them after all they'd been through. Nothing would take it away from them.

Chapter 22

Angela leaned back on the chair and laughed. "Stop, will you, or I'll choke on my rice cake. Poor Klaus, if he only heard you."

Carol was delivering a send-up of her own efforts to make conversation with Klaus when he had called by the previous evening to enact the South Kerry version of *Meet the Fokkers Two*. She'd met him briefly and awkwardly just once when he'd collected her mother to head to the airport for their trip to Rome.

"Well, strictly speaking, it's 'fokker' singular unless you count Timmy in," she said. "I nearly died when I heard Timmy coming out with 'No news?' to him. Precious little a German'd make out of 'No news?'. Not that I was much better. Well, when I heard myself going on about the weather, I thought we'd both keel over with the boredom. And that was before Timmy rowed in with his amateur forecaster routine."

Angela tutted. "Come on, Carol, sure you'd draw talk out of a stone."

Carol threw her eyes to heaven. "It's too much talk I got in the end. I made the big mistake of asking Klaus what he thought of Brexit. I thought he'd never shut up. To make matters worse, I was dropping with the tiredness. It took me all my time to keep my eyes open in a show of interest, moryah."

Angela gave a furtive look at the stairs through the open hall door. "Good job your mother's gone for a nap."

"Nap? She's probably sitting up in the bed trading in stocks and shares on the tablet or checking out some more flights for Klaus and herself after the success of the Roman holiday. How long is she back now?" She crossed the kitchen floor to check the calendar on the wall. "June 18th. It's a fortnight since their trip. The weeks are flying into one another. The longest day of the year is nearly in the door to us. I'm back four months now. Help!" She wheeled around. "Anyway, any news on your Prince Uncharming?"

Angela frowned. "Don't mind him. As you're studying the calendar, pick a weekend to go over and visit your bicycle man now that you have young Sharon to fall back on. She's as cute as a young fox. I never saw anyone to pick up on work so fast. Margot says she'll have a job done before you even think of asking her."

Carol nodded. "You're right about Sharon. That's the best sign of a worker: being able to recognise what needs to be done without being told. She's kept going between Margot and the place here. Do you see the interest she's taken in our neglected vegetable garden? Timmy is pure diverted with passing his knowledge on to her." A worried look crossed her face briefly. "Sorting out the car and the other stuff with the guards isn't working out as easily as we thought, though. Thank God for Eoin and his big heart. He's handling everything for free. He arranged for her to give a statement in Cahersiveen. He said it could be ages before they get back to her. He's hoping that she'll get off with a caution if she has a ball of money ready for them. The *cratur* is saving like mad."

"I hope it works out for her," Angela said. "She deserves a break. She's after making a real little home out of the old den in the yard. Not that she can nest in there for ever, mind you." A note of mischief lifted her voice. "But you still didn't tell me whether or not you'll nip over to London. The flights to Stanstead are half-nothing from Kerry Airport."

Carol smiled. "You're in an awful hurry to dispatch me. I don't know. I think it's a bit soon. I'd frighten the life out of him by trailing him. Anyway, I have to watch the pennies. Speaking of which, I'm going to head into Portmagee to flog two more Skellig paintings as soon as Herself gets up."

"Let me have a look at them," Angela said, heading into the conservatory where the two seascapes were leaning against the paint-spattered wooden bench.

In one, a yacht with its white sail pot-bellied in the wind rounded the black cliffs of the Small Skellig. In the other, flaming clouds offset the ebony darkness of both islands as the sun set.

"My God, you're a pure genius. These will fly out the door. I'll never get one off you at this rate."

Carol was chuffed with the praise. As hard as she worked on her paintings, she could never fully believe in their worth until she detected true admiration in another person's voice. "Don't worry, Angie, you'll be first on the list. I tell a lie. My business manager, Margot, is first in line. To think that I owe it all to her. Well, not all the credit. It was actually Oliver who suggested I try the Skelligs as a subject, but she gave me the push in her own gentle way."

Angela was still in matchmaker mode. "Ye're getting on like a house on fire with the emails since he went back. What's the latest from him?"

Carol wanted to share the store of happiness that the online relationship with Oliver was giving her, but she was careful about gushing. "You'll be sick of me going on about him. And, you know, I don't want to be floating around in this shiny bubble when you're –"

Angela wagged a finger at her. "Stop this instant. Just because I'm on Misery Street doesn't mean that you have to be tiptoeing around me. It'll do me good to have some of your shiny bubble rub off on me. Go on, tell me a bit more about him."

"Oh, all right so, but you have no one to blame but yourself if I get carried away."

"Good woman, start away. I'll make my excuses and leave when I can't bear any more of your loved-up chat."

Carol told her it was amazing how much more she kept learning about Oliver through the email messages alone. Just the day before, he'd told her that he was a big fan of the Bee Gees and the Pogues. He said he couldn't wait to show her the Japanese Garden in Holland Park. And the Orangery. He was just a couple of stops away from the Park on the underground. He went there whenever he had a spare hour. Now, when she thought of him, she pictured him ambling down pathways between ancient trees and glasshouses.

She told him she'd always wanted to go to Kew Gardens. He wasn't enthusiastic. The planes flying over there to and from Heathrow every few minutes were too much of a distraction, he said. She'd already told Angela that he had never married. She got the impression that there had been a significant relationship in his life, but he wasn't inclined to talk about it and, though she was curious as hell, she was going to let him come round to tell her in his own good time.

Angela was soaking it all up. "Go on. What else have you found out?"

"God, I don't know what else. We just natter away about

everything on the phone, but I prefer the emails. They're the next best thing to letters. I really miss getting letters." She thought for a few seconds. "Well, he's a tennis fiend and he's big into Grand Prix as well. He has an encyclopaedic knowledge of the players and drivers. And . . ."

"And the biggie," Angela interrupted, "his work. Did he spill any more beans on that?"

"The couple of pensions he built up while working as a broker in the City allow him to write. He's working on a project that he can't say much about at the moment. I know he still does freelance consultancy." She gave a hollow laugh. "That'll come in handy when I'm discovered as an artist."

Angela was thoughtful. "He could be with MI5 for all we know. Anyway, he's a good person whatever he's at."

Carol nodded. "The best thing about him is that he isn't all wrapped up in himself. You know the way some people couldn't ask you a question about yourself to save their lives. It's all 'me, me, me'. Well, Oliver's the direct opposite of that. In fact, he's asking about you in every second email. Speaking of which, let's have some of your news."

Angela started tidying away the mugs. "I'm all talked out. The latest bit of advice I'm following is that it's good to give talking a rest when it's only feeding oxygen to the fire and making it flare up again."

"You sure about that?"

Angela nodded. "That's where I'm now but, don't worry, I'll be pouring my heart out again to you yet."

"All I'm afraid of is that you're burying yourself in work and that you're not dealing with it."

Angela's tone was bitter. "Oh, I'm dealing with it alright. It's a bit like a hire-purchase plan. I'm taking it in instalments. The first hurdle is cleared. I've more or less convinced myself that he's not coming back and that it's for the best. If the marriage wasn't right, then it's just as well to let it go. No use in flogging a dead horse and all the rest of it. If it was right, he wouldn't be camping out with his flouncey down in Kenmare."

Carol was unconvinced. Angela was obviously paying lip service to the wisdom of calling it quits, but there was no way that she could be emotionally prepared to write off the relationship after all those years. Too little time had passed. But she wasn't going to come out and state her thoughts baldly. "Instalments are a good idea. Just don't feel you have to tick off the list at speed. Take your time. Anyway, moving swiftly along in support of your oxygen-deprivation theory, you might be interested in knowing that Oliver's next preoccupation after your marital woes is Inspector Arthur. He keeps asking if the verdict is likely to be delivered any time soon."

"And is it?"

Carol shrugged. "I can't see how he can postpone it any longer. He landed back again three days ago. He's on his third farmhouse billet since Margot ejected him. And there's nowhere left to inspect. Not to mind a new bingo hall to frequent. If he doesn't wrap things up soon, there will be a lynch mob after him."

"You're right. Every single Farmhouse woman is fit to be tied over him. I never came across the bate of him." She stood up and stretched. "I'll have to start yoga. God only knows what else I'll have to try to survive this."

Carol laughed. "Buy a bike and hit the road with me. I don't know myself since I took it up."

Angela was thoughtful. "No, I won't be taking to the bike, but I will find something. Annette keeps sending me text messages to keep me positive. I know it sounds corny but they really keep me going. She gave me a present of a great book too. It's all about seeing difficult experiences as opportunities to get you to grow, to make you a better person."

Carol groaned. "Give me an easy life any day and I'll happily live as a moron from here to eternity."

Angela punched her on the arm. "Look, I know half the stuff is daft, but I'll extract any idea that'll help me get through this. It's sink or swim. This week I'm thinking of all the negative stuff as fertiliser to make me grow as a person."

Carol smiled. "Well, you could fill a silage pit with the amount you're landed with. You're some woman. Come here to me." She gave Angela a bear hug. "You're a diamond. You are going to come out of this a stronger person. And when that *lúdramán* attempts to come crawling back to you, you're going to grind your heel into him."

Angela laughed. "He's giving me a wide berth at the moment. He probably thinks I'm reading more of my crime novels and plotting a violent end for him."

"Maybe you should alternate between the crime and the self-help. Revenge might be a form of personal growth too. I watched a film once where a guy was advised to leave revenge to God. 'Why should God have all the bleddy satisfaction?' was his answer to that." She glanced at the clock. "Mam should be up soon. I'd better get out the bubble wrap to prepare my babies for their journey to the gallery. I'll give you a call later and let you know if many of the others have sold since he last rang me."

Angela waved from the door. "You're on to a good thing, there. Keep it up."

Carol went to the kitchen window and watched her friend cross the drive to her car. She stood there until the car disappeared.

Chapter 23

"Where did you say she's gone again?" Timmy asked.

"*Arrah*, she went down to Portmagee with the paintings two hours ago," Mary sniffed. "I suppose she's having coffee."

Timmy was clearing the dishes from the dining room. "How in the name and honour of God did she forget this lot?"

"Do you have to ask? I know she's my own daughter but she'd forget her head if it wasn't tied on to her."

Timmy threw a look at the cat basket under the table. "She'll throw a fit if she sees her ladyship in here."

Mary was defiant. "I don't care. Poor old Sue Ellen arrived at the back door meowing to beat the band. She's older than myself in cat years. The bit of heat will do her good. I used always leave her in for a few hours in the day until that nuisance of an inspector fella came around."

"Suit yourself," Timmy said, "but she'll have to get a quick shift if anyone calls."

"How's that young Sharon doing over with Margot?" Mary asked, coughing. She beat her chest. "I'm killed from this. I think I caught the head cold on the plane coming back from Rome and it travelled into my chest."

"The young wan is playing a blinder, although they

were so busy this morning that she left the heat up too high under the rashers and they were like Taytos when the four Yanks clamped their false teeth on them." He laughed. "You should have heard the lecture Margot gave her."

"A blind bit of notice she'll take of Margot," Mary smiled. "That's unusual for the girl, though. I can't find a fault with her when she helps us out with the breakfasts. We had a pair of German girls last night. Hikers on the Kerry Way. Great English by them, but faces that'd stop a clock. The English couple were in the dining room the same time as them. You could cut the silence with the bread knife. For the life of me, I can't understand how some of these foreigners don't make talk with each other. You'd never get that with Irish people." She coughed again. "If this doesn't clear, I'll have to go to the doctor."

"Why don't you put up the 'No Vacancies' to give yourself a bit of a rest."

"Shure they're all Airbnb. You can't cancel them. There's scarcely a soul off the road. Anyway, the whole country has the cold. Nothing for it only let it take its course. Anyway, I wouldn't give the other houses the soot of it. To have no car outside the door and we on the Wild Atlantic Way."

Timmy was washing the dishes in the sink. "Well, mind yourself, missus. A summer chest cold is the worst sort. Once it gets stuck into you, there's no budging it." He paused. "Maybe a glass of punch might give you a bit of relief."

Mary brightened. "Good man yourself. Take the bottle out of the press there." She looked into the basket. "Oh, my poor *piscín*. I think she's picking up a bit, though."

Timmy had taken out the Power's bottle and was waiting for the kettle to boil. "I might make a glass for myself while I'm at it," he said tentatively.

"That goes without saying. Give me a lemon and a knife and I'll slice it. Half a spoon of sugar will do me. And turn up the radio there while you're at it. I heard no news all day."

"A big loss that was to you. It's nothing but that auld Brexit morning, noon and night."

The two of them sat there companionably listening to the radio that was playing at a higher volume than Mary would have liked. She knew Timmy was getting deafer and she made no comment on it. The music was so high that neither of them were aware of Margot until she was standing in front of them.

"Glad to see the two of you enjoying yourselves," she said, appraising the two glasses.

"Purely medicinal," Mary said. "Well, how's business with you?"

"I have four Americans for three nights," Margot said triumphantly. "They're *Star Wars* fans. They can't get enough of the place. I had a pair of English that were over for a wedding in Killarney and decided to make a holiday out of it. They're only one night, though."

Mary took a sip of her whiskey. She was peeved. "We had four but they were all one-nighters. That's the worst of the Airbnb as far as I can see."

Margot shrugged. "It's all business. And you can get Carol to change the settings to two or three nights minimum stay. Speaking of Carol, where is she?"

"I'm waiting for her to get back from Portmagee to do the rooms. Any time she goes down that drive, God only knows when she'll reappear. Is this inspector making any shape to wind up operations? If he doesn't pull out soon, we'll all be driven buckhouse."

273

Margot snorted. "That cuckoo. He refuses to tell me when he's leaving for good. Just when it looks as if we've shaken him off, up he pops again. I've a good mind to ring Fáilte Ireland, but I don't want to end up in any more trouble than I'm in already." Her voice sank a little. "Half the association is cool with me." She gathered herself again. "I don't know what Fáilte Ireland was doing when it sent him down. The man has me demented. I still can't say how sorry I am for sparking all this off."

Mary raised her hand. "Whisht, girl. Didn't we call it quits?"

Margot smiled gratefully but at the same time she couldn't help glancing around the kitchen. She sniffed. Mary could see she was holding herself in check. Thankfully, Sue Ellen hadn't been rumbled in her nest. The place wasn't as tidy as it should be. Carol had begun to rely on Sharon on the days she worked with them. It was obvious that the housework had got short shrift over the previous few days as she had concentrated on finishing the second painting.

Mary affected a fit of coughing to stave off any lecture.

"Mary, that's a desperate cough," Margot said, her face a picture of concern. "Timmy, when you finish that glass there, you might give her a hand around the kitchen."

Timmy smiled. "It's true what they say, Margot. You'd have the whole parish running and racing for you if you got half a chance."

"Who're they?" Margot said testily. "Come on, out with it."

Timmy knew he'd slipped up. He shifted in the chair but, just then, Angela rushed in, breathless.

"I had a call from Julia Sheehy. She's fit to be admitted. He landed on her doorstep just after the washing machine had flooded the utility room. On top of that, the sheepdog had got loose – the silent, deadly fella that steals up on you without barking. He was swinging off the hem of yer man's overcoat when she went to the door. She thought he'd read her the riot act but all he could talk about was some hall in West Cork where the jackpot hadn't been won in six months and he's staying another night."

Mary was stricken. "He'll hardly land back here to us. We're only expecting a call or a letter."

Margot was rooting in the press under the sink. "That's why I'm here. He told Julia something about repeat visits and mentioned this place and a few others."

Timmy scowled. "The divil carry him – still on the rampage."

Margot paused in her attack on the cooker with Jif. She massaged her temples with her knuckles. "I can hear the phone calls already. I can't take much more of this. I tried to ring Carol but she's not answering."

"I don't know what she has that phone for," Mary said. "The time you need her most is the very time she won't answer it. I don't know what she's doing flouncing around Portmagee when there's so much left to be done here."

Angela's eyes widened. "Mary, can Carol not have an hour or two off? No wonder young people are so slow to take over farm guesthouses and B&Bs when they're expected to be such slaves to the business."

"Angela, I'm surprised to hear you talking to me like that."

"Well, maybe it's about time I started surprising people, starting with myself."

Margot and Mary were looking at her in astonishment when Timmy called out from his vantage-point at the window. "*I think ye're all in for a surprise, ladies!*"

He darted across the room and threw a pink hand towel over the slumbering cat.

With that, Arthur made his entrance. He rubbed his hands together in obvious good humour.

"Again, I appear to have made my arrival in the middle of a summit. Or is this what you call a Rambling House? I was hoping to catch you and your delightful daughter on your own, Mrs O'Connell."

Margot took a step towards him. "My aunt is feeling a little poorly. That's why we're here to give her a hand. The farmhouse spirit – everyone mucking in together."

Timmy and Angela were feverishly wiping surfaces and putting things into presses. Not quite everything. Arthur's eyes swivelled to the whiskey bottle. Suddenly, the pink towel rose as Sue Ellen sat up and meowed. Mary and Timmy froze. Margot and Angela looked at each other in horror.

"Do I hear a cat in here?" Arthur asked, his face turning a plum hue.

"It's just the way the wind is blowing in the eaves," Mary said. "These old houses have such echoes – the least thing carries from outside. Sometimes it's like a woman wailing. I tell the people it's the banshee." She caught Margot's warning look. "Of course that's only if they're not of a nervous disposition."

Arthur clearly dismissed her explanation as the ravings of a madwoman. "Is your daughter here? I want to leave tomorrow and return home via West Cork. We can have our little chat if she's available."

Mary coughed loudly and he moved away from her. "I'm expecting her any minute now. But you can go ahead and talk to myself. We don't want to be detaining you." She coughed again.

"That's a dreadful cough. I hope you've been to the doctor."

Mary assumed what Carol called her 'Mother of Sorrows' look. "I wouldn't be wasting my money on a doctor when I'm not long for this world anyway."

Arthur sat down at the kitchen table and opened his briefcase. Margot dropped to her knees with the dustpan and brush. She found herself looking directly into the frank eyes of Sue Ellen who, with the towel snagged on her ears and falling down her back, had the aspect of a pink Madonna.

"*Meow!*" said the cat conversationally.

Margot jumped to her feet instantly and assailed Arthur with a barrage of talk. "To tell you the truth, we're all afraid that Mary has a virus and that it could be terribly contagious. Carol isn't too good either. Weak chests run in the family."

Arthur was rustling through his papers. "All in the genes, the genes. Take our family. My father wouldn't allow a dog or a cat inside the door. If he came within a foot of one of the creatures, he'd sneeze his head off. The same as if he snorted the contents of a pepper-shaker up his nose. And I'm the very same."

The cat meowed again. Angela made a pretence of dropping a fork under the table. She crouched down and pulled the towel over the cat again. Sue Ellen was having none of it. She reared up, pawing at the towel.

Meanwhile, Timmy was clattering a saucepan on the draining board.

Arthur looked at him strangely.

"Don't mind Timmy," Mary said. "He doesn't be well at times."

Arthur's nose twitched. He sneezed.

"Are you sure there isn't a cat in here?" he said, pulling a large white handkerchief from his jacket pocket. His nose trumpeted from behind it.

"I wouldn't let one of the creatures darken the door," Mary declared. "Since there's no sign of Carol, come into the dining room and we'll start our own discussion in peace and quiet."

Arthur emerged from behind the hankie only to disappear again with a loud sneeze. "I'm prepared to wait for her."

"You might be catching an April cold. Like myself. Come on now. We don't want to be passing on our germs to the others, do we?"

Mary made a production out of limping into the dining room.

"It's the damn hip," she said, addressing Arthur, who was sneezing in her wake.

Angela handed him a kitchen roll and closed the door firmly behind them.

Margot tapped Timmy on the shoulder and pointed to Sue Ellen, who was sitting up like a queen regarding her staff expectantly.

"Get that woebegotten ball of mange out of here before she multiplies before our very eyes!"

"But that's Sue Ellen," Timmy protested. "Her kitten days are over."

Margot was so exasperated she could only hiss. "*Out, out, out!*"

"*Alright, alright, alright.*"

"Oh, let me do it," Angela said, reaching in under the table. "You'll do your back in."

The dining-room door opened and Arthur came back in to retrieve his briefcase just as a regal Sue Ellen loped from the basket and took a leisurely stroll across the tiles, tail in the air.

"*Open the back door!*" Margot shouted at Timmy as she set off in pursuit of the indignant cat with the sweeping brush.

"I knew it!" Arthur said, storming back into the dining room.

Mary had her back to the kitchen and was blithely unaware of the domestic safari that had unfolded. "The news is not good. I can tell by your face."

"I can't imagine how you can read anything from my face – it's so contorted from this infernal sneezing. You needn't bother with the cover-up. I've just seen your feline friend emerging from her bed under the table." He tore off a ream of kitchen paper violently.

Mary was stricken. "It was just because the day was so cold and she's so old and Carol was on the missing list and . . ." She stopped wondering what to say next. "They're rarely in. Except for that time Jacinta snuck in the window and ended up in the bed."

Arthur may as well have been at the other side of Cahersiveen for all the effect her explanation was having on him. His eyes were on the sheaf of papers he was rustling through. "This hasn't been an easy decision. Even up to five minutes ago, I wasn't sure whether I would give you the benefit of the doubt or not. But I'm afraid the concealment of that cat under the table is weighing heavily on me."

Mary was raging. "These are isolated incidents."

Arthur produced an A4 sheet from the case with a

flourish. "I fear not. A copy of an email from one Chantal Guiton in Marseilles. It arrived around the same time as your former enemy now turned ally, Margot, emailed the Dublin office. Chantal was less than enchanted at the sight of a large black cat with its paw in a dish of butter in the dining room. Hardly a scene from a Kerrygold advertisement, I'd imagine."

Mary was deflated. "Lucifer. He has the heart scalded on me, climbing in windows."

Arthur rummaged in the bag again and produced a mousetrap. He waved it gaily in front of him. "I found this under the bed in . . ." he stopped to refer to a note, "in 'Chestnut', along with a sizeable amount of fluff." He waved the trap again. "Astonishing, given the omnipresent cats."

Mary's voice was weary. "Carol has an overactive imagination. She thought there were mice around in the springtime. She laid out a pile of traps. She must have missed that one when she gathered them up."

Arthur assumed a kindly expression. Mary's heart sank even further. Eoin always said that when a judge began his verdict on a gentle note, he feared the worst. The judge who gave you a dressing-down was generally the one who came in with a favourable verdict.

"The cats are a major black mark from a hygiene point of view," Arthur said. "But I'm afraid there are major difficulties with the bedrooms too – dampness, poor tiling in the en-suite bathrooms."

"Save me the litany," Mary said, squaring her shoulders. "Just give me the verdict. The bottom line is that you're taking my shamrock, aren't you?" Her voice had held firm until it reached the word 'shamrock'. Then it quavered.

"I'm afraid so until certain improvements are implemented.

Unless of course you're open to an alternative plan." He looked furtively towards the kitchen and dropped his voice to a whisper. "For a consideration, I may be prepared to overlook certain flaws and amend my report accordingly."

Mary blinked. "And what might this consideration consist of?"

Arthur examined his nails. "One thousand euro. Of course, this is strictly between the two of us."

Mary rose out of the chair as if she'd been stung by a wasp. "You can whistle for it, you blackmailer!"

Arthur's expression never changed. He snapped the briefcase shut, and gazed over the top of her head.

"Have it your own way but, be warned, if you a breathe a word of this, I will deny everything," he said in a voice holding no shred of emotion. "I simply gave you the figure for the estimated cost of upgrading an en suite. I can't help it if you're hard of hearing."

Mary's voice, when she managed to locate it, was supercharged with emotion.

"*Get out the door, you blackguard!*" she roared. "*I don't know what the world is coming to!*" She fired a sugar bowl at his retreating back, striking him smack between the shoulder blades. The bowl fell to the ground, miraculously intact, but the sugar scattered everywhere.

He streaked through the kitchen and out the back door with the others looking at him in astonishment. He passed Angela who walked in open-mouthed. Mary sank into her armchair with a face like doom. Margot picked up Arthur's jacket from the back of a chair and followed him.

Angela put her hand on Mary's shoulder. "The news isn't good. I can tell."

281

Timmy's face was grim. "Don't tell me he failed ye! D'auld maggot."

"Oh, but he did," Mary said bitterly.

Timmy threw down the sweeping brush with a clatter. "That's fierce scamping. How can they get away with it?"

Mary looked very tired. She leaned back in the chair and closed her eyes. "Rules and regulations. Standards."

"Regulations my arse," Timmy said. "The country is gone clane mad with regulations since we joined the Common Market."

Angela was searching for something consoling to say. "To quote yourself, Mary, it might be the best thing that ever happened to you. A blessing in disguise. You were going to have to think of retiring some day anyway."

Mary spluttered. "Retiring? A blessing? I'm disappointed in you, Angela, very disappointed. Next stop the County Home, I suppose."

"I didn't mean it like that," Angela said in a strangled voice. Her eyes were brimming with tears.

"Oh, sure I know you didn't, girl. You were only using my own words. Take no notice of me."

Margot was a ghost of her usual self when she came back into the kitchen. "I need a drink," she said weakly, leaning against the fridge.

Angela poured a half-glass of whiskey and handed it to her. While she turned to get some water, Margot downed the drink neat and began to speak in a monotone.

"He said there was an email from an American family who said I wasn't homely enough, that I didn't give them enough to eat, and that Richard wasn't their idea of a traditional Irish farmer. He said his stay confirmed everything they'd said."

Mary brightened. She struggled to prevent a smile. "You mean he failed you as well. Take no notice of him. You did those Americans a favour by cutting back on their rations. You should have told them it was a health farm. Do you remember the family?"

Margot's face was flushed from the whiskey. She held out the glass for a second shot, dutifully poured by Angela, as Timmy mournfully witnessed the last of the bottle being drained.

"I have my suspicions. There was this waspish crowd here not long after I opened in March. They almost held me personally responsible for the Skellig not being open at that time of year. The room was full of duty free, and they had a path beaten to the kitchen door for ice. The husband was throwing out questions like machine-gun fire." She put on an American accent. "'How did you afford to refurbish this house? What do you work at?' The wife had a face stretched tight as a bodhrán and she was like a presidential wife simpering at the husband."

The corners of Timmy's mouth curled down in contempt. "They're the last word altogether to go writing off letters like that."

Angela was thoughtful. "What I find strange is that they're not going on TripAdvisor. That's where the real —"

But nobody was listening to her, least of all Margot, who had built up a head of steam and cut across her. "Well, their letter chimes with our bingo fiend's view that my house is '*cold, sterile, devoid in atmosphere and lacking the characteristics of traditional Irish farmhouses*'. He adds for good measure that the orange juice could strip paint."

A broad smile lit up Mary's face like a sunrise but she

rapidly switched to sunset when she realised Margot was staring at her.

Angela had a light-bulb moment. "Do you remember telling me back in July about someone giving out about portion control? I mean that must have been a warning bell."

Margot shook her head vigorously. "That's neither here nor there. It's a guesthouse not a soup kitchen. You have to watch your costs. There's a long winter ahead of us. What really gets me is the assault on my personality. Cold, how are you! Just because I'm not prepared to listen to their life stories over tea and scones. Short of having a lobotomy, I couldn't change my personality."

"That would be a job in itself," Timmy said earnestly.

Margot eyed him coldly. "What do you mean?"

"Changing your personality," he said. He continued like a man advancing across the collapsing floor of a derelict building. "Well, you know yourself, you're a bit quick off the draw."

Angela dropped her head into her hands. Mary shot Timmy a warning look with as much conviction as the farmer who goes to bolt the stable door after he's seen the horse galloping down the lane.

"What's this?" Margot said. "*The Weakest Link*? For God's sake, I don't know what guests expect from us. A surrogate family? Is there some website showing cherubs opening the front door with a dusting of flour on their floral aprons and a framed certificate in psychotherapy in the hallway?"

Angela lifted her head and surveyed Margot with disbelieving eyes. "They're coming into a *family home*, Margot. That's why they book with us and not a five-star hotel. Yes, they're invading our space but that's what we sign up to. Like it or not, you're part of the package, part of the product you're always talking about."

Margot drummed her fingers on the table. Her face was fixed in a pout. "I know all that. And I can see the attraction for the visitors. I loved the agri-tourism experience in Sardinia myself. It's just that it's such a strain listening to people all the time. It's not really what I expected."

Something caught fire in Mary as she listened to her. "Well then, Margot, you shouldn't be drawing it on you, so. You never know who's going to walk in your door and what frame of mind they'll be in. The big warm *Ceád Míle Fáilte* with the tea and scones means so much. I've seen wans arrive as bitter as crabappples, but a bit of kindness brings them out of themselves." She could see that Margot's attention was elsewhere but Angela was nodding and willing her on. "You know the big bow window facing south in the sitting room? It's a real sun trap. I like to think that that's what I'm creating here – a cosy place with kindness falling like sunshine to bask in. They're looking for a different landscape but they find a more peaceful version of themselves."

Margot shook her head. "That's truly lovely, Mary, but with Airbnb taking over I'm afraid you're *The Last of the Mohicans*, an endangered species. Sentiment won't fill the bank account. That's the hard economic reality."

Mary took a deep breath. "This is a business. Just because I invest so much personally in it doesn't mean I'm running a social services centre. John, God rest him, never begrudged me a penny, but I always took pride in having my own few pounds. I never had to go with the hand out to him. There were enough women having to account for every penny. But women like me running the farm guesthouses always had their own money."

Timmy clapped his hands and Angela joined in.

"Well said, Mary! I'd be lost only for my own little business."

Margot brightened. "I have a new business idea, myself. I'll divide the house into self-catering apartments. I'll get the architect in right away. He can look over the stone sheds in the yard as well. A new project. I feel better already."

Mary's heart sank again in the face of Margot's enthusiasm for a new beginning that reminded her that her long association with Fáilte Ireland was doomed. "At least I stuck to my guns and never handed him over the money."

"Who?" Margot said, already walking her own property with the architect in her mind's eye. "What money are you talking about?"

"Who do you think?" Margot said. "That inspector. He demanded a consideration of a thousand euro in return for overlooking *certain matt*ers. I told him where to go."

"That's mad," Angela said. "There's something seriously wrong there."

"That's the height of blackguarding," Timmy said.

Margot jumped to her feet. "It's extortion, nothing less. It's criminal. I'm going straight to the sergeant."

Mary waved her hand. "Don't waste your energy. He'll deny everything. His word against that of a deaf old lady. He said so." Her bottom lip quivered.

Margot was halfway across the kitchen floor. "We'll see about that. If he's tried to take advantage of you, he could have done the same to other people."

The room was deathly silent after Margot's departure. Mary's voice was lifeless when she eventually spoke. "Did you hear her going on about the self-catering? They're made of money. Sure the farmhouse is only a hobby to her."

Angela yawned. "You have to admire her energy. She can't rest without a new project to pour her passion into. Please God, we'll all get a rest when she does." She laughed. "The only thing is that I pity the builders when she gets going. She'll break the heart of every tradesman who comes through the door at the rate she changes her mind about details and features. I've seen grown carpenters practically break down and cry over her quare notions about *features*."

Timmy laughed. "I walked in one day when the job on the house was nearly finished. I asked one of the fellas if he'd seen her around anywhere. Sez he, 'I didn't and I don't want to.' But, at the end of the day, she pays every single one of them on the button. That's much better than them serpents that are full of *plámás* and couldn't pay a bill to save their lives."

Mary smiled faintly. She had a faraway look in her eyes. "That's all very well for Margot to be launching into a new project, but what am I going to do if I don't have my people coming through Fáilte Ireland? I won't want for money, but I can't stand the thought of rattling around a big, empty old house on my own."

"You'll be grand out, missus," Timmy said. "You have the luck of one of your black cats. And the neck of a giraffe to go with it."

"He's right, Mary," Angela said. "You have your reputation built up over the years. People will come back."

Mary sighed. "I hope you're right. But it's the shame and embarrassment of it along with everything else. What are the rest of the women going to be saying behind my back? I was with Bord Fáilte from the very start, ever before they changed to Fáilte Ireland and started tricking around with the shamrock, making it look as if was one of those stretchy toys that children pull. It's like the ground is being swept from under me by people who don't know the first thing about me or all I've put into the place. And I'm worried about Carol on top of everything. I don't know whether she's coming or going. And what's Sharon going to do if we have less work?"

Angela was firm. "Stop tormenting yourself, Mary. Everything will work out. You know as well as I do that Carol might take a wobble every now and again, but she always lands on her feet. Her star will rise yet, mark my words. There's going to be great take for those Skellig paintings. I think she's valiant that she hasn't sold out on what she wanted to do."

"I suppose so," Mary said without conviction. "What's keeping her? She should have been back ages ago."

Angela implemented the old reliable therapy of making a pot of tea. She was pouring the first mug when the car crunched to a halt outside the window.

Carol came through the back door beaming and waving a white envelope. "Two more sold." Just as quickly, her good spirits evaporated when she caught sight of her mother's drawn face. She looked from one to the other. "What happened?"

"Our fine friend, the inspector, called while you were out," Mary said. "We're for the chop."

Carol exhaled. "Oh, my God, Mam, I'm sorry. I was hoping against hope. But, look, we'll do fine with Airbnb. Look how many people we've got through it already."

Mary was downcast. "But it's not the same thing, Carol. Airbnb is for the new ones coming up. I'm a Farmhouse woman all my life. It's like playing for Kerry and being told to leave the field. I feel so . . . " She gulped and her voice was lost in the tears.

Carol could feel the anger rise inside her. If she could find that fool, Arthur, she'd pulverise him.

Suddenly, there was a screech of brakes outside. Angela scarcely had time to announce Margot's arrival when she shot through the back door with a bottle of Prosecco by the neck.

Angela's heart sank. All they needed now was the launch of the new project. She steeled herself for some gross display of insensitivity.

"*You're safe, Mary*," Margot cried, her voice bubbling with glee. "*You're safe. We're all safe. Nobody has lost their approval. It was all a big con job.*"

Mary's jaw was slack. "What do you mean?"

Margot was ecstatic. "Our inspector was a conman! A conman or a sick man, I'm not too sure at the moment, but the important thing is that he was no inspector."

Her audience could scarcely believe the good news. The competing chorus of '*Are you sure?*' put Carol in mind of the crows.

Margot delivered the news in breathless, staccato bursts. When she related Margot's experience to the sergeant, he made a few discreet calls only to discover that five other Farmhouse women had the same experience. Three of them had handed over cash. He went on the Pulse system and discovered that one Athur McKeown was on the missing persons list.

"But there's no crime in being a missing person," Carol said.

Margot waved her hand magisterially. She had the floor and she was going to hold it.

289

"No, and I don't think he's really a criminal," she said.

She had directed the sergeant to ring Fáilte Ireland in Dublin and alert them to the fact that a man, who claimed to be an inspector for the organisation, was extorting money from their members. Carol smiled at the thought of Margot setting herself up as director of operations at the Garda Station and issuing orders to the mild-mannered sergeant.

It emerged that the said Arthur was the brother of a cleaning contractor at the Dublin offices and suffered from manic depression which kept him awake half the night. The brother had been bringing him to work with him to keep him out of harm's way.

Arthur was also a computer genius. Unknown to his brother, he had found a computer account that hadn't been logged out and gained access to a complaints file.

"It transpired there was only one email complaint in relation to this area – mine," Margot concluded sheepishly. "But he read the others and collated them in his fertile imagination to create other fictictious complaints about this area."

Carol whistled. "You have to hand it to him. He really put on a good show."

Margot nodded. "So good, in fact, that the Fáilte Ireland switchboard had several calls today from 'failures' like ourselves. The guards are out looking for the poor man."

Angela was overtaken by sympathy. "The *cratur*."

Timmy looked at her as if she had taken leave of her senses. "I'll give him *cratur* if I meet him. Hasn't he half the parish demented?"

Mary was jubilant. "The good news is that we're all fine. We'll put it behind us."

Margot thrust the bottle of Prosecco into Carol's

hands. "You're more adept at this." She winked. "You've more practice. I'll get the glasses."

Once the glasses were filled with the fizzing liquid, Margot proposed a toast to their deliverance.

"To good friends!" Carol said.

"To new beginnings!" Angela said.

"To my shamrock and Farmhouse women everywhere!" Mary said.

Timmy frowned as she struggled to add his own leg to the proceedings. Then, his eyes lit up. "To the Bread and Breakfast. Long may it prosper!"

And, as one, they all cheered "*To the Bread and Breakfast!*"

Chapter 24

Oliver's emails had become sporadic. There wasn't a peep out of him for two entire days. Carol told herself that she shouldn't have been rattling on to Angela about his earlier messages. It was as if she had tempted fate. When two of her own emails hadn't met with an answer, depression set in. Her heart lifted when a message did arrive on the third day, but it was short and stilted, basically an enquiry about the weather and how busy the house was. And now another day had passed without a message of any sort. She cursed the expectations raised by mobile phones.

She took herself up Bolus Head to see if she could shift her mood. She was missing him more than she should have. It was ridiculous how dependent she had become on the emails and text messages from him. So dependent that silence from him for two days could knock her off kilter.

It was evening time. The longest day in the year, 21 June, had drifted by three days earlier in the clasp of the heat wave. The sea was calm and flat under an oyster sky. She could hear the waves washing off the base of the cliffs below her. A faint cry of gulls reached her from the sea while the hoarse call of ewes was answered by the high-pitched bleating of lambs in the fields below the road.

As the road climbed higher, the grey expanse of Lough Currane appeared behind the houses of Waterville. Ahead of her, a red van moved between the green of scrubby fields and the grey lines of stone walls.

Newly shorn sheep were painted a sherbet orange. A lamb had escaped from a field to the road and couldn't find its way back in again. The ewe was running the length of the wire fence beside the road. The lamb kept pace, bleating all the while.

Carol realised how bad her mood was when a gold-coloured bullock with a mullet haircut fixed her in a stare and didn't break eye contact. She knew what lay ahead of him and he didn't. She realised she was overreacting because her feelings were askew.

Despite herself, she checked the mobile again. Nothing. Oliver's lack of contact worried her. She missed the jokey text messages, the way in which he could make light of the mundane details of her work in the guesthouse, his descriptions of London. She wondered if she had offended him with some flippant remark.

The last of the evening sunlight was colouring the cliff faces on Scariff Island and, beside it, Deenish. Way off on the horizon, the trio of islands, the Cow, the Bull and the Calf, were held in a pale frieze of light.

Her hand closed around the phone in her pocket. She stopped herself from taking it out and checking for a message yet again. She'd walk to the end of the road first. She was mad at herself. Everything was so beautiful but she was bothered. *Practise staying in the present moment. Yes, right.*

In a matter of minutes, the light deepened so much that windows of houses in Waterville and here and there on the mountainsides had become crystal shards. Shadows deepened in mountain pockets. The horizon was suffused with a heathery pink.

A woman came down the road and passed Carol without a nod. She was holding a mobile phone in front of her and speaking into it.

Even before Carol rounded the next bend, she could hear a commotion of voices. The reason for it soon became apparent. An American family was standing around a self-drive car that had sunk into a roadside dyke with a stream running through it. She stopped to offer her sympathy for what it was worth.

"We just arrived here at this rental home," the woman said, pointing to the bungalow inside the ditch. "We flew into Dublin this morning and we've been driving all day."

The husband was on his mobile to the owner of the holiday home. Carol wished them well and continued up the road.

She met a farmer out checking on his sheep. They passed a few words about the stranded Americans.

"Cars are always going into the dyke on that turn," he said. "Bad drivers. At least there's no harm done to them down there."

Carol took out her mobile to take pictures of the stone ditches and the plant life: fuchsia with indigo bells, clumps of foxgloves, lusty thistles, bedraggled nettles.

She passed the two ruined houses, backside to the wind, gables conscripted to take the storms. One small window high up on the gable faced out to Scariff Island. The door and the windows faced into the land for survival. The windows of Kilrelig National School, dated 1899, faced out to the sea. There had to be a message in that, Carol though because the school opened their eyes to the world.

Her phone rang. It was Oliver.

294

Chapter 25

Mary was sitting at a circular wrought-iron table beside the conservatory, fanning herself with a copy of *Ireland's Own*.

"This heat will have us roasted alive," she said. "Nearly three months now without a sign of rain. I never witnessed a July like it. It's desperate to the world to see the grass looking so yellow."

Carol was stationed at an ironing board set up beside her. The iron was plugged into an extension lead trailing from the dining-room window. She selected a sheet from the laundry basket at her feet and folded it in four, gripping the fabric under her chin as she completed the manoeuvre. "Most people are so glad to see the sun after the drowning we got all spring that they'd shoot you at the mention of rain."

Timmy arrived from the kitchen with a tray of mugs and a packet of chocolate digestive biscuits. He took a biscuit and spoke in between bites. "The farmers are driven spare. First of all they couldn't put the bashts out on the fields with the dint of muck. Now, they're running out of water and the news is full of talk of a fodder shortage. Wouldn't that give anyone cause for *ollagóning*? You can't win. Sure we had nearly five months of pure wet winter, a lashing of snow in March for good measure and

295

we're landed directly into this burning summer without a spring in between. Am I right?"

Carol continued ironing. "You're right, of course, but not everyone thinks of the farmer. People are just delighted to be able to go the beach. Well, at least we won't mock the Americans again when we hear them saying, '*Everything is so green*'. I love the sun but I hate to see everything so burned up. When you look at some of the fields of faded grass, you'd think you were out on the prairies instead of down here in South Kerry."

As Mary poured the tea, she caught Timmy's eye and gave a slight nod in the direction of the ironing board.

Carol waved the iron in the air. "Don't think I didn't see that look, mother."

Mary straightened herself in the chair. "I don't care whether you did or you didn't, madam. What are the people going to think if they drive up and see you cocked out in the open with an ironing board? We'll be mistaken for an asylum."

Carol ran the iron up and down the sheet lazily. "They're going to be overcome with admiration at my ingenuity. They'll be making videos and posting them on YouTube. This is the best summer we've had since seventy-six and I'm not going to waste any of this glorious sunshine."

"YouTube," Mary scoffed. "What will they be putting up on it next? The cat having kittens, I suppose."

Timmy bit into another biscuit – his third – and devoured half of it at once. "I thought it was the cat and her kittens that landed ye in the mess in the first place. I wouldn't go broadcasting yeer problems to the world if I were ye."

Carol breathed a sigh of relief when she placed the

final sheet on top of the pile neatly stacked on a chair beside her. She selected a fistful of pillowslips. She adored pillowslips. Not a bit of bother in them. The elasticated bottom sheets had been her nightmare until Angela shared a tip. Iron them on the bed.

Timmy gestured towards the two rental cars parked under the cool shade of the beech trees. "Who have we here at eleven o'clock in the morning? I thought they'd all be cleared out by now."

Mary tossed her head back. "They said they were Germans. *Mo léir*, they're not Germans a'tall. They said they'd have the breakfast at nine and they didn't come down till ten. We didn't clear their breakfast table yet because her ladyship here wanted to get a taste of the sun before it gets too hot." She pushed her chair further back into the shade. "Too hot. Did we ever think back in March we'd have this complaint?"

"As long as I'm in this house I haven't seen the likes of this crowd. Gemans, my eye. When they came down eventually looking for omlettes, they did my head in. Omlettes and cold plates. Now, they'll be all day leaving the room."

Timmy pulled his blue baseball cap further over his face. "Almighty God, missus, you get all sorts here, don't you? You could write a book. You wouldn't want to meet too many like that."

"Indeed'n I could write a book. The only thing is that people would think I was making half of it up. Truth is stranger than fiction."

Carol's stack of pillowslips was growing higher. She smiled to herself as she listened to the pair. She'd checked her phone early that morning to find a lovely WhatsApp message from Oliver with a smiley face kissing a tiny red heart in the air. She was so glad she'd taken Angela's advice to visit him for that couple of days at the end of June. They'd had such a good time. He'd lined up visits to the Tate and the National Gallery and an afternoon out in Grenwich as well as celebrity-spotting strolls in Holland Park. They'd got on like a house on fire. And, oh, the chemistry that had ignited. Now, he was on course to come over for a week in August. The putative Germans could come downstairs at tea time for all she cared. All was right in her world.

"At least they weren't fussy," she said. "They could have had their noses stuck in the air. They're a very cheery lot. My guess is that they're of Turkish descent. A lot of Turks migrated to Germany to work in the car industry."

"They're very tanned for Germans alright," Timmy said. He glanced towards the cars again. "Have you two carloads of them?"

Carol frowned. "Actually, the second car belongs to the lovely Spanish couple that arrived two nights ago. She just brought up tea and toast to him this morning. He's not feeling great. I'd better check on them if they don't appear soon. I thought he caught some bug in the heat but, as far as I can make out, he suffers from kidney stones. The English isn't the best. Thank God for Google Translate."

All three of them turned their heads towards the driveway as the sound of a car carried around the turn that was bordered with hydrangeas showing the signs of the long drought. Mary ran her fingers through her hair and brushed some crumbs from her skirt.

A shot of steam rose from the iron as Carol attacked the final pillowslip. "Don't assume the lady-of-the-manor posture just yet in case it's another gravel-cruncher stealing a look at the old pile and wheeling around again at the sight of the natives."

The trio relaxed again as Angela's grey Toyota Corolla nosed around the turn, all the windows open down to the last. Sharon was in the front seat, and Lisa waved wildly from the back. They'd been helping Margot again, and finished early because she only had one car. According to Mary, they might as well move over there. Margot hadn't lifted a finger since Sharon arrived. She relied on Sharon to do most of the rooms.

"Look who I found sauntering up the road," Angela said, banging the car door behind her.

Lisa ran directly to Mary and thrust a wild bouquet of fuchsia and montbretia into her hands. "I picked them especially for you, Mary."

"The ditches are full of them," Sharon said. "The orange and red are gorgeous together. Carol should paint them."

Mary leaned forward to accept the flowers and a hug from Lisa. Carol watched out of the corner of her eye. The little girl had her mother wrapped around her little finger. It was good to see. Lisa was a light in all their lives. She blessed the providence of the clapped-out car that gave up yards from them that rainy night that seemed so long ago.

Mary dispatched Sharon for more cups and a fresh pot of tea. "And you might make a start on the last table in the dining room when you get a chance. Have your cup of tea first."

Sharon shook her head, and turned to Timmy. "Do the hardest job first, isn't that right, Timmy? If I get all the work done early, I might bring Lisa to the beach in Ballinskelligs. Margot was so happy with the cleaning I did that she promised to give us a spin. She's going to

Waterville for a game of golf and she'll drop us off and pick us up on the way back."

"Make sure you put plenty of sun cream on or ye'll fry," Mary said.

Angela was wearing a broad-brimmed straw hat with a pink ribbon. Carol admired it. "Hats are really your thing. They suit you down to the ground. Whenever I put on something like that, I age about twenty years and I feel like an extra in *The Best Exotic Marigold Hotel*."

"A lovely Frenchwoman gave it to me. They were flying out from Dublin the next day and she didn't want to be carrying it. Some of the people are so nice. They appreciate all the extra little things you do for them. They make the job worthwhile." She pressed an empty mug to her flushed face for the coolness of the china. "I'm fit to melt. Normally, I love the heat but this is going on too long. Somebody told me that the lawns in the Europe Hotel above in Killarney are gone as crisp as cornflakes."

She was wearing a leaf-green polka-dot dress with buttons down the front. The colour set off her tanned face. She looked radiant, albeit in an overheated sort of a way.

Carol felt so happy for her. "I knew the weight was melting off you, but you never looked as good as you do in that dress."

Angela did a twirl. "Would you believe that I have it since before I married? It was shoved in at the back of the wardrobe. I couldn't bring myself to give it away because I paid a small fortune for it. One of the few dacent things I ever splashed out on. I never thought I'd see the day that I'd fit into it again."

Lisa clapped her hands when Angela finished her twirl. "You're like a model."

Angela reached across the table and tussled her hair. "Thank you kindly, little miss." She stood in the shade with her back against the grey stone and wrinkled her nose at the biscuits. "To think that I used to devour packets of them. Now, all I can see is the calorie count."

She sauntered over to Carol.

"Let me give you a hand," she said, stacking the sheets and pillow slips into the grey, plastic laundry basket. She dropped her voice. "You know it's all very well getting compliments about looking like a model, but I must be the best-dressed depressive in South Kerry. I'm hiding behind a mask."

Carol squeezed her shoulder. "You don't have to tell me. All the same, it's a damn impressive mask."

Angela sighed. "It's a wonder to me how a person can feel like a bucket of cold ashes inside and look good on the outside."

"Don't knock it, girl. Keep acting like you feel fabulous and one day you will."

"What day will that be? Will it be before or after I qualify for the pension?"

Lisa called across from the table. "I can hear you whispering. Tell us the big secret."

Carol put her hand on her hips in mock outrage. "Mind your own business, you little monkey. What a nosey parker we have in you."

Mary turned to the little girl. "You're dead right, Lisa. Whispering in company is bad manners. Remember that."

Carol was folding up the ironing board when Sharon rapped at the dining-room window. She yanked the sash window up and stuck her head out.

"The Spanish lady came down to me bawlin' her eyes out. She wants ya, Carol. She's after runnin' back up the

301

stairs again like a bat out of hell. I hadn't a clue what she was sayin' but I think yer man must be after takin' a turn for the worse. She kept sayin' his name and pointin' to her belly."

What a contrast from the views of Glenosheen for Pablo and Lidia as they looked out the windows of the Accident and Emergency Department, Carol thought to herself. Except for the relentless blue of the sky, everything was grey outside – paving, boundary wall, the terraced houses beyond it. A Tayto bag fluttered listlessly in a faint draught of air. This was her worst nightmare. Being stuck in University Hospital Kerry on a baking hot day.

A furze-yellow ambulance appeared with the light flashing. She'd lost count of the number of ambulances that had passed in the two and a half hours they'd sat there waiting for Pablo to be seen.

The windows were grubby with fingerprints mottled to become a grey skin. She remembered a newspaper story about a terminally ill patient who spent his final days gazing through grimy hospital windows. In his will, he bequeathed money to pay for a cleaning service so that every other patient could look through clear glass. She'd have shared the anecdote with her two guests but she baulked at the thought of what could get lost in translation. The initial interview with the triage nurse had been a trial in itself with questions issued in rapid fire.

"When did you last have a bowel movement?"

Pablo was nonplussed. Carol stepped in, rephrasing the question in slow motion. "You have a problem going to the toilet?"

His eyes fired with the light of comprehension. "I have nothing. No piss, no nothing."

"How would you describe your pain on a scale of one to ten?"

He was eager as a schoolboy to describe his symptoms. "Last night, pain bery, bery bad. Womit three times."

The nurse was clearly under pressure and the translation problems weren't making her day any easier. Carol intervened again in the measured speaking voice honed from years of dealing with people with broken English. "Pablo, she is asking you to say how bad your pain is now. If it's very, very bad, you say ten. If there is very little pain, you say one."

Pablo began to repeat how bad the pain was the previous night. The nurse was about to unloose her pony tail and sprint out the door and down the driveway into the great unknown.

"But how is the pain now?" Carol asked.

"Now, say it eez four."

Carol winced. Good man, Pablo, she thought, you can add a good four hours to the wait now.

The nurse handed him a plastic container for a urine sample. No translation services required here. They left the nurse's office and settled back into the hard plastic seats in the public area. She'd noticed a sign advising women to let staff know if they were pregnant. Superfluous, in Carol's estimation, given that they'd probably have given birth by the time they'd negotiated the waiting game otherwise known as the Irish A&E system. She was beginning to regret her kind impulse to drive the pair to the hospital in Tralee. Helping people was coded into her genes. She'd read somewhere that it was called the 'saviour complex'. She was hardly going to change now, but people would probably get on fine without her.

Just then a young man emerged from the inner sanctum pushing an old man in red check pyjamas in a wheelchair. At least he'd been seen. The waiting room was like the carriage of a commuter train. No one spoke. Most had their eyes glued to a small TV screen on the wall.

A line from the documentary caught her ear. "*I always used to hope that my mum would come back.*"

The next camera shot was of a house where the woman was abandoned as a three-year-old.

The storyline absorbed Carol until her eyes drifted from the TV to the signage stating that aggression or verbal abuse wouldn't be tolerated. "**Incidents will be recorded and may be reported to the gardaí when necessary,**" the notice concluded. She had a mental image of two young guards dragging a crazed version of herself off the reception counter.

A young mother came in with a buggy. Carol was shocked to see her set an oxygen cylinder on the ground beside it. The mother, a slip of a girl, adusted the oxygen mask on the little girl who'd begun to cry. "I know, I know," she said in a soothing voice. Carol's heart went out to her.

She asked Pablo to see his watch. "It's an hour and a half since they took your urine sample." He looked at her quizzically. "Since they took the piss."

To her surprise, he replied, "In Spain, it eez worse."

Lidia nodded and smiled.

She looked so elegant in her powder-blue linen shift dress and her matching open-toed sandals and handbag. Manicured toenails a sassy scarlet, of course. Her glossy black hair was knotted on top of her head. Carol estimated that she was in her late forties. Pablo had a few years on her or else the extra few pounds he was carrying made him look older. Lidia had a limited number of phrases and a disconcerting habit of laughing heartily at the most inappropriate junctures. Carol's inner bitch was tempted to say 'I'm coming to hospital myself next week for a double leg amputation' to test the reaction.

Pablo had inherited the family jewellery business in Valencia. Lidia's jewellery was discreet – a fine chain of gold circles at her throat, a slender watch bracelet with a diamante face, a cluster of diamonds and a gold band on her wedding finger. Carol daydreamed about what it would be like to have an adoring husband who looked after all her material needs. He'd probably drive her round the twist.

The voice of Lidia's adoring husband brought her back to reality. "I worry about you because you lose all the day. I am tired because I sleep nothing. Worry about the pain."

No wonder there was such a population drain from South Kerry. Up to a two-hour drive to Tralee, depending on where you lived, hours waiting in Casualty when you arrived. And God help you if you needed an ambulance. With ambulance control re-located to Dublin, conveying place names was tortuous. And postal codes weren't always accurate. Throw in patchy phone reception in some valleys and you were really struggling.

God help the foreigners who made their home around the Ring of Kerry. Many's the dream of *A Place in the Sun* hatched on a heavenly day in Derrynane, Ballinskelligs or Valentia, was destined to degenerate into *A Place in the Rain* and hours driving to hospital, cinema or dentist.

"Princess Beyoncé O'Driscoll," called a nurse, who had emerged through the magic door to the treatment area. The name was a dead giveaway even before Carol saw a copper-curled girl of about seven and her parents, members of the Travelling community, disappear into the inner sanctum.

Pablo groaned. "*O Dios!* No medicine, and the pain goes up, up, up!"

Lidia sat on the edge of her seat and stroked his face.

"You should have told them it was a ten," Carol said grimly.

Pablo explained that he'd been drinking two litres of water a day to stave off the kidney stones.

"Maybe you should have been drinking more," she said.

"Maybe go to the sea with Lidia," he said.

"Why?"

"For to drink the water." He gave a rueful grin.

Carol smiled despite herself. She checked the phone again. Over two hours had passed since they'd seen the triage nurse. Her stomach was rumbling. Where in Airbnb's small print was there a warning that you might be required to become conversant with the inner workings of the plumbing of a middle-aged Spanish man?

Pablo took out his mobile and watched something online. Lidia looked at the TV. When a nurse emerged yet again to call another patient through the 'magic door', Carol didn't dare hope it could be Pablo. But it was. She wanted to somersault across the open space beside the rows of chairs.

Inside the door, the corridors were like a field hospital lined with trolleys and chairs. Some people were on their own, others had relatives keeping vigil. What struck Carol was the absolute weariness etched in the faces of the sick. A woman rested her head on the shoulder of the man beside her. From a cubicle or a room came the pitiful sound of a child wailing, '*Mammy, Mammy!*' Carol had heard people giving out about the Government and the health system since she came home. Now she could see what they were talking about. And the recession was supposed to be over. *Hello?*

Pablo was escorted to a cubicle where a doctor, possibly Indian, began the entire rigamorole all over again. "When did you last have a bowel movement, sir?"

Carol groaned inwardly.

Next stop was the X-ray unit where she read a notice for the domestic abuse organisation, ADAPT, pinned on a notice board. **"Just because there's no bruise doesn't mean it's not abuse."** She thought of the victims of domestic abuse who'd sat on the same chairs waiting for X-rays.

By then, Pablo was attached to a drip that looked as if it would take forever to empty. The smell of coffee reached her from a vending machine. She'd chance a cup no matter how awful it was.

Mary was still up when they arrived home at quarter to nine that night. She ladled up plates of Irish stew to the three of them at the kitchen table.

"The next politician that comes to the door canvassing will get tally-ho from me about that cursed A&E," Carol said. "It's like purgatory, a place you suffer in until you gain admittance to the heaven upstairs where you get the best of care."

While they were eating, Mary's face took on a preoccupied look. Carol asked her what was up.

"I had a phone call from George while you were out," she said.

Carol trained a pair of questioning eyes on her.

"Later," her mother said, a finger to her lips.

Chapter 26

Carol's brother and sister, George and Michelle, existed somewhere out there on the periphery of her consciousness. And she was happy enough to leave them out there where time and distance had consigned them. There were no bad feelings, she knew they'd be at her back if ever the need arose, but their paths had diverged widely and contact was sporadic.

The family had extended to include the in-laws or, as Carol preferred to call them, the out-laws.

Michelle and Frank met in Dublin when she was training to be a primary school teacher and he was a rookie guard fresh out of Templemore. The night club, Copper-Faced Jacks (Coppers to regulars), was heaving with nurses that night, so it was nothing short of a miracle that Frank hadn't hooked up with someone from the Rotunda or the Mater. Carol knew this story off by heart because Michelle repeated it almost as often as she did Frank's name.

In any social situation that called for an introduction, Michelle's catch cry was 'We're MichelleandFrank'. Whenever Carol slagged her about it, she put on a hurt face.

There was no doubt but that Michelle was a catch – huge green eyes, a headful of black curls that she was continuously trying to straighten, an immaculate sense of style, a lady to her fingertips and, behind the dreamy demeanour, the ruthlessness of a lioness when it came to defending the pride.

Frank was a tall, intense man with a permanent five o'clock shadow and an expression that suggested that he was concentrating on solving the next serious crime. He missed being good-looking by just a fraction.

Frank still had his First Communion money, as the saying went. Not that he needed to draw on it. An only child, he had inherited two farms in Mayo. There was the singular disadvantage of an overbearing mother who thought Michelle indolent, but she was a safe distance away in Bohola.

Carol admired Frank for his devotion to her sister, but Michelle had that effect on everyone since she was a child. She exuded a helplessness that made them do things for her before they even realised what was happening. Everyone except Carol.

"I'm not her slave," she used to protest to her mother. "How come you're always asking me to do things while she's lazing around the place?"

"Ah, but you're way bigger," Mary said. "Michelle's practically a baby. Wait till she catches up."

But Michelle never really caught up fully, even though, lured by the prospect of a wage, she did her share of bedroom-cleaning and breakfast-serving. Frank, when he came along, became her servant-in-chief. When the children, Isobel and Frank Junior, were born, they hired a housekeeper, Maureen, a capable widow strong enough to mix concrete. Michelle kept on teaching, and eventually retrained in Special Needs.

Frank Junior had a wild streak that Carol took a secret delight in. Isobel, her godchild, was quiet and dreamy. Her nose was perpetually stuck in a book, a trait that Carol indulged with gifts of more books whenever she could.

George, a ball of restless energy, was big into suits and sunglasses that were always on top of his head even after the fall of dark. He was an accountant with a mania for property development. No recession or downturn could touch him. He was so secretive that none of the family knew the extent of his portfolio, but they all knew about the block of penthouse apartments in Salthill thanks to the loose talk of a garrulous Galway solicitor holidaying in Waterville one August. And then, Olivia, George's wife, let slip after a few G&Ts too many at a Confirmation, that they had a block of student accommodation in Limerick. The look he shot her!

It was all very well being tight as a clam about your own business but George would go down your throat for a piece of information. His idea of conversation was an artillery round of questions. Carol felt like chewing a fist of multivitamins before any inquisition.

She genuinely admired Olivia but she didn't know how she stuck her workaholic husband. Olivia worked three days a week as a dentist's receptionist. Well, an orthodontist's receptionist. There was a difference. George was proud of that. "I've plenty of money and she doesn't need to work. But she's that type of woman."

Olivia was a golfer. She built up a wide circle of friends through the club. More often than not, she holidayed with them. George hated to be away any longer than four days. Any breaks he did take were always built around Bank Holiday weekends to capitalise on the extra day off work.

He was so busy that Carol wondered how they found time for each other. Evidently they did because the result was Gerard, aged ten and going on fifty. He came with that rarified manner of speaking and self-assurance that was part of the territory of certain only children.

Even though Carol had been wrecked from her day in the hospital with the Spanish couple, she couldn't contain her curiosity when Mary announced after Pablo and Lidia had gone to bed that George had rung requesting a 'family meeting' the following Saturday.

"What's ating him now?" Carol asked her mother. "I suppose he'll want a set of accounts submitted in advance. He's probably worried about his inheritance, given that he sees me installed in the ancestral home."

Mary wagged her finger. "The cheek of you. Inheritance. I've no notion of going anywhere soon. I suppose the next thing is that I'll find the house in the property section of some paper."

There was an edge to her words that stopped Carol in her tracks. It was strange to hear her mother sounding vulnerable. She was uneasy. "Ah, Mam, this isn't like you. What did he say to set you off?"

Mary had picked up *Kerry's Eye* and her face was obscured by it. She rustled the pages before throwing the newspaper back on the table impatiently. "He was harping on about the Airbnb. He says that you're drawing too much on me and that I'm not able for it." Her voice cracked. "He succeeded in confronting me with what I'm successfully dodging – most of the time. The fact that my energy isn't what it used to be, that I can't take on everything that I want to . . . "

Carol felt guilty. Mary was voicing what she'd been thinking herself. The commissions for the Skellig paintings had drawn her away from the housework more often than she wished. She had noticed Mary looking tired, but she didn't want to admit that she was the cause of it. "I am doing a lot still and Sharon is taking up the slack when I'm painting." She could hear the defensiveness in her own voice. George would drive a coach and four through her explanations.

Mary frowned. "That's another thing. Sharon. George was twenty questions about her. I'm afraid he must have heard something."

Carol's heart sank further. She dreaded the thought of the pow-wow on Saturday. Mary told her that George had picked up a cancellation at one of the holiday homes on the grounds of the Parknasilla Hotel outside Sneem. Michelle and himself would drive over to Glenosheen while Frank golfed and Olivia went for a spa treatment.

Carol couldn't help herself. "I suppose they thought I'd charge them. Parknasilla. Frank must be having a nervous breakdown at the thought of shelling out for that. That fella would live under a stone. It has to be a deal. He'd sleep in a shed here before he'd pay the full whack for that luxury."

Mary rubbed her temples. "George came at me with such an assault of talk, I'm not even thinking straight. I don't want to hear another word about this meeting until they land. We'll make it up as we go along. We'll be fine."

Carol pretended to agree. She knew they'd be tiptoeing around the elephant in the room for the next few days. Even without a conversation with her brother, he'd made her feel so inadequate. The disturbing point about the whole thing was that he probably had a point. She'd sleepwalked into the whole Airbnb undertaking, never expecting it to take off so quickly.

Even though a continental breakfast was the basic requirement for Airbnb, Mary had insisted on cooking a choice of the full Irish or omlettes because the guests coming to them through the Farmhouse Association would be having that anyway.

"You can't make fish of one and fowl of the other," Mary said.

Most of the Airbnb guests were willing to pay extra for the full breakfast but the added morning work was clearly too much for Mary. Carol hadn't insisted strongly enough that she stay in bed because, in truth, she knew she'd never manage to cook all the options on her own.

She'd squared it off in her mind, telling herself that Mary was a businesswoman and got a kick out of the house coming to life again. But maybe she would have been as happy ticking over with the trickle of people that booked in through the Irish Farmhouse Association.

The last thing Carol wanted was to be made feel like a charity case. God only knew what George and Michelle and the out-laws had been saying about her already. *Three deep breaths, three deep breaths.* She'd need an oxygen tank by the weekend at the rate at which the madly negative thoughts were beginning to swirl.

There was the usual small talk around the kitchen table as an opener. Carol dutifully enquired about the children, work and whether there was much change in Dublin and Galway. In turn, George and Michelle asked her how she had found Italy. Nobody mentioned Matteo. Carol thanked her lucky stars that they hadn't heard about Oliver. They were holding back on discussing Airbnb and all the extra work it was creating. There was so much that couldn't be mentioned – yet – that she felt like a conversational no-fly zone.

Michelle and George were like figure skaters cutting lavish, swirling loops around her. She played along, knowing that before long they'd be closing the circles and gliding towards the inevitable vortex waiting to suck them all in. As she waited, she wondered how her mother would deal with it. Who would call the meeting to order?

There was a lull in the conversation finally. All the pleasantries had been exhausted and no one had the appetite to ignite another round of superficial questions on topics in which they hadn't the slightest interest.

This was it. They knew that it was time for business. Everything else had functioned as a superficial clearing of the throat. Mary didn't let the silence lie for long. As she rapped her mug on the kitchen table, she reminded Carol of Judge Judy.

"Time to get down to business. No more beating around the bush. I'm sure everyone else is looking forward to dinner in Parknasilla as much as I am."

Carol had done her best to convince Mary to take up George's offer to spend the night in the stately old hotel outside Sneem. Mary had told him not to be wasting his good money, that she'd prefer to sleep in her own bed. Privately, she'd told Carol that she was afraid she'd be worn out after the family meeting.

Carol would have given her eye teeth for a couple of nights there. The hotel was straight out of a Victorian novel with its limestone turrets and sash windows looking out to sea, its old-world-aura of varnished wood, deep silences and landscape paintings. The very hands of the clocks seemed to move more slowly there.

She loved visiting Parknasilla in winter especially. The lounges with their open fires were perfect for sinking into an armchair and burying yourself in a book. No wonder the playwright George Bernard Shaw had spent weeks there in ninteen hundred and nine writing a play, *Saint Joan*.

When Matteo had visited, she dreamt of a night or two together in the old part of the hotel, but he had baulked at the price of it. She should have stood her ground but, looking back, it would have served no purpose. He'd only have sulked and taken all the good out of it.

Her mother's voice brought her back out of her daydream. Mary was opening up the discussion with an even-handed approach that would have done a UN diplomat proud. *On the one hand. And then again on the other hand.*

Carol could see George's knee bobbing up and down under the table. He was itching to get his spake in. And in he did come, again with a patient tone reserved for the misguided who were in need of enlightenment, of which he possessed vast reserves.

"What you're saying is all well and good, Mam, but only up to a point. You say you're happy to fall in with Carol's plans for Airbnb for the moment, but what Michelle and myself are concerned about is the long-term strategy. Isn't that right, Michelle?"

Michelle's glossy locks bounced as she nodded her agreement. She'd obviously had a cut and blow-dry in honour of the summit. Carol hadn't brushed her hair since the morning. Or had she fallen yet again among the ranks of the forget-to-brush-their-hair women? She would have given anything to break into the discussion at that point but, Michelle, his deputy, was primed for lift-off. It was a skilfully choreographed piece of work honed over the phone and, presumably, on the spin across from Parknasilla.

Michelle was nervous. Her face was flushed. "We don't really want to interfere. It's just that we . . ." She cleared her throat.

"Go on, Michelle," Mary said helpfully. "I'm not going to bite."

Carol could see that George was dying to get stuck in again, but he had to present it as a two-hander. It was one of those times that Carol wished she had someone at her back, a partner or a friend rooting for her in the corner. She thought of Oliver, calm, measured Oliver. Then again, he might have stuttered and faltered in the minefield of family tensions. She'd instructed Mary not to feel she had to defend her. Above all else, she was to present what suited her own needs.

Michelle ventured out again. "The last thing we want to do, Mam, is to interfere in your business, but we're concerned that there's no long-term plan and that you might end up in a situation where you're under too much pressure."

Mary nodded. "Yes, I can see exactly where you're coming from, and I do appreciate your concern." She sounded as if she was warming up for another 'but on the other hand' when George turned to Carol.

"The problem is that we had no warning about this. There was no consultation. I get the impression that you're making it up as you go along."

Carol flared inwardly. She dug her fingernails into her palm to contain herself. He'd identified her Achilles Heel. Yes, he knew exactly the right button to press, but she wasn't going to react. "I'm sorry if I didn't consult you both but I felt it was something to be worked out with Mam. I didn't think really."

His voice was tinged with ice. "You didn't think, did you?"

Michelle realised that the 'George Lite' – the watered-down George – was wearing thin. She shot him a warning look. "I'm sure that everything can be sorted out without a problem once we all have a clearer picture where this Airbnb business is going."

Carol was grateful for the intervention. The last thing she wanted was confrontation with George. She could never handle conflict. She took her note from Michelle's conciliatory tone.

"If the two of you think that I'm trying to cut inside you, then you're wrong. When I saw the increased interest in this area because of *Star Wars* and the Wild Atlantic Way, I thought it would be a shame not to capitalise on it. I suppose I was thinking of the old days when the house was so full of life and people." She looked at Mary. "And you were all for getting some of that atmosphere back again, weren't you, Mam?"

Mary looked taken-aback to be drawn into the discussion again so soon. She squared her shoulders. "A big part of me hated to see the business I had worked so hard to build up dwindle away, but I was more or less resigned to the fact. When Carol suggested the Airbnb, I said to myself, 'Sure what harm can it do for a summer?'"

Carol relaxed. That was a reasonable point of view. She could tell by George's body language that it wasn't what he wanted to hear. His foot was now flicking rapidly under the table. He clearly wasn't patient enough to wait to hear what the 'other part' of Mary's view on the project was. He was dealing out another hand in the hope of a better result.

317

"Leaving the Airbnb aside for a while, Mother, Michelle and myself are worried about this young woman and child you've taken on board. I mean, what, if anything, do you both know about their background? It's a big risk to take in strangers like that."

Mary's eyes narrowed. "I take exception to that, George. I'm known far and wide as a sound judge of character. Sharon is a lovely young woman, as honest as the day is long. And she's doing a great job of bringing up that little girl on her own. Sharon is paying her own way between the work she's doing here and over in Margot's. And she made a tidy bit of money with the flowers and vegetables she grew in the garden."

At the mention of Margot's name, Carol wondered if George had wheedled any information out of her. Or was it a careless remark of Timmy's? A bit like the Stasi files that became available for inspection after the fall of the Berlin Wall, Carol chose to align herself with those who declined to see who had ratted on them in case it was someone close to them and they'd regret the knowledge.

George was definitely armed with insider information but he chose to circle the topic. "We all know you'd buy and sell us when it comes to taking the measure of people, but that's not what I'm on about. I've no doubt that she's as sound as a pound, if that's what you tell me. But the problem is the crowd that she'll have following her. You have no guarantee what she'll draw around the place. In this day and age you can't be too careful."

Carol's heart sank. He was voicing the fears that she'd pushed to the rear of her own mind. Judging by her mother's face, he had the same effect on her. *Bingo*, George. All they wanted now was a self-fulfilling prophecy. It was at times like this that she wondered why she'd ever come home.

Mary pushed back her chair and folded her arms. "I don't like the turn this discussion is taking. To be honest, I'm tired of it. A person would be better off if they didn't own a single stick of furniture. All that's driving the three of ye is the same old jealousies that had ye arguing as children. '*It's not fair. She got that and I got nothing.*' I'm plain sick of it and I don't want to hear another word about it."

Carol felt affronted. "I don't want anything off you, Mam."

Mary raised her hand. "All three of ye will be well taken care of, don't worry. I just don't want anyone coming in here telling me my business. I'm not fit for the home yet. And I won't be for another while. When I do want help – and that day will come – I will ask for it. In the meantime, all I want is the three of ye to keep the peace. If that's not too much to ask."

There was a sullen silence around the table.

"Well, is it?"

"Of course it isn't," Michelle said brightly.

Mary looked from George to Carol. They nodded.

Carol caught up a white teacloth and waved it. "Truce."

All three of them laughed.

"That's more like it," Mary said. "Now, we'll pull ourselves together and go over to the Parknasilla and play happy families for the sake of the in-laws. And maybe if we put our heart into it, we might just become one." She smiled. "For a weekend anyway."

Chapter 27

Portmagee's single street of houses reminded Carol of a chain of red, blue and purple toy blocks glowing at the harbour's edge. It was only nine in the morning but the day already had the makings of yet another deadly calm July scorcher. The stretch of sea between the village and the Skellig Experience Centre at the other end of the Valentia Island bridge was as still as a bucket of water.

She asked Oliver do the talking at the reception desk in the centre when they went to pay for their boat tickets shortly before nine o'clock. She was wearing sunglasses and a baseball cap. She got a kick out of being mistaken for a tourist and enjoyed observing the change in the way locals spoke when they dealt with visitors. Like the day in May when she had gone to visit the circular forts at Over the Water outside Cahersiveen.

"Would you like to hold a pet lamb?" a man in the car park at the fort called Cathar Gheal asked her. He pointed to the soft, woolly mite with a black head nestling inside a blue van's open back doors.

"No thanks, we have loads of them at home, boy," Carol replied.

The look of astonishment on his face was worth anything. He clearly assumed she was a tourist before she opened her mouth.

Oliver asked the man behind the counter what were their chances of seeing the puffins on Skellig. The man assured them they'd see lots of adult puffins flying between the ocean and their burrows where the chicks, small balls of grey feathers, were waiting to be fed.

"The adults spend much of their day standing sentry at the mouths of burrows a stone's throw from the steps leading to the monastery at the top of the island," he said, laughing. "When I die, I'm coming back as a puffin. I've never seen anything so popular with the women."

Carol had never been on the island between May and August when the puffins came ashore to nest and rear their young. On her very first trip, she had made the mistake of sitting over the diesel engine during the eight-mile voyage to the islands. She spent most of the trip getting sick over the side of the boat while stolid continentals munched sandwiches. How she had longed for an immobile concrete road or footpath! Anything but the relentlessly rolling swells. Her clearest memory of that first trip was the relief of setting foot on the rock solid pier in Portmagee afterwards.

Second time out, the boat left behind a mist-shrouded peninsula only to sail into a world of brilliant sunshine and enamel blue skies on the Skellig. Much like the skies overarching the harbour as they waited for their boat to arrive at the pontoon. Still, she was taking no chances. Several trips had been cancelled the previous week because of rough seas. She sucked on a sliver of root ginger as her insurance against nausea.

They were reminded at reception that it was a four-hour round trip and that there were no toilets on the island. The man added with humour that the new type of visitor attracted by *Star Wars* generally had no knowledge of the Skellig's history as an ancient centre of pilgrimage.

"We've been asked if there's an elevator or a gift shop out there," he said, throwing his eyes to heaven. "I was even asked if Ryanair lands there."

Oliver suggested they have coffee while they were waiting. Carol glanced longingly at the sandwich display. She'd skipped breakfast for fear she'd end up feeding it to the seagulls.

The café wall, overlooking the harbour and the village of Portmagee on the far side of the water, was made entirely of plate glass. They watched a red fishing boat make its way in from the open water, a screaming cloud of seagulls whirling above it.

A grey-haired man sitting at the table beside them pointed to the boat. "He was out all night fishing."

He introduced himself as Jackie, a former fisherman and assistant to the skipper on their Skellig boat.

"Where are ye from?" he said. "I suppose ye're on holidays."

Carol didn't need a crystal ball to divine the twist the conversation was going to take. She kicked Oliver under the table. He was a talk show host's nightmare when it came to conversaton. It was like kick-starting an old motor cycle into spluttering life.

Jackie waited.

"*Ehm,*" Oliver said. "I'm from New Zealand originally but living in London."

"London, I see, faith. London Town. I had a brother over there in Kilburn. He spent so much time underground laying pipes that he refused to be buried. Up he went in a ball of smoke."

Jackie rattled on a while longer about the brother. Carol was daydreaming until the conversation swerved violently.

"Are ye married?'

He may as well have asked Oliver if he was a cross-dressing pole dancer. Oliver blinked furiously. Carol thanked God for the sunglasses.

Jackie looked from one to the other.

"We are actually." Oliver's voice was deadpan.

Carol fixed her face in what she hoped was an expression of infinite tenderness and gazed at Oliver.

"Have ye children?"

They shook their heads in unison.

"Are ye trying?"

On cue, the three of them burst out laughing.

"Sure I'm only blackguarding," Jackie said.

Skellig, a place at the edge of the world, was home to a community of monks from the sixth century onwards. It was estimated that a dozen or so hermits lived on the rock at any one time. Likewise, there was a regulatory twelve passengers on board the boat: eight French adults of mature vintage, a young American couple, and Carol and Oliver. Whether the Americans were married, had children or were trying was never established.

To the right, the low island cliffs of Bray Head rose to green fields where a herd of ebony, gold and cream cattle grazed. The trail of a jet was a broken skein of wool trailing on cobalt.

"The Skellig is a lovely spot on a fine day," Jackie said. "Ye have the besht day in the year."

Carol knew the French couples hadn't a clue what he was saying between the throb of the engine and his accent.

The young American guy was sitting right beside him.

"Really?" he said, doubtfully.

Jackie studied his earnest companion. "Wan of them anyway."

The boat ploughed on, cleaving the sea into a white swell. Carol's father had taught her the names of the islands but she had forgotten a surprising number of them. Jackie filled in the gaps. Puffin Island, looming on the left, was set so close to the headland that it was difficult to discern where one ended and the other began. Around the corner was Saint Finian's Bay.

"The swells were so high lasht week that we had to come back in by the bay inshtead of the middle of the harbour," Jackie said.

Carol thanked her lucky stars for the table-flat sea stretching out on either side of the boat.

As they left Bray Head behind for open water, the islands of west Kerry came into view. Tiaracht of the lighthouse. Innisvickillane, once owned by the Irish Taoiseach Charlie Haughey. Carol had a vague idea he had died while she was away. The name of the third island escaped her, but Jackie was already coming in with the answer. "*Inis na Bró*." He pointed to two inky smudges on the far horizon. "And there are the Blaskets."

Oliver was taking photos left, right and centre.

"You'd double for a Japanese tourist," she mouthed in his ear, "only that you're such a beanpole." She put one hand over the lens playfully. "If you don't come out from behind that lens for a bit, you'll never connect with the elements."

He dropped the camera to his knee. "You're right, but it's just so incredible I can't help myself."

"Wait till *Sceilig Bheag* rises up, you'll be shooting for all your worth and I won't stop you."

324

Carol made some small chat with the Frenchwoman beside her.

"I think the Skellig is our version of Machu Picchu."

"Yes," the woman agreed. "We are so lucky to make this voyage." She added that they were going to the Cliffs of 'Mohair' next.

Carol smothered a laugh.

Carol knew of old that the smell of *Skellig Bheag*, the smaller of the two islands, often carried to the boats on the wind before it came into view. That was because it was home to an estimated 39,000 pairs of breeding gannets every summer. God bless the gannet counters, whoever they were and how they managed. Whether it was the direction of the wind or what, there was no whiff of the birds to announce the jagged rock that towered out of the sea like an underworld creation. Gannets' droppings or guano spilled down over the black stone. Carol searched for a description of the thousands of birds screaming in the air around the cliff faces and needle-like peaks, but her métier was paint. She trotted out the old reliable image.

"Remember what I quoted to you during that first walk of ours? That the islands are like two vast cathedrals rising out of the sea? This is the first."

Oliver, enountering the rock for the first time, was hit full force by the sheer raw impact of the appartition that could have doubled as a backdrop for Hitchcock's *The Birds*.

He shook his head. "This is one incredible cathedral. It's as if a wedge of Himalayas was dropped into the Atlantic covered in guano instead of snow."

The gannets crowded every available ledge. Only the sheer, inaccessible cliff faces remained black. At one end of the island, the sea had cut a cave through the rock. The remaining arch looked like a teapot handle.

On the far side of the island, another cave, tall, slender and as geometrically proportioned as a church window, had been wave-carved from the rock. The skipper cut the engine and the boat drifted towards the base of the cliff. The heads of two seals were barely visible above the water.

The engine roared into life again and set course for Skellig Michael. They passed underneath an eighteenth-century lighthouse set on the clifftops.

"I heard tell that a fierce storm blew so hard once that the windows were blown clane out of that lighthouse as high as it is," Jackie said.

He pointed to the modern lighthouse and a row of small cabins that the Skellig guides slept in. And then they were climbing the steps from the small pier up to a rocky clearing where a crowd clustered around a guide giving a safety talk.

"Take your time, watch what you're doing," he said. "Unfortunately, people have fallen. There have been fatalities."

While they stood there listening, puffins fluttered overhead between the sea and their burrows, their wings flapping like those of humming birds. Their little orange feet were splayed out flat behind them as they whirred by.

The guide looked up and pointed to a passing puffin. "That particular motion of their wings gives them an advantage over the bigger birds in windy weather. It allows them to hover at the burrow's edge until the right moment comes to dart inside." He noticed people getting impatient to head for the stone steps. "Nearly done. Remember, no one should leave the steps to get closer to the burrows because your weight could collapse the earth and bury the puffin chicks alive."

Carol shared the impatience of the others. Their boat would leave again at two o'clock. The talk, a new addition since her last visit, had been introduced in response to two deaths in falls from the steps. She had read the news reports online in Italy.

The guide finished with another warning. "Remember: *take care, take your time*. If your boat has to wait ten or fifteen minutes, they won't mind."

Carol and Oliver were among the first to ascend. The steps were steeper than she remembered. Her chest tightened. She was relieved to see that Oliver's breath was slightly laboured as well. He was preoccupied, a little distant, and she missed the usual ease between them. She concentrated on the puffins. At the first clearing, they stopped beside the tall rock stack called the Wailing Woman, behind which the white summits of Sceilig Bheag floated in an expanse of blue.

The next section of steps didn't feel as bad and, before she knew it, they were inside the monastery walls a good five minutes short of the estimated twenty-five minutes to get there.

Carol frowned at the sight of crowd milling between the beehive huts.

"Puck Fair," she muttered.

But, Oliver, a Skellig 'newbie' had never seen the place in quieter times and wasn't fazed at how busy it was. His mood was lighter. She was relieved.

"I'd like to see the interior of one of the huts," he said. "Is it allowed?'

Carol nodded and led the way up a short flight of steps to the largest hut. Inside, it took their eyes a minute or two to adjust to the darkness. No one else had followed them. They were both silent in the cool of the gloom. Soon, they heard a faint humming sound.

"Do you hear that?" Oliver said. "It sounds more like a bird than bees."

Carol listened intently. She pointed to the lintel and whispered. "It's coming from here. It's like the noise a hen makes in protest when you pick her up to collect the eggs that are under her. Somewhere between a purr and a growl."

They bumped their heads together as they peered into the crack. They could see nothing. Carol felt giddy. She brushed her lips off his and laughed. "What would the monks think?"

"I'm sure we'd have their blessing."

"A fine stiff penance more likely. Come on out before we're struck down."

The sunlight was blinding outside on the monastery rampart. There were people everywhere. Carol tried and failed to get a sense of the sacredness of the site.

A young woman addressed the group and introduced herself as a guide. She began a talk on the history of the smaller rock and the gannets, explaining that they only settled where there were no humans.

"I think the rock is like a great big snow globe," she said.

Carol dug Oliver in the ribs with her elbow. "That's exactly it. The woman's a genius."

"The male and female puffins separate in the winter to spend their time at sea off Newfoundland," the guide said. "In summer, the monks used puffins as a source of food because they were easy to catch."

The voice of an American woman rose from the throng. "How could they eat those cute little birds?"

"They're still eating them in Iceland," the guide replied.

The monks had quarried tons of rock by hand between the sixth and twelfth centuries to form the terraces and to build the monastery on a south-facing slope that had a micro-climate all its own once you stepped inside the walls, she explained.

Carol whispered to Oliver. "Every single step was hand-carved by the monks. Imagine. And there are three different stairways to the ocean."

"Incredible," he whispered back.

The guide was distracted suddenly. Carol turned her head to follow her line of vision. A young man was perched halfway up one of the stone huts.

"*Get off the structure, please!*" she called.

He replied in French and didn't budge. He seemed unsure how to get down. He wasn't getting any sympathy.

"*Descendez, s'il vous plait,*" the guide commanded.

After the talk, the daytrippers melted away towards the exit archway and the steps down to the boat. Only Carol, Oliver and the young American couple remained with the guide.

Carol was elated. "Isn't it great that ours is the last boat off the island? I never thought we'd be so lucky as to have this practically all to ourselves."

Oliver smiled feebly. He twisted his hands nervously together. Carol made a mental note to ask him was he OK when they got back home. She didn't want to spoil their day on Skellig. Maybe she shouldn't have kissed him in the stone hut. She'd have to keep herself in check.

She followed on as he clicked his way through the stone structures, each view unimpeded at last. She met the guide again at the graveyard plot and asked her about the purring noise they'd heard between the rocks.

"Oh, that's one of the storm petrels. They nest inside. But the ravens are daring and they've learned to follow them in. Come on and I'll show you."

Carol looked around for Oliver. He was standing on an upper level looking out to sea. She shouted to him. The guide led them back into the large hut and shone the dim light of her mobile into the lintel crevice just long enough for them to see the the tiny storm petrel eyeballing them.

"I bet the ghosts of the monks are happy that some creatures are enjoying the shelter of their work," Carol said.

The guide agreed. "We get manx shearwaters in here too. They come out in the dark and fly all around like bats."

Oliver checked his watch when they were out in the daylight. They still had forty minutes left to get down to the boat.

"Let's stay here as long as we can," he said. "Who knows when we'll be back?"

Carol was overtaken by a tenderness when she heard him say 'we'. So much meaning packed into two small letters. The niggle of anxiety passed. She was overthinking as usual.

"I've found something interesting in the upper wall," he said. "I want you to look at it."

"Just a quick look so. I want to take my time going down the steps and to get proper pictures of the puffins with no people around."

Oliver was already striding ahead of her up the short flight of steps. When she caught up to him, he pointed to a space between the stones. A dart of irritation prickled. She'd told him their time was limited.

His manner was edgy again. She glanced at the space to humour him. "If it's another storm petrel . . ."

"Look in deeper." His voice was almost a croak.

She crouched down, took off her sunglasses and peered in to humour him. There was a small red box wedged in the space. As she prised it out, she turned around to look for the guide. "Whatever we find will have to be reported. Someone could have lost this."

Oliver looked so serious. "Aren't you going to look inside?"

She was losing patience. "Give me a chance."

She opened the lid to discover a blue stone surrounded by what looked like diamonds. The sun caught their sparkle.

Carol was hopeless with jewellery. She couldn't tell bling from the real thing. "I bet it's a prank. Nobody in their right mind would shove a sapphire into a stone wall."

Oliver held out his hand and she slid the ring into his open palm. He might make a better job of assessing it. "What do you think?"

"It's the genuine article."

"How can you be so sure?"

"Because it belonged to my mother. And my grandmother before her."

Carol had barely time to digest what he said when he shot down on one knee with such speed that he banged the knee on the bare rock. He was wincing with pain as he said, "Will you marry me, Carol?"

Her shoulders shook. She was convulsed with laughter. She didn't know whether it was shock or his expression. She wanted to stop but the tears started to flow.

Oliver stood up. Stricken, he replaced the ring in the box, avoiding her eyes. Carol sprang forward and threw her arms around him.

"Where are you going with my ring, you daft, daft man? *Yes, yes, yes!*"

Doubt was written all over his face. "Do you mean it? Are you sure?"

"Of course I'm sure. I'm so sorry about my reaction, but it must be the first proposal ever where the man practically kneecaps himself in the process."

Oliver rubbed his knee. "I certainly hit it a bang. I'll have some bruise."

Carol held out her hand. "When you're finished dealing with your wounded knee . . ." She laughed again. "Bury my heart at Wounded Knee."

Oliver stared her out of it. "Would this pass as a wounded look? Come on, Carol, be serious for a moment at least."

She inhaled deeply, wiped the tears from her eyes with her sweatshirt sleeve and gave him her brightest smile. He placed the ring on her finger. It was loose. She held her hand up to the light and twisted it this way and that to enhance the sparkle. "It's astonishing. This is astonishing – the whole thing." Then, she handed it back to him. "You mind it, please, until we take it to Killarney to get it properly sized. There's no way I'm going to be responsible for this heirloom bouncing off a rock into the Atlantic."

Suddenly, the guide was calling them. "Do you two want to spend the night on the island?"

They waved to her and headed for the doorway leading out to the steps. One or two flights down, they saw two puffins perched on a flagstone directly beside the path. They stopped to snap them.

Carol laughed. "There we are – Darby and Joan."

"Who?"

"It's just a saying. A description of an old couple who fit well together. Every old sock finds an old shoe."

"Marvellous! First of all, she laughs when I propose. Then, she calls me an old sock."

They picked their way down the steps carefully, stopping a couple more times to photograph the sentry puffins looking out to sea.

"Do you think that we'll be going our separate ways for the winter and meeting up again in the summer?" She was a few steps below Oliver and couldn't read his expression.

"Obviously, we'll have to work out the practicalities."

"Feck the practicalities. I want to drink champagne."

On the final stretch down to the boat, she asked him about his earlier lapses in contact.

"I was afraid I was going to find myself back in the situation that I got stuck in with Matteo."

They were off the steps and walking side by side on the terrace path. Oliver stopped and took both her hands in his.

"Carol, I would never treat you like that. I just got this irrational fear that you'd meet someone else. An old flame maybe. I can't do half-measures. Either I make a commitment or I back away completely. I couldn't leave myself open to losing you. It was a big step, and I wanted to be sure that you felt the same way. I know I couldn't be sure of that unless I took the gamble and asked you. But it was such a daunting prospect that I backed away those few days to gather my courage."

"No more backing away," Carol said sternly. "Just speak your mind no matter how afraid you are. I just can't take being left dangling in limbo."

He continued the explanation on the descent. His friend, Archie, noticing the morose silences and the dark circles under his eyes, had said, "Man, you look like a racoon. What's up?" After much prodding, Oliver confided his dilemma. Archie was unequivocal. "Go for it, mate. Otherwise you'll spend the rest of your life tortured by 'What if's'. What's more I can't face a lifetime down in the local looking at your mug."

The expectant faces of the others looked up at them from the boat bobbing on the swell beside the pier.

She linked her arm in his and turned her face to the sea wind. She inhaled the peace of the edge of the world and prayed to the spirits of the monks for a blessing and a protection from any maurauding 'Vikings' intent on robbing her new-found equilibrium.

Chapter 28

"You're joking."

Angela had been looking straight ahead at the boats moored in the lee of the little marina by the sea's edge in Knightstown, lulled by the tinkle of the mast cables and the play of sunlight on the water. Her head spun around, her face a picture of disbelief.

"You are joking, aren't you?"

Carol expected some smidgin of surprise but she was miffed at the strength of Angela's reaction.

"Oliver and myself got engaged," she repeated. "Don't give me that beware-the-beast look. You were the one that kept telling me how gorgeous he was."

"I know I was, but you can't blame me for being surprised. With the speed of things, I mean. This is the end of August and you only clapped eyes on him back in March." She barked out the questions. "When, where, how and, for the love of God, why are you only telling me now?"

For once, it was Carol who was concerned about the volume. She glanced around her. The crowd chattering in the garden of the Royal Hotel were, to all appearances, holiday-makers, as were the scattering of people strolling at the harbour's edge, but you never could tell where locals might lurk with ears cocked for gossip.

A knowing look replaced the shock on Angela's face.

"Don't tell me you're . . ."

Carol burst out laughing. "Oh for God's sake, I *am not*."

Children were dive-bombing into the water from an enormous inflatable raft. Their voices carried in the warm evening air. The crew of a yacht that had drifted into the Marina minutes earlier were busy on deck with ropes as they tied up. Angela had been musing what it would be like to sail all the way up to Galway or Dun Laoghaire when Carol dropped the bombshell.

"It was the day we went to the Skellig last week. He took me completely by surprise. Up in the monastery of all places. It was a wonder I didn't keel over the edge in freefall."

"That's four days ago. How did you keep it to yourself?" Angela said. She caught Carol's left hand. "And what about the ring? Have you got one?"

"Aisy, girl, aisy! Give me a chance. We agreed that we'd tell one good friend each for starters. You were the obvious choice. Anyone else would think I was stark raving mad. Although I'm beginning to think that even you have doubts about my sanity." The glow from the secret she'd been hugging to herself dimmed. "Aren't you happy for me?"

"Of course I'm happy for you. Stand up there, you daft clown, until I hug you."

The car ferry had clanked into the pier and a stream of cars was passing by behind them. Carol noted a few local faces. "Will you stop or they'll say we've definitely turned, and it's no wonder that himself left you."

They sat there and chatted, the heat of the evening wrapping round them.

"You'd swear we were in Greece or somewhere, it's so

336

warm," Angela said. "It's really lovely when you can sit out like this in the summer, instead of being bundled up in fleeces or being stuck inside a window looking at the rain dripping down. Anyway, go on, tell me about the sparkler."

The ring had been deposited in a Killarney jewellery shop to be re-sized, Carol explained. Angela admired a picture of it on her friend's phone.

Without the ring as a concrete sign, the engagement had dipped in and out of fantasy in Carol's mind. That was one of the reasons she had been impatient to tell Angela, but it had been impossible to find time to get away from the house and talk to her on her own.

Out walking over the previous few days, she'd felt so much at one with the blue sky, the orange and scarlet ditches and the hazy mountains. It was the exhilaration of stepping out over a cliff and abseiling down to the ground, of leaning low over the spray as a sailing boat saluted the sea, of skiing into the dazzling whiteness of an Alpine slope.

"I'm just so alive in myself," she said. "And the most important thing is that it feels completely right."

Angela asked when she was going to break the news to Mary and everyone else.

"We're going to leave a respectable interval. Christmas, maybe. I really couldn't cope with the sermons about rushing in and all the rest of it. Imagine Margot calling me aside and giving me an earful. Oliver was all for telling Mam before he went back but I persuaded him to keep his powder dry. That's as long as she hasn't guessed it. Sometimes I think that woman can X-ray my mind."

They were reluctant to leave the bench and drive home. They made their usual pact to wait until the next cloud would cover the sun, knowing that it would turn into the next cloud and the next one after that. They fell silent and watched parents calling children from the sea, the sail boat crew sharing cans of beer on deck, a teenage couple strolling hand in hand along the harbour wall. The smell of a barbecue mingled with the oily smell of seaweed in the low tide.

Carol sensed a shift in Angela's mood, a hesitation as if she wanted to say something.

"Penny for your thoughts."

"Don't talk to me about thoughts, girl. They'll be the death of me. I'm awake in the middle of the night turning everything over in my head. Even when I drop off to sleep, I wake again at about six, and he's the first thought in my mind." Her voice was charged with nervous energy. "Anyway, your news is a great distraction. I'll warm my heart from it."

"I'm always saying the same old thing to you, Angela, and I hope it'll eventually sink in. A person can only do or give what they are able for at any moment in life. Be patient with yourself. Things change. Be open to the possibility of being happy again one day." She laughed. "Will you listen to me? I'll be lining up for a certificate in counselling next. If only I was so wise about my own affairs."

Angela sighed. "I have an entire care team watching over me. Annette wants to convert me to Buddhism, she swears by it. Margot is drilling Mindfulness into me. 'Label your thoughts. Let them go.' Theresa has just dropped me off a brochure for autumn night courses. As far as I can see, Buddhism and Mindfulness are basically the same craic, only that there seems to be more money to be made out of Mindfulness. To be honest, Margot's caper is working a bit. When I can put my mind to it."

Carol stretched her arms over her head. "I wouldn't knock anything that works. Just pick and choose what you want out of it." She yawned and shifted on the seat. "The wood is going through my arse. I suppose we'd better head back."

Angela fixed her with a serious look. "First, do you mind if I ask you something?"

Carol grinned. "Of course you can be bridesmaid."

Angela didn't laugh. "I wouldn't be your friend if I didn't tell you that I'm delighted for you and worried about you all in the one go. I know it's the old story, but is it possible that you are rushing into things?" She took a breath. "On the rebound."

"I don't mind you saying that in the least. Between emails and phone conversations, Oliver must have put the same question to me a dozen times."

"And?"

"Of course I'm rebounding. A hare tearing up Bolus wouldn't have the same bounce as me." Carol caught the dismayed look on her friend's face. "Don't worry, I'm being carried by a good, positive and kindly energy that will carry me nowhere but the right destination."

Angela threw her eyes to heaven. "You sound like someone delivering a script for one of those TED talks that I'm being bombarded with on WhatsApp. To be honest, it's too airy-fairy for me. Come on, Carol, I just want to be sure that you're not deluding yourself. Oliver is lovely but it's not always wise to rush headlong into things." She sighed. "Look where it got me. The main thing is that you have to be sure that you're not deluding yourself. Or Oliver for that matter."

Carol's face darkened. "Come on, Angela, who can be sure about anything? The amount of affairs and marriage break-ups I've heard of since I came home. Fellas that you'd think butter wouldn't melt in their mouths at school blazing through Tinder, playing the field and still keeping their feet firmly planked under the kitchen table. And the women! Sure Timmy was only telling us the other day about this wan, a pillar of the community, *ating* the altar rails every Sunday, married to a hard-working, honest saint of a man, and she off dancing in Cork somewhere every weekend with a no-good rake from Killorglin who would drop into a dead faint if he had to look a day's work square in the face."

Angela sighed. "Oh then, I know I'm not wanting for company when it comes to those stories. Maybe you're right. I can't imagine Oliver doing anything to hurt you."

The sun had distilled into a brilliant red disc burning in the west against an apricot sky. The light was ebbing.

Carol stood up and faced Angela. "Look, I won't stay here all evening boring you, but let me explain something to you before we go. And I don't know whether it will set your mind at rest or torment you. This is a gamble, but it's a calculated gamble. Oliver and myself have weighed up the odds in so far as we can. We're engaged but we're holding off on the wedding. I wouldn't even leave him draw down the subject of a date."

"Well, that's reassuring," Angela said, her voice doubtful at the same time.

"Hold on to that, so, because what I'm going to say next might rattle you a bit. Every disappointment I've been through to date has done nothing but convince me of the value of the art of delusion. You know when you see

340

a couple in the first flush of love? They're intoxicated with the happiness of it. They haven't a clue in the world what's coming down the road to meet them. Sometimes it's good, sometimes it's woeful. But I wouldn't for one second take away that happiness from them, even if it was built on sand. There and then, it's happiness pure and simple. If I'm deliriously deluded now – and something tells me I'm not – it's the best feeling in the world. I'm savouring every single minute of it. And when I'm beached in the day room of an old folks' home some day, I can look back on this time and, what's more, relive the sheer joy of it. If this is delusion, bring it on and let me knock what I can out of it."

Angela shook her head. "That's the maddest thing I've heard, but you're very convincing. You should audition for a TED talk yourself."

"Sure, I was considering it. I have the title and all. 'Practised in the Art of Delusion'."

"You'll drive the world mad if you get half a chance."

"It might be no bad thing. Sure we're only half-living most of the time."

Angela stood up. "You're a pure tonic. Once I get my head in gear, I'm going to get back into living too."

Carol whooped. "That's our Angela. I'll hold you to that. In fact, I'll be right behind you pushing."

They walked along the shoreline towards the car. The sun had slipped from sight, leaving a burning red sky in its wake. Seagulls were screaming and fighting over scraps thrown from the pier by a couple with three young children.

"Come on," Carol said. "Let's drive up Geokaun Mountain to see the rest of the sunset. In the right light the view up there would take the sight from your eyes. Even if we only get ten minutes of it, it'll be worth it."

Angela caught her enthusiam. "Of course it will. Just one last thing. I don't know how I'd have managed over the past couple of months without you. Of all the years that you could have come home . . . It must have been fate that carried you back to us this year."

Carol turned the key in the ignition. "Everything works for a reason. You can drag good out of the worst situations." She revved the engine. "Just watch me. I'll drag good kicking and screaming out of this calamity that's latched on to you. Or maybe it isn't a calamity at all. It could be the best thing that ever happened to you."

Angela made a play of shaking hands with Carol. "Hi, I'm Thelma. Come on, Louise, let's head off into the sunset. Just make sure you don't drive over the cliffs at Geokaun."

They booted down the road laughing, the radio turned up to the last.

Chapter 29

Contemptuous eyes darting out of balaclava slits. Shouts. "*Where is the fucken money? Come on, you useless auld wan!*"

Names. "*Dried-up bitch!*"

Words she wouldn't even repeat to the gentle female garda, who came to take a statement.

There had been two of them that she knew of. It was suggested that a third could have been sitting in the car, ready for a speedy get-away.

It was a game to them, moves all rehearsed and played out before with other poor *craturs* like herself, no doubt. She was a rag doll pushed from one to the other across the kitchen floor until they tired of the play.

There was no ring of the doorbell. The front and back doors were securely locked from the fall of dark. Carol had warned her before she left. But doors were no deterrent to the likes of them. Windows held their own weakness. Just a quick smash of glass and the catch was exposed. She'd heard nothing.

It was the second weekend in October. The house sign was down and stored away for the next season. If there was to be another season. Carol had taken Sharon and Lisa on a weekend break to Clonakilty in West Cork as a treat. A schoolfriend of Lisa's was going with her parents who insisted on driving them all in their people carrier.

Mary had refused to go. She told them she'd savour the peace and quiet. She'd been expecting Klaus to fly over from Berlin that weekend but she'd mixed up the dates. When she waved the car off, the house felt very quiet but she settled into baking a porter cake to distract herself.

"Hello, missus." The disbelief when she turned to find them behind her. The black balaclavas were the worst.

"You might help us out a bit, missus. We're short of cash. Look on it as givin' to the poor. Lovely big house like this you mustn't be short of a bob."

She went directly to the yellow china hen. She was so relieved that she'd ignored Carol's advice not to keep cash there. At least she'd be able to get rid of them.

One of the pair pushed her to the side, grabbed the notes and threw them on the table. "That'll do for starters."

Mary's stomach lurched. "Please go. You have the money. That's all I have in the house."

"Ah come on, missus. You can't expect us to settle for that. You must have something else for us." He pinched her arm. "Now, don't make me lose it. You wouldn't like me when I'm cross. I go mental, like. Just give us a small bit more and you'll make it easier on yourself."

Suddenly, he pushed her sharply. The fear. Push, push, spinning from one to the other. The reeling in her head.

"Catch her if you can. What if we miss? An awful pity to let you fall. Wouldn't it be shockin' altogether, missus?"

And the second fella took up the chant, though he sounded half-hearted, as if he'd been fed the words and wasn't too keen on them.

Back he came, the boss man, the main voice. "An old bag of bones. You'd break up like a bundle of dry old sticks."

The words of the Canadian visitor sounded out in her mind as clearly as if the woman was in the room. '*Bon courage.*'

She repeated them over and over in her head but, yet, the nausea rose in her stomach. *Dear Lord, don't let me get sick.*

Bull and Bird, she christened them. Bird, the lackey obeying the orders of the Bull McCabe, the bully in John B Keane's play *The Field.*

When she felt she could take no more, the Bird caught her and pushed her down into the chair. She fell with less force than she had expected. Still, she didn't cry. *Bon courage. Bon courage.*

In her desolation, she thought of John. *Oh, John, where are you when I need you?*

The Bull leaned in over her, fingers boring into her shoulder. His breath was foul. Stale tobacco and the stomach-churning smell of halitosis. She took minute breaths.

"Now, we don't like this either. The sooner it's over, the better for all of us." He dropped his voice, adopting a chummy, conversational tone. "You know I've been in nearly every jail in Ireland. My mate here has only seen Cork."

He placed his mouth directly on her ear. The warm, moist breath sent a shiver down her spine.

"*Just tell us where the fucken money is!*"

The shout made her jump. Her heart was a mad heifer bucking at the end of a rope.

When she began to speak, her voice failed her. She coughed to clear her throat. "Everything was there where I showed you."

"Everything," he said, pointing to the yellow china hen. He gave a manic laugh. "*Chook, chook, chook!*"

He swept the pile of banknotes from the kitchen table to the floor. "The miserable guts of two hundred quid. I didn't drive all the way down here for that. I wouldn't wipe my arse with that."

He dashed over to the worktop, caught the yellow hen, raised it high over his head and smashed it to the ground. "That's what I think of your poxy hen. Come on, now. An old bird like you must have something better stashed around."

The memory of the day John gave her the gift of the hen lay in lemon shards all over the kitchen floor. And the cruel eyes were boring into her.

The Bull pulled her roughly to her feet. He stood there clenching and unclenching his fists.

"What more can I give you?" Her voice was a croak.

"What more can she give us? Is that what you said, love? You'll have to speak up. You should be able to work that out for yourself. Hold up your hand there like a good girl."

Mary was confused. She hesitated. He grabbed her two hands. The veins ran in thick blue lines. She'd always hated her hands. They were old hands even when she was young. That's why her wedding and engagement rings were the only rings she ever wore. Surely they wouldn't?

"Get them off her good and lively."

"But they won't come off. That finger's swollen with arthritis. I haven't taken them off in years."

"Don't give me that shit."

The Bird spoke up. "I'll use washing-up liquid. That'll do the trick."

Mary pleaded with him. "Oh please, don't. It won't work. I've tried it so many times."

She squeezed her eyes tight as he twisted the rings, the lemon smell of the liquid making her sick. That innocent smell of soapy plates, suds and sparkling glasses corrupted. She thought of the poor dentist who was taken hostage years before by the IRA and had his finger cut off. She shivered.

"*Stop, will you stop!*" she screamed. "*All I have is some jewellery. There's no cash.*"

Bird dropped her finger. Bull's eyes narrowed to slits. "No cash. How many times have I heard that? I don't suppose you have the crown jewels stashed away upstairs by any chance?"

Mary rubbed her finger. The skin was red but it hadn't broken. She took a deep breath. "There's a gold sovereign pendant. And I have a ruby eternity ring. There's four or five valuable pieces. The rest are just gifts from my late husband and my children. They're not worth much apart from sentimental value."

The grey eyes glinted. "Gold. That's what I like to hear." He brought his face close to us. "But if you're lying about the money and we find out . . . " The menace of his words hung in the air.

The Bird linked her up the stairs. His superior went ahead of him, singing, 'Here comes the bride!', a manic energy crackling from him.

"For feck's sake, keep it down," Bird said uneasily. "You're wired."

"Get over yourself. Who's going to hear us? We're out here in the asshole of nowhere and they're all away for the weekend."

Mary stiffened. How could he be so sure? Just how much did he know? And who told him?

The jewellery box was on the dressing table. She'd never had any call to hide it. It was an inlaid mahogany box that Carol had brought home from Morocco one

New Year. The key had long since disappeared. No need for keys in Glenosheen.

Bull tipped the contents of the box out on the bed and riffled through them with his nicotine-stained fingers. A handful of gold chains. The sovereign in a gold setting. He paid most interest to the coin, the antique ring set with rubies and opals and the gold pearl earrings. She winced when she saw him stuff those pieces into his jacket pocket along with an ancient charm bracelet that she'd put together when she'd worked in Killarney.

He hesitated over the dented silver pocket watch that John had inherited from his father. She'd meant to give it to George. Her heart sank when that followed the other pieces.

"Look at this baby," Bull whooped, scooping up a gold Bulova watch with a slender bracelet.

Mary felt so tired. If the watch bought her release, let it off with everything else. She never thought she'd see the day that she'd be thankful for arthritis. At least her rings were spared. She recited the 'Hail Mary' to herself. Wrong choice of prayer. *Pray for us sinners now and at the hour of our death, Amen.*

But the jewellery did satisfy them in the end. Bull had an eye and he knew the worth of the sovereign pendant.

She cursed herself for not wearing the panic button. She had a habit of leaving it in the bedside locker or on the shelf over the bathroom sink. Once she found it, she could raise the alarm. The mobile was somewhere in the kitchen. As soon as they left, she'd lock herself in the bedroom. No such luck.

"Down the stairs again, missus," Bull said. "Get a move on."

"I'm so tired. Please let me lie down. You've got what you wanted."

Boss pulled her by the hair. "What part of 'Come on' don't you understand? You might have something else for us downstairs. A few more rolls of money tucked away somewhere. Get your brain in gear."

"Easy, willya," Bird said. "Haven't we got enough? That goldie necklace thing alone should settle the score. I can't owe you much more."

Bull smacked him across the face with his open hand. "Less of the lip now, boy, if you know what's good for ya. And don't go talking business in front of this wan."

The Bird muttered under his breath. He pushed Mary ahead of him on the stairs. She stumbled. He reached out to catch her but she lurched out over the final four steps and landed on her side on the tiled floor. Her right temple and hip hit the hard surface with a crack. She knew she was in trouble with the hip, but maybe the fall was a godsend. She'd play dead.

With her eyes closed, she listened to the panic of the pair.

"For feck's sake, why couldn't ya keep a hold on her?" Bull shouted. "If she's done for, we're in deep shit."

Bird found some fight in himself. "You shoulda left her in the bedroom like she asked. We've enough got. But nottin' is ever enough for ya. Sharon's gonna kill me over this."

Mary froze. She nearly cried out despite herself, the feeling of betrayal was so sharp.

"Will ya shut up, ya big cissie! Pity about your bleddy Sharon. Anyway, how's she to know you were anywhere near this place?"

"She'll put two and two together! She's heard Lisa tell me over the phone that they were all going away to Clonakilty!"

Mary concentrated on taking minute breaths. She stayed absolutely still. At least Sharon hadn't deliberately sold them out, but George's words came back to her, '*It's the crowd that follows them.*'

"Get the money in the kitchen and we're outa here," Bull shouted.

"But what about her?" Bird said. "We don't know if she's dead or alive."

"And I'm not waitin' around to find out," Bull said. "We'll have burn rubber till we're well past Killarney. Leave her, I tell ya."

Mary could hear the stairs creaking. Then, she felt the weight of a duvet pulled up to her chin.

There were steps in the hall and a cold draught as the front door opened.

"Will ya come on, Darren, or I'll lave ya here for the pigs to find," Boss called.

The door slammed again. Mary opened her eyes. She tried to get up but pain seared her hip.

Darren.

Chapter 30

Lisa's study desk in the corner was the first thing that caught Carol's eye when she opened the door of the den. The purple china jar of felt markers, the Tiffany lamp, the notebooks arranged so neatly at the side, the little troll with orange hair, all the brightly coloured drawings arranged in a montage on the wall behind it. There was hardly a single picture without a sheep or a rainbow.

Carol had spotted the pink desk for sale in the Saint Vincent de Paul shop in Killorglin when they were fixing the room up for Sharon and Lisa. It came with a matching chair. It was the first of many treasures they'd found in the charity shops the three of them had combed for bargains. "One man's rubbish is another man's gold," she'd told Lisa.

Between them, they had created a cosy living space with lemon walls, blue-and-green curtains and soft furnishings. All created on a shoestring budget.

Lisa had begged them to buy a bright red armchair they'd seen in Vincent's, a charity shop in Killarney.

"But the room is choked with stuff," Sharon said in exasperation. "We won't be able to move if we get that. You couldn't swing a kitten in there as it is, not to mind a cat."

Lisa's face was stamped with determination. "We need red. And a purple cushion too. We'll have all the colours then."

The light dawned on Carol and Sharon in the same instant.

"You're making your own rainbow," Carol said.

"We'll have a real rainbow room," Lisa said. "Won't it be great, Mam? Sleeping in a rainbow. We won't have to go chasing any rainbow to find the end. We can make our own."

Sharon thought of the day they stopped the car at the County Bounds on their journey to Kerry. Did she ever think back then that they could be so lucky?

She crouched down, caught the little girl and swung her in the air. "I found the rainbow's end the day I got you."

Carol insisted on paying for the red chair. "My treat."

Sharon rooted in her bag for her purse. "You can't. You've done enough for us already. I've got extra money now from selling the flowers and the veg in the market."

Carol shook her head and headed towards the counter. "Save that for when she goes back to school. This is my treat. I sold two more paintings last week. A bargain basement armchair won't break the bank."

Now, the cheery red of the chair glowed at the heart of the deserted room. She ran her hand over the velveteen covering, but it brought cold comfort. She sank into the seat and looked around, her heart as empty as her surroundings. The sight of the dolls, the books, the stacks of jigsaw puzzles and games, and the fluffy toys discarded on the bed and on the floor cut her to the quick. All the signs of a hasty departure.

Her head ached. She pressed her fist against her mouth. Her throat constricted as she imagined what it must have cost Lisa to leave without so many of her *Frozen* books and dolls. At least her collection of LOL dolls were small enough to carry. When Sharon had started earning, she'd bought her one every Saturday.

They'd left the previous evening. Sharon had got a

friend of hers to drop them to the train in Killarney. Carol had been visiting Mary in the hospital in Tralee and hadn't seen them leave with the bags. When she'd returned home after ten and seen no light in the window, she'd presumed they were asleep. She found the note that morning when she'd gone to the door of the den to remind Sharon that the offer was still open to move into the house for the winter. She'd read the note so many times since that the paper was wrinkled. The spelling reminded her only too painfully of the plans they had made for Sharon to start a literacy course with the Kerry Education and Training Board.

Deer Carol,

Thanks so much for everytin you dun for me and Lisa you will never no how much it ment to me I no what you said about not blamin us and all that but im goin mentel tinkin about Darren and the damege he dun comin around here and hurtin Mary. if I never cum here it never wuda hapen I swear on me mother's life I told him notin but its stil my fawlt if we wasn't here he wudnta com here. Lisa knows notin about what reely happened it was her talkin to him on the fone that gave him the idee that you wer rich and that he cud find muney to pay bak the skum bag that was leanin on him for muny for drugs and he beged me and beged me to let him talk to her a few times, sed he was beter agen. I shud have lisened to my gut and turned him down but he beged and beged. he was all questshuns about the place. I stil don't know how he made out were we were but the gard thinks he got on to somewun in

353

Cahrciveen or Kilorglan i can't stay here for the
shame of the trubel we made. I will call from Cork
to see how Mary is getin on this was too gud to be
true. I was afrade it wudn't last. I hope Mary will
get beter fast. I can't stand to look at anywun
around here in the faces with the shame of wat
hapened please don't try to get in tuch with me. we
dun you too much bad.
luv
Sharon xxx

Carol pulled the door out behind her. She dreaded to
think where they were in Cork. She hoped it wasn't a
hostel. When she got back inside, she rang the guards in
Cahersiveen for the third or fourth time that day.

"Can't we not report them as missing persons?" she said.

"I'm afraid not," the sergeant said. "Once she left a note
saying she didn't want contact and she got in touch with
you saying they were OK, I'm afraid my hands are tied."

Just as she was finishing the call on the landline, her
mobile rang. It was George – again. She'd lost track of
how many calls she'd got from him since Mary had been
admitted to hospital. She hoped the heat had worn off his
rant. She was disappointed.

He had her over a barrel and he was taking full advantage.

"If you had listened to Michelle and myself when we
warned you but, oh no, you were off on another of your big
save-the-world missions. Well, I hope you're happy now."

Carol let his voice wash over her. Whenever he paused,
she wearily inserted the regulatory apologies. They were
heartfelt. She had gone and messed up everything. Good
intentions counted for nothing. The image of her mother's

bruised face against the hospital pillow swam in front of her burning eyes. She looked so fragile in the bed.

"You're one hundred per cent right, George," she said. "I never got anything so wrong in my life before. I'm sorry." Her voice shook. "Look, I'm not going to be able to continue this conversation. I'm not hanging up on you, but I'm going to have to put the receiver down."

"Wait," he said. "I'm upset about Mam and, right, I'm firing on all guns. I don't want to make you feel worse than you evidently are feeling. I'll be down about twelve tomorrow. I know I'll be talking to Mam on the mobile in the meantime but tell her that I'm asking for her."

The thought of seeing George face to face was the final straw. Carol put her face down on her arms on the kitchen table and wept. Just then the mobile went again.

"Oh, Oliver," she sobbed. "I'm drowning in all this. Mam's injuries are bad enough. Her hip is cracked. Have I told you that already? At this stage I'm so tired I don't know what I've told anybody. But the guilt of feeling so responsible is killing me. I can hardly go to the shop with copping these accusing looks from people. And then there's the worry of how Sharon and Lisa are managing in Cork."

Just the sound of Oliver's voice at the other end of the phone soothed her.

"Guilt and blame won't make Mary one jot better," he said. "You're going to have stay strong to be of any use to her. Take a break from blaming yourself. You were doing a good thing taking Sharon and Lisa away for the weekend. You didn't send those two criminals to your house. Rural crime is a fact of life in most societies today. It comes to every second door sooner rather than later."

Carol drank in his words, not totally believing in them

355

but absorbing the comfort of knowing that he was there rooting for her.

"I'm so mad at myself for my lack of common sense," she said. "George was right to warn me but I wouldn't listen to him. The worse thing is that it's my mother who has to pay for my stupidity. And, on top of that, I hate conflict. George will be the least of my worries. The locals will be gunning for me for drawing this trouble on top of them. Nobody remembers anything like this happening in Glenosheen before."

Oliver tried to calm her. He admitted that what had happened was extremely serious but she wouldn't make it any better by bowing down under it.

"You have to be strong," he said. "You have that strength inside you. I know it. Tiredness magnifies everything in the brain. Make yourself a good stiff hot toddy and get into bed. Park all your thoughts until the morning. I'll be over in forty-eight hours. I booked the flight before I rang you."

She began to cry with relief.

"That's not exactly the response I expected, you silly woman."

Carol blew her nose. "The silly woman says thanks. That makes me feel so much better."

"Now, take Dr Oliver's advice and get to bed. I love you."

"Yes, doctor. Love you too."

Her head was pounding. She dissolved two painkillers in a glass and knocked them back.

On one steep slope of the valley where the light was a rare visitor that never lingered long, no farmer had ever attempted to shift stone or scree. No man or woman had dreamed of coaxing another green patch from the slope with crowbar, spade, brute force and fertiliser. Intead, the furze lorded over it.

Yellow-blooming furze so thickly clustered that it was a green and mustard prickly quilt sheltering foxes, badgers and hares, and teeming with bees in summer.

No living soul in the valley had ever penetrated the heart of it. There were stories that there was a fairy rock in there, that the 'good people' danced on top of it at night-time parties, that in the morning they all filed into a tunnel that led down into their own little village of houses and wells and patchwork fields where snails drew ploughs, and birdsong and light filtered down from holes between the furze.

Even the baying beagles that coursed through the winter valley in a river of yelping brown and white skirted the furze thicket. They never dared to venture a wet nose beyond the edge, no matter what musky scent carried from it on the wind.

Carol was down. She was knocked back and winded, in despair at her own foolishness. She longed to hide away from everyone. She wormed her way into the centre of that yellow slope and curled up in a ball in a powder-dry earthen chamber deep below the green and spiky thorns, blossoms glinting in the spaces above, a yellow sky arching over the green thicket.

She took deep breaths of the coconut-toffee fragrance of the flowers baking in the sun. The yellow air penetrated deep into her lungs until it made its way her bloodstream, becoming a liquid brightness dissipating the heaviness that weighed her down. She slept in a warm golden, healing haze from which she didn't want to wake.

All the splintered torment fused into one bar of gold pulsing inside her. She woke in the cold bedroom, sure of herself again, ready to take on whatever was coming towards her. She would make things right.

Chapter 31

"I don't want a party."

"What do you mean you don't want a party? You have to have a party."

"I don't want the fuss, Angela."

"Well, we want the fun."

"So, I'm supposed to have a party I don't want in order to keep everybody else happy?"

"Exactly."

"It'll cost an arm and a leg. I can't afford it."

"It doesn't have to cost a lot. We'll all pitch in."

"Anyway, it's too late now to go organising anything."

"It's the middle of October. That gives you at least eight weeks if you go for the second weekend in December."

"Come off it, Angela, I don't have the heart for it, after everything that happened to Mam. And Sharon and Lisa taking off like that."

"They're the very reasons you need a party."

They had parked in Portmagee, walked across the bridge and headed out the road towards Bray Head to take advantage of the spell of mild, sunny weather that had set in.

Scarcely a leaf had fallen from the trees, and the ditches were rubied with haws and rosehips. Blackberries were holding on here and there, a shrivelled version of their earlier glossy selves.

A farmer hailed them from the gateway of a field as they passed.

"Morning, ladies. It's a mighty spell of weather. If this month held fine, it would shorten the winter for us."

Every second person was full of predictions that the autumn sunshine would last for a week or more. It was part of a national willing suspension of disbelief, a coping mechanism to deal with the vagaries of the weather.

"I need a party now like a hole in the head. Sure I'm Public Enemy Number One around here – 'the Connell wan that drew the Cork druggies down on us'."

"Anyone with a grain of sense doesn't blame you. Think of all the cards and calls you've been getting for Mary. And all the offers of drives to Tralee, the casseroles that are lifting the lid of the deep freeze. Like everything else, you'll be forgotten before long. Someone else will take the limelight. Are you going to face into your forties with a defeatist attitude? Come on, Carol girl, shake yourself out of it."

"My good woman, you're doing my head in. I never had you down for a party animal. Then again, you're full of surprises this weather."

Angela laughed. "I'm full of surprises all right. Leasing the farm was the best decision I ever made. OK, money will be tight for the winter but the feeling of freedom is unbelievable. I'd never have switched from dairy to dry stock, anyway. It breaks my heart every time I see a cattle lorry on the road, taking them away to the factory. And they only knowing each others' company and the ease of the fields up to that." Her voice lifted. "I can't wait to head over to Gearóid for Christmas. Seán nearly has more money saved than myself. He has a shopping list as long as your arm made out. Imagine seeing New York with all the Christmas lights. And the Rockerfeller Center with the big tree. Thank God, we can stay with Agnes in Jersey City. The trip is dear enough as it is."

Carol was so happy to hear Angela talking about Christmas so enthusiastically. She'd always dreaded the season of good cheer either because Brian was on a spree or he was on the dry and as cranky as a bag of cats.

"You've rounded the corner," she said. "That awful frown has melted away and your eyes have the old light back in them. And the figure on you. How much have you lost now?"

Angela struck a mock pose with one hand on her hip and the other behind her head. "Ah sure I'm falling away to nothing. Just over two stone gone."

"I hope you're not set on losing much more. Otherwise your face will be gaunt. There's nothing worse."

"Don't worry. I have only a few more pounds to go. Speaking of faces, you should have seen the look on Brian when he saw me in the red polka-dot dress at our last meeting. Plus he turned green when I mentioned New York. I made sure to draw it down every chance I got."

Carol affected a look of concern. "God help us. The poor cratur is probably saving hard for baby stuff. When's she due?"

"I think it's about the middle of January. We don't mention it. You wouldn't believe how well I'm dealing with it now. I just let it go – most of the time. I wouldn't be human if I didn't have a downer every now and again. Anyway, I have better things to think about, haven't I? I'm googling New York every night."

As they climbed the gradual slope towards the old

tower on Bray Head, a fleet of puffy white galleons had come to a halt across the western sky, becalmed in its passage through a day devoid of wind or breeze.

Inside the dim, damp tower, the glassless windows framed views of the Skelligs. Carol took pictures with her phone.

"I just love the contrast between the darkness of the stone and the blue of the sea and the islands," she said. "It's like a natural canvas and frame."

Angela agreed. "Star-watching from the middle of Staigue Fort must be the same. I'd love to do it some time. In fact, I will do it. I'm signing up for the next astronomy course the Dark Sky Reserve puts on. I put my life on hold for far too long."

The determination in her voice made Carol turn around from the window. "I don't know how that poor woman will fare with the lovely Brian but I think she's after doing you one hell of a favour by carting him off."

Angela didn't smile. "She might or she mightn't. You wouldn't know till afterwards. But there's one thing sure: I'm going to do myself every favour I can from here on in. No man or no woman will ever again dictate what I do or how I feel. This is my new motto. I am the master of my own fate/I am the captain of my soul. That's another gem that Annette rooted out for me. It's from a poem called 'Invictus' that Nelson Mandela used to like. If it's good enough for Nelson, it's good enough for me. I can't remember the name of the fella who wrote it, but more power to his elbow. I wouldn't have chosen to be on my own in a month of Sundays. It's a bummer. But the upside is that I have the compensation of living life on my own terms, of having a home free from conflict. Best of all, I have peace of mind. I'm not waiting for the next upset, the next disappointment to sweep away the good phase I was hoping against hope would last."

Carol clapped her on the back. "I want to be your manager when they're signing you up for motivational talks. Life is a game of swings and roundabouts, isn't it? I gave the summer trying to heave you out of the dark hole. Now, I'm the one that's struggling. I thought I had a handle on it the other morning, but I'm in relapse mode today."

Angela hugged her. "You'll turn this to the good yet. Just have patience. And you have Oliver to help you. So stop whining."

On their way down the hill, she raised the topic of the party again.

"I know I'm like a dog with a bone but I really think a party would be the ideal way to bring the valley together in a positive way after the shock of the burglary. It could be a thank you for the way everyone rallied round. And wouldn't it be an ideal way to announce your engagement and celebrate it?"

"You're selling it very well. When you put it like that, I'm tempted to go for it. I'll ring Oliver and see what he thinks."

"There's no need. I rang him already and suggested the fifteenth of December. It's a Saturday. Sure you have him wrapped around your little finger. He's all for it if you're happy to go with it. I know the actual birthday isn't until the twenty-third, but you can't have it running right up to Christmas, especially since I'll be flying off to the Big Apple. God, what I kick I get out of saying that. Yahoo!"

"Emailing my fiancé now, are we, to set the date for a

party I hadn't even planned? What were you saying earlier about not allowing anyone to dictate to you? You put Field Marshal Margot in the shade."

The October sun was warm on Carol's face. The sea air and the walk revived a sense of hope in her. Mary was battered and bruised but she had survived the ordeal and was due to be released in three days' time. Carol would collect Oliver in Kerry Airport on her way to or from the hospital in Tralee. There was so much to be thankful for. Yes, she *would* celebrate.

Margot took charge of the food. She opened a computer file to match all her Farmhouse friends with a dish. As a back-up, she used a clipboard, ticking off every name as they confirmed. Each person was advised to label their bowls and plates and to make sure to take them home that evening.

Mary insisted on paying for the meat and fish. "We'll be the talk of the parish if we don't cover the main costs ourselves. They'll have us down as charity cases otherwise. Salads and desserts, I can just about justify but not the main dishes."

A host of volunteers was enlisted to roast legs of lamb in their own ovens and to boil whole hams, all funded by Mary, despite Carol's protests. The hams were to be cooked with a generous dollop of cider in the water, and finished off in the oven with a glaze of honey, wholegrain mustard and cloves. Each Farmhouse woman was to turn up to the Community Centre on the morning of the party and set the joints of meat on a table that would serve as a carvery.

Through the pop-up gallery, Carol had made contacts

with other artists and craft workers in Iveragh and the Beara Peninsula. She sent out an email inviting them to the party. In lieu of gifts, she asked them to make decorations from shells, driftwood, slate, seaweed, stones and the general fruits of beachcombing.

For her own part, Carol requested empty jam jars and decorative bottles to be dropped off at the house. Most of the jars were used to make candles. The bottles and the remainder of the jars were set aside to be filled with posies of rosehips, holly, haws, ivy and whatever flowers had survived in the garden and ditches.

In September, she had made gallons and gallons of elderflower wine, intending to give bottles of it as Christmas presents. Instead, it would be used for the party. Other than that, it would be a BYO event.

She bought lengths of hessian to create four separate wall hangings festooned with fairy lights, lengths of driftwood and evergreens.

Two photographer friends put their heads together to assemble a variety of props, including picture frames, glasses, hats and joke sets of fake noses to take fun pictures.

Carol bartered two of her finest Skellig paintings with the local hotel to provide the cutlery, plates and glasses for the day. She decided against a band.

"Will you go away out of that, one picture is fine," the owner said. "If I took two, they'd have me down as a pure robber."

Carol couldn't get over the warmth with which people responded to the party. Friends were falling over one another with offers of help and with ideas.

"I had forgotten how decent people are," she told

Angela and Margot at one of their weekly 'campaign' meetings to assess how things were going. "It was worth having the party for that alone – to experience the sheer goodness of people."

Margot looked up from her clipboard list. "I find the same. You have to go away to appreciate it. I know neighbours have grown more distant since women have gone out working and life has speeded up, but scratch just lightly beneath the surface and you'll find that old parish spirit. What was the Irish word they had for it? The gangs of neighbours that used to gather to help with the haymaking and the harvest or any other big job that needed doing?"

Angela put her hand up. "Please, miss, I know. It's *meitheal*. Do I get a star for that?"

Carol smiled at her. "You're some goose. Yeah, *meitheal*."

"Less of the chat now or we'll get nothing done," Margot said. "What are you doing for music?"

Carol said that an old school friend of hers in Waterville had volunteered her music-mad son to make out a play list and act as DJ later in the evening.

"If there's a band, people won't be able to hear each other speak," she said. "There's nothing worse."

"That makes sense," Angela agreed. "Would you be up for some set dancing later in the evening, though? I think I could rustle up an accordion player. Come to think of it, I know a harpist down near Sneem. I'd imagine she'd jump to the chance of a good party."

When Carol insisted on a donation to charity instead of personal gifts, Margot tutted. "Spare us the Joan of Arc routine. Are you out of your mind? Think of all the lovely vouchers people give. Afternoon tea in the Parknasilla, a spa treatment in the Europe, dinner in the Bianconi."

Carol was hearing none of it. "I want to make a donation to the Valentia Ward at the hospital in Tralee. I've become so aware of rural isolation and depression since I came home that I want to support a mental health service."

Margot was gazing over the top of her head. "Can anyone tell me where I can get my hands on a can of spray polish pronto?"

"What are you looking for that for?" Carol asked.

"To shine up that halo of yours. What else?"

Carol's main reservation about the party was the stress it might create for Mary. Her mother had put on a brave face when she came home from hospital, but there was a nervousness about her. She couldn't bear to be in the house on her own. That's what pained Carol most – seeing her once independent mother robbed of the feeling of safety within her own four walls.

George and Michelle had visited twice *en famille* since the burglary. They wanted Mary to go and stay with them for a while but she said she wasn't up to it. To be fair to both of them, there had been no recriminations after the full-force storm of emotion in the immediate aftermath of the incident.

"I'm just glad she is still with us," George said. "It could have been so much worse."

And though they may have had reservations about the birthday party, they maintained a diplomatic silence.

Klaus, to his credit, played a blinder. Carol developed a new affection and respect for the stolid German when she saw how often he visited and the care he showed her mother. There wasn't a day when he didn't ring at least once. And then there were the parcels, most of them no larger than a book but exquisitely wrapped. The gifts varied: a notebook, a volume of poetry, a bottle of body lotion, hand-made soap, tickets to a concert in the National Concert Hall, a CD. When Mary opened the packets of kindness, she relaxed and blossomed.

Klaus was at one with Mary in his enthusiasm for the birthday party which, to Carol's immense relief, had proved to be a welcome distraction to her mother and an ideal way to divert her mind from the distressing memories that had her crying out in her sleep. Carol felt an immense gratitude to Klaus for rowing in behind the preparations for the party. She had confided the idea to him on the phone one evening shortly after she had broached it with her mother.

"Of course, it is a good idea. Mary needs to forget what has happened. And this is a big event in your life, Carol. Certainly you must mark it. I will assist you in whatever way I can."

It was Klaus who came up with the idea of having a photographic montage of her life from childhood up. He suggested that Mary go through the photo albums and the endless shoeboxes of unsorted photos to select the best images. He supplied the technical expertise, scanning them and transferring them to a CD to run on a loop during the party.

And then there was Timmy. In ways Carol felt that he was jealous of the bond between Klaus and his mother, that he felt supplanted in her affections. He disappeared whenever the German visited.

Mary laughed when Carol confided her suspicions.

"Don't be ridiculous. How could anyone come between Timmy and myself? We've soldiered too long together."

Still, she did take Carol's words to heart and she was extra solicitous about Timmy. And Carol figured that she must have said something to Klaus. On the rare occasions that he did bump into Timmy on his weekend visits, he went out of his way to ask his opinion on different matters and made sure to tell him how highly Mary thought of him and to thank him for discovering her the morning after the burglary.

It had been uncanny, really. Timmy had sat bolt upright in the bed that morning at six o'clock in a cold sweat. He had woken from a vivid dream in which he met Carol's father, John, who told him that Mary wanted to cross over to him but that it was not her time, that she should go back.

Driven by a sense of foreboding, Timmy got up in the pitch black and went straight out to Glenosheen with no idea of what he would do when he got there. He had a spare key but he rarely ever used it. When he went around the back of the house, his shoes crunched on the broken glass. The curtain was blowing in the half-open window. He went in and made his way to the hall, switching on very light as he went. He found Mary under the duvet in a crumpled heap. All she could do was cry when she saw him kneeling beside her.

After the burglary, Timmy was like her shadow. If ever Carol wanted to go out, she simply had to ring him and he'd be over to the house.

Mary and himself missed Sharon and Lisa keenly. They kept hoping that the mother and daughter would come back. Not a day passed that they didn't draw the mother and daughter down in some conversation, reliving memories and laughing at things Lisa used to say. On Mary's instructions, Timmy would turn on the Dimplex heater in the den for a few hours every day. Carol wanted to pack their things away in boxes but Mary wouldn't hear of it. Timmy backed her up. "*Arrah*, give it until January anyway. Sharon might come back when the fright of it wears off."

The party had thrown him at first. He couldn't think of a single thing to contribute.

"All the women can cook and all your arty farty friends can do those fancy decorations," he said. "Margot is the commander-in-chief. Your mother and Klaus have the photos in hand. I don't know what to be doing with myself." Then one day he shot up the drive on his bike, his whole self tensed in high voltage. "I have it, I have it. I'm going to get you the grandest Christmas tree you ever laid eyes on."

Carol was elated. "Oh Timmy, my head was so set on the birthday that I didn't even think of a Christmas tree. That's brilliant."

When Klaus arrived on the next visit, he congratulated Timmy on his brainwave and handed him a small box. It contained a set of two dozen metal candle-holders fitted with tiny red candles. Timmy was nonplussed.

"They're for your tree," Klaus said.

"You mean you can go and put real candles on a Christmas tree," Timmy said, turning some of the holders over in his hand. "Isn't that the best thing ever?" He laughed. "As long as we're not the cause of burning down the community centre."

Late one night, Carol could scarcely speak for the

yawns that swallowed her words when she rang Oliver. "I'm run ragged from it all. The main thing I'm afraid of is that people will only turn up out of a sense of duty. Apart from worrying that I might be causing hassle for my mother, that was the big reservation I had."

She prattled on for ages before she noticed that he wasn't responding very much. "Well, that's enough chat out of me, Ollie, my love. What about you?"

The pause on the other end seemed endless. The tiredness fell away. Her brain sharpened to an anxious clarity.

"Can I run something by you, Carol?"

"Of course, fire away," she said, faking a confidence she didn't feel.

Chapter 32

The Saturday of the party dawned wet, wild and stormy, thanks to the arrival of an unwanted guest, Storm Deirdre, in a fit of bad temper and agitation.

Carol woke to the sound of the wind howling around the eaves, rain hurling itself against the window and Oliver snoring beside her. It was pitch black. She switched on the radio beside the bed just in time to catch the Six O'Clock News bulletin announcing powercuts, flooding, swollen rivers, hazardous driving conditions and the assorted delights of a routine December day in globally warmed Ireland.

"Wonderful, just wonderful," she said aloud. "Should we call it off?"

Oliver sat up, blinked sleepily and stroked her cheek. "They didn't call it the Wild Atlantic Way for nothing. Unless the day degenerates into an all-out hurricane, we'll go ahead. After a year of these storms, I imagine people will just shrug it off."

"I don't know too much about that," Carol said. "I can't get over the extremes of weather since I came home. I certainly timed my return right. Rain and drought and storms. It's biblical stuff really."

"All you're missing is the plague of locusts," Oliver said, his voice hoarse from sleep.

"Oh, then, I'm ruling nothing in or out. A regiment of frogs is probably massing."

The party was due to start at twilight with the guests welcomed by the flickering of jam-jar candles on the roadside ditches and all along the path to the front door of the community centre.

Carol sighed. "If the wind holds up through the day, the jam jars will be blown clean across to the shores of Manhattan. I can see them twinkling on the Hudson. After all my hard work making them."

Oliver lay down and closed his eyes. She knew she couldn't sleep again with the worry of the day. When she switched on the bedside lamp, he groaned and pulled the duvet over his head. Men! The world could be teetering on the edge of a precipice and they'd insist on having a sound sleep before dealing with anything.

The light of the lamp reached just as far as her dress hanging on the open wardrobe door. Just the look of it soothed her. What an antique beauty! She had fallen in love the minute she had clapped eyes on it in the designer swop shop in Tralee – soft off-white cotton embossed with a subtle biscuit-coloured pattern of leaves and flowers, a scooped neckline edged with scalloped lace and a border of pale apricot gauze dropping from the hemline to bring the fall of the fabric just below her calves.

And that wasn't all. Painted on the centre panel of the dress were two nosegays of pink rosebuds and, just below the neckline, two single rosebuds. The delicate shoulder straps were further works of art. Three on each side – one chain of tiny rosebuds on the outside, a band of lace in the centre and another chain of lemon buds on the inner edge.

In the same shop, she had found a pair of elegant,

peach-coloured slingback shoes embellished with two soft leather roses. When she had tried on the dress and shoes, they fitted like a dream, and the colour heightened her complexion.

"They were waiting for you," the shopowner said in genuine awe, no need for false admiration to move the stock along.

When she heard about the special occasion, she reduced the total price from two hundred and fifty euro to two hundred.

"It's strange but that dress has been hanging here so long that I've become attached to it," she said. "Countless women tried it on, but it never seemed quite right. To be honest, I was glad that it didn't suit some of them. They weren't the right fit. I think you have the right spirit for this elegant lady. You're a perfect match. You'll give her the home she deserves."

In the gentle lamplight of the bedroom, Carol gazed across at the dress and visualised the original owner as she had first set eyes on it in a shop window and coveted it. She imagined the pleasure of trying it on, turning this way and that in a front of a long mirror, scooping her hair up with one hand, the excitement of seeing it packaged in tissue on the counter and tied with ribbons, the joy of seeing the admiration in a lover's eyes.

"I'm going to do you proud today, my vintage belle," she whispered.

Oliver had resumed his snoring. She leaned in and kissed his brow.

Carol's friends were stoic. The cars arrived from about 4.30pm onwards, wipers swishing and headlamps illuminating the driving rain in their beams. Women and men made olympian dashes to the front door with raincoats over their heads while the drivers parked. The few hawthorn trees in the ditch strained landward in the teeth of the wind. No one bothered to line out the candles.

Oliver and Carol greeted every new arrival. Slowly, the windows condensed, and the tables filled up with food. Timmy was on sentry duty beside his tree. He hadn't been allowed light the candles for health and safety reasons.

"This country is gone to the dogs with Health and Safety," he said with a grim face. "You couldn't piss crooked with them."

But the tree still looked magnificent, bedecked with decorations that Carol had made from seashells, pine cones and hand-painted pebbles. And the red unlit candles in their brass holders. The tree was crowned by a figure made from scallop shells.

Fairylights twinkled in the hessian wall hangings that were topped with branches of sea holly. Hand-made mobiles twirled from the ceiling. The tables were dotted with dried flower arrangments, hand-painted sea pebbles and driftwood.

The room hummed with conversation. The harpist valiantly competed with the background noise. The accordion player had more luck with his strident notes. Most of the conversation was like a weather report as people traded information on the damage of the day – trees down, areas without power, rivers bursting their banks.

Mary was like the Queen Mother receiving her subjects from the depths of an armchair parked beside the fireplace with the fake coal fire. It pleased Carol no end to see the warmth and regard that the neighbours lavished on her mother, who was making light of the burglary with every enquiry.

"You're a gallant woman to face down those blackguards," said an elderly man leaning on a stick in front of her. "Hell isn't hot enough for the likes of them."

"There must have been somebody watching over me," Mary said. "But I tell you I wouldn't wish it on my worst enemy."

"Is there any account of how the guards are getting on with them?" the man asked.

"Oh wisha, Diarmuid, I wouldn't hold my breath. The biggest blackguard of the pair was out on bail. The usual story. I suppose they'll get off with a rap on the knuckles."

The man shook her hand. "I know what I'd do with them. I'd give them holly if they ever landed back here again Anyway, you're safe and well, fair play to you. The story could have been a lot worse."

An army of women moved between the kitchen and the tables, serving tea and coffee, topping up plates from a seemingly endless supply of sandwiches, quiches, savoury pies, cakes and desserts. Cloud-light pavlovas, heart-shaped biscuits and towers of brownies, trifles and cheese cakes crowded the dessert table.

Most of the women were members of the Irish Countrywomen's Association, commonly known as the ICA. What they didn't know about cooking, baking and catering wasn't worth knowing.

Mary, an ICA veteran herself, had insisted on baking two of her specialities. Her Poteen and Cider Cake was prepared a day in advance of baking by bringing the dried fruit slowly to boiling point in cider and allowing it to cool overnight with a dash of poteen added for good measure. Every November, a cousin from Cahersiveen arrived with a bottle of poteen that, he swore, was the best of stuff 'imported' across the County Bounds from the Coolea area, famed for its traditional music and its illicit spirits. Mary's Porter Cake contained a half pint of Guinness. Angela brought her own Irish Coffee Cake topped with whipped whiskey cream and chopped hazelnuts, and an enormous bowl of Tipsy Cake, which was really a sherry trifle lifted out of the ordinary by her home-made custard.

Oliver joked that the gardaí could breathalyse the guests on the strength of the desserts alone.

Margot roasted two legs of lambs and finished them with a breadcrumb, rosemary and Lakeshore mustard crust.

The biggest surprise of the lot was Oliver, who revealed that his grandmother in Christchurch had taught him to make Christmas cakes. When she got too old to mix the ingredients herself, she had told him what to do. Mary handed him her well-thumbed copy of *All in the Cooking* to use her favourite cake recipe. Again, a liberal shake of the bottle of poteen went into the mixture and a little more was poured over the finished product.

"Aren't you a great baker for a man?" Timmy had said, admiring the cake. "I can remember wan time when Mary's Christmas cake dipped like a trench in the middle."

"Timmy!" Mary said.

He put his hand over his mouth. "I'm sorry, missus, but it's the God's honest truth. Not that it made a blind bit of difference to the taste."

Mary sniffed. "I'm glad to hear that at least."

Timmy's delight at the news that Klaus couldn't make the party because of family commitments was ill-disguised. Carol found that she was genuinely disappointed that he wouldn't be there. The regret was as much for her own sake as her mother's. Over the past couple of months, his kind nature had been unstinting. And his thoughtfulness had extended to her party. He had rung the owner of the Skellig Chocolate and ordered a consignment of chocolates for the party because he knew she adored them.

The hall was already beginning to fill when Angela carried a heavy cardboard box inside and, on Carol's instructions, placed it under a table just inside the hall door. Inside the box was a cake that Carol had ordered from a novelty baker in Killarney. She was saving it until later. Carol had already placed a large carrier bag under the table on which there was a guest book to record the names and messages of the well-wishers.

The first hour of the party passed in a blur while Carol moved from one group to another greeting friends and introducing Oliver. Michelle enveloped her in a cloud of Dior perfume and silk when she hugged her. They posed countless times for the two photographers. After a while, she noticed that George was the only member of the family missing. She felt a prickle of anxiety. Surely he hadn't taken exception to her having the party in the community centre? It would be just like him to consider it not grand enough. She questioned her mother as casually as possible about his absence.

"Oh, with all the fuss, I forgot to tell you that he rang this morning," Mary said. "He told the others to go on ahead because he had to check out a property in Limerick on the way down."

Carol was crouched over a pram admiring a baby when she felt someone tapping her on the shoulder. Margot caught her by the elbow and guided her halfway down the hall.

"Don't look now because it will be obvious that I'm talking about him but, when you get a chance, there's a man standing just below the toilet doors by himself," she said. "He's wearing a light grey check suit and a pink tie."

Carol guessed without looking whom Margot was referring to but she kept her expression neutral.

She waited for a few moments and then nonchalantly scanned the hall until she had the man in her sights.

"Well?" Margot said.

"*Mmm*, he looks vaguely familiar but I can't place him. I think I might know him from Waterville."

Margot tutted. "Well, I've made a few enquiries and not a single person knows who he is."

Carol laughed. "Maybe someone ordered me a stripper as a surprise."

"Carol O'Connell, have you no taste?"

"Where's your sense of humour, girl? If he's a gatecrasher itself, so what – there's no shortage of anything."

Margot's eyes narrowed. "My suspicion is that some arm of the Health Service Executive has sent him to check out the kitchen for hygiene standards. I hope the community centre isn't going to end up in hot water."

"*Arrah*, you have an over-active brain, Margot, there's probably some harmless explanation. For the love of God, don't go tackling him. Anyway, it's time for me to make my speech, I suppose."

She waved to Oliver at the opposite side of the room. When they met in front of the fireplace, she noticed he was carrying a book, but she was distracted by the sea of faces looking expectantly towards them.

Margot darted up and hissed in her ear. "Where's the cake? You're supposed to be blowing out the candles at this stage."

Carol just grinned at her. "I'll be doing things a little differently – as usual."

The rows of people to the front of the crowd had fallen silent but the hubbub still percolated all around the back of the hall. Margot headed through the crowd with a glint in her eye. Shortly afterwards, the chat fell away.

Oliver stepped closer to Carol and winked at her. It was the reassurance she need to get started. She took a deep breath.

"Since most of you are standing, this is going to be short and sweet like the proverbial ass's screech. I want to thank you all for coming here to celebrate with me on a day that no normal person would stir outside the door. Special thanks to my army of cooks, bakers and decorators for the magnificent spread, and for turning the hall out so well. Most of you know that I came home from Italy and into the snow and the rain back in March. It's been an eventful return, to say the least of it, with a few unexpected twists and turns along the way. But at the end of the day, it's good to be home. It's good to be back among your own." She paused to steady her voice. "We had a terrible experience in Glenosheen back in October, one that shook us to the very core. To be honest, it will take us a long time to come from it. But you stood shoulder to shoulder with us. You're still there for us. We

380

will never forget the kindness and the support. From the bottom of my heart, thank you one and all. Above all else, I want to pay tribute to my mother for coming through it so bravely. She's a model of courage and strength to us all."

Cheers and thunderous applause burst from the gathering as Carol finished her last sentence. It went on so long that Carol melted into tears. She turned around and hugged her mother.

"I'm beginning to feel like an over-emotional diva at the Oscars. But, don't worry, we're nearly there. Presents are secondary to your presence, but, if you want to make a contribution to the Valentia Ward at University Hospital Kerry, there's a white bucket up there beside the Christmas Tree. None of us gets through life without some challenge or another. And it's good to be able to support the services that help people make the journey back to wellness." She laughed. "That's my worthy bit over now. Unfortunately, there's some more. I want to acknowledge the support of Oliver here, my better half. Plus he has an announcement to make."

She looked at him quizzically as he stepped forward with the book in his hands. There was a picture of the Skelligs on the cover. When he held it up, she read the title, *All Along the Wild Atlantic Way* by James Montgomery.

Carol could scarcely believe her ears as he spoke. He explained that he had always written travel articles under the name James Montgomery, but his dream had been to write an entire travel book. On the strength of a series of articles in the *Financial Times,* he had been commissioned to write a book on the Wild Atlantic Way.

"I've kept it a secret even from Carol until publication because I wanted to present the finished article as a gift, if you like, to her and to you, the people of this exceptional area. So this, my dear Carol, is my birthday gift to you."

He opened the book and read from the inscription page. "'*To Carol, a kindred spirit under a Skellig sky.*'"

Wild shouts and 'yahoos' burst from all corners of the hall.

When the din died down, Oliver spoke again. "Permit me, if you will, to read a sliver from the section on Iveragh. '*The chaotic charm of Glenosheen, a Victorian farmhouse screened by towering beech trees greened by ancient rains, is a breath of fresh air in an accommodation sector blighted by so many soulless Airbnbs where you are met by combination key boxes rather than smiling faces. Owner Mary O'Connell is a formidable presence presiding over the family's farm guesthouse to which she has been welcoming guests for over forty years. She is a veritable fund of knowledge, generously dispensed.*'"

Wild applause greeted these words of praise.

Silence prevailed again, and he continued. "'*Mary's artist daughter Carol moves effortlessly between the easel and the dining room to serve up one of the best breakfasts I have encountered on my travels.*'"

Carol caught her mother's eye and mouthed 'effortlessly'.

Oliver looked out on the crowd. "Shall I go on?"

The chant of "*More, more!*" reverberated through the hall.

"'*The valley of Glenosheen sweeps down to the Kerry coast where waves warmed by the Gulf Stream lap infinitely long beaches. And dominating the horizon are the jagged Skellig Islands rising under immense skies. If you are looking for sterile perfection, mass-produced spas or town centre Airbnbs, Glenosheen is not for you. But if you want a breakfast served on fine bone china, a marble fireplace in your bedroom and the sound of birdsong to wake you in the morning, this is your dream hideaway.'"*

As Oliver snapped the book cover shut, he put his hand up to stall any other applause. "If you'll bear with us, Carol and I have one final surprise. To prepare, I would like you to make a large circle around the centre of the floor, please, and clear a passage, if you may, for the gentleman at the end of the room."

As the crowd parted, the man in the grey suit and pink tie walked forward carrying a large Gladstone bag. He had recruited one of the local men to move the table that had been inside the door and to place it in the middle of the floor. As he did so, Oliver stood beside him and Carol and Mary made their way down to the door. Carol bent over the carrier bag she had stored under the table and took out a white shawl dotted with pink rosebuds that she had hand-painted herself. She draped it around her head and shoulders. She reached into the bag a second time and took out a bouquet of rosebuds and baby's breath.

Linking Mary's arm in hers, she started to walk slowly up to the table which had been transformed by a white lace tablecloth and a lighted candle in a crystal holder. Angela's hand flew to her mouth in astonishment. She ran across the floor to the accordion player and whispered in his ear. He immediately began to play 'Here Comes the Bride'.

The man in grey beckoned for two chairs to be placed at the side of the table. He knelt over the bag he had placed behind him and took out a wine box and a hammer. Heads turned at the sight of the hammer, but, by then, the guests were in throes of astonishment fatigue.

Oliver hugged Carol and Mary in turn as they reached the table. He guided Mary to her armchair which he had repositioned at the edge of the crowd. Then he took Carol's hand and they sat on the two chairs.

"My name is Trevor Ryan and I'm the celebrant engaged by Carol and Oliver to conduct their humanist wedding ceremony today," the man in the suit said. "Now, I know you came here expecting a birthday party but I hope you will be pleased to have a wedding thrown in for good measure."

He opened two ring boxes, took out the wedding rings and held them over his head for everyone to see.

"I'm going to pass the rings around now," he said. "You'll all have the opportunity to hold them, make a wish for the couple or, if it's your belief, say a prayer for their future happiness."

Timmy stepped forward. "You're a brave man. There's no guarantee them rings will make their way back up to you." His words were rewarded with a gale of laughter.

The celebrant spoke some more about the wedding day. He explained that Oliver had fallen under the spell of Skellig Michael and proposed there in August.

"The altitude has that effect on people, all right," a man at the back of the crowd quipped.

The laughter stopped abruptly when the celebrant took the hammer from the table and circled the floor, tapping his palm with it.

"Now this might appear to be a strange implement to introduce to a wedding ceremony," he said, "but all will be revealed."

He turned back to the table, replaced the hammer and picked up two envelopes.

"Here we have two love letters written by Carol and Oliver to each other," he said. "Neither of them have read the other's letter. The letters are a reminder of the good qualities they see in each other. We are placing them in this wooden box with the bottle of wine."

He slid the cover shut on the box and called Oliver and Carol to the table. They took the hammer in turn and nailed the box shut.

"Here they stand in the flush of love," the celebrant said. "There are possibly couples among you, though, who realise that even the most loving partners do argue. And what we have here in front of us today is an antidote to any falling-out. There may come a day when Oliver and Carol will have such a serious difference of opinion that one or both of them will want to turn their backs on each other and gallop out the front door. At that point, they will open the wine box and drink half the bottle between them. Then, they will read the love letters and finish the last drops of the beaded Hippocrene. At that point, the argument will be forgotten and the light of love will be restored to their eyes."

Angela whispered to Margot. "Brian and myself would have needed a warehouse of wine to survive our marriage. There would have been no call for a hammer the bottles would have been out of the boxes so fast."

The rings made their way back to the altar, borne by a teenage girl with waist-length black hair. The celebrant read the wedding vows and invited Oliver and Carol to place the wedding rings on each other's fingers. In the background, the accordion player and the harpist softly played the old Irish ballad 'Grace'.

"I now pronounce you man and wife," he said. "You may kiss the bride."

The hall was convulsed in applause yet again, and a tide of well-wishers engulfed the bride and groom. Among the first of them was Angela.

"You divil," she said, "you absolute divil. How did you keep this secret from me?"

"With great difficulty. I was absolutely dying to tell you but Oliver and myself agreed that Mam would be the only one to know that this party would double as our wedding day."

Angela hugged her. "I'm just so happy for the two of you."

Just before Carol was swept into the arms of a tall countryman, she asked Angela to bring up the cake box from the end of the hall. The cake, when it emerged, was a work of art. Soon, an admiring circle of people had gathered round the replica of Skellig Michael with a tiny bride and groom perched on top.

Carol and Oliver were posed with a knife to cut into the Skellig when the main door swung open to admit some latecomers to the party. The sound of a child's shoes thudding across the wooden floor and a girl's voice calling out her name made Carol look beyond the photographers. She blinked.

"Carol! Carol!"

For a couple of seconds, she was disbelieving. Then, she realised it truly was Lisa sprinting towards her. Sharon hung hesitantly behind her. And coming up the rear were Klaus and George, wearing the broadest of smiles.

Carol knelt down and scooped Lisa into her arms. Mary beckoned to Sharon, but the young woman was stuck to the spot and sobbing. Klaus put his arm around her and gently led her forward. Sharon stood in front of Mary, her face tilted resolutely to the floor.

Mary rose to her feet. "Come here to me, girl. Give up that auld crying." She folded her arms around her. "Where did ye get to, a'tall, a'tall? We're dying with the lonesomeness since ye ran off."

Sharon sobbed into her shoulder. "I'm so ashamed for what Darren done. You must hate us."

"Sure that was nothing to do with you, girl. You weren't to blame for what he did. And from what I could tell, he wasn't the ringleader. It was the other latchico."

Sharon stepped back. Her face was red and swollen. Klaus passed her a handkerchief. She blew her nose noisily. "I never wanted to come back after what happened but . . ." She looked around to George and Klaus.

George stepped forward. "In fairness to Klaus, he spent the last week ringing every agency, hostel and hotel he could possibly think of in Cork. God only knows what class of a phone bill he'll get. He didn't really want to to meet the pair on his own, so he enlisted me to go with him. We'd have been here a lot earlier only it took some persuading to convince Sharon to come down."

Sharon nodded. "I still don't know if we should be here. I'm afraid people will be givin' out to me and they'd be right to. The shame of what happened is killin' me." She began to sob again.

Lisa's face was stricken at the sight of her mother's upset. She wrapped her arms around her waist. "Ah Mammy, don't cry. You should be happy that we're back again. I missed everyone so much."

Carol tousled the little girl's hair. "You're dead right, Lisa. And we're so happy to see the two of you again. I kept waiting for you to come back. It's like a dream come true to see you here. And I bet you're starving, aren't you?"

Lisa nodded.

"You sit down here with my own mammy, because she's been storing up an ocean of hugs for you, and we'll bring you some yummy food, OK?"

Lisa nodded. "OK."

Mary sat and patted the arm of the chair. "Sit down there, pet, and tell me all your stories while they fill up a plate of goodies for you."

Sharon wiped her eyes with the back of her hand. A smile flitted across her face at the sight of Mary and Lisa together but it disappeared almost as quickly.

Carol placed her hands on Sharon's shoulders and looked her straight in the eyes. "If anyone says a word to you, they'll have me to answer to. Nobody is going to force you to do anything against your will but, if you're willing to come back here and give life in the valley a second chance, Glenosheen will be your home until you get a house of your own."

Sharon looked at Carol uncertainly. "I don't know what to say. I don't know if I could land back with ye after what happened." Then she looked at Mary and tears sprang to her eyes again.

Mary reached out and took her hand.

"Sharon, look at me. Carol and myself have talked this over so many times since you disappeared. There's a home here with us for as long as you need it. Maybe we're being selfish but Lisa has brought us so much love." She laughed. "And you're not so bad yourself. But Carol is right. It's your decision. Take your time and think about it. In the meantime, go over there to Margot and she'll find a plate to feed you up."

Carol turned around to see George and Klaus staring at her. Their eyes passed from the shawl to the bouqet to the wedding ring.

"What in the name of God . . ." George began.

Carol beamed. "*Arrah*, the day turned out a bit differently than people expected."

THE END